THE MARIONETTE MAN

TABLE OF CONTENTS:

Prologue: The Lance of Harmony.

Chapter 1: Things Left Unsaid.

Chapter 2: For All Our Lost Time.

Chapter 3: To Sleep, Perchance to Dream.

Chapter 4: The End of an Era.

Chapter 5: A Loud and Obnoxious Series of Bangs.

Chapter 6: Everything Works in Circles.

Chapter 7: The Lies We Tell Ourselves.

Chapter 8: Fuel for the Frying Pan.

Chapter 9: Down in Flames, Up in Smoke.

Chapter 10: Purely Semantic.

Chapter 11: Something Important About Cats And Bags.

Chapter 12: Come Whatever May.

Chapter 13: Ragnarok.

Chapter 14: Hair of the Dog

Chapter 15: A Love of Masks.

Chapter 16: Better Than a Poke in the Eye

Chapter 17: A Harsh Reality.

Chapter 18: Every Dog, Every Day

Chapter 19: Out to the Black.

Chapter 20: The Worst Possible Outcome

Chapter 21: The God of Death.

Chapter 22: The Long Slow Goodbye

Chapter 23: All That Remains.

Chapter 24: Black Humour.

Chapter 25: The Marionette Man

PROLOGUE: THE LANCE OF HARMONY.

"Harmony and peace aren't always the same thing. You can't always shoot for both."

The *Lance of Harmony* floated motionless against the backdrop of the void, lit amongst its fellows by a hundred thousand shining stars sparkling across the Milky Way.

It rested as a ship apart from the pack, a smaller frigate of division two – the G.O.D. rapid response fleet under direct defense orders from the High Council of the Gods itself. The *Lance of Harmony* was waiting above *Blend*, of course. It was waiting for the fleet admiral's order to open rifts through space and rush to defend a world of no importance - *Petronova*, near the neutral territories.

The green light was signalled across the fleet comms, with the *Lance of Harmony*'s Captain acknowledging the chain of command by giving his own orders, to begin the process of charging the enormous rift generators deep below-decks. The heavy humming and vibration began almost immediately.

"Weapons primed, Captain Brass."

The Captain nodded acknowledgement, and the ship's engines burst to life, rattling *The Lance* forward at his hand mark, driving the ship forwards into a miraculously formed bright circle of white light ahead of it. The bulk shifted, corrected, and stabilized as the gravity generators lightened and pulled the ship in all the proper ways.

The bow of the enormous vessel softly sank into the white unknown.

At two kilometres long, the *Lance of Harmony* was a mere dwarf next to the fleet rifting all around it.

"Hangar Bays one through thirteen, prep for deployment."

His orders barked fast, efficient - weapons, engines, shields, fighters, crew, all readying for the battle to come, the minute they emerged into the space above *Petronova*. Reports had been vague, few and far in-between. Nothing but hostile unknown through the bright white light of the rift ahead.

The white light enveloped the outside of the bridge around their view as the ship passed through the joining of space, and suddenly there were gasps and an immediate sense of panic.

The Captain knew something was wrong even before communication links were fully re-established and the FoF kicked in. Alarm klaxons sounded, and immediately foreign and completely unidentified friend or foe markers blipped into existence on consoles across the whole bridge, bright red dots with projected trajectories and intercept patterns. Each one was emblazoned with a small question mark.

"We're through Captain, rift generators spinning down."

It didn't matter. The Captain had been expecting to emerge with the rest of his division to a few enemy ships at best, perhaps a small invasion fleet trying to land ground forces for a raid. The Black Armada, that age-old mortal enemy, often hit hard first, and cared about casualties and counterattacks afterwards. They were known to feed lives and resources to slaughter, just for the demoralizing effect it had on civilians and soldiers of The G.O.D.

Instead of the expected, what happened all around the *Harmony* was chaos.

The rapid response fleet was under siege, with ships all around *The Lance* being torn to shreds, holed, broken, and blown to pieces by a carefully orchestrated defense that simply shouldn't exist. Gun batteries from below, sent enormous arcs of bright light upwards, signalling shots from clusters of both orbital and planetside positions of massive railguns spread across the entirety of the planet, with additional missiles from unknown vectors arcing into ships all around him, decimating the rest of his division.

"No contact from the Admiral's carrier, Captain. Orders?"

This was wrong. So wrong. Too many red flags for Captain Bradley Brass. There was simply no way the planet could have been invaded and re-entrenched so quickly. The planet-side batteries usually took months to repair and resupply following a takeover. The foreign friend or foe beacons that should be marked as different Black Armada icons entirely. They shouldn't exist in the systems, and yet there they were. And the sheer number of enemy ship and fighter formations that were rapidly closing in… There was no time. No time at all. Even if the Guardians of Destiny fleet had superior numbers before rifting in, the enemy had been waiting, and those numbers meant nothing now.

This battle was already lost in the first salvo.

"Pull us out of the carnage. Swing wide above that wreck to port and have our starboard guns fend off the fighters. Head for the closer of the two moons for a slingshot maneuver."

The ship lurched even despite the artificial gravity, and communications finally came online.

"Sir, the admiral's carrier is down, and the fleet is scattering, trying to escape the planet-side batteries. We've already lost most of the fleet. It was an ambush."

It was somehow reassuring to have someone else state the already obvious.

"Engines to full once we clear the wreckage, avoid those missiles, Knowles."

The ship swung wide around the venting wreck of the nearby battlecruiser *Borealis*, with the *Harmony's* bridge crew trying hard to ignore the screams and cries for help echoing across the comms networks. No sense in stopping to help survivors and winding up in the same spot.

Several missiles soared around the *Borealis's* wreck and spattered across the *Harmony's* invisible plasma shielding, shocking it into rippling visibility, a bright sky blue. The shielding was still new to many aboard, and was a special boon for such a small retrofitted frigate, but it held. The Captain nodded at the pilot to continue increasing thrust. There was a hesitant moment as the ship shuddered then, and the plasma shielding bubbled as a sphere around the hull flashed from bright blue to a viridian green. The Captain looked to the older crew woman and her partner sitting at the defense console.

"Railgun round amidships at starboard Captain. The plasma shielding held, but it won't take another one unless it gets some time to recharge."

He checked his data pad. The trajectory of the shot had come from a pair of larger battlecruisers moving to intercept. Both of them appeared again with that same mysteriously absent FoF tag. Not even marked as unknown! Just a simple question-marked symbol with no lettering. He ordered the ship to swing around again, the batteries along each side of the ship flashing rapidly in a rumbling rhythm as shells and missiles fired off through the void. Usually, even a single battlecruiser would have two or three frigates outgunned, but with the planet-side batteries below narrowing their hunt, and the rest of the enemy fleets closing rapidly, there was no choice but to feint and run for the nearby moon, praying they could be quick enough to put the desolate meteor-cratered sphere between the *Lance of Harmony* and the railguns far below.

"Attention G.O.D. fleet. You are outnumbered and outgunned. Surrender immediately and you will not be harmed further."

The communication on an open channel was unexpected. The Black Armada rarely took prisoners, preferring war trophies in lieu. Strange, that they would allow an entire fleet to surrender before it had been mostly reduced to scrap.

Almost immediately there was a reply, but not from the *Lance of Harmony*.

"All Guardian ships, this is Captain Princep of Division three. I order you to keep fighting. I repeat. KEEP fighting. Any Captain who surrenders their ship will be court martialed and summarily executed."

Well, no need to answer the enemy then.

Obviously, the enemy had intercepted the transmission, as whatever restraint the enemy had been using was immediately thrown to the solar winds. The two larger cruisers on intercept course for the *Lance of Harmony* began launching more missiles and fighters en masse, including space-rated Agatha transport boarding craft.

"Deploy every last piece of equipment we have, including all fire teams. Get them planetside if we can. Cut gravity once they're away. And divert the fusion engine output to speed up cool down and recharging of the rift generators."

The first half of the order was futile. It was intended to save the lives of a few individual fighter and dropship pilots along with some soldiers in exchange for the lives of those remaining aboard the ship. With the transmission, it was no longer a mystery why more railgun rounds hadn't pierced the *Harmony*'s shield already in minutes past.

Regardless, the enemy's soft spot for surrender had bought him the time he needed to begin rounding the moon's gravity well. The tug of additional planetoid gravity pulled on the crew softly in addition to the ships' active anti-gravity generators. Doubt furrowed his brow as he pondered the approach vector.

Would it buy them enough time?

Two more railgun rounds sailed by, their trajectories marked in yellow on various screens.
Warning shots, perhaps, but even with the threat of the gun batteries planet-side safely tucked behind the moon, the *Harmony* was at a disadvantage, with its engines and stern showing a visible backside to the enemy. If only mooning an enemy could make them stop shooting. The *Harmony*'s own railgun was bow-mounted, and there was no way the frigate could swing around in time to get targeting coordinates before it was scuttled.

Another railgun round skimmed dangerously close to the port side of the stern, and the plasma shielding shimmered back into view, this time changing color from green to yellow to red in the span of a millisecond, and then it vanished without so much as a rattle as the gas dispersed in a cloud. There was a loud alarm from the defense console, confirming that the shield had indeed fizzled out completely and would require several minutes to recharge.

The Captain thumbed his wrists, feeling for absent cufflinks that he had shipped home only days prior on a gut feeling. Would his son and wife miss him? Or would they move on quickly as he assumed they would? The worry in the back of his mind was impossible to ignore, even during a situation like this. More memories, and an old dream he had cherished, it all flashed before his eyes, now forever out of reach. All of it was impossible to shut out, like a stream of consciousness that wouldn't cease. His crew were likely having similar thoughts.

Bodies moved on autopilot as brains froze in quiet recognition of the looming end.

He knew the outcome of the battle, and had run the math in his head. The foolish and arrogant orders of a soon-dead senior Captain had decided the ending of this story.

He and his crew would die.

As the ship rounded the other side of the moon, more foreign ships were waiting. His ship had no A.I. and there were only the rudimentary blue and red lines projected in basic estimations, criss crossing across the screens in 3-D.

The lack of any clear path for the ship to follow through them answered his question of where to go next. The rift generators were still recharging.

He stroked his thick black beard with a left hand, shaking his head in solemn sorrow.

And then, eyes blazing and watery, tears running down his dark cheeks, he resigned himself to fate.

Wiping both the sweat from his forehead and the tears from his cheeks with a sleeve, he gave the order to fire, a fruitless defiance of the enemy stationed on all sides of The *Lance of Harmony*.

Breathing stopped.

The world paused.

Then, the enemy fired back.

CHAPTER 1: THINGS LEFT UNSAID.

"Our greatest regrets always involve those we leave behind."

When Arthur Brass turned twenty, everything changed.

His mother. The war widow. Never remarried.

How many years of good relationships with the government under Guardians of Destiny protection and the secret police had there been? And suddenly she just magically becomes a target?

Fake. Had to be.

Nothing she did directly was treasonous, and his poor mother hardly fit the description of the enemy painted in the propaganda – she was hardly the portrait of a half-naked, frothy-mouthed berserker screaming the name of the Immortal God-Emperor Xex! As far as Arthur knew, there was no secret altar to the Black Armada God-Emperor in his mother's closet. But… As far as the British state and the Guardians seemed to be concerned, this poor war-widow was the direct cause of a string of recent losses to the Black Armada. They suspected she was harboring the location of terrorists or some such ridiculous notion, perhaps? There was some conspiratorial undercurrent to it all that Arthur couldn't place, but which definitely felt wrong. Somehow, she was to blame for the burning of entire worlds at the hands of the enemy? Or for the lack of recruitment for the army? The gods themselves knew what else!

The secret police got rough, that *is* how it all started.

His mother was answering questions at the front door, in the same polite and reserved tone she always put on. There were two of them. A man. A woman. Dressed in the same white combat armor - the matte white plasticky stuff designed to soften explosives and stop bullets. The man had his cap tucked under the crook of his arm, with the other hand resting on the holster of his stun gun. His female partner was off to the side, voice recorder held out lazily as the other set of fingers fiddled with her tight bun.

Pristine.

Official.

Arthur listened to the murmur of the voices from where he was laid up on the couch watching television – some distance down the hall. The soft light from outside in the cold sun filtered down the hallway and framed his mother in a white-box halo. The officers were mere shadows beyond the threshold somewhere further. This specific cop had been getting more and more aggressive each passing month in his advances, while his mom continually spurned him each time. What reasons did he need for his power? His partner seemed exasperated throughout it all, but uninterested in ever stopping him. It worsened. And worsened. The passes became more obvious. More forceful.

Different types of hunger will do things to a person, it seems.

His mother barely raised her hand to scratch her cheek and the officer moved in frustration and anger, backhanding her across the face with lightning speed. He heard the slap echo in the open air. A crispness to it. Clean. Brutal. Found himself moving up and off the couch in under a few seconds, sprinting to the door as his mother crumpled against the doorframe. Saw nothing but red hot anger.

His mother was a tall spindly woman, who had no weight to cushion such a vicious blow. Yet even as she fell, the cop merely stood over her, his hand still raised - as if she were a dangerous drunkard at the pub ready to rise again and take a half-cocked retaliatory swing at any moment.

His partner was frozen in shock, clinging to the recorder like a vice. Arthur sprinted past the entryway closet towards the door. The female officer stepped back, dropped the recorder, reached for her stun gun. As he approached, she seemed conflicted, to have no clue what to do next – frozen in place. She had been drawn into this fiasco whether she liked it or not. Both seemed to be oblivious to Arthur's initial approach, locked in the moment of escalated post-violence shock.

Arthur didn't stop to think, nor could he. Rage flooded the system. The stocky, muscled, twenty-year-old was acting on pure adrenaline and instinct, fuelled with nothing but anger. The kind that settled in the bones, the kind that built up over time. Even in that brief span of time, through the haze of fury he knew he would do anything to protect her.

His first punch hammered into the secret police officer's neck as the officer glared down at his mother, efficiently doubling him back and over even though the younger Brass had meant to clock him square in the chin. Neither white-clad officer had even noticed him get up from the couch in the shock and flurry of the backhand.

The new threat moved the second officer to action. Gave her a target. She reacted just as quickly in retaliation, Snapping the holster and slamming him back into the wall with her Kevlar and plastic-coated forearm. Something clicked in his neck as her armor pressed into his windpipe. A half-second later she was stabbing a crackling stun gun barrel towards Arthur's torso with her free hand. Arthur, pinned as he was, couldn't move against the wall. It caught him in the gut easily, knocking his wind out with a crackling punch of electrical power even as he struggled to fight back.

A futile attempt at regaining the advantage.

His mother screamed then, amidst the sparking and snapping of two live stun guns and the fighting and shifting of white armor.

It did nothing.

Neighbours shuttered their windows.

The officers, calm and calculating now, regarded Arthur as the newest, biggest threat. Forgetting Angela Brass, his mother, entirely, they descended upon him like a pair of hungry vultures. Arthur was zapped again and again, each punch of electricity jerking his muscles into tightening knots. An eternity collapsed into seconds as he collapsed to the deck of the apartment complex walkway, feeling cold linoleum press into his left cheek. He flailed - jerking and spasming uncontrollably.

The two standing over him merely shifted into kicks as he dropped, catching him in the ribs and limbs repeatedly as his mother sobbed in horror in the doorway, bleeding from her lip pressed against the door frame. He could only wheeze and hack up blood and spittle as they delivered blow after blow into the tender flesh of his stomach, his neck, and his face.

His muscles were still twitching from the stun guns as he curled up feebly to protect himself, merely trying to survive the brutal beating. He lost consciousness at least once.

It was only after he had been sufficiently bruised and bloodied, lying on the ground in a half-conscious pile of angry purple on his light brown flesh that they hauled him away to the cruiser, dragging him most of the way - leaving smears of blood. His grey hoodie was stained with blood and dust, his split lips and broken nose drooling blood. He already knew he was missing at least one tooth in the back.

Before they loaded him into the patrol vehicle, the first officer, his own neck a vibrant purple from Arthur's initial punch, dropped a sopping wet white rag over Arthur's mouth as his partner clicked the cuffs behind him.

"Does this smell like drugs to you?"

The officer chuckled at his own grim humor, eliciting a panicked glance from the other female officer. One of Arthur's eyes was already swollen shut, and he tried in vain to hold his breath as the cloth was forced against his face. Yet he could only struggle weakly as he smeared his own blood across The Union Jack and the G.O.D. Helix emblazoned next to each other on the matte white paint of the door. The male officer smirked, amused at the defiance, and slammed his stun gun a final time into Arthur's ribs.

Out of anything he had ever endured, getting hit with these was the worst pain Arthur had yet experienced in his naïve little life. It hit like a punch, and then for good measure rattled his brain around as he tightened his lips, and bit into his tongue. The hazy sweetness dotted his taste buds from the cloth fumes, mixed with the savory taste of blood and metal. Unphased, the officer's gun barrel jabbed again a second time and Arthur gasped, unable to help himself. It felt like only half an instant before the drugging sunk in, and then everything crashed to nothingness.

He woke up, some number of hours later. Everything was caked in a crushing darkness, and every part of him ached.

He panicked at first - thinking they had beaten him blind, before feeling the edges of a cot, and then the cool chill of a concrete wall and floor. Realizing he was in a jail cell, his anger flared again as his eyes adjusted ever so slowly to the murky void.

How dare they do this to him.

Rolling over, the sharp, immediate pain let him know that moving too quickly would be difficult. His entire body hurt, and Arthur could feel the cold stickiness of his own still-drying blood on his skin and clothes. Most of it was from a clotted gash on his forehead that the officers had not bothered to attend to. A lesser amount appeared to have dribbled from the searing hole where one of his molars used to be. He could still feel the blood weeping from the chasm where the roots had ripped from his jawbone.

His forehead would likely have a scar.

Still, much the opposite of his expectations, the cell itself was clean, dry, and relatively plain. Once his unswollen good eye had adjusted to the murkiness, seeing that no window was immediately nearby, he slowly explored the space. He had to get ridiculously close to see much, especially with one eye swollen shut - but there was new white paint on the walls, overtop of where previous occupants had scrawled things. Hell, he could almost make out the dark edges of letters beneath the new coat, but with the pitch-black, Arthur didn't have the patience to decipher what some other dead convict would try to tell him.

He fully expected execution, as was common for the false charge of treason.

His eyes eventually adjusted just enough to the murk and Arthur eased himself up, wincing at his injuries. Every movement was torture, and his head was pounding a tattoo-headache drum beat on the inside of his temples. Still, the cell seemed brighter with every passing moment. Arthur sat back down on the cot, feeling incredibly alone. He tried his best to procrastinate from the feelings welling up inside his chest - glanced here and there - at the stainless steel toilet, at the sink, at the shower stall, (which surprised him, but which he was thankful for nonetheless.)

Eventually there was nothing left to do but think. Surely his 'crime' was serious and the charges impossible to contest. Regardless of his noble intentions towards defending his mother, he had attacked two officers of the "British" secret police. But oddly, the eerie silence of the prison he found himself inside implied a distinct lack of other residents. Aside from the faintly echoing sounds of doors opening, there were no human noises other than his own body and the crisp sterile smell of cleaning chemicals, which made him nervous. He certainly would not have enjoyed it if the cell reeked of piss, but he was certainly curious as to why they would scour the cell so clean for a single prisoner? The chemical smell was fresh and pervasive. Bleach mixed with something tinged in lavender. Maybe he was going to be in here for a while, rotting as the G.O.D. plotted him towards an execution or "disappearance."

It quickly dawned on him that he may have been transferred to a different jurisdiction, further up the bureaucratic ladder. He'd likely be more firmly in the grasp of the Guardians of Destiny proper. His British citizenship would be worthless, here. Was this par for the course? Or was it perhaps that the offending officer had friends in positions of power?

Of course, the G.O.D. could do whatever the fuck it wanted. Made sense to him, as it was likely why the officer in question could get away with hitting his mom so overtly in the first place, even with a female partner bearing witness to the event.

No, it was probably even simpler than that. The officer may have had the Union Jack on his uniform, but the uniform and car were all coated in matte white for a reason. White was the color of the Guardians of Destiny. The G.O.D. The gods themselves. Immortals who had ascended beyond the aging process, developing powers via strange and mysteriously guarded secret rituals.

What could the British Government do but bow and pray before a bigger brother?

Reflection was incredibly easy for Arthur when it dawned on him that he may not survive the rest of his sentence. The sheer wall of regret he had been quietly carrying and drowning in alcohol before that point was impossible to ignore, let alone try to sort through all at once. He forced it back down to save his psyche; took his thoughts elsewhere. Hours upon hours spun past. Without even a clock to mark how long he had been here, all this figuring and thinking was quickly becoming aggravating. A strange brew of "what-ifs" and self-pity was flooding through his brain.

Then a flash of why the empathy was so strong.

Arthur's Mother, of course.

His mother would likely have been apprehended as well, taken somewhere else to await her own false charges – likely mocked up for "striking" an officer. Oh god, would she die too? His own death he could stomach, but his mother was wholly innocent!

He forced himself to think away from that descending spiral. Away from his mother. Back to himself.

Perhaps Arthur would finally get to know his father in death. If that was where he was headed. Would his dead old man be happy or disappointed to see him in the afterlife so soon? The Guardians told the people through mass media that they were simply the voice of The Creator. That any religion could offer a path to salvation and enlightenment if a person showed enough reverence and faith in something.

But what did he truly believe?

Did he really believe in all that Heaven and Hell bullshit? What was the point of following a religion if the gods were walking and talking in the world around them? Who was there left to worship as a Muslim or a Christian if the one energy being "*Creator*" that everybody, even the gods seemed to believe in... Well *The Creator* was just plain missing in action!

And really? Fuck the immortals!

How dare the *Creator* show up and give those almighty bastards the power to rule over the rest like Arthur and his mother! Living like slaves or ants under the gods was stifling enough, even with the illusion of free government and self-determination. It all made his skin crawl. Pissed him off even further as he stewed on it all - spiralling out in the quiet dark.

Perhaps life was all just a big joke!

Those born outside the highest echelons of power and wealth and any other measurement of worth were doomed from the start. People like him were cursed, weren't they? They'd never accomplish much of anything - aside from being lap dogs for these assholes. He thought back to all the service jobs he had worked to buy things that never lasted. Food. Alcohol. Club covers.

Human capital had a price, and each life could be stickered with a price tag and used up until the job was finished or the human broke. Did the immortals just see normal people as meat? Cows, fattened up to be ready for the slaughterhouse?

That's what had happened to him, right? He had broken. He let his anger get the better of him.

The existential crisis of the jail cell was cleansing in a way. Arthur was forced to think about what he might have wanted for himself had this little "incident" never happened. Had he ever wanted more than to take care of his mother and then burn out bright once she was gone? One last blitz of coke and alcohol on a Friday night, followed by a shotgun shell to the back of the mouth – providing he could find one? Burning out bright itself was an amusing notion. It felt like a consequence of too many moth and lightbulb stories from his youth.

"Easy is as easy does?" Honestly… What did that asshole, his dead dad know, that Arthur didn't?

More hours passed. Arthur slowly came to decide that his anger should be a tool, not a hazard, and so he tried to brainstorm ways in which he could turn his flaws into useful quirks should he make some magical prison breakout happen. The looming terror of prosecution and subsequent death kept prodding him out of his newfound philosophy, however, as did the ever-present pain in his body. The spiritual journey towards enlightenment would take a lot more than a few hours of quiet contemplation. One quickly grew tired of the existentialism of it all. The constant ache of injury denied him any easy sleep, so he at least made a point to wash off the dried blood as best he could in the tiny metal sink jutting from the concrete wall.

Arthur languished for what felt like days, sleeping on and off in short bursts at all hours as much as the pain would allow. The break in being trapped alone with his thoughts came in the form of an officer in white garb. Lights clicked on and off with proximity as he marched down the long row of cells on either side of the hallway. Arthur heard him coming long before he reached the cell. A younger man with soft brown eyes and hair swept to the side, clad in the same white combat armor the other two officers had been wearing. Possibly was Arthur's age, judging by the shitty goatee he was struggling to grow. He was formal, and clearly reciting a script someone had made him memorize. He clicked his heels together, then spoke to the cell as if Arthur wasn't inside, informing him of the charges laid out against him.

They were all fitting with Arthur's expectations as false charges go.

Assaulting an officer, disrupting the peace, public drunkenness, crimes against the state, and the biggest nail in his coffin, which he assumed would ensure a thoroughly fixed trial: disrupting the war effort.

Bullshit!

"Do you understand the charges?"

"Of course I fucking do, fake as shit or not."

The officer didn't reply to the sarcasm, simply turned and left, and Arthur was left to sulk in his cell. Was it ever too late to change these things once they got rolling? Or was almost every court case a foregone conclusion at the whim of some god-loving bureaucrat?

Despite his inner fears of torture or an oft-expected informal bullet to the back of the head, he wasn't approached again, and never found himself executed in the dark, all alone..

Occasionally an officer would walk past his cell down the line, but they would neither look at him nor acknowledge his presence in the empty row of cells, apparently more interested in the empty cells around him. He tried calling to them once or twice, only to be met with cold silence or feigned deafness.

He did wake up one night with the strange sensation of being watched. He was faced against the wall, and feeling the quiet airflow of someone breathing, pretended to roll over in his sleep. A brown-skinned man with jagged black hair at all angles lingered there outside the bars, peering in at him through the metal.

Arthur made an effort not to stir, and pretended to sleep for a little longer, but when the man remained, he finally dropped the sleeping façade, and sat up to speak to the jagged-haired man.

The stranger only rubbed his chin and wandered off down the row before Arthur could say anything.

"Hello? Who's there?"

No answer, only the slamming of the iron doors at the end of the cell block. In the murk, realizing none of the lights had come on like they were supposed to with the proximity sensors, Arthur wasn't able to get a good look at the man either. He supposed he was a lawyer or bureaucrat, likely appointed to be prosecuting or defending him. A fake show of actual legal process. The sandals and informal wear had shown him how little was expected, of course.

Arthur detested being so helpless and so thoroughly institutionalized.. Everywhere else in his life, his wit and his fists were good enough to settle any dispute. Now he was a faulty product, just like his schoolyard bullies had tried to prove all those years ago. The knowledge of this new failure drowned out the lingering dregs of his hope. He'd pushed down so much that he had figured he was the exact thing the system wanted – another braindead binge-alcoholic fixated on the basest urges in life. That was what the people in power wanted, right? Easy to control sheep!

He wasn't some dissident intellectual who disappeared by night, found floating in the river months later. Or was he? As far as he knew, he had been playing the game correctly, even if the game was indeed rigged from the very beginning by actual gods.

A few more tense days of boring silence swept past, and the same young officer arrived to present him with a court date. As by magic, within the hour he was quickly transferred to a more typical prison, and then even more quickly shuffled through the traditional British Justice system with a speed that implied clear-cut help from up above. He barely had time to take stock of his surroundings or try and make acquaintances in several different British prisons over the next few days. Within three days of getting his court date, he found himself in the courtroom, clad in a green and yellow boiler suit and secured firmly with chains and shackles around his wrists and ankles, all linked with a tiny silver chain emblazoned with the Guardian Helix. It made sense for the charges they had levied against him, false as were. He was to be painted as a dangerous menace to society, a terror to himself and others, strange, angry, drunkenly belligerent.

The trial was a sham, of course, but it somehow felt to Arthur like it was far more important than it should have been, like he was a deranged serial killer or a bomb-planting wartime terrorist. His reflection had dwindled down to a numb acceptance – the fantasies and what-ifs were gone, as was all the fire and anger that once spurted from his nostrils. He felt numb and defeated, erased in the face of this wall of bureaucracy.

The courtroom itself was largely empty save a handful of people. It was a hilarious turnout for such gravely inflated charges. The two officers involved in the incident and their state-salaried lawyers were present to serve as witnesses. Arthur's mother, thank god, was sitting in the public section of the court, although of course she was barred from taking the stand as a witness herself.

On seeing her there, relief washed over him. A sort of release. He could die in this state of being comfortably numb, knowing she was safe. That he hadn't taken her out with him. There was sparse turnout otherwise - the bailiff, the prosecutor, his state-appointed British counsel, and then the judge himself.

A handful of extended family members who he barely knew

consoled his mother in the public section. Outside of the courtroom floor proper, Arthur took note of the gorgeous brunette woman up in the gallery taking notes with a pen and pad. Clearly young enough to be a law student, maybe twenty at most. Slender and prudish. Soft olive skin. She was suited up like a lawyer or a librarian in a dour black skirt, legs crossed, and a prim and proper blazer over a white blouse, complete with meticulously-bunned hair and thick, black-rimmed glasses.

She was stunning.

Sharp features and unblemished skin save for the small scattering of freckles across her face and hands. She mostly wrote notes, so he could ogle her without her noticing.

Arthur couldn't lie, he tried for half the proceedings to imprint her memory in the back of his head, as she'd likely be the last non-guard, non-family woman he'd ever see again and she was one hundred percent his type.

It felt like a fun little game, one last librarian to wiggle his eyebrows at. It helped that she looked familiar, but that only put notions in his head – remembering past dalliances and memorable one night stands. She resembled one of many partners from his past, and he found himself pretending she was them, even. Come to see him burned as a last sort of scorned lover's spite.

But her colleague, well, it killed the fantasy somewhat.

Beside her was a younger man - about twenty-five in a light grey suit and black tie, a tad less meticulous than his counterpart. His long blonde hair was tied back in a rough ponytail, and he looked completely bored. He occasionally reapplied a bright red cherry chapstick while examining himself, mostly his hair, in a small pocket mirror. The scent wafted down ever so slightly to the point that Arthur began wrinkling his nose whenever the chapstick re-emerged. To make it worse, in and around his beauty routine, Blondie wasn't bothering to stifle his loud and frequent yawns, clearly audible in the near-empty court.

Fucking law students. The suit thing was starting to bug Arthur. It felt like all this professional dress held some sort of magic power over him in his ugly prison coveralls and manacles, as if his difference in appearance was enough to declare him guilty before the behemoth of the crispy-clean legal system and those feasting upon it with their eyes like hungry gluttons. Even his mother was wearing a nice dress with a plethora of fastened G.O.D. paraphernalia against her clavicle. Who knows if it was genuine belief or just some vain hope that demonstrating bureaucratic worship would help. Arthur grew hot and angry again thinking about how a woman with a bruise across half her face and a split lip would still play pretend, even though he knew she was probably doing it to try and help him with lesser charges in some way.

The bailiff read the charges, the same ones levelled at him in prison, and the proceedings began.

Arthur kept glancing up at the two in the press gallery, as both of the young law students seemed listless, sure that this trial was already a joke. Arthur sighed loudly every-time they whispered frantically to each other, drawing looks from both Judge and Bailiff.

Just get it over with, yeah?

Let him take the memory of the cute young brunette to his lonely cell before whatever was preplanned - be it a prison sentence, an execution, or some other punishment the bureaucrats had already decided all played out. Assaulting G.O.D. personnel could carry a sentence of death depending on the who and the where, as per the treaty with Britain.

He found himself anxious, distracted, and fidgety.

The blonde man would lean over and whisper in the brunette's ear every so often, to which she'd either nod curtly or wave him away dismissively. She never stopped jotting down notes, even while listening to the old grey-haired Judge rattling off statutes and legal precedent. It didn't really matter if the folks in the gallery were law students or state propagandists. He just knew it bothered him that what could signal the end of life as he knew it was some amusing farce for these stupid young fucks.

The blonde man leaned in for another whisper, and he just couldn't help himself.

"Can you two stop fucking around?"

The moment of silence that followed his callout dragged on for an eternity in the silent courtroom, as the judge continued obliviously looking over some documents. The woman took great offense to being thrown in with her friend, and glared back at him, leading the blonde man to grin mischievously. The call out had startled almost everyone, with the bailiff overreacting by dangerously shooting his grasp to the holster of his gun, regardless of the cuffs and chains that trapped Arthur's wrists and ankles together. The judge finished the page and glared down from the stand at him with a cold ire, drumming his fingers in annoyance. Nothing else was said, and the awkward and stuffy silence quickly descended again. His mother shot him a look of disapproval, tinged with fear.

Arthur shrugged back at her, rattling his chains softly as he scratched his stubbled chin.

Court proceeded.

As expected, both officers denied having ever come into physical contact with his mother, despite her sitting there in the courtroom with a blatant purple bruise on her cheek, one very poorly covered with makeup for some reason. They didn't even try to plead self-defense or say she struck first, they just lied on the stand entirely. Even the female partner wove such a complicated string of lies that Arthur couldn't keep up. The prosecutor thus accused both his mother and him of having falsified injuries and initial testimony.

The only reason she was free was her marriage to one Captain Bradley Brass, now deceased. A war hero or some such. Arthur opened his mouth to protest – to reference the fact that his mother was denied a role as a witness, but catching her eyes, a subtle shake of the head cowed Arthur into silence. The evidence piled on in stifling amounts, some of it shown in the courtroom, and some of it viewed by the judge alone in his rear chambers. He longed for a drink more and more as it dragged on, even if just a shitty lager.

It continued across several hours, ranging from poorly edited security camera footage at the far end of the apartment complex walkway, to the elaborate lies - a pair of false and clearly rehearsed testimonials from the two officers.

Arthur grew sick, just wanting it all to be over. He had resigned himself to his fate.

The judge at one point did speak to his mother's bruise as hard to falsify in passing, but seemed to understand that it wasn't his job to contradict the G.O.D. or to question the testimony and evidence provided by the Guardian secret police. At some points, the woman up in the gallery did make Arthur's heart flutter here and there, tutting loudly at some of the more preposterous and obvious lies from the officers. Arthur was grateful for her sudden turn in his favor, and the support silently endeared him towards her over the course of the proceedings.

It would be awfully hard to not objectify her in his dreams.

If he got one more night of rest, that was. The televised executions of traitors and war criminals were often held on the same day as the trials. The news only showed mostly blacked-out images of firing squads, and then always cut out to commercial as the bodies fell.

Nothing seemed to stop Mr. Ponytail from keeping on with his whispers and yawns beside his new eye-candy, though.

Arthur couldn't help but take a great and secret pleasure in the possibility of cuckolding the young man in his fantasies, afterwards.

Near the end of the trial as the judge meandered back into the recesses of the courthouse to begin the process to actually decide Arthur's fate, Arthur's old friend Billy popped into his brain.

Billy's dogged desire to get as far away from G.O.D. influenced London and Great Britain finally made sense to him. America might be a patchwork of loyalties to either side of the war, helping to keep Earth largely neutral in the conflict, but that move towards danger also ensured safety somewhat from the exact thing that was happening to him now. It was his fault, really. He had been stupid for not evacuating his mother from Britain sooner, or at least securing himself a prominent, visible role or career somewhere so that the two could have been safer.. Beaten down over his life, he had ceased thinking that any way out was even possible. That was the worst mistake, maybe.

He considered name-dropping his dad perhaps in some brave interjection while the Judge waffled in the rear chambers, but he never once honestly assumed his dead father's position would save him. At least he could have tried, instead of simply resigning himself to his fate like a weakling.

His own fucking apathy had doomed him, most of all. If he had bothered to do something with his life, perhaps he could have saved his mother. He could have bought land in the last few bits of countryside up north in Scotland, far from the police, from the mess of society, and from the bureaucracy. Somewhere out there on the frontier in the neutral colonies of The Milky Way, perhaps. A little ranch on the edge of colonized space. Pirates and raiders be damned, the risks still seemed better than this. He could have given her a garden to preoccupy herself. Yet, instead of filling the caretaker void his father had left behind, he leeched off his mother like a pathetic infant child until now, when he pulled her down with him.

The judge finally wandered back to his seat at the head of the court after what seemed like an eternity in his rear chambers, and Arthur prepared for the worst. He was settled on the idea that he would either be put to death or thrown in a cell to rot for the rest of his life - what he assumed was the standard verdict for assaulting G.O.D. officers and enforcers, amongst the very least of his false crimes in terms of scale.

He simmered in his anger and helplessness, staring at the floor until the judge emerged and coughed to draw the attention of those dozen-or-so bodies present. Arthur's pathetic pre-assigned defense attorney, a sniveling glasses wearing stick of a thing, had vanished during an earlier recess, and had not even bothered to return. An open-shut case, of course. The silent watcher from his cell had never materialized, likely refusing to even chronicle or witness such a pittance of a case.

Yet another bureaucrat.

The prosecutor was an older black gentleman in a three-piece suit. Dressed to the nines, he served as just another fixed segment of the whole song and dance.

The judge in his white and black ceremonial robes stalled at the last moment, and after recapping the evidence and the charges, stared down at Arthur with dark brown eyes. His light brown skin-tone almost matched Arthur's despite the liver spots and lines of age.

He continued to stall in the closing silence, seeming to be weighing something deep within himself - his wrinkles creasing further with some mysterious and quiet thought as he bored his gaze down into Arthur from his seat. An older man, but one probably long since used to the injustices of the system.

Arthur expected no mercy from an established crony like this.

His face was stern, and Arthur found he couldn't hold the man's eyes for very long, as he kept falling into the guessing game of whether he was bound for execution, disappearance, or life in prison.

Arthur gave up, trying to avoid his gaze by staring at the older man's nameplate to his right.

The honourable Judge Joseph Undelwood.

CHAPTER 2: FOR ALL OUR LOST TIME.

"Bending and Breaking are not mutually exclusive traits."

As the anxiety faded, Arthur embraced the anger rising within his temples under Judge Undelwood's withering gaze. He was quietly and resolutely angrier than he had ever been in his entire life before that point. He directed this cold seething anger and defiance upwards towards this older black man representing the entirety of the G.O.D. establishment, who met his silent wrath head-on with a dignified indifference.

Undoubtedly, the Judge was accustomed to years of defendant anger and despair, for his voice hadn't quavered even once.

Undelwood's voice was different in the sentencing - deep and knowing. It was the voice of an old, powerful man - one used to decades of doling out unfair punishments at the behest of his everliving masters.

"Arthur Brass."

The younger man sat up straight in his prison attire, clinking his chains emblazoned with the helix motif ever so softly.

"Based on the charges levied at you, contrasted against the oddity of the evidence, I'm going to give you an option, Mr. Brass."

The first words were tinged with an oddly warm tone, even as Arthur tried to avoid his eyes and direct as much quiet hatred as he could up at the golden-etched nameplate. The two up in the gallery bristled, and sat upright as well - suddenly at attention to the judge's change in mannerism.

"Largely due to the strangeness of the evidence, but also due to your family heritage, having had such a distinguished captain of the Guardian Navy for a father... I will grant you an exception to the terms of life imprisonment or execution that would normally accompany the charge of striking an officer of the Guardians of Destiny. This is assuredly not a regular circumstance under the United Kingdom's treaty with the Guardians proper. Not to mention the larger charges, for which I judge you to be "not guilty." The evidence is shoddy and obviously manipulated. I stand by my professional duty to uphold the law, regardless of who may or may not be in the room."

There was a heavy weight to his words. And he paused for a moment, mulling something over. Arthur could see Undelwood's entire focus was pointed directly down at him, and the Judge was trying hard to shut out everyone else in the room in order to make this moment an important one, with as much gravity and truth as he could muster.

"Arthur Brass, regardless of the events before it, you struck an officer, of that there is no doubt. Still... I have no direct power to punish officers of the G.O.D."

He steepled his fingers together.

"As a Judge of The United Kingdom, I'm giving you two choices as a result of both the testimony presented at this trial as well as the bruises clearly visible on your mother's body. In fact, I'm quite perplexed at such a bizarre injury, one that she could not have given herself without great effort. There is self-defense somewhere in this case that is not being addressed and I am unable to place it anywhere truly rational. I suspect foul play in my courtroom, which greatly offends me."

Arthur gaped, at a loss for words.

His eyes slowly slid back to Undelwood's from where they had been burning holes in the placard to his left. Panic, shock, relief, fear. Every emotion in the book cycled through him like a carousel strapped with a jet engine. The two officers looked ready to jump out of their seats, but the Guardians of Destiny pin on the judge's right breast was undoubtedly the only thing keeping them quiet. The bailiff stood quietly, a small smirk on his face at the tension between the judge and the secret police. The two in the gallery were apparently riveted by the sudden turn of events, the woman fuming visibly at the judge's lack of reverence and likely also at his refutation of G.O.D. authority.

Great stuff for a paper, or an examination or some shit though, Arthur was sure.

"Either you accept the initial verdict of life imprisonment without parole, ignoring what should be an immediate execution as per the charges of assaulting an officer under the treaty, or alternatively..."

The courtroom hung on his words and the pause that followed.

"You may walk away with a clean and untarnished record, provided you immediately enlist in the G.O.D. Naval Academy as your father did before you. Choosing the second option will allow me to waive all charges against you, insofar as you successfully graduate from the Academy and enlist as an officer for a single term of 5 years. I do this as a justice of the people - as allowable by the initial treaty, article twelve, subsection thirteen, between His Royal Majesty of Britain and the Guardians of Destiny. I acknowledge the role of the latter as a higher power and protector of the entirety of the human race. Serving time as per conscription rules in lieu of jail time is an option for every citizen, although it has not been invoked in some time."

Undelwood paused, carefully choosing his words before he continued. The pause was interjected by a loud click from all of the microphones dangling haphazardly around the courtroom, almost simultaneously. The soft droning noise of electricity and the attached chirps of feedback from courtroom A.I. stenographers had disappeared as well.

"I also hereby acknowledge for the record that this is highly unorthodox. It is not often that a family legacy takes such a sudden and stark departure from a father's noble service toward the greater good of our species. I met Captain Brass once, and I could tell that he was an honorable man, even in the brief passing moments I met him. I feel this story can still be moved back towards that path. Penance may be paid to the gods, gifted as this opportunity passed down from father to son. I am of course taking a risk by gambling on your character, but after the G.O.D.'s recent losses, the need for Naval officers is high, and enlistments have tapered.

The officers looked nervous. Arthur's mother gaped.

"I would hope to see this trend of restorative justice become the norm. You can pay for your crimes with time served, and aid all of humanity with your service by protecting us from the threat of the Armada's hordes. I offer this choice to you as part of my duty towards the twin law of both The United Kingdom and The Guardians of Destiny, the latter of whom protect all of humanity from those that would do us harm."

Arthur almost chose life in prison in his moment of shock and in his lack of comprehension, somehow seeing this act of charity as merely a convoluted plot to swell the G.O.D. ranks.

Conscription under a different name!

After all, serving immortals was always a life sentence regardless. One would be unlikely to survive a full five years. Of course, he already knew the lackeys of immortals rarely ever outlived their ageless masters. The choice was between service or confinement for the rest of his shortening life.

His choice had been reduced to a black and white painting of toy soldiers playing war upon a painted backdrop of stars.

Hell, perhaps suicide was still an option?

Arthur looked back at his mother sitting in the public section of the court, meeting her eyes and trying to catch some possible meaning or answer from her worried expression.

The G.O.D. was corrupt as hell. Walking around as religious saviours, pretending to guide the entirety of humanity, when everyone knew the stories. Wealth! Decadence! Immortality!

People's lives were reduced to mere playthings. To be thrown away in some false crusade against a great evil. It wasn't much of a secret how nepotistic and steeped in cronyism the gods were.

After however many thousands of years, they were likely all well-versed in playing favorites. Every bar-room hero told stories of harems, consorts, and every weekend warrior's favorite - the binge-weekends of legend! But no matter how deep the corruption ran...

He continued locking eyes with his mother, seeking some sort of sign. Her worried expression morphed into a worried smile, and a simple nod. After looking at her for a few more seconds, the bruise being the clearest and most noticeable thing on her face, he turned back to Judge Joe Undelwood.

If it ensured he could protect his mother with such a status...

He nodded up at the older gentleman, which luckily for him the judge interpreted as an affirmative to the offer laid out before him..

"Then I do, in fact, as a justice of the nation of Great Britain, pardon you of all other charges. Your good standing as a citizen of this country and a servant of all humanity shall be upheld via service to our glorious protectors, The Guardians of Destiny. For a period of five years. May the gods themselves decide your new fate, Arthur Brass."

At the conclusion of this strange verdict, with warmth seeping forth from the Judge towards Arthur, the courtroom echoed with a slam. The woman up in the gallery had slapped her notepad on the seat beside her loudly. Immediately she and her blonde-ponytailed companion descended into hushed whispers, heads bent together like daffodils. Her blonde companion was visibly irritated, his ponytail shaking feverishly a single time.

They paused, then stood up to hurriedly leave when they noticed everyone below in the court staring up at them.

The core group involved in this bizarre turn of events remained in the courtroom for a time - Arthur's mother, the bailiff, the judge, and Arthur himself, with Judge Joe Undelwood citing at him an endless list of stipulations, conditions, legal jargon, and other issues that would be necessary pending his release. Five years was surely just a number on a piece of paper, and there were plenty of loopholes that would ensure his service for much longer than that, it sounded like.

"I will take the vast majority of these formalities upon myself, having rendered such an... Irregular verdict. This is to avoid outcry from the press and other authorities as pertaining to G.O.D. nepotism or favoritism. I will perhaps even be forced to intervene directly to avoid an appeal should they dislike my push for restorative justice in this new age of Armada-Guardian treaties and neutral unaligned planets. I will be your direct supervisor in this process, of course."

His words did not offer the relief that Arthur assumed was intended, due to his already-racing brain. But he was indeed released from his shackles, and freed almost immediately afterward into his mother's care.

The first thing he did was get blackout drunk, of course.

After that, Arthur was given a period of two months to get his affairs in order and to heal up after his 'accidental fall' that had occurred right before the trial. Arthur would be required to report to Judge Joseph Undelwood directly, quickly coming to know the judge more personally as his sponsor. It was Undelwood who had signed up as his primary sponsorship nomination into the G.O.D. Naval Academy on Venus. Arthur was struck with how much he didn't know about the world of politics or the greater galaxy beyond London.

It all seemed so bizarre, and he couldn't help but wonder if the Judge had known his father more closely than he let on before the captain's death, possibly through the military or some other such passing connection. When would a judge and a Guardian naval captain have the chance to meet?

It was the only explanation for what felt like being gifted a second chance via this elderly stranger.

Nepotism disguised as kindness, perhaps?

Arthur couldn't help but be suspicious of it, and remained skeptical at best. Perhaps, he figured, this Judge Undelwood was merely padding the end of his career with a sappy story about leniency and reforming hardened criminals unto a life of greater good at great personal risk. Or maybe he just wanted a favor owed? The man was feeding him into the ranks of the Guardians of Destiny after all, so for all it probably mattered to the Judge, Arthur would likely die in the war anyway in some backwater engagement above a farming or resource world. That was the usual story for the boonies, as far as he could know.

Most applicants to the Naval academy hoping to be considered for officer positions were required to have had prior military or navy experience, and also to have an army, navy, government, or other higher ranking political or military G.O.D. contact as a sponsor, which was in his case - Judge Undelwood.

But Arthur was not stupid.

The fudging of this rule worried him.. He was being fed to the meat grinder rather than shot in the head or kept in a prison cell, to become some useful product of his warped society. He found himself wondering who had sponsored his father upon his initial entry to the academy, and how long he had served even before his own admission on Venus.

Arthur would have only been a year or two old when his father first applied. He was forced to consider that he would be entering the Military Industrial Complex of an organization beyond the country of his birth, where he would be risking life and limb in an active and ongoing war across a good swath of several arms of the Milky Way. He would finally see for himself the horrors he had tuned out for so long in the media, whilst fighting in a near-fanatical religious organization whose overarching goal was to nebulously guard the "destiny" of humanity.

But what did that truly mean?

This revelation of sponsorship made him curious as to how much sway judge Joe Undelwood kept. His admission was never questioned by anyone he talked to, and every single one of his documents was signed not by the Judge himself, but instead with a single "H" scrawled in a lazy print - half on and half off the dotted line.

An alias of The Judge, perhaps?

For all he was worth, Arthur did what he knew to do best and pressed his fears and worries down to a dull roar at the base of his spine. Anxiety crept through his body like poison, tensing his jaw and brow at all hours of the day. This was a second chance, hell, multiple second chances, all rolled into one clusterfuck of bureaucracy and secrecy. It was also a chance for him to change to become the sort of man his father might have been, a foggy story of "once upon a time" over a decade ago.

Arthur never expected leaving to be so easy. He had already been fired from his daytime advertising job due to his sudden absence – somehow, they had never even been informed of his initial arrest, and much to his surprise, there was no record post-pardon that he had ever broken any law, let alone been incarcerated or charged with anything.

Whatever Undelwood had quoted really made things strangely easy throughout the process.

He knew there must be a secret pipeline to all this. Perhaps it happened constantly enough to feed the immortal hunger for manpower while remaining largely unknown in society due to the one way trip. Still, he was chuffed that his face wasn't plastered across every news feed in the country, even if it did make the entire fiasco seem all that more unfair in how it had played out.

Arthur couldn't help but fall into a conspiracy theorist mindset that the G.O.D. had been recruiting this way for years under the radar. But was it really any better to choose an unjust execution over what amounted to illegal conscription by a greater foreign military power?

At least one had a chance at surviving to live a normal life, with one option of the two presented to him.

He thought about running away at times, maybe escaping to one of the Armada favored states in America like Texas, or to a country like Russia that had declared itself steadfastly neutral towards any of these shadowy immortal bastards out there in the galaxy. But with his mother's safety on the line indirectly, he couldn't dare turn back. Even if he could escape and somehow his mother was miraculously left alone in peace, the Guardians were a group of immortals that ruled just over a quarter of the damn galaxy!

According to the history books in school, rapidly rewritten when the gods revealed themselves to the public decades ago in the forties, they had gently nudged, shaped, and guided all of humanity from the shadows, entirely in secret somehow - for tens of thousands of years. Surely that meant they had eyes and ears everywhere, and one of their agents would find him no matter where he hid should he flee. It was inevitable, he guessed.

All paths now led to the Naval Academy on Venus.

The two months prior to shipping out flashed by as a long series of goodbyes to everyone he had ever kept somewhat close around him.

Save his mother, oddly.

Even as her bruises faded, she kept her distance, even actively avoiding him around the apartment. It broke his heart, as in his mind he had made the decision for her. He figured this was likely to protect his feelings, but it still hurt like getting smacked in the heart with a brick.

The day before he was scheduled to leave, his mother broke the imaginary wall she had erected between them, and brought him into her room with the subtle curling of a finger in his bedroom door frame. She sat him down on the bed and stared into his eyes with her hands on his shoulders, taking a very long time to gather herself.

"Arthur, before you go, I want you to know a tiny bit about

what sort of man your father was."

She opened her bedside table and pulled out a small red cedar box, stained with an amber hue. Inside were a pair of tiny silver cufflinks, which he recognized as his father's from all the older man's formal Naval photographs.

They had never matched the other officers in any of the pictures, as cufflinks weren't officially required as part of the uniform, so they were clearly out of the norm for being in most dress uniform photos.

As he held them, he trailed his thumbs across the cufflink's swirling cursive letters. "AB" was etched cleanly into both, perched almost precariously above a tiny sailing boat engraved in the silver.

A reminder of his son, whilst Captain Bradley Brass sailed across the spaces between stars.

"Your father may not have died in an enormous conflict with honors being given out left and right posthumously, but he fought very hard to keep you safe back here on Earth, even as the Navy forced him to stay away for longer and longer out in the colonies or fighting on the edge of *The Black*."

She closed his hands with hers, pressing the cufflinks into his palms with a soft sigh, and a feeble smile. She was clearly struggling, and had been building up to this moment emotionally.

"When your father and I were young, we wanted to sail the world. The *Junktown Blues* was the sailboat we bought to do it, but then your father lost his parents, and he had to sell it to cover costs for their passing. Later, when he started his own merchant line with the Junk and Rumblers Guild out to the far colonies, he named the old freighter he bought after that sailboat. He never made enough money as a trader to take the time off and buy another boat so we could see our dream to the finish. The second *Junktown Blues* has been in drydock for years."

She paused, staring into Arthur's soul through his eyes for a single, eternal moment.

"I think you would have loved growing up on the high seas. Maybe it would have helped, because I so often have no idea what to do, and I'm just so paralyzed with doubt. I sat here and did nothing as you drowned for all these years."

She was crying now, but batted his hands away steadfastly when he tried to reach over and wipe her tears.

"I can't help but blame myself for all this."

"Mom, no…"

"And then Brad took that Navy job. He worked so hard. And he loved you so much. Then tours got longer and longer. The time we were all supposed to share together never came."

More sniffles. The emotions he had pushed to the base of his spine itched, trying to escape their cage. He could taste the sour tang of craving.

Throwing back a rougher whiskey was usually the cure for this emotional stuff.

"I know that your father didn't die in the front-lines of the war, Arthur. I'm not stupid. But after the Navy took him, he did everything that was asked of him to the letter.

He set his jaw.

"He loved us so very much through it all. I know this isn't what you wanted, baby. But no matter what happens - when you serve your time, please, please promise me Arthur… Promise me that you'll never let go of your dreams like we did."

Arthur gave her a big hug and held her there for a long while to let her cry it all out, with her face buried into his shoulder. Her porcelain skin was frail – like wrapping paper to the touch.

A lifelong struggle with anorexia.

He couldn't fathom how such a spindly, frail woman like her could be so damn strong on the inside. Here he was, a strapping young lad, who simply couldn't keep his emotions or his drinking problem in check worth two shits. He admired his mother eternally for that inner strength.

The two stayed like that for a long time, the latter half in silence as they both quietly cried, and then did their best for the rest of the day to pretend that things were normal.

After a fitful sleep, he left the next morning - after kissing her on the cheek and giving her another long, silent hug. The momentary frailty he had seen the day before was gone, replaced with the same quiet power and resolve he had always known from her.

A façade in action.

Arthur found that you always remembered people for either their greatest strengths or their greatest weaknesses.

His mother, he always remembered for her strength.

"Good luck out there Arthur."

She pulled him close.

"I'll always love you. And I'll always be rooting for you out there."

Her final words to a child lost to war.

CHAPTER 3: TO SLEEP, PERCHANCE TO DREAM.

"When the only direction to go is up, you often tend to go up."

Arthur was exasperated with the monotony of travel.

It was only made worse by the fact that Judge Undelwood was only able to arrange a traditional civilian space shuttle for his journey to the academy on Venus, damning him to almost thirty-six long hours of silent recollection.

It was actually quite fast by more archaic standards, but felt slow all the same.

The war economy had rendered most space travel expensive, and even G.O.D. budgets could be constrained. Cold-fusion engines were fast, but any ship large enough to be outfitted with a rift generator could simply open a rift. Folding two points in space-time together could have gotten him there in just a few minutes after initial boarding rather than the hell of such a long flight. He managed to keep his thoughts in his head for the most part, despite being stuck next to a particularly chipper and pudgy young applicant.

This infuriating, stupid younger man went by the name of Gidder, and Arthur finally shut him up after fifteen minutes of throwing angry one word replies back at the new irritant. It was a blessing then, when Gidder fell asleep and snored loudly for the general remainder of the trip.

Arthur never bothered to ask for his last name.

There was a brief, frustrated panic when Gidder woke up somewhere in the middle of the journey to ask where they were, but at the cold angry silence from Arthur, he sighed and turned back towards the window and the stars outside and promptly fell back asleep.

The universe had grown infinitely large to tiny little humanity in the past few centuries, not that many of them knew about it until relatively recently. Each star twinkling outside the window was another beacon, a possibility out there to be some distant solar system. Each one just might be home to hundreds, if not millions of people – humans who had never known Earth for generations in the earliest colony seeding back in the 1700's.

A strange thought - that while the majority of humanity were barely sailing the seas, the gods were shooting cryogenically frozen colonists through prototype rifts to colonize the nearby arms of the Milky Way.

Who was still out there? Lost without contact now that the rest of humanity had acclimatized to the speed of merely linking two points together.

Arthur tried to imagine them, growing up on distant terraformed planets and learning about Earth in textbooks while everybody back on the actual homeworld hadn't a clue they ever even existed in the first place. The propaganda and illusions of primitivism had run so deep, for so long, that only the highest council gods really knew when the first colony ships went out, all those hundreds of years before proper rift travel was established.

For all Arthur knew, after training on Venus, he'd be travelling to planets that people had been living on for centuries. Hell, he'd hardly know the names of them yet… Although that was probably due to the fact that he never paid much attention in geography or astronomy class. As far as humanity knew - aliens didn't exist out in the black. Even The Black Armada was originally just a splinter faction of the Guardians of Destiny, stabbing them in the back way back in the 1800s sometime.

That gave Arthur pause.

The idea of an evil empire out there worshipping some god-emperor, especially a god-emperor who had betrayed and eaten the real Creator….

Well…

Arthur paused just long enough to fondly hope in a streak of misanthropy that should humanity ever meet real intelligent aliens, the bastards would blow both the Guardians of Destiny and the Black Armada to smithereens, even if he had to die with the rest of humanity to have it happen.

His old mobile was a piece of junk, without any civilian comms buoy relay to connect to without paying out the nose. He hadn't been provided with any G.O.D. military communication devices yet, so to bide his time and avoid interacting with pudgy, annoying Gidder he stared out into the sea of stars twinkling in patches of blue and yellow against the black. Without the pollution of London's city lights to block it, the Milky Way stretched out like a giant rolling wave outside the viewport, and the weight of it finally hit him that this was his first time leaving not only his own homeworld, but the homeworld of all humanity.

He was sure it had been one hell of a shock some three or four decades ago when the Armada and Guardians popped out of the woodwork to say they had been secretly exploring and colonizing the stars for centuries. It must have been a second, equally jarring shock that just as soon as they had materialized, they also casually explained: "Oh just so you know we're actually at war with each other and have been using your dumb earthling caveman societies as proxies the whole time."

There was a numb hilarity to that – that while most of humanity's best and brightest on Earth were figuring out how to sail the terrestrial oceans - centuries behind the immortals and their lackeys, the gods were already soaring out into the black in their starships, plopping down terraforming machines, transplanting Earth ecosystems, and somehow abducting swaths of the best and brightest people in the night, all to colonize alien worlds.

It had to be certain that some of the kings and queens had been in on the deal somehow. Bowing before gods seemed like a thing a monarch would do...

Perhaps it wasn't geniuses, it was instead various crews of convicts or undesirables, people like him - being shipped out across the galaxy. That's how Australia was colonized by the British, wasn't it?

Well, silver lining, at least the colonies had no local population to displace and commit genocide on outside of the colonists themselves.

Fucking immortals.

Fucking G.O.D.

"The Guardians of Destiny."

Proclaimed "protectors of all humanity and their shared future."

Granted superhuman abilities by some energy being on a fucking whim.

Agelessness, with insane regeneration from wounds and ailments beyond any normal human body. And even gifted a manipulation of the very energy and matter in proximity around their bodies – a trick bestowed by some mysterious energy being – "The Creator" back in pre-history to guard a nebulous future.

How much of the grandiose, religion-infused story was true, and how much was false? What had been carefully concocted to ensure that people like him remained firmly in line and serving?

They could be killed of course. Even Arthur knew immortal did not quite mean indestructible. You'd see it in the news every so often, that minor gods one one side or the other had been killed in action.

There was always a day of mourning when the G.O.D. announced that some lesser god in the local hierarchy had been struck down in the line of duty. But new gods popped up all the time, slowly worming their way up the ranks towards the mysterious ruling council itself. Whether they were born, grown in test tubes, or created with some strange magicks, well...

Arthur could only guess.

Thus, Arthur's thoughts raced ever onwards - building elaborate conspiracy theories and alternate histories to wile away the travel time. It was kind of fun to invent new titles and gods that may or may not even exist.

The shuttle plodded along at what seemed like a snail's pace to him, despite really being a relatively quick trip for such a small shuttle without a rift generator. Arthur knew how big space was, but he figured that in all the time the gods had been out here, humanity would be better already as a species at getting around.

When one could just crack open a big white hole in space-time, easily wormhole-linking two points, everything else would of course seem slow by comparison.

When Venus finally appeared as a slowly growing yellow dot in the distance, a sense of elation overcame him and a subtle but ever-present black pit of fear grew in his gut. He wasn't sure if it was the shifting gravity as the shuttle's artificial source battled the true gravity of Venus, or his own fears. Regardless, he wanted to push the feelings down to the bottom of his spine, and the gentle tug of gravity doubled down and made the pit appear all the worse.

At first glance, Arthur was surprised that Venus hadn't been terraformed somehow, from its initial deathtrap status as a planet.

Sulphuric acid droplets in the clouds, bone-crushing pressure, crazy pressure-cooker heat, and wild atmospheric storms higher above the surface proper weren't exactly great for the average human's health.

The G.O.D. Naval Academy proper was on Venus' northern pole, where the storms were worst of course, and the shuttle was, (as expected,) slow to navigate through an enormous security blockade in orbit even before they ever hit the howling winds and insane heat. The security process involved docking to orbital space-elevator connected stations, guarded by at least two G.O.D. battlecruisers. The checkpoint security searches occurred two separate times at two unique orbital checkpoints.

The checkpoints made sense to Arthur. The Guardian military had been attempting to consolidate its power on the Solar System for a number of years after the recent treaties with the Black Armada. The treaties declared Earth's Solar System as neutral ground. The only proper neutral ground outside the neutral territories. As such, Arthur had expected a full body scan or two, but... The border guards went as far as to individually inspect every item of baggage via scanner. Each checkpoint took over an hour for the mere half-dozen passengers due to the supplies freighted belowdecks.

The enormous kilometres-long battlecruisers loomed in the viewports the whole while, each equipped with enough firepower to shred the tiny transport shuttle into a hundred-thousand pieces of debris. Venus was never exactly a top tier military installation, and was more so an outpost campground for officer-fodder-in-training, so he was perplexed as to why they were so obsessive about security. Surely no military secrets were stored in-system, right?

The Black Armada had been at war with the G.O.D. for centuries. The current year - 2092 was staring down the end of the century with no resolution to this war in sight. Hundreds of years of war - ongoing since the 1800's sometime, with the two sides opposed based purely on their innermost philosophies of religion and power structures.

Maybe there had been peace talks over the decades. Likely in secret of course, as they didn't want to alert the masses, but probably always at a level far above all the plebeians down on good old "Terra."

It bothered him that this bitter, angry, meat-grinding Guardian military machine would likely be his life from here on out.

Five years had to be a scam, right?

Really, just because the birth system of Humanity was 'secure' didn't mean the Guardians of Destiny had won the war or were even really routing out spies. Was every second recruit into the academy a terrorist? Shouldn't the gods be more worried about the bureaucrats that worked for them…?

Arthur became even more irate when the guard searching his bag took out his tiny travel bottle of shampoo and tube of toothpaste and chucked them, citing a hoarse and gravelly rendition of 'No Liquids.' It was as if the guard forgot that the planet the station was orbiting was covered in deadly clouds of sulfuric acid... Lots of liquid in the clouds down there that either of them could take a bath in!

Arthur was allowed one respite – as Gidder was escorted off the shuttle into the airlock of the station. It was a silent monologue of vitriol for Arthur – as this one guard was to be his last target, allowing for a final venting against the establishment before falling in line and trying to be a good little G.O.D. puppet like they wanted him to be.

He silently swore it to himself.

Private Muniz, by his black on white name tag, was rifling through his boxers and whisking a handheld detector of some sort over each folded pair in the bag as a second woman stood and watched. This whole search act to Arthur was a justification of the big picture, if one connected the dots.

There was an agony in that.

The G.O.D. had never even tried to hide the history of control, that it had secretly been manipulating the governments and rulers of the world for most of recorded time. Religion was an easy answer, pointing at the holy word of The Creator, conflated with the original Abrahamic God most people worshipped. Established religion usually allowed for easy coercion into a greater narrative of course.

The gods managed to sweeten this fact up with the argument that it had ensured the safety of the majority, and had already prevented hundreds of genocides, despite the blatant and even aggressively encouraged travesties of two world wars and the colonialism-based warring before it.

And then the massacres that followed the local mining insurrections on Mars over forty years ago, just before it all went public.

Ultimately, an organization full of immortals so arrogant as the Guardians of Destiny hardly cared what he thought of his undies being searched.

The propaganda reinforced this notion of deference to greater powers to anybody still listening. All the media touted to ordinary mortal folk like him was that the vile Xex, the tyrannical "God of Control" and former Prime Triumvirate member, would go to any length to desecrate what the Guardians stood for.

So who truly ruled the "Central Universe?"

To Arthur, even the notion of being the center of all universes in the multiverse was laughable.

There was only one Universe as far as he could see, so how the hell could it be the Central one?

Did they think people were stupid?

Well, of course they did, but where would Xex have come from, with his army powerful enough to challenge the gods if not from the G.O.D. itself? The whole immortal shtick was rotten any way he looked at it.

Arthur's tendency to zone out was making it difficult for the female guard to ask the occasional question, as she was often having to ask it twice before Arthur snapped to attention and answered.

Did that make him suspicious? Did they even care if he wore boxers or briefs?

Rumours abounded, and the few friends of friends he had met at parties who operated within the more illegal of British circles had guaranteed him of the Black Armada's actual existence. One buddy of a buddy had even boasted in Arthur's specific company that he had sold guns to a person who had identified themselves as an Armada agent. He had assumed the guy was an idiot for saying such out loud at the time and wondered why the secret police had not scooped *him* up long before.

And here he was! Arthur Brass, the everyday citizen, now knocking at the doors to the gods' military industrial complex!

How did the secondary players like the corporations and guilds get around these sorts of searches to get into places like Venus?

The U.S. based *Sunbelt Suppliers Company* dared to openly pursue trade with the Armada in the majority of its' contracts, despite apparently "neutral" global markets post-treaty. There was certainly profit in the intense war production economy. *The Whiskeyjack Company* out of Texas was rumored to deal with the Armada too, but nobody ever had much proof as they paid taxes and tithes appropriately…

Private Muniz finally let him off the hook, but he also failed to bother repacking anything with any tact. Arthur was then marched aboard the station for secondary screening shortly after Gidder. It was only after a half hour of harsh questioning that Arthur was deemed safe, and capable of rejoining his few other peers to continue the journey down to the surface beyond the naval blockade.

As the shuttle made ready to undock, Gidder was still nowhere in sight.

Apparently being stuck in thought and aloof to the guard's questions was rude, but perhaps it also marked him as simple-minded enough not to get pulled aside and properly strip searched, as was likely the fate his pudgy comrade recruit had been delivered unto.

The shuttle plodded onwards after the last academy enlister had been screened or vanished, in roughly equal numbers.

Tight stakes on Venus, apparently.

The pit in his stomach was expanding and contracting, and

his throat ached for the burn of something with a high alcohol content. A vodka-soda on ice would have been sublime!

Venus was dotted with high atmosphere listening posts and low orbit defense stations, due to the similarities of its upper atmosphere to Earth. However, breaking orbit was slow and dull for safety reasons, and the descent gave him more than ample time to read and reread the *Caution! Barrier may be extremely hot on re-entry, please do not touch!* sign on the window.

After the initial descent through the roughest part of the storms swirling the northern pole, it was actually kind of idyllic to watch the yellow clouds drift past as the shuttle skipped the remainder of the high winds, the acid, and the pressure by skirting the edges of such chaos.

As they roamed the skies at supersonic speeds, Arthur could feel destiny drawing closer at the same rate of speed as the academy.

The academy proper was carefully hidden within the vortex of clouds that swirled around the mountain ranges hidden beneath the tumultuous northern pole. It was a dangerous location, even more so than the rest of Venus below the skyline. It made perfect sense to Arthur from a tactical standpoint, though. The storms and circular wind patterns around the poles guaranteed isolation and protection.

The real danger of Venus was its deceptively opposite surface level.

The shuttle began rocking and jolting the minute it dipped too far below the clouds for the final drop, with *Maxwell Mons* looming in the distance. While the intense winds of the planet died off the higher up one got, the intense pressure and heat closer to the surface made existence inside a tin can like the civilian shuttle incredibly dangerous.

Tension rose at every creak or groan of the cabin around him.

A single blown seal, or a malfunctioning airlock could cook or crush a person in seconds, and every cadet including Arthur was thoroughly scared stiff with all the ways one could die on that tiny yellow ball full of anger.

He was never a religious kid, but he prayed to any and every god that might be real, even some of his own creations, with each jerking motion of the craft. A secondary set of prayers was devoted to the hope that the Gravity Generator would keep running to offset the pressure outside, and that the hull and heat shields had no missed leaks to allow the heat to seep in and cook them alive.

Arthur could hardly see out the window to the dimly lit plains below, but could see rays of light from somewhere far below the shuttle's trajectory, as beaming searchlights shone upwards to guide the descent. They must have been somehow shielded from the pressure and boiling heat, to last so long in such an antagonizing place.

They got closer down towards *Maxwell Mons*, the main nesting site of the academy, and he could start to see the plains around the mountain chain a little better.

Giant squat machines were strewn across the landscape, spewing whitish clouds of what he assumed to be recycled nitrogen and oxygen into the air in hopes that mankind might be able to live a little less mortally on the surface one day without the pressure and heat.

It was a valiant effort, trying to terraform such a hostile world, as most people knew that usually colony worlds were selected much more carefully to avoid wasting excessive resources during the terraforming process. The solar system was hardly friendly outside of Earth itself. But it made sense to try and better colonize the home system, for sentimental reasons.

Who knew science from school would actually come in handy?

All around the enormous plateaus and around the mountain peaks, Skyjacks dipped and dove in patrol patterns, each equipped with acid coating and pressure shielding. The small defense drones darted to and fro, weaving vapor trails in some complex dance only the simple Class 1 and 2 artificial intelligences themselves understood.

Every single piece of the machinery on Venus was carefully protected from the planet itself, serving as a sort of defense even without the battlecruisers up above and the ground defenses down below.

Despite her brutal appearance, seemingly unchanged since a runaway greenhouse effect festered and ran rampant millions of years ago, Venus had lightened up, if only a little due to the ongoing terraforming attempts. The clouds had thinned enough over the past half century to let more light in.

The atmosphere was indeed slowly changing.

Still, Venus was definitely a long way from being the next Earth.

Terraforming was surely an expensive task - and choosing planets that could be terraformed in days, weeks, or months must have been preferable to worlds like Venus, which might take centuries more work before humans could ever hope to walk freely on the surface. Arthur figured that perhaps one day when the pressure and heat abated more, seeded plants could help filter the carbon dioxide from the planet instead of the enormous cloud spewing machines that belched white vapor in long trails all around him.

For sabotage or perhaps depressurization reasons, *Maxwell Mons*' Guardian Naval Academy and the other secret installations built into *Ishtar Terra* had no windows that he could see in the rocky yellowed exteriors. Only the spotlights leered up at the shuttle.

The notion of being safer in the depths of a mountain was a temporary reprieve from the certain deathtrap that was this civilian shuttle. How many runs had this hunk of junk made to and from Venus, each time getting a little more banged up or corroded by acid until it eventually crumpled like a soda can sunk under the deepest parts of the ocean?

A few more careful minutes, the white searchlights were finally matched with other beams of light - all of varying colors; blues, reds, and greens.

Landing lights.

The window was illuminated brightly enough that he had to look away.

"Attention all passengers, prepare for final docking at Maxwell. Please double-check that you have all your belongings, as any items left behind will be discarded under G.O.D. biohazard security protocols."

Arthur let out the breath he didn't realize he had been holding for several long seconds.

Arrival was enough to send relief shooting down his limbs in waves of blood and a dangerous sense of finality to his journey. He grabbed his duffel bag from the overhead compartment and joined the small queue that was forming towards the rear loading bay gangplank.

"Blast doors sealed and pressurized, all passengers please get ready to disembark. Please follow the directions of any and all G.O.D. personnel upon descending the gangplank. Thank you for flying with *In-System Charters*."

There was a loud clunk, and the shuttle clanged twice in unison with something outside.

The queue began to move, with the various bodies slowly filing through the opening airlock and down the ramp. Arthur was puzzled when he first emerged into the hangar, as instead of the grey, yellowish metal and rock he had expected, the entire hangar was lit up with a bright nighttime interior.

The line of recruits passed from the shuttle's gangplank onto a second story catwalk, then through and above the main hangar. He was somewhat spellbound to see the beautiful nighttime cityscape of Tokyo broadcast via hologram along the walls and outside every one of the "windows," as if they were all magically back on Earth. He didn't guess it to be Tokyo at first, if not for the gold subtitles softly shimmering in the night skies above the enormous cityscape - filled with hundreds of seventy-plus-story skyscrapers and interlaced with various sky-traffic.

Someone up ahead began barking orders, clearly a drill instructor. The small line followed the voice, winding past rows of white Agatha aircraft transports and other such G.O.D. machines of war, most gleaming white and marked with the same glossy anti-acid sheen to ward them from the harsh Venusian atmosphere. The bright pinpoint lights of arc welding could be seen amongst some of them.

The wide, spacious hallways burrowed through the mountainsides, and the holographic projectors broadcast similar fake scenes as the hangar onto all the walls of the installation, with specific "environments" depending on which hallway or room one was in. Arthur guessed it was on some sort of daily or weekly rotation.

Mesmerized by the holograms, Arthur realized somewhat late that the drill instructor's yelling had gotten closer, and each recruit in line was being sorted, ordered to follow the colored lines on the floor based on their enlistment, with Red, Blue, and Green, leading to specific areas.

Thanks to the wait in line for his turn, he was able to watch the beautiful holographic scenes all around him, broadcasted along almost every surface save the roof, floor, and signage. The rolling sands of the Gobi Desert were splayed out across the hallway, with gently blowing winds pulling wafting sprays of sand from the tops of each dune to scatter down the valleys of tan, beige, and yellow.

They were processed and quadruple checked yet again, albeit more lightly by G.O.D. footsoldiers. It felt like the umpteenth-time, but at least the scenes changed every little while along a particular theme, with engaging mock-ups of both the familiar and the foreign. Some hallways and rooms hosted unique scenes - kelp forests, coral reefs, and tropical beaches like those of the various atolls of *Dhekar-Qiraj*.

The cafeteria displayed a series of vast windswept plains with lightning strikes across a grey cloudy sky, *Ashes of Sunrise*. Here and there, the myriad of fantastical scenes loomed - enormous crystal spires, or endless windswept oceans dotted with volcano vents appearing from the waves. All of it was interspersed with dozens of other foreign worlds.

It made him feel incredibly small, with such a wide variety of colonies and vistas across the Milky Way. It seemed different somehow when projected around you so photorealistically instead of being broadcasted on a television or computer screen during a news broadcast.

Arthur neared the front of the line, and was soon ordered down the green line to his room – Delta-44. There was no idea what to expect, as his bunkmate was still pending, but he did his best to settle in and grit himself for the worst.

The first few days were mostly processing, interspersed with basic testing. The recruits were tested for both physical and mental issues, and yet Arthur's fascination was still on the holograms and screens. Another volcanic island chain, complete with beachside bunkers, a snowbound planet, and a vast grid-work space station hanging in empty space near a fiery red star, full of docked battlecruisers and trade ships.

Everywhere, there were countless new images of everything possibly imaginable.

To much amusement - during the routine cardio physical, a test that consisted of plodding along on a treadmill at a solid jogging pace, another recruit was also lost in the images. He was gazing over at massive metropolis slums spewing grey smoke, before mistepping, eating shit, and tumbling into the wall behind the treadmill.

The strength test was a struggle, having not done much training outside of infrequent running for the past several years. But the mental tests were easy to excel in using any modicum of outside the box thinking. He even caught one of the officers in charge of testing chatting with a lab technician shortly after he pointed out the error in one color matching puzzle. For the briefest moment, the officer smirked, eyes running Arthur up and down.

Was his father ever smiled at, just like that?

The shouting of drill instructors marked the arrival of more transports over the next few days as the semester started in earnest for the new enlistees. Two days after the first tests, an enormous lecture hall served as the home base for a beginning of the semester introduction with the rest of the class to be. First came the rundown of the planet itself, which most of them had already researched or experienced firsthand themselves, many on the flight in.

Deadly heat, crushing pressure, and certain instantaneous death was lurking on the surface, meaning they would likely never leave the facility unless it was to leave the planet proper or to visit one of the orbital or high atmosphere installations.

Next came the facility itself.

Of course - most of the naval academy was carefully excavated for kilometres upon kilometres throughout the *Maxwell Mons* mountain range proper, extending farther out underneath the surface of Venus - buried deep within the mountainside or beneath the plains around it.

This was by design, in case of orbital bombardment somehow piercing the natural defenses of the polar vortex and intense wind, heat and pressure that seethed over the outer walls of the mountain fortress around them, however many kilometres thick.

Only the military hangars and the communications areas were above ground - reinforced, double-sealed, heat treated, pressurized. Both were off limits to the cadets outside of pre-authorized comings and goings for training. Flight training on smaller transport and fighter craft like Justices, SW-80 Protectors, Agathas, and Sophies would take place from their second semester onwards.

The very bottom levels of the academy were dedicated to research and development, and also strictly forbidden to recruits unless they had a damn good reason for being there, with of course, the regular rules holding in place for such a visit - orders or authorization.

Arthur was beginning to see the extent of the bureaucracy that fuelled the Guardian war machine. Discipline and adherence to bureaucracy. A strict set of rules to follow, with threats for those that strayed from the rigid structure and expectations.

Another hour of codes, regulations, and expectations later, involving such restrictions as a lack of alcohol and narcotics outside of leave time, a blanket ban on unregistered and unvetted communications, and other such facts on traditional military or academy tidbits.

Finally, they were released from the lecture.

Residence advisors, the same shouting voices who simultaneously filled the role of drill instructors and ranking officers above them acted as escort. Each last-name group quickly settled into the habit of following the orders of their specific instructors to new quarters further down the facility in a long line of dormitories reserved for first year enlistments in a dozen different specializations. Seraphs, Chayots, Pilots, Officers, Spec Ops.

And so on.

Arthur did as he was told - smart enough to comply, ensuring his best to obey.

The trip consisted largely of being barked at by armored and masked Shock Trooper Infantry enforcers. They were hardly comforting to Arthur and the other greenhorns, largely due to the incessant screaming and the lack of hesitation with which they butted the recruits with rifle ends if they dared slow down or step out of line. The standardized gas-masked helmets of the troopers were intimidating enough without the screaming.

He tried to avoid eye contact with their visors. Each G.O.D. Shock Trooper wore the same general combat armor – matte white plasticky stuff with the Guardian helix on the left pauldron and ranking and awards on the right. Bulky plating bulged on the larger areas, the torso and pauldrons, whilst ceramic plating was molded into the armor outline itself. The helmets were pressure sealed to the neck, with the gas-mask filter giving them a terrifying appearance, as immaculately white as they were.

Arthur found it incredibly difficult to pay attention, struggling to process it all between all the images around him of worlds he had never visited, and playing witness to the general abuse of those suffering nearby - those too slow, or not efficient enough.

At first, the academy sent him spiraling with the strange duality of existence as both a University-style place of learning and as a simultaneously tough-as-nails military training installation. Most of the folks around him, unlike himself, were completely unphased due to previous experience in the various military branches of the G.O.D. or from the armies and navies of their origin countries, as superficial as they were.

The only contingent that seemed to echo his own existence in the lineup was the very small minority of rich kids or political spawn that were being thrown into the system due to catastrophic fuck ups involving grotesque amounts of privilege. They were luckily the ones being abused in lieu of his own punishable absent-minded daydreaming.

For Arthur, now far away from the quiet passivity of the shuttle and his slow life back home on Earth as an alcoholic lush, well… He had to be on his toes at every second, constantly prompting himself out of daydreams that in normal circumstances would consume most of his waking hours with questions and "what-ifs." The pace had already changed quite drastically! He was woefully unprepared for military life, a target on a level even below the most regular of academy greenhorns.

He managed at avoiding a rifle butt, and any direct chastising outside of a single scream at him to close the gap between the enlisted member in front of him and the fronts of his own boots. But he breathed a hefty sigh of relief upon reaching the dorms again. They were each asked a series of questions yet again within their dorm quarters in the presence of their new bunkmates – mostly pertaining to any allergies or medical issues that the physical testing could have missed.

He found he very quickly adapted to answering quickly and properly, ending each sentence with "sir" or "ma'am" as appropriate. There was a ferocity with which the drill instructors freely berated and battered the trainees with for any smidge of imperfect or lagging obedience.

The Class 1 A.I. assigned to their room was ordered to set an alarm for 0500 hours the following morning, but they were otherwise ordered to stay in their bunks and to not wander, outside of bathroom use, which was a shared dormitory-style facility at the end of this floor's hallway.

Arthur collapsed onto the nearest bunk, not sure if they had been assigned or left to freely claim one. Almost immediately, a face popped down into vision from the bunk above, which belonged to the friendly bald man on the bunk above him who had remained silent during the questioning.

"Hey, rookie! Officer training, by the insignia?"

The beefy man faintly resembling his father from the photographs was dangling by the waist from the bunk above him. And he was grinning.

"Yeah."

"So, where you come from before now?"

"Camden. London."

"Army? SAS?"

Arthur gave him a confused look. Which was met with another wide grin.

"Hoo boy, you're a true greenhorn, then! Welcome to the party…?"

"Arthur Brass."

"Private Tyrone Wells, from the 630th. Nice to meet you, rookie! Army or Navy?"

Arthur tentatively shook the hand offered down to him from

above.

"Navy."

"Another charity case from death row, eh? You from a political family, or just flush with cash?"

Arthur gaped.

Well, it answered some of his conspiracy theories about the bureaucracy based on those beaten back in the lineup.

"Neither. Dad was a Captain. He died a long time ago."

"Hey! Look at us, orphaned brothers! Doing the great Creator's work!"

"Yeah, I'm uh... Not that religious."

"Hey, no worries brother. I've got enough for the both of us. You can serve him, and I'll handle all the praying on your behalf."

It seemed sincere, and it was a nice sentiment. Nobody had ever prayed for him before.

"Where are you from, Tyrone?"

The larger man swung down from the bunk. He was a fucking brick of a man.

"Well, Detroit, originally. Survived on the streets when my dad died at thirteen. Enlisted at eighteen to find a way out. Or maybe it was the big guy who helped me find my way out."

He pointed at the roof, and winked.

"Served long then?"

"Ha! Can't you tell by my youthful face, my man?"

A pose, then. The woman in the top bunk across from them chuckled. The other girl in the bunk below her had already fallen asleep, breathing in the deep throes of dreaming - clearly wiped out by the intense initiation process.

"I'm just kidding man. I'm twenty-five. And yeah, sat on the front lines out on a half dozen worlds in the neutral territories, just waiting to get shot at. And after a few years I didn't think I'd see any action - but then the 630th got pulled from the neutral territories, dropped in hot on Jikos during a fucking invasion! Lost a few good buddies that day. Been hot on and off ever since. I've definitely shot a motherfucker or two in my time, having put down a few of those crazy, axe wielding fucks in the name of The Lord."

He wasn't quite sure how to respond.

"Jikos? Three years back?"

The woman swung her legs over the bunk, looking down at the two men as a cat might gaze down from a high shelf with only partial interest.

"Yep, thereabouts. You there?"

A grim nod.

"Flying a Sophie, the fucking deathtraps that they are, dropping you grunts planet-side. A Tyrant on a flyby caught my engines just as I was clearing the low rises, would have been toast if not for the squad I had just dropped off. Berserkers were almost through the glass when they showed up with their Seraph leading them in. Saved my ass, then let me tag along until I could hitch a lift on the Agatha bringing their reinforcements. Hell of a fight, eh?"

The larger man nodded solemnly.

"One helluva fight. Creator must have had plans for you! What's your name, miss?"

"Sally. Sally Weathers."

Arthur couldn't help himself. He laughed out loud, sitting up and breaking the solemn mood. It was all so surreal. The sleeping girl stirred, and both of his new comrades gave him a quizzical look, broken by a hearty guffaw from Tyrone.

"I get it! Pilot named Weathers? That's pretty good!"

The tension broke again. Tyrone clapped him on the shoulder heartily.

"Don't worry buddy, you'll see action soon enough. Might not laugh that hard if you make it out alive with a new story to tell!"

Arthur felt his heart sink. Of course. He was literally laughing at two combat veterans swapping war stories. What a fucking idiot!

"Sorry, I need a drink."

"Haaaaa, you really are a greenhorn, arentcha Brass?! Everybody knows that shit will rot your liver! You gotta hit that green stuff instead! Not too much, mind you. Knew lots of smart guys back in the day who became potheads and now they're dumb as bricks!"

Tyrone Wells' positivity and enthusiasm was infectious. Arthur couldn't help but smile wryly back at him.

"What're you shooting for, Wells?"

"Power Armor. I'm gonna become a Seraph or a Chayot if I can get there. I'd take a Sentinel or a Harbinger, but those Harbs are walking target practice for air support and orbital strikes. Just need my officer ticket, and then after some experience in the Armored Corps, I'd like to get chosen for The Hand of Wrath or The Hellions!"

Weathers whistled.

"Pretty high hopes."

Tyrone drew a crucifix across his chest, apparently never losing his hope or positivity.

"How about you, Weathers? Want to get out of the flygirl business and into a nice cushy command gig?"

Sally flopped back, her legs kicking gently against the bunk.

"Captain a Battlecruiser or a Carrier, if I can. Maybe a destroyer. I've been carrying you grunts around for a decade. Thought it was finally time for an upgrade."

"Well, how about you, Brass? How are you going to serve The Lord?"

Tough question. And Arthur didn't feel like spewing out his whole life story just yet.

"Maybe a captain, like my father. He commanded a battlecruiser, as far as I know. I think the last one he served on was called *The Lance of Harmony*. Not a fan of the big, flashy, drawn out names though, if I can be honest."

Both Tyrone and Sally nodded sagely.

"Uh, you folks are spitting out all these names. I have to admit I'm not really that well versed yet. I tried to cram before shipping out, but…"

That smile. It was fucking infectious with positivity.

"Aw, don't worry baby bird. The Creator smiles on the ignorant, so that the righteous may lift them towards heaven! I got you. I can be your adopted momma bird."

He wasn't quite sure what to make of being called a baby bird, but as Weathers was smirking from what he could see of her face, he didn't immediately protest. Seemed like humor was one of the ways to cope with all the shit the two had seen.

"Seraphs are the big white lanky suits of Powered Battle Armor. With the spurs extended they look like four-eyed rabbits, kinda. They can jump a couple of stories no problems on those spurs of theirs! Four slitted eyes, two on each side. Angel wings engraved on the back near the main thrusters. They can flip a tank, crush a man's skull to dust. They're walking fucking heavies!"

One could tell that Tyrone was passionate about armor.

"Chayots are even bigger – they're the bulky ones with the red lines and icons of The Lord all over 'em. Red on white. Walking artillery, baby! Only the most devout of his children get to rain down his righteous fire from above! That's what I'm really shooting for! Although flipping around in a Seraph, or hanging tight in a Sentinel or Harbinger…"

"Don't get too excited, Wells. I've seen those things blow from the air. Any one of those fuel canister strings rupture, the chain reaction sends a fireball up into the air a hundred feet as they all set each other off. Walking death traps, those Chayots."

Weathers was grim again, clearly worried for him.

"The Creator protects, my good-miss-Weathers. And the faithful shall all serve him again in Heaven. Ain't nothing as bad as the streets were. Had to sin a dozen times over just to eat some days."

Arthur was certain that Tyrone's default setting was "smiling." How a combat veteran could be so smiley with such a hellish life-lived was simultaneously fascinating and terrifying. He would hate to ever see the big man pissed off.

"Well, we're all first years here. Same page. So once you learn to fly, Wells, maybe you'll get a taste for life in the skies."

Wells grinned at her tone. Arthur could tell he came from a good place, even if the fanaticism was a bit overbearing.

"Anybody down for a game of cards before we call it a night? Feels just like basic training all over again! Watching the slow-pokes getting a rifle butt always makes me laugh. I had to work really hard to keep it in when Brass got screamed at for lollygagging. This kid... Daydreamer, arentcha Brass?"

Arthur felt his face flush a darker shade.

"Yeah, Rummy?"

Tyrone and Sally were nice enough. Sally was about thirty-five. "A distinguished older lady" as she put it. Had been flying for a decade all across the fronts. The two taught Arthur more over the course of their rummy games, explaining hierarchies, bureaucracies, and the various units they had faced or fought alongside over their careers.

It felt so impossibly large in such a ridiculously short amount of time, and he couldn't help but feel like a stupid kid, with this experienced soldier and a skilled pilot helping him learn the ropes over a game of cards. He probably learned more about the Guardians from the games of cards than he did in all the cram studying he had done up until his departure for Venus.

Weathers won handily, and they retired for their early roll call.

Time and learning were funny like that.

He quickly got to know his bunkmate, Tyrone Wells, even better over the next few weeks.

Wells was fixated on success through the hierarchy, to an insane degree. He had everything mapped out, and he freely shared his plans with Arthur throughout the first two intense weeks of classes, physical training, arms training, tactics classes, and Guardian history seminars.

The last of them was dry, told in broad strokes of colonization, military engagements, annexations, and politics.

"See, Brass…"

They were running the dish pit one night, as every two rooms had a kitchen rotation, a sanitation rotation, and a quartermaster rotation under the quartermaster herself. It cycled like clockwork.

The G.O.D. seemed to love hierarchy and holistic inclusion, ensuring that the soldiers were actively helping support staff and acting in subservience to them while on rotation. It was definitely a clever way to build comradery between the military personnel and the regular paid staff.

"If you're smart, you find a patron. Play the zealot. Start with a god somewhere lower down, and then prove yourself capable and loyal enough that you're snatched up by somebody on the council for one of their personal units. I'm planning on reaching up as quickly as I can for someone on the council. Maybe even Serania, The God of Control herself! It would be the ultimate honor to serve the last remaining member of the Prime Triumvirate blessed by God himself."

"Right…"

Just what Arthur was looking forward to of course… Working alongside *religious zealots,* bowing before the immortal gods, and singing hymns to the "OG Creator" all day. Still, Tyrone had real drive, and Arthur hung off him like a barnacle as much as he could, grilling him for his own sake about military protocols, shit he should watch out for, and the like. Tyrone was Army, not Navy, but the two were closely intertwined, and Arthur found he could rely on Wells for emotional support more than most – a godsend, pun intended, for a man whose normal reaction to emotion was to bottle it up deep inside himself and drink off any of the lingering aftereffects of feelings.

Settling in was actually fairly quick and easy overall. While he was officially out of the British Government's control and into the hands of the Guardians of Destiny proper by that point, little had changed in terms of how he lived. The structure of the system actually helped him regulate, hilariously.

This was all with the small addition of open brutality for any disobedience, and a strict set of regulations attached to his very living existence, of course.

The same regimented government systems he was used to back home and at work in Britain were present - carrying ID cards everywhere, showing up to work on time, and addressing superiors with religious reverence. All the same scenarios quickly hammered themselves into place with different names and more stringent formalities.

Perhaps the gods had played a role in how it had all evolved back in the UK. Aside from a pledge of loyalty to the G.O.D. - he wasn't bogged down with paperwork or other abstract bureaucracy outside of following direct orders.

It was as if they had the system fine-tuned for speed and churned through manpower as quickly as they received it. It all seemed to confirm his initial suspicions about the nature of the meat grinder.

In the first month, he was well aware that new identities as production line soldiers were very much instilled as truth. If any of them forgot, the drill instructors and professors reminded them.

The first intro lessons were constant reminders of wartime and battlefield fuckups leading to death in the meat grinder. The direction and wisdom of the gods was to be followed, for the greatest losses had always come when direction from the immortals was absent.

When an ascendant was active on the field, the Army and Navy followed their orders.

Period.

This risk of great loss was not only for themselves, but for their crewmates and the worlds they protected too, with simple fuckups slaughtering hundreds if not thousands of others at a blink.

The frequency of these reminders perturbed him, putting the fear of failure somewhere deep in the back of his skull. It never fully settled down deep with the other emotions. It was almost as if they were building up a faultless martyr complex inside the students, which made him curious as to how many ships and lives were lost every day and how many of the enormous dry-docks across the Galaxy would be needed to ever rebuild them all.

How many G.O.D. soldiers were annihilated thoughtlessly each day to make such grim drill instruction necessary?

After the settling in period, the deeper schooling began, and Arthur was immediately at a disadvantage compared to the majority of the other applicants, most of whom had the gruesome, yet mystical privilege of their previous military experience.

Where he was forced to read his textbooks every spare moment to catch up on even the most basic protocols alongside military terminology, the rest of his fellow students raced ahead, placing far above him in most tests and practice lessons.

Tyrone, bless his heart, helped him every step of the way and explained the reasoning behind some of the more obscure concepts and regulations, but he still felt dragged along in free fall, constantly watching for an Advisor to wander into his room and expel him from the academy for poor performance.

"Nah, see, the Blackout Contingency is for when you're stuck somewhere and can't get out. Maybe you're trapped on a scuttled ship, or pinned down under fire as the eggheads evac. You make your peace with The Creator, and then you bust up everything of value, delete A.I.s if they can't wirelessly hop somewhere else safe, purge records and intel, that sort of thing. Then you fight to the last man. But it's not called a Blackout, usually you hear it called in code over the comms or the Friend or Foe system. Your targeting icons will suddenly swap certain green or grey friendlies to square red targets to 'black them out.' So listen for something like 'we're going dark at yadda yadda.'"

Wells was fucking brilliant. He would definitely pass his tests to become a Chayot.

The only opportunity Arthur had to recover was in tactical challenges, which were essentially mock battles with only a few specific winning outcomes. Here, creativity was encouraged over anything else, and thus he succeeded where his peers failed due to their concentration on the specific scenarios they had learned, or due to the traumatic wartime experiences they had endured.

Both Army and Navy were often intertwined, with small rivalries popping up here and there as Naval officers treated Army units like fodder for an overall mission success. The idea of "anything goes" in a fight was the one thing that came easy to him. It was the only avenue in which he succeeded above others, by doing whatever it took to survive and succeed at all costs.

In quiet moments reserved for study, he found solace in the 'Coral Forest' wing of the academy, which was essentially the student-accessible research wing. The floating kelp forests and soft pink and blue hues on the walls helped him cope, especially when he started to have small panic attacks whilst imagining the raging heat storms above.

The scenes were labelled to be from *Tsunami's Wave Crest Upon The Horizon*, long and ridiculous as the Guardian naming conventions usually seemed to be.

The safe coral forest study space was his lifeline outside of Wells, Weathers, and the other member of his quad, a quiet yet skilled engineer, Katarina Prabst.

Anxiety like this was rampant amongst many of the academy students, but the system failed to care or acknowledge that any one individual might be suffering mentally or emotionally. Insofar as nobody hurt themselves or those around them, nobody in the system ever cared to check on them unless a serious allegation was brought up that required questioning. The psychologists that sat in offices down on the cubicled floors only ever popped up if somebody was reported to be a danger to themselves or others, and thus most unhealthy coping mechanisms festered, completely unchecked.

It felt like more of an ass-covering than any genuine care.

The nature of the world above got his anxiety going the most. Every drill instructor constantly reminded the recruits that they were only a few kilometres from near-instant death via heat and pressure, which was enough to keep them all hopped up on the adrenaline of fear, and Arthur's flawed coping strategy of bottling everything up was finally starting to fail him.

The colorful fish and brightly colored coral were the things that soothed him enough to keep working. He studied there so often that Tyrone often had to make the trek to come check on him..

It was his worry for Arthur that poked at him, he confessed, driving him to come, to stretch his legs, and to ensure Arthur hadn't up and offed himself. An odd boon for Arthur in this isolation amongst the kelp was that he made friends with many of the graduate student level research staff as they went about their business. They would stop to chat with him as he sat hunkered down on a bench studying or watching the looping screens of swimming clownfish in silent reverence.

"Brass, you've got a future in the research and development division!"

"Take a break, kid. No use rushing to war."

"Arthur, I'm headed to the cafeteria to grab a coffee, want one?

And so on, and so forth.

His closest confidant outside Tyrone throughout the process was his sponsor Judge Undelwood.

Due to Joe's privileged status, tied to the G.O.D. but employed by the United Kingdom on paper, the older man could arrange video calls as he pleased, despite the dense acidic clouds of Venus making communication slightly sporadic and difficult without careful scheduling.

He spoke to his childhood friend Billy or Billy's wife Rebecca every once in a blue moon, but Billy's job reporting on the front-line colony worlds for CNG, the Central News Group, rendered him unable to maintain connection for long, or even to guarantee his own safety due to constant security blackouts on non-military communications.

Sometimes the two would be mid-sentence when the feed would cut-out, as explosions and gunfire would echo in the background. Billy would quickly say his goodbyes and vanish, his movements and position obscured by misinformation and the official propaganda that Billy himself helped shape.

Time passed quickly in a consistent schedule, with the forced structure of the academy pushing Arthur ever further into his work, where normally he would have slacked off and lacked motivation with weekend binge drinking procrastination.

Months rapidly progressed into years.

Two years into his multi-year degreed training program, before he would start his five years of service proper, Arthur participated in a few studies and experiments sponsored by *The Eye*, the G.O.D. Black Ops and intelligence division.

A few of the friendlier graduate students put him onto it initially, all of which would supply him with extra academy course credit.

Judge Joe Undelwood on the other hand? He did NOT approve.

"Arthur, *do not get caught up with The Eye.* They operate without any oversight, and while I can step in and grease the wheels of any bureaucratic process you could potentially become embroiled in, I couldn't possibly help you further should things go sideways."

"But I could finish a full year early with enough of this extra credit, so isn't a year of my life worth the risk?"

A "harrumph" from Joe marked his frustration with the younger man's eagerness for risk and devil may care attitude.

"Well, you can make your own decisions, you're an adult. But even if it's just research, I wouldn't touch anything that section of organization is involved in with a fifty-foot pole. I'm already sticking my neck out for you. I absolutely *cannot* do much more. Do I have to remind you that your current trajectory could make you a target for recruitment? It is incredibly hard to say no to a spy and saboteur agency when they want you as a minion."

"I'll just say no. I'm already training to serve in the Navy, so it's not like I'm spitting on their boots, I just have a plan already. It'll be fine, Joe."

Even Arthur knew he was being arrogant for the sake of speed and progress.

"Well, when you find yourself assassinating some neutral territory crime lord or politician on suspicion of them being an Armada asset, a fat lot of good I am!"

An awkward pause.

The Judge clearly cared a lot about the younger man's wellbeing, which confirmed Arthur's status as some sort of bleeding heart salvation complex for the older gentleman.

"How's that religious friend of yours? The one wanting to become a Chayot?"

"Tyrone? Yeah, Wells is good. He's ahead of me on pretty much every fucking test though, which is annoying – especially since I'm finally starting to break out into the upper half of the standings. The dude is crazy smart. I bet if he hadn't joined the Army, he'd probably be a professor or something somewhere by now."

"Good, good! I'm glad you finally made a friend!"

They blathered on trivialities after that.

Arthur ultimately decided to ignore Undelwood's advice for the sake of both building possible contacts and earning the credit towards faster Academy graduation. It was just too big of a carrot to pass up. And it would only be a month or two.

Things were simple enough for the tests – he would do basic physical exercises and endure countless bio scans of every individual part of his body. Every so often he would have blood taken or be asked to spit in a test tube. They would occasionally inject him with what looked like blood or a clear liquid with the viscosity of jellied ooze, an "immune booster," they told him.

There was one experiment in which they stuck a large gauge

needle with a weird glowing sensor attachment into his chest through his ribs.

It hurt like hell!

There was a tiny bit of silvery liquid in the needle when they pulled it out and he felt ridiculously overtired for a day and a half afterward. Suffering from slight pain due to the hole in his rib muscles, Arthur asked one of his regular graduate student acquaintances what the hell it was for the next day.

Apparently, that test was to analyze his "soul core resonance" – some technical gibberish that Arthur could hardly interpret as actual research. The experiments seemed pointless, as in Arthur's own naïve sense it was the sort of strange, biogenetics science the gods had been doing for over a century and a half already. What could they possibly learn about the human body that they hadn't already learned by almost a hundred years into the second millennium?

After all, prosthetics and cybernetic body parts were extremely popular, and new industries were capitalizing on the demand. Not that he had the cash for such things nor wanted to go through invasive surgery.

His decision to participate in the tests came back to bite him in the ass, of course.

Things got hectic extremely quickly when one of the many experiments he had signed up as a guinea pig for was halted mid-session in a flurry of bureaucracy and armed soldiers.

It was the first time he ever saw a suit of Seraph power armor in person, as a squad of fully kitted-out, glossy white Shocktroopers stormed the lab, pointing a variety of slug and plasma guns at both the lab technicians and Arthur himself.

They screamed at everyone to get down as they swarmed the lab, which immediately intimidated the eggheads into cowering submission. Everyone complied, save Arthur, who was unable, strapped as he was to a medical bed having his heart monitored.

The Seraph came in last, as the remaining few scientists were being handcuffed and pressed to the floor.

Tyrone's "rabbit legs" comments made sense, as the streamlined, elegantly sleek suit of white power armor had to fold the leg spurs down on all hinge points to fit inside the doorway to the room and loom over his prone form. The four glowing slitted eyes stared directly into his face where he sat strapped onto the gurney.

Each eye hummed a soft red, and he could hear the chatter of comms from within the helmet. In one hand was the handle of a melee plasma weapon, large enough that if activated could slice him in two with a single cauterizing stroke. A large sidearm sized big enough for the suit's hands hung from a magnetic clamping holster at the hip.

He was terrified. The suit seemed alien, with how smooth the lines were, how quiet and soft the artificial muscle fibers moved, how the servos and additional pneumatics of the limbs hummed and whined with engineered precision. The gangly form loomed over him, analyzing him closely.

"Name?"

"Arthur Brass, sir."

"Rank?"

"OR-1, sir. Naval Stream Student."

"Hmph. Stay there."

The Seraph rose again and began barking orders in a tinny, heavily processed voice to get those handcuffed up and moving to the transport. Arthur noted the simple black eye painted on the collar of the armor. Filed it away for later.

Strapped down as he was, Brass was left alone as each of the graduate students he had been friendly acquaintances with, and others he didn't know as well, were rounded up and filed out the door as prisoners to be interrogated. A single Shocktrooper was left to guard him, eventually being relieved by his own familiar drill instructor.

"You're not in trouble, Brass. You're just the test subject."

Yet his debrief felt more like an interrogation.

After numerous hours of questions, mostly on what he remembered being said or done in the tests, it was revealed by his drill instructor that there had been a subversion of rank from somewhere up the chain, using the academy's resources and facilities as a front for what he called *Eclipse*, a research group representing a defected Guardian Scientist.

The instructor didn't specify much beyond that, but brought him before a panel of G.O.D. interrogators along with other volunteer students who had also signed up for the tests as extra credit. Arthur was questioned and scrutinized on and off for the next several months, having to report to the panel again and again as they tried to track down how the *Eclipse* experiment could have been running underneath the Guardians' noses without anybody realizing it.

The establishment didn't seem to be targeting Arthur specifically for once, seeing him as the brainless cattle in the test, innocent of guilt.

But they did perform their own tests of course to see if Arthur and his cohort had been brainwashed or bugged. Yet despite volunteering for almost every experiment over the last few months, Arthur emerged blameless, unbelievably with his reputation unscathed and without being tortured along the way. He even got most of the credit!

He had expected at least *some* torture.

Arthur was oddly happy he had become a mere number, as just another student in the academy.

Serendipitously for him, several young grad students in their first few years of study were quickly drummed out of the academy as a result of the fiasco, with the focus of the political and security fiascos centred entirely on them. He was saddened to see some familiar faces vanish, but was simultaneously glad that he had not become better friends with them.

Time flowed ever onwards, like water through a sieve.

"Arthur, my boy!"

The video call had been arranged by Undelwood.

"I have some good news to share!"

He broke up into static for a full minute as Arthur patiently waited.

"Am I back?"

A thumbs up.

"So the good news is that I've accepted an offer to move up to the Supreme Courts of the Guardians of Destiny, representing their colonies and the peoples beyond Earth!"

"Congratulations, Joe. So what does that mean, exactly?"

The Judge had put on a few more wrinkles in the years Arthur had been slogging his way through the academy on Venus, but it seemed much like Wells, Undelwood was as chipper as ever, committed to some nebulous greater good.

"Well, I'm giving up my U.K. citizenship, for one! But I'm also taking the oath to become a citizen of the G.O.D. proper! I'll remain here in London of course, as so much is done remotely nowadays, and the majority of my workload will be reviewing caseload documents and ruling on cases without in-person trials. So quieter I suppose, but with much more gravity! That means I'm also going to be overseeing military trials of course."

Undelwood blathered on, explaining the nuances of the paperwork and the scope and scale of duties as Arthur found his eyes glazing over.

"Anyways, I just thought I'd let you know that I may have less time to chat, as this new position has me working just beneath the council itself, which will ensure I perform my best with all possible due diligence!"

"I'm happy for you, Joe."

He was, truly. This strange older mentor who had saved his life in a roundabout sort of way...

Well, they had become close.

His mother only ever communicated with him by letter, and outside of book club updates and volunteering quirks at the local library, she had written less and less over the past while. The letters came first every week, then every month, and then not for longer and longer stretches of time. The silence persisted even when Arthur wrote first or tried to call and send messages.

Undelwood was an invaluable ally to have in lieu, as he fed him constant updates – the general scope of the currently stalemated war, the inner workings of high-profile cases, and even updates on small borderlands skirmishes with pirates and other such interesting G.O.D. Naval deployments.

Many of the pieces of news were often classified and not subject to too much discussion, despite the sketchy yet secure nature of their contact through guarded channels and encrypted network links.

Arthur trusted the man, as he had no-one else to trust in a position of authority, but he was constantly wondering who Judge Joe Undelwood really was, and thinking back to what his signature had meant. Was it his moniker? A code-word? A friend of his? How had *The Eye* or some other internal bureaucratic force not swept down on either of them for discussing this crap? Especially after the lab experiment incident? What did Joe truly want?

Undelwood was also growing older at a rapid rate beyond his actual years it seemed, and despite applying to be a god ascension candidate several times, he was declined again and again by the bureaucracy, and of course by those specific gods up above that were directly in charge of such selections.

Immortality was still a hunger that many attempted to sate. Like Joe, thousands of others applied or were automatically selected every year to become gods, as even with modern medicine and technology, the average lifespan still couldn't break 140.

The grotesque and overwhelming death rate for ascendants was seemingly worth the risk of living forever, frozen in time.

Even more unexpectedly - news about his mother came not long after, without much forewarning.

From what Judge Undelwood told him, she was found in bed, with an unfinished glass of red wine on the bedside table, and three times the lethal dosage of an industrial painkiller present in her body, taken orally as pills.

There were no words.

Arthur was broken.

He was only slightly calmed by the fact she had chosen to pass in peace, without pain. It helped that no matter what awaited her, in his mind his father would be there with arms outstretched.

The gods loved to abuse religion to justify their own ends, but part of Arthur hoped she found whatever it was she believed in. She had been quietly religious, as her family before her - not that she ever attended church. But with the speed of the academy, Arthur could hardly stop to mourn, with his life beginning to speed ahead whether he liked it or not.

Had she been slowly reducing contact over time to soften the blow?

He took the mere two days of bereavement leave he was allowed, and did his best to pick up the broken pieces of the life he had lived before Venus. Having Joe and Tyrone helped, and the careful guidance of the Judge kept him steady.

He coped as he always did - drowning his sorrows with as much whiskey as the canteen would let him buy on leave time - culling what little savings he had even further.

The Judge ensured everything would be taken care of back home on Earth. In his kindness, his "H" moniker succinctly arranged and paid for her funeral.

Arthur couldn't even attend.

The act was almost a silent method of apologizing for inadvertently robbing him of the last of his two parents.

It rang hollow, unappreciated, as Arthur sunk into depression at having missed his own mother's funeral.

He could only gape at her disappearance as he journeyed into the unknowing abyss of a new life.

His only lit candle back at home on Earth, snuffed out before he was able to stop it.

CHAPTER 4: THE END OF AN ERA.

"Some of us struggle so hard against the whims of fate that we fall right into the parts it may have foretold for us from the very start."

The rest of his time at the academy was a blur of keeping his head above water both literally and figuratively, as the lessons began to encompass physical tests in large training arenas as well as more complex mental exercises and resilience building techniques. It seemed that managing one's breath for extended periods of time was crucial to survival in any low oxygen or underwater environment. A handy skill if one were to be exposed to the vacuum of space, such as during ship-to-ship combat.

Still, Arthur always hated those empty-lung and breath holding exercises the most.

The intensity and demands of the academy spiralled ever upwards, and he found himself mastering skills that before he would never have dreamed to be possible.

In Arthur's third year, Tyrone graduated with honors as an ordinance specialist, surprisingly early due to his aptitude, and rejoined the army with the Armored Corps for the rest of his enlistment. Arthur couldn't help but feel the loss, as he was close with Sally and their other bunkmate Sarah, but had been almost inseparable from the bigger man, like an adopted older brother.

He said goodbye the night before he left, full of smiles and pep talk.

"I leave for the garrison on *Dhekar Qiraj* tomorrow, buddy. Listen, you just keep doing what you do best and you'll rock the exams and all the other bullshit for the next few years. And then maybe I'll be jumping out of something you're flying soon enough!"

More smiles from the bigger man.

"I don't know if I can do it without you Wells. I feel like I'm falling apart.

Tyrone Wells of the 630th frowned, which for him was an extremely rare occurrence.

"Man, you seem to think you're weaker than you are, Brass, and I haven't been able to figure it out for the life of me. You've been here for almost three years now. You studied your ass off harder than anybody else I know. You can captain a ship or run any position on a bridge, and you clearly get the gist of fleet maneuvers for later in life, when you're a crotchety old admiral. Quit beating yourself up. You're gonna be fine, brother."

Tyrone held the moment for a beat, letting it sink in, then brightened, and clapped both arms around Arthur in a bear hug that choked the breath from Arthur's lungs.

Damn, was Tyrone strong!

"If you ever get some extended shore leave, come visit me if I'm not rocketing around the borderlands in a suit of armor, okay brother?"

That hug lasted an eternity, and then the next morning Tyrone was gone.

He wondered if Tyrone Wells of the 630th would be the only real friend he would make other than Billy. He was terrified to lose Wells, either as a casualty to the forever war itself, or to the bureaucracy and sheer vastness of the Galaxy.

Tyrone was barely gone a few days, when a new dorm mate, Ryan, moved in - a dour white man with a large beard. He and Arthur got along well enough, but he didn't feel the same connection as he had to Tyrone.

So as he often did of course, he fell into old habits.

He drifted from the research wing to the bar in the canteen, studying while drinking any chance he could get. It seemed to make the time pass quicker, and he became convinced somewhere along the line that the alcohol helped him study.

He also threw himself into various aircraft and ship simulation exercises with vigor, as it gave him something to obsess over that wasn't studying or drinking. Luckily the simulators almost always had free space outside of class time proper.

Time raced on, as it always tended to do.

In his final year of the degree, with intense effort and time, (and curbing the drinking just barely enough) he passed most of his exams and mock battle practicums with flying colors. Whereas most young students drank and partied with each other on the weekends during their allotted 'leave time', Arthur maintained his solitary life - with the exception of one or two particular Friday nights where he fell back on post-high school experience and demonstrated for some second years at a dormitory party how to properly ingest an entire 6 pack worth of beer in one good beer bong chug. He had one hell of a hangover the next morning, but it was worth it for the admiration it bought from his younger peers.

Feeling that good on ego and intoxication had to be illegal somewhere. He was finding that after several years, he had finally somehow overcome the resentment towards him from some of the regulars at not having previous military experience. Thank the gods.

At his graduation ceremony, which coincidentally fell on his 25th birthday, Judge Joe Undelwood attempted to act as a foster parent and attended the event in full G.O.D. Regalia, which included a ceremonial sabre and a white military uniform.

Arthur found it hilarious and chuckled openly at the older man's pomp and circumstance, which the Judge defended lightheartedly. Despite his very short stint in the G.O.D. Army as a youth, Arthur discovered that Judge Joe Undelwood had been a soldier back when the organization had still been secret. It explained some of his prestige, and some of his pull within the circles he operated between.

Undelwood even made a point to publicly show affection for him on camera by giving him a big hug upon his descent from the stage. For Arthur, there was a moment of warm and fuzzy relief at being held. After all, Arthur had grown to love the man in a strange, fostered sort of way, as unlike his mother's distant, aloof form of love, the Judge was a brash and open man in both his actions and his feelings. He always showed Arthur a type of genuine affection that Arthur had never really known from his prim and proper mother.

It was nice, in a way.

How could a hug have so much power?

It was only upon freeing himself of Joe's grasp that he noticed the newer man behind the two of them, that the Judge was apparently putting on the show for specifically. He was an olive-skinned man with unkempt black hair splayed out at all angles. He looked Polynesian as best Arthur could tell, unsure of which of the dozens of frontier and colony worlds hosted which specific emigrant cultures. There was no secret token of identity, dressed as he was in a simple black suit with a flat white tie. It was emblazoned with a simplified Guardian Helix embroidered in black.

In a sea of white dress uniforms and formal wear emblazoned with pins, regalia, medals, and other outward tokens of grandeur, the lack of pomp and circumstance, and the simplicity of his formal wear seemed odd. Arthur felt he recognized him and the striking dark-skinned young woman in the red dress beside him from somewhere.

Without a formal introduction, however, Undelwood quickly whisked his young charge away through the crowd to the bar. Arthur became lost in the festivities of the moment and didn't meet up with the odd couple until the reception afterwards when he was well and thoroughly drowned in hard-bar liquor.

The older man in his forties was polite enough, and despite talking with him jauntily about which alcohols were great with orange or pineapple juice, he never fully introduced himself as more than a councillor, and insisted on being referred to by his title at such a formal event.

With Arthur's four-years of isolation and his general lack of political knowledge, the man and his date were quickly lost in the crowd thanks to the drunken mess that Arthur Brass quickly became.

He didn't remember much after that, although the woman on the councillor's arm had been stunning in that tight red dress.

The reality for Arthur was that his journey was still beginning. He had only just graduated from the academy, and was oddly saddened when he realized he was leaving behind the beautiful holographic screens and brutal outdoor landscapes of *Maxwell Mons* and *Ishtar Terra* for what was soon to be the cold depths of space.

While he was relieved to soon be soaring through the vacuum of space, over being caged down inside the pressure and heat of Venus' atmosphere, part of him also missed the safety and security of education's narrow scope and scale. A week of time with the Judge at his London home was all he could be provided, as the clock had now begun ticking on his five years of service.

Contrary to the typical assignments of newly commissioned officers into members of the bridge crew serving active ship captains... Arthur's exam results and mock battle practicums had picked him out of the crowd despite his rather lame showing in other areas throughout the rest of his school years. Much to his surprise, he was assigned as the captain of a relatively tiny, but newly completed G.O.D. Patrol frigate, the *Asalia*, tasked with patrolling a relatively quiet stretch of the edge of G.O.D. controlled space near the neutral territories.

Not wanting to waste the manpower or resources however - the bureaucracy almost immediately kicked into overdrive, deploying his new skills and officer ranking in a roundabout fashion.

They planned to use Arthur to temporarily fill in for a shore leave.

Arthur was thus temporarily assigned as a communications officer for a Navy Support Ship, the *Jalapeño Gold*, which he would serve upon until the Support Ship could rendezvous with the *Asalia* at a drydock facility called *The Transcontinental.*

Departing from Judge Joe Undelwood's home was sombre.

It spoke to his solitary nature, though.

The Judge had been called away for "an emergency" for the second half of the week Arthur was provided to prepare for his coming deployment.

He ultimately boarded the Aggie transport that would deliver him to his temporary assignment entirely alone, with no fanfare or waving handkerchiefs to bid him adieu.

His temporary ship was docked outside The Hub, a massive, cloaked space station in high orbit around Earth. The first time he saw the *Jalapeño Gold* through the cockpit windshield of the Agatha, moving in slow geosynchronous orbit, he was stunned.

He had seen movies and pictures of the kilometres-long starships before - long cylindrical bricks of steel lined with thrusters, gun batteries, and enormous deployment hangars along the sides.

In person?

Awe-inspiring.

And he already knew this Support Cruiser to be a smaller vessel compared to other types of ships like Battlecruisers or Carriers. The *Jalapeño Gold* seemed to stretch on forever to either side as they neared the double rows of hangars held fast against the vacuum with energy shielding. Arthur was starstruck. The prow at the front bore an enormous set of underslung railgun rails, jutting crudely like tusks. The four enormous engines at the stern vibrated with a powerful blue energy, mighty enough to force the enormous metallic bulk onwards through the void.

The squat, jutting observation tower sat above where the bridge was normally positioned in the center of mass. A careful consideration for maximum protection via the ship's armor and blast doors. It featured an array of antennae and communications equipment, which to him resembled a crown of sharpened spikes at this immense distance. Each hangar and porthole emitted a soft white glow from within, lighting up the sides of the greyish bulk like a nighttime cityscape.

Arthur figured it to be at least a kilometer long, and a quarter at least as wide as tall, but what transfixed him more than the size were the armaments. He eyed up the cavernous railgun shaft jutting from the bottom bow of the ship more closely, and the arsenal of gun and missile batteries dotted along both the sides as well as the top and bottom of the ship.

He was almost leaning over the pilot's shoulder now, and the older man did his best to ignore this touristy passenger as he rattled off a series of landing codes and military security key-phrases asking permission to dock in a clear hangar.

How could anything that possessed that many guns ever be destroyed? It was like a fat ovaled out cylinder strung up with guns as a tree might be with Christmas lights.

The Agatha was directed to dock in Hangar A-12 on the approach, and the pilot shifted course to align with the uppermost of the two rows of hangars along the port side, culminating in slowly prodding his Aggie's nosecone through the energy barrier of the correct one.

The twin engines of the small aircraft whined as they found the pull of artificial gravity beyond the barrier, but soon enough the craft pushed through, gently floating overtop a row of Justice fixed-wing fighters, and descending like a feather between two yellow lines painted upon the floor with yellow lettering marking it for new arrivals.

The Agatha settled gently with a soft trampolining of the landing gear, and the pilot nodded back at the sliding doors that were hissing with depressurization. Time for him to grab his gear and disembark before the pilot was off to his next scheduled pickup or dropoff.

Poor pilot, doomed to an endless list of things to be moved across the solar empire of the Guardians of Destiny.

He felt his feet hit the floor of the hangar, happy to feel the familiar pull of any approximation of Earth's gravity. His stomach rumbled at him happily - zero gravity could get disorienting after a long enough time floating in it, and no amount of clocked simulation hours could ever truly settle that uneasy feeling of vertigo in his stomach. The pilot gently nudged past him, clapping him on the shoulder as he passed.

"Good luck."

A mutter, and then he was gone, walking briskly towards the blast doors leading beyond the hangar and into the maze of corridors and rooms stretched out within the enormous frame of the ship. Arthur watched him go for a second, almost immediately distracted by the arrival of a bipedal mech at the hangar entrance, a stripped-down space-variant of Harbinger.

The small thrusters on its arms, legs, and torso flared on and off in short bursts to slowly bleed velocity as it neared the energy barrier of the hangar. It eventually slowed to a crawl and reached out, gripping onto a large metal handle on the outside lip of the hangar with one of the two three-fingered metal hands. The enormous slug rifle in the grip of the other hand was quickly clamped into a locking mechanism on the back of the hips, and it began placing a footpad onto a second metal railing outside the energy barrier, like a swimmer using a ladder to climb from the pool while still soaking wet.

It was a delicate task that Arthur could appreciate the mobility of, with the pilot inside maneuvering the several tonne machine gently - easing the enormous weight through the blue energy wall until the gravity within caught it fully.

The machine settled the first footpad onto the floor with a heavy clanging of metal on metal.

He was gently jostled aside as several deck crew rushed past him to assist the pilot - who stomped the mech into position between now familiar yellow lines. She clambered down the various rungs fastened to the back of the machine, and Artur was finally startled to motion, managing to avoid the deck crews and various other personnel that were bustling here and there as various pieces of equipment came and went from the port-side hangars.

It was crazy to think that this one hangar was only one of twenty-four in total, twelve on each side in two rows of six. Each cavernous hangar space was full of hundreds of individual Navy and Army personnel. It was a constant hum of activity - fuelling, doing maintenance, and working through other such routine tasks across dozens of unique pieces of aircraft, military hardware or armor.

Being awestruck at the enormity of the Guardians of Destiny war machine would likely be his new normal.

Well, it was definitely not lost on him as a new type of normal.

Moving to the hangar exit and following the signs in English towards the bridge, Arthur was as professional as possible to his crewmates and his temporary captain once on board and settled into his new role as one of two bridge communications officers positioned in the bridge and observation tower above the ship's bulk. The crew had an easy enough task, as it would be making a simple troop deployment run along a G.O.D. shipping route that would eventually stop to resupply the *Transcontinental* itself with a fresh deployment of personnel. The goal was relieving the workers moving to and from shore leave aboard the enormous dry dock where the *Asalia* was in the final stages of being completed.

Their first rift jump was equal parts terrifying and exhilarating, as nothing Arthur had ever experienced before beyond the simulator missions and scenarios.

All his years at the academy could hardly prepare him for the actual event of his body being moved through a torn hole in spacetime, connecting between two distant points. The intense vibrations of the enormous rift generator built specifically for the task near the main drive engines scared him slightly, as they began warping the gargantuan amount of space between the plotted entry and exit points.

The dull rumbling of the engines and the rift generator in tandem awed him at first, with the latter crackling to life and sending shivers down his spine and goosebumps across his body as spacetime twisted and crushed in on itself ahead of the *Jalapeño Gold*. It had him transfixed in a way that could never be explained in a mere textbook at the academy, as the white rift materialized ahead of the ship.

The exit point of the first rift was clear, of course.

That was part of his job as a communications officer, in addition to monitoring all shipboard communication to and from the Support Ship itself. He was required to "phone ahead" in a sense through A.I. policed comms buoys, each with their own micro-rift generators to allow transmissions and communications to flow freely at key broadcast and relay angles.

All this communication using the Friend or Foe systems was to ensure that the *Jalapeno Gold* wouldn't be slapping a hole in space-time into a problematic location - the middle of a fleet or the core of an orbiting planet, or some such place. Airspace traffic control was usually left up to the planet or facility being travelled to in question, but the world they were traveling to first was a bit of a backwater military outpost, *Brokeback Gorge*.

The actual rifts themselves amounted to opaque white holes lined with razor wire. Pilot precision and advance notice of arrival was key. If you didn't pass through the rift while perfectly centered in the middle of the jagged white circle...

Well, there sure was a lot of space being crushed between the two points being linked together.

Anything careless enough to connect with the edges of the jagged circular rift would shear its' matter apart like a wire cheese cutter through butter, scattering the atoms across the entirety of the condensed space anywhere between the two points. And it would happen to any matter on almost a monomolecular level, no matter how dense your armor plating was.

The only saving grace was that it didn't seem to ignite a true nuclear reaction by splitting the atoms, as it merely cut along the contact point and left the two pieces stranded halfway across the galaxy from each other depending on angles or the exact point of rift failure.

Arthur was awfully glad he hadn't been assigned as a pilot for his first excursion out to the black.

Each ship large enough to be capable of hosting a rift generator had one calibrated and sized to its specific girth and weight class, with plenty of extra breathing room generated for the ship and any close-by spacecraft in a tight formation to slowly pass through the rift without slicing in twain by connecting with the edges. Precise piloting and a clean entrance and exit were key.

Obviously, this whole process would be exponentially more difficult in combat situations, and he feared for the day it might occur even as he experienced it for the first time.

Arthur found himself praying that his father hadn't died due to such a simple mistake as perhaps the hand-eye coordination of enormous amounts of tonnage through a rift.

He confirmed their exit point vocally to the bridge, which was clear as relayed by the comms buoy A.I.

The captain gave the order for the engine room to spin up the engines for thrust while maintaining the rift generation with the precise XYZ coordinates delivered. There was a loud crinkling noise somewhere in the depths of the ship behind the bridge, like a hundred thousand cellophane wrappers and tinfoil sheets softly being rumpled up by hand into balls all at the same time.

The crinkling was accompanied by a deepening rumble, and a few seconds loss of gravity as the enormous fusion reactors diverted power from the gravity generators to the rift and propulsion engines. With several pulses of bright light in the kilometre or so distance ahead of the ship, the rift was ripped open properly and stabilized into place, emitting a bright white light that was hard to look at directly even at this distance.

It was like staring directly into the light of the sun.

The *Jalapeno Gold*'s engines accelerated slowly, and the huge bulk of the Support Ship lurched forward, the navigation computer plotting a course for the pilot straight through the center of the jagged white light.

The bright white light enveloped the bow of the ship before long, slowly devouring the length of the grey cylinder until the wall of solid white light passed across the bridge itself outside the viewport.

Arthur flinched as the white wall of light passed outside the viewport but found himself unharmed as it continued on past the bridge and they emerged through the other side.

As soon as it had surged across the outside of the bridge, Arthur found a sense of distance in his first rift jump - realizing the white wall behind them had never really moved, and the simple illusion of being overtaken was false.

Only the ship had ever actually moved.

He could still feel the ship's forward momentum and rumbling engines behind him, and the rift generator and the engines were still crackling away as the back half of the vessel followed them through the gap. But now the scene before them had changed, as a dusty green and mostly brown planet with dark patches of blue ocean and soft white clouds reared up in front of them and the Earth they had just left behind was now nowhere in sight. They had blinked across a good chunk of the galaxy in a mere minute or two.

As the back half of the ship continued to lurch through the portal behind them, a sense of wonder overcame him. There were always stories of course, about old creaky rift generators failing halfway through transit, with the ships in question being sliced clean in half - like sausages caught beneath a falling cleaver.

There was a grotesque notion of solitude in this - with either half of such a ship being caught god knows how many light-years apart. He'd hate to be the person standing right on the edge of that portal when it failed, with a collapsing bridge guillotining through that portion of the ship and anyone unfortunate enough to be positioned near the precipice.

What would it feel like to have your atoms scattered across two conjoined halves of space, if you felt anything at all while you were split in two on a monomolecular level?

"Pay attention, Brass. I know you're green, but we still have to transmit our fleet codes to let the colony know we're friendly."

Duty before daydreaming.

"Yes sir."

Arthur jumped back to work – yet another head case session interrupted by the reality of transmitting encrypted Friend of Foe targeting data. A crucial necessity after rifting.

Brokeback Gorge was quick and easy, and soon enough they were rifting again.

It was his first time outside the solar system, and he became more tense and robotic the further they got from the home world of humanity, terrified of making a mistake or losing his concentration at a pivotal moment after the one initial lapse. His crewmates noticed his increasing uptightness at each

Naval Base and refueling station they stopped at, all the while getting further and further away from the Earth towards the Northeastern spiraling arms of the Milky Way.

The time came when *Jalapeño Gold* eventually arrived at the *Transcontinental,* about a week after their initial departure from Earth. Due to how closely he worked with the navigator, he knew the drydock was somewhat within striking distance of the front lines, which added some subtle fear and excitement to the journey, at least in false anticipation.

Most of the journey was so far excruciatingly boring, involving waiting in orbit around planets or space stations as streams of smaller transport and resupply craft scurried back and forth between the location proper and their Support Ship. It was further delayed by the gratuitous amount of bureaucracy involved, as manifests were cross-referenced, logged, and filed away into the hungry maws of paper pushers hiding away in office buildings somewhere within the realms of the core worlds and military bases of the G.O.D. As one of two communications officers, he was responsible for sending the various reports and digital documents as the go-between.

It was monotonous work.

He was filing the final reports from the previous stop when his replacement arrived, a perky non-binary kid a year or two below him in age, who swept in with double Arthur's energy, pomp, and circumstance.

He was getting used to these slow transitions, and this one was shockingly similar to his arrival to the *Jalapeño Gold* a week prior, being devoid of much else beyond a formal salute exchanged between him and the captain. It did not take him long at his bunk to gather his things into his duffel bag and disembark via one of several departing Aggies flitting back and forth with supplies and personnel between the Support Ship and the *Transcontinental.*

This leg of the journey, short as it was, was finished at last, with the *Transcontinental* sprawled out across the void of space like the skeleton of an unfinished skyscraper before his tiny white Agatha.

A dozen ships in various states of construction and repair were moored between the various spindly and intersecting lines of the drydock station, with several more defensive ships floating motionless in waiting defense nearby. Some of the bigger cruisers were scarred and blackened, clearly having seen recent combat to be docked here.

Tucked inside one of the smaller girder docks, was the *Asalia*, the petite cousin to the *Jalapeño Gold*.

Finally! His new home for the next while.

Perhaps his coffin if things went wrong.

The *Asalia* was in the final stages of preparation for departure, and he was one of the final chess pieces it needed to begin the long patrol route from *The Transcontinental* at the eastern tip of the Milky Way's arm westerly along the edges of Guardian-controlled space.

They would be cutting across both the Outer and Perseus arms of The Milky Way, skirting the edge of the front along several uncolonized planets closest to *The Black*, The Black Armada's debris and wreckage strewn chokepoints and plotted bottlenecks that defended access to their inner territories. This would comprise most of their route, before *The Asalia* would begin looping back along the Orion Spur to complete the last leg of the patrol along the sovereign and ungoverned neutral territories.

The hangars were open - to onload or offload personnel, supplies, equipment, and his own person, along with a few others who would be joining his mostly new crew. As he had checked in via the dry dock proper, the previous captain who was in charge of the ship during construction was expecting him.

He met her at one of the airlocks leading from the station onto the *Asalia* proper, taking only a short time to transfer from his Aggie and to use one of the *Transcontinental's* multidirectional cargo elevators.

The captain saluted.

"It's your first command, right?"

Arthur nodded shyly, and they both dropped the salute.

She edged in closer, lowering her voice.

"You're on a fairly dangerous route, anything can happen out along *The Black*. You'll be a long way from any backup in the event anything happens. So stay sharp out there."

They shook hands and she turned to go. He paused, taking a deep breath to fight the rising sense of overwhelm while watching her as she strode away, removing her hat and shaking out her bun.

He let the breath out in a long sigh, and turned to settle in, first finding his captain's quarters, which were rather spacious compared to his shared bunk aboard the *Jalapeño Gold*.

Once he had unloaded his duffel bag, he moved upwards through the ship to the bridge built directly into the forward prow of the *Asalia*. It was a precarious location compared to the central bridge of the *Gold*, designed for visibility, speed, and evasion rather than much actual defense.

He did a quick lap of the bridge, currently half-manned with temporary staff, all waiting for relief. They were all mostly handling the minutiae of departure prep.

A request from *The Transcontinental's* administrator to meet with him was waiting, relayed by a helpful younger man with a big ginger beard. Happy for the chance to stretch his legs, Arthur meandered down through the airlock, asked for directions from a passing technician, and eventually found his way to the administrator's office.

The administrator was an older man, clearly quite comfortable in his long-time job managing the dry dock administration and the various projects *The Transcontinental* was responsible for completing.

"Tea?"

"Please."

They moved to sit across from each other, the desk hosting a small, framed picture of a happy little black-haired toddler playing in a sandbox.

"Captain Brass, I have some bad news for you."

The commander hadn't really even waited for him to finish sitting down before he unloaded it.

"The *Asalia* is a wonderful ship, and she'll be a lovely frigate to captain. However, there have been some delays in the final 'touch-up' stages of construction due to delays in materials shipments. The *Jalapeño Gold* is not only delivering you yourself to the *Asalia*, but also many core components and other superficial parts to complete some final touches on the frigate."

"So what does that mean for me? Do we have a departure date?"

"Oh, we have ample space here for you and your crew in temporary workers' quarters, and once they install the bunks and water filtration systems, you'll be good to go. I've already informed G.O.D. fleet operations of the matter, so all we can do is wait, I'm afraid."

All smiles, as if he did not have a care in the world. He occupied a very cushy position indeed.

"Don't get me wrong of course. The ship itself could fly out of dry dock tomorrow, but what many don't know is it's not the assembly or the operation of the ship itself that takes the most time, it's all the finishing touches to make it livable for the crew. Bunks, sinks, shower stalls, artificial leather covering for crew seats, I'm sure you understand, no? I wouldn't want to send you out across the stars with an improperly equipped frigate."

Arthur nodded, but on the inside, this example of the bureaucratic side of the war machine almost made him laugh with its disregard for resources and wealth. Artificial leather for a kilometer-long number of seats? Were they insane, if not at the very least wasteful?

Having water and a place to sleep made sense, but he was suddenly eager to see what other wastes of money the Guardians of Destiny had thrown at the *Asalia* in a lavish display of comfort in wartime. Was it meant to coax them into a false sense of security? A final huzzah in a space born capsule hotel before the ship exploded out on the edge of civilization somewhere?

With a few more exchanged pleasantries between himself and the administrator, he hurried up and waited.

His remaining crew soon arrived on other ships passing through, and he did his best to beat back his looming sense of dread and anxiety, moving to have coffee with the crew whenever possible.

He started with several engineers that would be working in and around the rear of the frigate, either as overseers on the rift generators or the engines. These were the crew responsible for any one of the dozens of systems and subsystems on the *Asalia*.

The waiting gnawed at him, and now that he was officially "deployed," he just could not find comfort in a hard bar drink like he was so used to doing previously. Captains were expected officially to always remain sober outside of shore leaves. He'd have to wait for his *actual* shore leaves, not just the Venusian Academy "weekend leave" that he was used to. And worse, it would take several months to finish the patrol in order to get that magical time off. The engineers, and other crew were nice enough, so he coped as best he could with the aid of caffeine. And his quarters were well-stocked, hilariously - seeming to acknowledge the official bureaucratic rules as separate from the reality.

The crew was small, due to the *Asalia* being a relatively diminutive warship designed mostly for escort missions and scouting, or to be deployed under the command of larger vessels as part of larger fleet actions. But the lack of crew aboard the frigate also enabled the ship to qualify and receive the funding to host a relatively intelligent A.I. construct.

The waiting meant he was also able to chat – somewhat poorly, with this Class 3 Artificial Intelligence, Bruno, who was installed on the *Asalia's* central network. Arthur was extremely relieved to have an A.I. running things behind the scenes, even if Bruno was rather low on the "class system" and therefore not as complex, self-aware, or emotionally intelligent as a Class 5 or 6 might be at the upper echelon.

A ship had to be pretty large or at least important to justify a Class 5 or 6 A.I. onboard, something he learned from Bruno. The prohibitive cost of programming them with deeper and deeper layers of intellect coding, and similar costs for providing escape avenues for them to download away to in larger combat situations made it too unaffordable otherwise. Arthur had to scoff – fake leather for the seats but not a higher class A.I. to maximize their performance? Did the Guardians of Destiny really want an efficient Navy, or were they just expecting to throw money, resources, and manpower at the Armada to win the war?

Was it all a ruse to stimulate the Guardian economies at the end of the day, by playing into a war of attrition?

He was sure there was a military strategy for actual combat situations, but as a new product of the bureaucracy, he wasn't particularly inclined to trust any pencil-pusher who lacked the actual experience in the field. They just wouldn't know what to prioritize, clearly, especially where money was concerned. The bloat of the Guardian workforce in terms of bureaucracy and logistics was staggering when he quizzed Bruno on the numbers behind it all. The system was so reliant on such logistical nightmares of accounting and cyclical investment that it was a miracle the war machine was able to even sustain itself.

When the *Asalia* was finally outfitted properly and subsequently cleared for departure, it was christened with its pre-designated name rather lethargically in a makeshift ceremony involving the *Transcontinental*'s administrator, Captain Brass, and a handful of dry dock workers.

Arthur was lacking in any real excitement. He was sick of waiting and had finally beaten back his nervousness and anxiety, being ready to escape the monotony of *The Transcontinental* and venture into the unknown, regardless of how far it might be from Earth or how much closer it would be to the dangers that lurked out in the dark beyond.

The *Asalia* finally launched with a fully finished interior and a full crew the day after the christening, readied with provisions, munitions, and navigation data via Bruno.

And fake leather seats of course.

They were finally ready to patrol through the cosmos.

The small size of the frigate and her crew combined with the vague patrol and scouting path, implied a long, slow journey.

They had been assigned only a few required stops for resupply and reporting, which allowed Arthur relative safety from The Black Armada and the majority of the conflict, despite being so close to their territory to the east.

As a result of their safer route, however, it would also put them out of contact with the rest of the G.O.D. for long stretches at a time, far from any comms buoys outside of the required rendezvous locations. He was also only limited by these specific checkpoints timewise, so with no real timeline for the route, he was free to pursue secondary G.O.D. objectives as he saw fit.

These objectives consisted of scanning gas giants and barren unexplored moons and systems for resources, while leaving probes to act as dragnet spies for Armada activity, despite the probes having longer communications delays back along the micro-rift route. With each rift jump the *Asalia* made, he grew more and more comfortable with the idea of space travel out here in the void – an amusing realization for a man who had only joined the Navy out of a life or death ultimatum.

Their communications back to the core worlds vanished completely on specific portions of the journey, near dead zones without nearby relays. Arthur therefore found his new-found captaincy very sporadic in terms of work.

Some weeks he was bored senseless, with absolutely nothing to do aside from the small acts he performed towards slowly getting to know his crew. Other weeks he scrambled to proof or sign forms and paperwork of all kinds to send back homeward to the core worlds in the short bursts of contact they were able to get. The *Asalia* had one or two person secretarial and science teams on board in addition to their solo communications officer, but even with their and Bruno's help, it was constantly a crunch period when he was required to report.

While getting to know the hundreds of crewmembers elsewhere on the ship was actively a more difficult goal, he got to know his bridge crew especially well as they had plenty of time to chat on the bridge whilst drifting out in the black.

This was especially true in the deadtime it took to roam specific star systems in shorter rift hops and wait for the *Asalia's* rift generators to cool down after each jump. While he was never too forthcoming about his history, especially as far as his choice to join the G.O.D. Navy was concerned, he constantly asked outward facing questions and pulled out the life stories of the people under his command.

In return, he shared with them his Academy experiences, and stories from his reckless teenage years in lieu of the stories of his short jail time and potential political problems through associations with Judge Joe Undelwood.

His first mate was a young woman named Jacqueline Harp. She came from a rather poor family, which seemed to be a trend in the G.O.D. She had enlisted in the Navy as a means of supporting her folks back on Earth. Her Canadian heritage came as an amusement to him, as some of his British slang was picked up on almost immediately. They'd joke around, somewhat unprofessionally at times, by poking fun at the other bridge crew with sloppy Cockney and rural Canadian accents.

She had risen quickly through the ranks due to intelligence and humility, even though she had only served a few years before entering the academy proper. She had been shuffled from ship to ship after that, never getting the chance to truly prove herself. It seemed unfair that despite her skill and knowledge, she had been denied a captaincy while he was thrown into one immediately.

The nepotism and cronyism of the Guardian establishment was somewhat easy to see if one merely pulled back the wallpaper. The Judge and his connections simultaneously made him feel guilty and unworthy.

Their navigator was a middle-aged man named Hammad Aziz. Aziz was cheerful and upbeat, having come from the joint-territories in the Middle East dominated by the Saudi-based New Islamic Brotherhood, a staunch supporter of the G.O.D. While Aziz was very talkative, especially about his home in the conglomerate state made up of previously Islamic Arabic nations long-since conquered and headed by Saudi Arabia, his religious beliefs steered them away from conversations on the Creator and on the G.O.D. higher ups in general. He was much more secretive and staunch about his faith than Tyrone had been.

It was for the best, Arthur suspected, but he still always pondered how Aziz truly felt about his work. The Guardians loved to use religion as a recruitment tool, and Islam had locked horns with the Guardian-backed Christian Churches on more than a few occasions throughout history, despite sharing the same prophets and God on paper.

This rivalry under the same banner was visible in full force. Hammad had served for over fifteen years and yet never once was promoted, despite several tours of duty out on the frontier, many involving active ship combat. Arthur couldn't help but feel sorry for him and this subtle persecution. He felt like he shouldn't have been a captain reigning over such talented people with so little actual experience.

Of course, it was not just Hammad that made them shy away from belief as a conversation topic. Not many were willing to openly discuss the Creator for fear of somehow committing some blasphemy, or of planting their foot firmly in their mouths. Even the act of acknowledging the energy being the G.O.D. revered so deeply within their belief system was difficult due to the nature of the war.

How could such a powerful creature or entity be gobbled up by a mere former servant, this "Xex, God of Control" if it were so omnipotent and omniscient?

And the question only deepened when one considered that Xex had been ascended by that same being itself in the first place. The whole mythos was all very mysterious, and hundreds if not thousands of conspiracies were manufactured every year based on it all. The G.O.D. propaganda machine mostly framed it in terms of a betrayal of the wholly benevolent energy deity, which made it easy to continue fighting the apparent evil of The Armada. Xex declaring himself a god-emperor and seeking authoritarian rule of the entirety of humanity also made him extremely easy to paint as a villain of course.

The subtle authoritarianism of the Guardians was apparently preferable by most to open dictatorship by someone who claimed to be the only true god in terms of power.

Not that the grunts like him would ever know the true story of how everything played out those hundreds of years ago, right? Arthur had soon conjured up more than a few conspiracies of his own during the first few weeks of the patrol, given ample enough time to daydream as he did.

The *Asalia*'s small size allowed for a smaller number of staff other than Aziz, and Harp, and Captain Arthur Brass was able to cultivate an atmosphere that was fairly informal. He liked them all. Next in line after Harp and Hammad was the senior comms officer Victor Hammond, a G.O.D. enlisted American ethnicity from the core world - *Holy Roman*. After him was their pilot, Jonathan Halevy, an outgoing Israeli from *Blend*. They all had vastly different upbringings from him, especially those from the colonies and the Guardian core worlds outside Earth, and he questioned Hammond and Halevy constantly on what it was like to grow up on an alien world so far away from the cradle of mankind.

Most G.O.D. Ships were required by military code to include a Science and Intelligence Officer on the bridge itself, who on their small ship was also their weapons man. However, despite the famous cloak and dagger nature of the position, being so close to The Eye, they found their man, Lieutenant George Durand, to be quite charming and outgoing. Instead of a slim and scary operative, Durand was a cheerful and portly Frenchman, always ready to pipe up with a crude comment or interject with some old wives' tale from his upbringing in the southeastern French countryside.

It contrasted Arthur, Harp and their jests quite well.

Even though he found himself quite a bit younger than most of the bridge, only older than Harp and Halevy individually, he felt he transitioned quickly from nervous and anxiety-ridden to being quite at ease in his role as captain, probably due to the incredibly slow working environment and the relative lack of anything really important to do outside of paperwork.

There were Naval and Army drills, perhaps. Every ship of course had a contingent of the G.O.D. Army on board, and despite their frigate's size they still staffed two full Shocktrooper companies.

On top of this, the *Asalia* hosted a full row of hangars on both the port and starboard sides, equipped with the typical G.O.D. air and spacecraft like Agatha all-purpose gunship transports, Justice fixed wing fighters, and a few other one-ofs. But all this equipment languished for weeks outside of training sorties, and in talking to the Shocktroopers, they grew weary of all the sitting, cooped up onboard with not much to do aside from gamble, work out, or wile away the time in virtual reality simulators or more archaic mobile games due to the lack of connectivity outside The *Asalia* itself.

The further they got from the *Transcontinental,* sporadic events did pop up, breaking the monotony of the patrol. The *Asalia* crossed paths with a couple of freighters coming from Armada turf that were quickly boarded and dealt with as per protocols.

The freighters were very much operating outside the scope of treaty-protected companies or the largely untouchable Junk and Rumblers Guild membership, carrying nebulous cargoes consisting of heavy narcotics and weapons shipments, both moving northwest across the galaxy towards the neutral territories. There was also the occasional security check on one or two passing trade ships, which were moving goods covered under the treaty or who were operating with the protection of one of the various neutral groups like the Unitary Mercenary Guild.

He felt like a border security guard more than a frigate warship captain.

Everything was boring, safe, predictable.

Easy.

Quiet.

Until all hell broke loose, of course.

CHAPTER 5: A LOUD AND OBNOXIOUS SERIES OF BANGS.

"Trouble always shows up when it's least expected, drinks you out of house and home, and then lingers well past the appropriate hour to leave, annoying all the other guests."

Six months into his patrol, during a particularly tough round of twenty questions between himself and Halevy, they were caught entirely by surprise.

The radar station started flashing and the ships' Friend or Foe contact sirens went off. The *Asalia*'s A.I. Bruno caught something on long-range scanners. Victor, just coming back from a trip to the canteen for a round of coffees, rushed over to verify.

Regardless of being a relatively stupid Class 3 A.I., Bruno had correctly identified, marked, and put the whole frigate on alert for an enemy contact. It was a relatively distant battlecruiser, clearly tagged in the ship's FoF system as Black Armada, not merely as another one of the neutral smuggler ships or freighters that they had dealt with previously.

All spacecraft were required by the treaty, even in wartime, to tag themselves with a friend or foe tag as pertaining to their respective faction or company. These could be faked, spoofed, or hidden via a blackout or comms scrambling of course, but this ship was clearly Armada, and there was absolutely no logical reason as to why it was here, nestled in as it was so close around this tiny hunk of rock. A moon orbiting a nearby gas giant of soft yellows and oranges.

The cruiser was in a stationary position, low to the surface on the edge of what should be G.O.D. Space. The rocky moon orbiting the gas giant was one of only two actual features in the system around a large red giant star.

The *Asalia* had passed by the gas giant a half-dozen times already, using it as a waypoint on their patrol route in their zigzagging back and forth path.

Every time before now, it had been the same barren rock devoid of atmosphere, of any valuable resources, and more obviously of any life. If it wasn't already charted months back, the moon would be easy to lose in the radiation spewing forth via the solar winds of the red giant, or the gas giant's storms.

Bruno had been lucky enough to detect the cruiser's Friend or Foe tag by mere coincidence: The battlecruiser had dropped radio silence and a communications blackout to broadcast an encrypted Armada message back to the northwest towards the neutral territories. The process consisted of launching a small micro-rift buoy, and then a second buoy past that, back east, presumably towards Armada space.

There was no way of knowing if these were permanent comms buoys or temporary ones, as some could be much more expensive than others.

Arthur considered waiting for help, but there was no way of knowing how long the Black Armada would hang around, or if reinforcements were coming to meet up with this single scout. Hell, if they noticed the *Asalia* before the frigate could take the initiative... It would be bad news.

Since he had no clue what the encrypted messages had been via the buoys, he had no inkling as to their purpose there on the small moon either.

"Any sign they've noticed us?"

Hammond shook his head in the negative.

Arthur was pumping with adrenaline, holding clenched fists and feeling the thumping of his heartbeat pounding away in his head. With each whispered update or reply, his voice wafted as almost a whisper of itself.

It was silly on his part, because sound of course couldn't travel outside the bridge, let alone through the emptiness of space with no matter to vibrate through…

Hammond was stone-faced, whilst Harp was clearly doing her best not to cry. Arthur couldn't see Aziz's face, but *Durand was fucking smiling.*

God damn intelligence operatives.

He informed the rest of the crew via internal loudspeakers of the situation, hoping that they were close to being ready at stations after Bruno's klaxon-based warning. It was expected that the entire ship was ready to go at-stations at the drop of a pin.

This was a Guardians of Destiny Naval vessel, after all.

"No sir, they're motionless, and even their engines are offline."

Within mere minutes of the first alert, the ship was indeed crewed, and they were on their way to investigate, and to likely engage the enemy.

Pretty stupid of course, for a small frigate like the *Asalia* to go after a full-sized Armada battlecruiser that easily outclassed it in size and equipment three to one, but clearly nobody else would be coming from the core worlds anytime soon.

The adrenaline had his pride surging. At all costs, he wouldn't be a coward in his first actual engagement with the enemy.

This was an incredible opportunity if he played his cards right.

Arthur ensured the order was given to go dark, bringing the engines down to a whisper and shutting down all communication both to and from the *Asalia* outside of local hardwired networks. Every section was given strict orders to stay stealthy by any means possible, a full ship-wide blackout.

The beauty of small ships was their ability to be sneaky. And Captain Arthur Brass planned to use every smidge of that infinitesimal advantage he could.

A cold sweat beaded on his brow.

As the two enemy buoys finally zipped away in a burst of radiation via tiny rifts generated by the cruiser, it meant time was ticking. There could be reinforcements on the way for an attack.

Perhaps this was just a scout ship clearing the advance routes for an attack or invasion fleet.

Bruno ensured that he recorded a copy of the two sets of encrypted messages being broadcast by the buoys before they rifted, to be sent back towards G.O.D. space at Arthur's orders. When it was possible to do so without giving away their element of surprise, of course, hidden alongside some carefully timed solar-wind radiation.

Arthur quickly typed out a hastily written contact report as well to go alongside them.

Bruno also catalogued the encrypted Armada messages for their own limited one-woman coding division, although as a frigate the *Asalia* was restricted to just the one decoder and a couple of low-ranking software techs on board. One hardly expected anything important to be deciphered anytime soon with only three bodies and Bruno's split attention on the case.

Their approach was painfully slow.

The gun batteries bristling from the enemy ship spiked up as dangerous silhouettes against the grey surface of the moon like porcupine spikes, easily doubling the armaments of the tiny frigate on approach. Arthur swallowed the lump of spittle that had been building up against the back of his throat as he held his clenched jaw tighter than he ever remembered doing before.

Venus had trained him well enough – he knew the only way to avoid being torn to pieces by the larger and better equipped ship would be to catch the cruiser by surprise before the situation could devolve into an old-fashioned "Wild West" style shootout. The larger ship could easily outgun their tiny little frigate - should the Armada be quick enough to spin themselves even partially and launch a broadside salvo with their various missile and anti-ship batteries. There was also the risk they'd charge and fire an assortment of smaller rail guns and armor piercing rounds with more functional degrees of fire than the main two guns.

The *Asalia* lacked fancy systems that came standard on larger G.O.D. ships or the smaller frigates used by The Eye – things like Contact Cloaking or Watchdog Aversion systems.

They didn't possess any of the more expensive tricks that bigger and better ships used to keep themselves hidden at all.

So, Arthur's strategy was to commit to this - the oldest trick in the book.

A good old-fashioned sneak attack from behind.

If they screwed it up, the small frigate also lacked defensive plasma shielding, meaning any actual accuracy from the Black Armada in what was called a slingback volley...

Well, it would likely render the *Asalia* an airless husk drifting through space in very short order.

The *Asalia* crept back towards the rock at a snail's pace, quieter than a feather in the absolute silence of space. Nobody said a word, with almost every single member of the crew holding their breath for ridiculous periods of time. Most present on the bridge itself jumped whenever someone exhaled suddenly.

The plan was simple enough, but needed extreme caution and precision as they slowly advanced around the far side of the tiny moon in an extremely low orbit in order to catch the cruiser from behind. They were moving as slowly as the *Asalia's* engines would allow them while still keeping it aloft via their gravity generators, fighting against the gravity well of the moon.

A tense hour of this ever-creeping waiting game passed, with everyone aboard praying they wouldn't be caught in a lucky scanner sweep. If any of the crew got anxious and moved too soon or too quickly in springing the ambush, the enemy cruiser might get their plasma shields up, quickly soaking any damage, and would then have enough time to react and scuttle them in return.

It was pure luck the cruiser remained motionless, close to the surface the whole time. Why it was here was a mystery, and at any moment it might begin to move.

Arthur's plan of attack was standard as far as ambushes went, operating straight from the academy playbooks and the number of battles in the simulator that he had executed in virtual reality. It had the *Asalia* slinging around the planet's gravity well, using the momentum of the gravity for a rapid hit and run attack on this sitting-duck enemy.

One brutal salvo of railgun rounds at a close enough range to punch through possible shielding and the hull together.

One clean run. It was all they needed.

The weapons crews were ready, waiting for Captain Brass' specific commands before they started firing up their systems and began the process of coming out of the emissions blackout to hit this enemy full force with everything the frigate had.

Not that it was much as far as battleships went.

If the *Asalia* failed, either by messing up the sneaky approach, or if they couldn't disable or destroy the cruiser in one salvo, they'd try to run as fast as they could and hope to lose them with a series of rapid-speed rift jumps back along their patrol path. They'd throw out comms buoys back towards the core worlds as fast as their rift engines would let them in-between jumps to scream for help.

There was no outside way of tracking where a ship went after it rifted, aside from clever guesswork along known travel routes or via intercepting communications, so maybe they could just make a clean escape if everything went to hell.

Captain Brass paused, hesitating, as the distance in kilometers slowly trickled down on each display monitor, with "distance to FoF target" visible in a popup to each of the bridge staff around their other monitoring duties.

They crossed the threshold of vision, and the battlecruiser slowly crested into view above the surface.

It was still motionless as they glided forwards, growing in size ever so slowly as they neared.

Everything clicked into place for Arthur, like one of his mock battles at the Academy, and the emotions at the base of his spine surged into action rather than distraction. The adrenaline kicked up a notch and blood vessels popped visibly from his clenched temples.

"All right, it's time. George on my mark, I want you to fire up all our weapons systems, go hot, and do your best with Bruno to aim for their engines. We only have one chance to scuttle them before they get everything back online, turn around, and blow us the hell out of the sky."

"*D'accord*, Captain."

His focus was on the edge of the planetoid's horizon where the tiny grey cylinder of the enemy vessel rested.

They all waited for their target to come into clearer view over the dark grey surface of the rocky world.

Seconds crept by.

What happened next was a catastrophe.

"Sir, we have a fleet transmission blasting through here. Comms Buoy just rifted in at our last known position, asking for a status update. They're blowing our cover."

Arthur swore, loudly, punching the air as he did so, with something along the lines of "cunts!"

From there the situation exploded.

Even as Bruno began playing the fleet transmission, basically what amounted to G.O.D. fleet command demanding their status - the Black Armada intercepted the encrypted broadcast and the distant ship sprang to life. Tiny white and yellow lights winked into visibility along the sides of the battlecruiser even from this distance. Red and blue lights on the tips of the various comms antennae and gun batteries also began to flare into sight.

It was in the beginning process of warming up its engines. The previously dark ship was sparkling to wakefulness. They had definitely intercepted the transmission, that much was sure, and it was enough to wake them up for at least a look around to see whom that message was intended for.

Barely a minute passed, and the battlecruiser's engines flared to life, with the long cylinder beginning to rise and spin slowly towards them.

"Captain, the enemy has detected us with a FoF sweep, and is beginning to lock on with weapons. Engines at half, looks like."

Hammond's warning came suddenly, as various lines began to appear on the main battle-map - holographically projected in 3D space from the large console in the center of the bridge. Bruno was calculating trajectories and attack and defense vectors as quickly as the Class 3 could manage on top of his other duties. The Armada cruiser wasn't moving as quickly as Arthur had expected, only using engines and thrusters at half power thus far.

Either it was waiting for a targeting vector to fire on them, or was unable to, which told him with how slowly it powered up that it was splitting its power resources for some reason. FoF alerts wailed, as the battlecruiser slowly brought weapons systems online, targeted back towards the *Asalia*.

The alarm klaxons blared again as Bruno sounded the warning across the frigate to brace for incoming fire.

Both possibilities in his mind were bad news.

If the battlecruiser was devoted to some hidden task requiring excess power from the engines, either sending out a distress buoy or spinning up rift generators, he'd possibly be neck deep in reinforcements, and as they had already lost the element of surprise, allowing it to shoot at them was hardly an alternative while they waited for the gap to close for their much smaller effective range.

Whelp.

So much for getting close enough to punch through the shields in one volley.

"Durand, OPEN FIRE! All other batteries - target the enemy vessel and fire at will."

George did not waste time following orders.

The frigate hummed beneath their feet, as both the engineers, gunners, and Bruno worked in unison to light up the enormous railgun in the bow. Electricity buzzed in the air around them and hair stood up on end as the huge rails underslung beneath the bridge began sending electric current surging through the length of the giant magnetic accelerator rails. The simulator hadn't replicated the charge in the air like this, which was a novel new experience for him.

The bridge froze, and then the whole of the *Asalia* shook with recoil back towards the engines as the enormous magnetic accelerator along the bow finished charging and lit up with a bright arc of blue and yellow lightning.

A twenty-tonne, depleted-uranium-core slug crossed the space of kilometres in a matter of seconds, the engines straining to continue velocity against the backward force of the projectile.

Guardian technology had mastered the basics of such simple physics as recoil centuries ago.

The railgun round did drop in velocity, as the bright flash of the slug arced through and was pulled downward by the gravity well of the moon, but Bruno and Durand had accounted for that.

The first round was en-route and on-target.

Objects in motion, stayed in motion with no force to stop them, and any kinetic round fired in open space with no gravity well or source of friction would sail on at insane speeds for what could be eternity until it hit something else out in space.

The slug seemed to move in slow motion from the bridge, while in actuality crossing an enormous distance towards the enemy.

"Missile pods, now. Target the engines in case the railgun misses. Halevy, take us as low to the gravity well as you can without sucking us in or slowing us down. Prepare to jig right, defensive maneuvers."

His ship shifted under his feet as they hit the first gentle tug of gravity from the surface below, even through the power of their own gravity generator. The bow arced downwards towards the rocky surface, even as the first railgun round finally connected and the Armada Battlecruiser's plasma shielding erupted in a concussive blast of rainbow coloring as excited gasses rapidly changed states of matter.

"Shielding confirmed, sir."

In under a second it changed color, shifting from blue, to green, and then cascading in color all the way down to red and then nothingness at the point of impact. The plasma defenses had clearly failed, dissipating and failing outwards in a wave of red-orange color as the railgun round sheared through the energy field and buried itself into the hull of its stern, close to the engines.

There was a brief pause as the numerous orange flares of missiles arced out into view towards the enemy, launched from the *Asalia's* batteries along the length of the hull behind the bridge.

Silence.

And then an enormous eruption plumed outwards from where the slug had impacted into the battlecruiser's hull, as the transfer of energy from the dense slug blew an enormous battle wound into the enemy vessel just ahead of the glowing blue engines.

The bridge cheered together as one.

Even from this great distance, they could see streams of

debris and other shrapnel pouring from somewhere within the superstructure, vented outwards into the near-vacuum of space from the damage. A good sign, signalling the battlecruiser was losing atmosphere from within. It was a clean hit, but still not the precise ambush attack he had hoped for, thanks to command's completely unexpected blunder.

He was trying not to seethe even thinking about it, tasked as they were with finishing off the enemy.

"They still have some engines, captain. They're turning on us slow, attack vector."

The cruiser had begun launching its own missiles, while also deploying fighters, transports, and other armor from the numerous hangars along its' sides.

"Launch all our Justices and Protectors. Harbinger pilots and fire teams defend the hangars from boarders. All anti-air batteries, you have permission to fire at will."

Arthur scrambled his own fighters along with the *Asalia's* various missile and aircraft countermeasures, fearing he was too late already - having held them from launching to ensure the ambush succeeded. The *Asalia* was mostly outfitted with older model Protectors and Justices, the basic fixed wing backbone fighters of the Navy, so he feared for the worst.

Missiles bloomed into hundreds of orange fireball-flowers around the Armada battlecruiser as the swarms of traditional payload rockets were lit up on approach in swaths by the opposing air-defense batteries. Across the hull of the battlecruiser, the streaming lines of yellow tracer rounds arced up and out into space by the tens of thousands.

The cruiser's plasma shielding was desperately trying to recharge, failing repeatedly at wrapping around the structure in a wave of struggling red-orange energy, flickering helplessly and giving out to the sucking hunger of empty space, again and again.

"Keep firing, Durand. Aim for the stern. Clip those engines."

"Aye Sir."

The rails jutting out from beneath them flashed again and again every dozen seconds or so as the weapon fired, pulling them all backwards against the straining of the engines and gravity generator. The G-forces were surprising for a gravity-generator equipped craft like the frigate.

The second waves of missiles neared, almost completely invisible individually at this great distance. The battlecruiser's anti-air batteries couldn't possibly stop them all, however, and perhaps a third of the *Asalia's* missile salvos finally connected with the areas around the railgun wound. Dozens of small orange flashes, one after the other, bloomed against the hull, sending sprays of metal up and out into the gravity well of the moon. The ship kept turning, but just as Arthur was expecting them to reach the attack vector as drawn by the holographic projector, to return fire and destroy the *Asalia* with a single salvo, there was a second eruption from within the large grey enemy ship somewhere near the railgun impact.

A lucky missile hit, perhaps?

"Their fuel cells are going, sir. We must have struck close enough to the engines to cause a failure. It's spewing radiation."

Arthur's jaw dropped as the Black Armada battlecruisers' engines simultaneously cut out in a final flare of blue propulsion, and gouts of orange and blue flame began belching from the railgun hole near the back of the ship. He almost fainted watching the slow-motion eruption, as having taken itself out of its own stationary low-orbit, the bulk of the enemy ship was now slowly being sucked down into the gravity well of the planet without the help of its engines or gravity generator to stop it from falling.

"Sir, they still have fighters closing, and are still trying to empty all their missile pods."

He snapped back to the battle at hand.

A good omen, but it wasn't over quite yet, despite the falling cruiser.

The anti-gravity generators of the ship must have kicked back in somehow, because the descent of the enemy was gradually slowing as it was wrenched down by the gravity well. The hulk came to a slow stop, frozen above the rocky surface below at an odd, janky angle, still unable to move without engine power proper.

An injured beast was almost more dangerous than a healthy one.

They would likely do everything to survive, now.

The captain of the enemy battlecruiser would play the cornered animal.

Still, a single attack fighter or a stray missile striking a critical point could cause the same danger for them, especially as their ship's bridge was located front and center on the bow of the frigate.

Hell, they might easily be scuttled or suffer the same fate as the Armada cruiser if their own engines were crippled somehow. Being smashed into a rocky backwater moon in the middle of the empty frontier, taken down with the last gasps of a dying enemy was not exactly how he wanted to die.

"George, continue to compromise their hull with the railgun, weapons free. Have the anti-fighter batteries pick targets defensively. Hammond, get our e-jammers up, have all our pilots focus on the small craft and ignore the cruiser's rail guns now that they can't turn to fire their main gun at us. Halevy, pull us up out of the gravity well. Make sure those fighters don't go for our engines. Bruno, calculate enemy weapons vectors for Halevy to help us dodge."

The enemy ship was opening up at the *Asalia* now with everything it had left, sending smaller railgun rounds out from the smaller broadsides awkwardly facing the frigate. Each miniature railgun round arced towards the Asalia in bright streaks of light, most missing completely due to the smaller vessel's range and evasive movements. All save one glancing blow sent grazing along their port side. It shook their teeth, with several batteries near the top decks shearing off in strings of metal. Some casualties of course, not that accurate reports would come until after the battle.

The battlecruiser was still perched there, mostly unmoving. It continued billowing blue and orange flames from the stern, as Durand and Bruno working in concert sunk three out of seven more railgun rounds in across the broadsides. The Black Armada battlecruiser was trapped - a sitting duck, doomed even whilst hanging in mid-fall above the grey craggy surface below.

While a lack of engines prevented the enemy from turning further to face the *Asalia,* to unload their own main railgun or plasma weaponry outwards at the tiny frigate, it still had hundreds of aft guns, capable of peppering them with shells and smaller caliber rounds of all types.

The segmented streams of light from two sets of weapons batteries flashed back and forth between the two enormous shapes above the star-backed moon, as several hundred shells, missiles, railgun rounds, and plasma arcs each minute rocked back and forth between both hulls.

There were several more muted rumbles from somewhere below the *Asalia's* bridge, although none were as serious as the initial railgun strike. Each still signalled the frigate to be taking damage.

Seconds stretched magically into eons.

The railgun finished cooling down yet again.

And George Durand promptly sunk another uranium slug deep into the damaged stern, close to the initial wound.

Almost immediately, the battlecruiser's anti-gravity generators failed in a brilliant flash of white light, going nuclear in a sudden blink. It was a spectacular sight, watching the behemoth warship half-erupt into a blue and orange fireball up against the backdrop of the gas giant behind it.

Simultaneous with the billowing explosion, it slowly sank downwards, as if the tablecloth holding it up from the descent had been ripped out from under it and there was no table left to catch the fall.

The next several minutes were harrowing.

The *Asalia* trembled with every remaining missile strike, and the battlecruiser's last surviving fighters moved to engage the frigate in a frenzy of zealotry, attempting to pull the frigate down alongside the cruiser. Their tactics rapidly degraded into last-ditch kamikaze style suicides, as befitting the standardized Black Armada tactics upon losing the advantage and losing any hope of a clean victory.

These last few suicide attacks were largely ineffective, but there was a realization on Arthur's part as their anti-aircraft guns and Justices mopped up the remaining attackers that the battle had been won.

George continued to lead the offensive efforts of the *Asalia*, peppering the enemy ship with even more railgun slugs as a final precaution. Soon enough, they watched as the battlecruiser split into two fractured pieces, with the remaining intact section of bow dropping last, a venting shell falling helplessly over the course of a slow minute.

Eventually the two pieces finished slamming into the rocky grey crust of the planet below and breaking further on impact. The bow was largely intact, with the holed stern nearby shattering into a fragmented mess of superstructure, belching atmosphere, debris, bodies, and flame.

The *Asalia's* defense gunners and munitions crews had done an incredible job of protecting the engines and bridge throughout the skirmish. Initial damage reports established that the rumbles Arthur had felt were largely only superficial damage – mostly black pockmarks and otherwise minor armor and hull damage.

The *Asalia* was now less than perfect in appearance, but was still fully functioning in terms of operating systems.

The enemy fighters throughout the battle had been pushed by the frigate's batteries into strafing her hangars and midships, which only caused minor damage at best.

Without anywhere to return to land, those not as dedicated to the Black Armada cause as the more brainwashed kamikaze pilots were now attempting to flee into a higher orbit around the gas giant as the *Asalia's* contingent of fighters and weapons batteries hunted them down.

All in all, they had indeed lost a handful of lives, mostly those of fighter pilots and the few crew who were manning now-destroyed gun batteries.

Arthur focused on directing their pilots and defenses at the last few fighters flitting away from the *Asalia* trying to escape, even as he gazed down at the broken battlecruiser and watched the ship die a final death. The superstructure was actively venting atmosphere in several streams of debris - alongside occasional bodies shunting outwards from a variety of hull breaches and the largely destroyed stern section. With no power from the engines or generators to seal blast doors, a lack of atmosphere would suffocate or pull survivors out from aboard the wreck, at least those not already prepared for the vacuum.

Arthur winced at the thought of that, as the shell belched neon-blue plasma from the railgun holes speckled across what remained of the stern. He felt a strange sort of pity for those he had killed, and held onto a lingering sense of dread and loss for the few they had lost aboard the *Asalia*.

Now that they were temporarily safe, the adrenaline of the battle washed out of him in a wave of nausea. But he still had work to do to mop up the mess and call for help from the Guardians of Destiny core worlds - hopefully before any more Armada reinforcements could arrive.

Their fighters came back from the final hunt with remarkably few additional casualties, and he made a quick note of the list. Only counting a grand-total of six pilots deceased from the approximately thirty of their fighters, and three deaths from amongst the crew aboard the *Asalia* manning gun batteries, it was still a roaring success overall.

He hated the fact that he had lost any lives at all. The deaths were on his own shoulders as well as partially upon the heads of fleet command, even if only accidentally.

He felt the weight of those deaths as captain, knowing he had made the choice to engage the enemy while he could, instead of choosing to run and cry for help.

It would likely be a burden he would continue to carry and process.

But the crew had done well and followed orders perfectly. When provided the list of casualties, he found he still couldn't recognize all of the dead by name, despite knowing a few of the names and faces from the canteen.

It was a hard thing to do, even for the captain of a small frigate like the *Asalia,* which was host to hundreds of crew members. He resolved to memorize and honor them just the same, to carry them along with him in a sense.

Arthur had faced death or imprisonment only a short time ago as a guaranteed outcome, so perhaps it was better that at least these Guardian souls were able to go down fighting instead of expiring via such a feeble end as an execution.

There were still a few unknown variables, with Arthur still fearing somehow that this easy victory was merely a ruse.

The thought lurked in Captain Brass' mind that there was still something dangerous aboard the scuttled cruiser, or that it could somehow still attempt to call for backup as a final curse against this small frigate who had waded into battle beyond its station.

It was very much like beating a dead horse to scour every possibility, but being his first actual battle outside the academy simulations, Arthur figured that being safe was better than being sorry.

Lucky enough, the reinforcements this strange scout might be leading never arrived, despite the initial fears. Arthur ordered comms buoys sent back towards the core worlds to inform them of both his initial contact report as well as the outcome of the battle itself.

It was starting to look like the battle was truly over.

Captain Arthur Brass and the *Asalia* had actually won!

CHAPTER 6: EVERYTHING WORKS IN CIRCLES.

"Understanding that you're in the eye of the storm doesn't really protect you from the other half about to hit."

"Sir..."

Harp's voice after the shooting had finally ceased was stunned to say the least.

"We just scored a kill on an Armada battlecruiser with... A frigate a third of the size... And under a dozen casualties..."

They were all forced into a deep, thoughtful silence by her statement, and Arthur realized the scope of what they had truly accomplished.

It was only his first tour of duty as a G.O.D. Naval Captain, on a backwater patrol route along the frontier.

And yet, he had captained the *Asalia,* all alone on the verge of Guardian territory, into a near-perfect victory against a far bigger ship.

This had been no skirmish against pirates, or another illegal-trade takedown, but an actual naval battle concerning the real war in their home territory.

This had been a defensive maneuver for the sovereignty of

Guardian space..

And they had won.

"We... We're heroes..."

Arthur waved George's sentiment down, rapidly doing the calculations for various outcomes in his head. He quickly began recognizing that the battle, no matter how impressive a win - was a small piece of a larger puzzle he'd soon have to figure out in depth.

"We still have work to do. We have to collect our dead, and be prepared for Armada retaliation. This'll mean nothing if the Armada shows up with more ships and kills us while we're cheering. But I do have to say... All things considered? Good work, crew."

The smiles bloomed across their faces for a moment, and they returned back to work with fervor.

The medical section was quickly filled with crew members who had suffered mild injuries. Those hurt bore an assortment of injuries ranging from cuts and scrapes, to small crush injuries, or in one case, even serious impalement by debris. The *Asalia* only had a single ship's doctor, and his medical staff were quickly overwhelmed.

But nobody onboard had died outside of those few fighter pilots who had perished, and that was the important part of it.

Arthur's next order of business was to deploy salvage and investigation crews into the cruiser after they had completed the task of recovering the bodies and craft of the fallen pilots, or what remained of them.

He felt sorry for the crewmembers who were designated such a grisly task.

Brass had learned to fly most small craft via simulation in his academy education, and his flight record for Protectors and Justices was rather poor. He pitied those forced into the thick of inter-ship battle in such aged models of fighter.

Their two squads of Shocktroopers went into the enemy wreck first, clad in their pressurized breather gear for zero pressure environments requiring sealed body armor. Arthur had ordered them to check the broken husk of the Battlecruiser for intelligence, survivors to take prisoner, or other useful data.

After the team had secured the wreck and declared it safe - with all hands lost, George went in with a small intelligence team to try and extract what they could from computer systems or the shipboard A.I., whilst carefully avoiding the unstable stern section.

They also convinced two of the Armada pilots who had attempted to escape into surrendering, using threats of force.

The few others still in orbit?

The frigate's fighters ensured any remaining enemies were hunted down and destroyed.

The enemy Tyrant fighters were far too small to possess rift generators, and from where the remaining two pilots drifted in-system, post-surrender, they were easily escorted to land in one of the undamaged hangar bays.

Not all Armada personnel were brainwashed martyrs for Lord Xex of The Black Armada, it seemed.

The acquisition of two undamaged Tyrant fighters and their pilots to interrogate would likely impress the bureaucracy. Arthur did feel a twinge of guilt when he learned one of the pilots was only 18. Perhaps the young girl had merely made a poor life decision and would hopefully not be tortured or worse upon transfer.

It was a futile hope, but allowed him to move on to other

matters.

Two hours after their initial attack, G.O.D. ships called into the system by HQ from nearby bases and trade routes started showing up, rifting in a safe distance away from the planet. He spoke to several captains directly, many not believing him at first - that such a small frigate had actually scuttled a full-size Armada cruiser. However, after getting closer and aiding the salvage and intelligence work, several began to praise him and his ship, much to Arthur's quiet pride and subtle embarrassment. After all, the crew had been as much a part of the victory as he was, and having the weight of it laid upon his shoulders alone was disquieting.

Apparently, this tiny victory was a bigger event politically for the Guardians of Destiny than he had initially thought. A few minor gods working within the bureaucracy even started contacting him as early as a few hours after the event, congratulating him for such an enormous victory against the hated enemy and for a steadfast upholding of the reputation of the G.O.D. Navy.

He had no idea who half of them were, as they never bothered to formally introduce themselves, but as gods they most definitely ranked higher than him, and he politely and subserviently played the role of "yes-man".

Despite the flurry of activity all around the *Asalia*, the next few days crept by slowly and the Armada seemed disinterested in recovering the lost ship or sending reinforcements of any kind, as if they had never clued into her disappearance in the first place.

Arthur did recall that his crew never intercepted any outbound transmissions after the initial buoys, so perhaps the enemy captain had made an error or been fearful of transmitting so close to G.O.D. space. Maybe they had been overconfident, sure that command over a larger and superior ship class guaranteed a victory against any brazen enough to interfere? The countless guesswork at the bizarre turn of events drove him mad, as absolutely none of it added up.

As per its goals, George's team unlocked the secrets of the enemy vessel after literal days of decoding. As salvage work progressed, it turned out that apparently the Armada vessel had been a scouting ship with a plethora of navigational data, including many previously unknown resource worlds recently plotted into its systems along the edges of G.O.D. space and the Neutral territories.

George's previous capture and relay to HQ of encrypted data shortly before the battle proper also caused another flurry of activity in several ministries, especially those concerning resource extraction and colonization. When it turned out the transmission only contained a tiny fragment of what the ship had actually discovered, it intensified further.

There was no backup fleet pending, or anyone to even really discover the scouting ship had gone missing anytime soon. So - to the victors would go the spoils.

Arthur tried to divert as much of the attention away from his own person as possible as the event started circulating within the bureaucracy. After the *Asalia* had finally been allowed to leave the planet, and the salvage work was safely in the hands of other ships and teams, he made sure most of his bridge crew were allowed some rest and leave time before his own needs were addressed.

Naval combat itself was turning out to be fairly rare with the treaty in place, with the current stalemated state of the war and all. Only the Army ever seemed to see real combat these days - mostly on the neutral territory colonies or the border worlds. Save for rare Armada raids, and the ever-present threats of pirates of course.

Despite repeated attempts by the G.O.D. to contact him for a full debriefing - even as he attempted to continue his sporadic patrol picket, he wasn't given new orders to return to one of the core worlds proper or to stop patrolling, which he found both intriguing and at the same time alarming. Many heavily encrypted messages would reach the *Asalia* only to be decoded as mere queries to their current location, or they'd be questions about his personal status or his remaining crew that hadn't been transferred to relief ships for leave.

The odd scenario, and equally mysterious setup that precluded the actual victory was covered across most G.O.D. favored news networks for weeks on end. This was from what few broadcasting frequencies they could pick up on key locations throughout their patrol, and for a while this odd trend continued of lacking any direct orders - even while news coverage continued to increase. They answered every question that HQ asked them, but were ignored when they asked for new orders or any direction at all.

Nobody on the *Asalia* was stupid, and after discussing the ambiguity at length with his bridge crew, it became apparent that the central council of gods itself was conjuring up what their fate might be back inside the safety of the core worlds.

The *Asalia* had rustled with the hornet's nest of bureaucracy, and this time the topmost figures of power were tasked with trying to decide the frigate's fate.

Just as Captain Brass started to worry that the *Asalia* would be a prime target out in the black for Armada revenge - to crush Guardian morale, things changed yet again.

Their patrol was suddenly revoked, and he was given orders to return to the inner G.O.D. colonies for debriefing, as the pendulum continued to swing nebulously. The *Asalia* was put in drydock, and Arthur Brass was given months upon months of shore leave on the core world of *Holy Roman* while the G.O.D. upper echelon tried to decide whether to promote him, hide him away via a sideways demotion, or disappear him altogether, particularly as Arthur had put several more prominent Naval captains to shame by highlighting their recent failures.

It made sense with his bizarre victory against superior odds.

Regardless, *Holy Roman* was a beautiful world, with an incredible hybrid skyline of familiar blue skies, striking modern skyscrapers, gothic style abbeys, and art-deco buildings. It felt like being home on Earth, while still being completely alien.

The Guardian economy confused him the most, and used a currency of imaginary G.O.D. credits, rather than individual paper pounds or dollars. The concept of credit cards had been normal back home, but he found the conversion rate was terrible for what remained of his personal UK savings. A completely cashless society bothered him somehow, as if there was no real value behind this artificial plastic.

This wasn't to say he was poor however - he had mostly ignored his personal finances while out on patrol, so he had accumulated several months' worth of captain-grade pay in a two-week ongoing cycle that he could now utilize freely, if he could figure out how the damn credit systems worked. Paper or coin monies truly were non-existent, and somehow the special Navy card he had been given to use his money, directly withdrawn from his new military savings account…

Well it not only conferred unto him a military savings discount, but also some bizarre measure of notoriety and respect.

He came to detest being referred to as "Captain" Brass at every shop or bar he made a purchase at, and felt it alienated him from the common folks around him. He had become the G.O.D. soldier amongst the masses who simultaneously respected and feared him. And many were beginning to recognize him from the news.

Unfortunately, just as he was getting comfortable with the temporary barracks apartments and the strange neo-militarist cultures of Holy Roman, the war machine finally made a decision, and barely a year after he had set out to the frontier, he was shipped back home to *Earth*.

He was allowed to return to the home of Judge Undelwood, and was also given relative freedom for approximately a week. Of course, when asked if this was shore leave or something else, he was refused an answer by his direct handlers, each of whom had changed every day or two throughout *Holy Roman* back to *Earth*.

Eventually one of the bureaucrats handling his case let slip that he would be required to make a media statement of sorts for his actions aboard the *Asalia*. This accidental reveal doomed the poor bureaucrat of course; as Arthur had a different handler to report to the very next morning. The previous person had vanished entirely.

Perhaps the bureaucrats were so tight on the reins for fear of their own jobs and lives, just like he was?

When finally asked if he had any preferences for the reporting of his "valiant" efforts, he demanded as politely as he could that were he to be officially interviewed, Billy Shotcroft would have to be the one to do the interview.

It was organized and settled within the next day. Then the shore leave was extended for an indeterminate amount of time, adding artificial time to his five-year sentence.

The fact that the CNG was already established as the network of choice for most G.O.D. propaganda sure must have oiled the gears to help him achieve his weak request. He had honestly just done it to drag Billy out from harm's way and pull the man back to *Earth* where he could finally see his friend again in person, god knows how many years later.

The G.O.D. wasted no time of course in picking up his "heroic" and "fearless" suicidal attack as one of its primary spears of propaganda in the months following a particularly nasty defeat on a fringe world in the neutral territories. Thus, his interview was suddenly deemed incredibly important to the higher authorities, and even by Serania herself, head of the whole organization, who was rumoured to be involved by the Judge in passing.

He was never one for remembering faces.

Arthur was cautious, as it was generally wise to fear the "Frosty Bitch Up Yonder" for her famous brutality and complete lack of empathy towards the organization's enemies or traitors.

Her meddling was almost always veiled, according to Undelwood.

Shouldn't one fear the only human other than Xex himself who had been kicking around for something like 75,000 years?

Arthur did a little research when he could, but there was surprisingly little info about her available online outside of obvious Armada propaganda or anti-god satire. He finally found a picture by accident in a newspaper article from twenty years prior, and immediately he was sure he had seen her somewhere, on a billboard or something at least. If the picture was legitimate, she was a cute brunette with thick, black-framed librarian glasses.

Cute in Arthur's eyes anyways.

She was the only member of the original *Prime Triumvirate* to still live and breathe on the side of the G.O.D... When it came to light through his research that there were only two of that original trio left, just Serania and Xex, he was a tad worried. The Trio were the heirs of the Creator and all, and they were the ones who had founded the original Guardians of Destiny in the first place almost a hundred thousand years ago. Jikos, the third member, had died fighting Xex on *Lamentation Day*, hundreds of years before Arthur was ever born.

Spooked was the least of various emotions to surface when he realized he was caught between two ancient, immortal gods.

He became somewhat paranoid after that, sure that someone, somewhere, was monitoring his searches online. But the "God of Justice" was discussed as a topic almost constantly anyways from what he could tell.

Being known across the Universe as a black-hearted bitch didn't really do wonders for a fan base, despite her wealth, beauty, power, and immortality. It seemed the most religious of Guardian factions revered her, while the rest were skeptical and guarded - seeing her as a fanatic zealot herself.

It took several weeks of daydrinking through shore leave until one day it finally hit him, and he couldn't believe how fucking stupid he had been.

Serania was the brunette from the court that day all those years ago.

...

Fuck.

And not only was she there all those years ago, but she had also been openly pissed when he was freed from execution or life in prison.

And he had told her to shut up...

What the fuck sort of conspiracy shit did he find himself in here?!

Who the hell was Undelwood working for? What the hell had his victory whilst captaining the *Asalia* really meant? Was it all just a setup? Had he killed Guardians instead of Black Armada aboard that cruiser?

His mind raced for hours afterwards, and the anxiety was almost too much to bear. What if he had just killed himself a second time, indirectly?

But... If Serania really wanted him dead, wouldn't he already be a corpse? It could be staged as some overdose of pills, or a quiet, manic-depressive suicide.

And who was the long, blonde-haired man?

Arthur resigned himself to fate, and vowing not to explore any further, he helped himself to the judge's extensive liquor cabinet even further. He drank himself to sleep that night on the finest highland scotch he could find.

He was "nudged" by a handler to leave the Judge's home closer to his interview, which meant he was shortly after escorted by the secret police in their white uniforms to an armored car, and "encouraged strongly" to take up residence in one of the guest rooms of the CNG tower downtown for a 72-hour period before the live broadcast date.

It wasn't a bad deal, really.

He was getting fed up with his current housing arrangement, and becoming more and more paranoid and suspicious of the owner, Judge Undelwood. It was a strange and awkward duality, in somehow simultaneously trusting Joe based on how far he had worked for Arthur's wellbeing, but being frightened of the implications of his unknown connections.

He tried his best again and again, but failed every time at sorting out his feelings of trust, love, and possible betrayal by the older man who had supported him thus far.

The change of scenery was thus a mixed blessing.

The Judge's place itself had been very 'old modern' and had the faintest smell of old man to it.

The Central News Group apartment on the other hand, was blank, open, and beautiful within its beautiful new tower in the heart of downtown London. The movement over the last twenty years for higher ranking executives of companies to live in the upper tiers of buildings they worked within was to his benefit, it seemed. Glass on two sides looking out over the city, pristine white walls and roof, marble floors and countertops, white leather couches, and white carpet.

His confinement to the tower was a tad irksome, but to keep him docile, he was promised that after the interview, that he would be given a second extended shore leave.

He hoped "extended shore leave" wasn't code for a permanent retirement of the "murdered" kind.

His "nudge" to the tower, which had undoubtedly been carefully organized by the G.O.D. with help from the British Government, was rushed and uncomfortable. Upon arriving, he found the tower itself was surrounded outside and filled within by armed and armored G.O.D. Shocktroopers in lieu of CNG private security. These Shocktroopers in full armor fully patted him down and thoroughly inspected his bags of course, and upon entering his new temporary abode, there was an ominous sign - pristine white lilies and a very expensive bottle of vodka that graced his bedside table.

The smell of the lilies overpowered the bedroom.

When he looked closer at the bedside table with the gifts, Arthur noticed there was a plain piece of white paper resting underneath the bottle. The paper was blank, save for a capital "S" scrawled in seemingly perfect cursive in the direct centre of it.

It was at that point that he was completely aware of the far-reaching ramifications of his actions.

The guards and the tower apartment were Serania's blessing or curse, based on how one interpreted them. He highly doubted the Black Armada would work so hard to assassinate him for the loss of one ship, no matter how powerful the propaganda was that worked towards it, so this whole process of delaying his life must have been Serania showing him how much power she truly had over his life. She also clearly grasped the full extent of his little stress-related drinking problem too. It was as if the vodka was the subtle nod to a choke chain she could yank at her own whim.

He took it that the gift of lilies alongside the bottle was either a thank-you note or a sweetly worded threat, as his actions had made him both a target of the Black Armada, and also of everyone he had sullied within the G.O.D. proper.

The "S" was obvious. She wanted him to know who held his leash, one that only a true dog of the military could wear.

He started on the vodka almost immediately. He found to his pleasure and relief that it lacked any sort of poison, and promptly got to know the armed doorman outside the apartment quite well in short order, due to being denied permission to leave the tower for errands on more than one occasion during his stay.

Of course, his "errands" were alcohol runs, but aside from the initial gift of fermented grain, he was locked in tight, even when he volunteered to leave with an escort of soldiers.

Billy showed up exactly forty-eight hours after Arthur, and with only a few carefully rationed dregs left of the bottle of vodka and horrible dread in his gut most other times, Arthur was elated in the brief exchange they were allowed. Billy Shotcroft was a merciful break in the monotony of his imprisonment within the news tower.

Billy and Arthur were able to chat for the majority of the evening when his friend arrived, over a fairly elaborate dinner in one of the conference rooms. They kept their talk civil, for obvious reasons, catching up on missed time and focusing mostly on the food.

Digging into a juicy, medium rare steak and pile of creamy garlic-mashed potatoes with asparagus was an incredible luxury for two men used to the hardships of military rations and nutrient paste.

With a reload of the same stunningly smooth vodka that Billy brought with him, the night eased into a state of inebriated relaxation, before Billy drunkenly retired for the night elsewhere in the tower.

Tomorrow?

Well, best not to think about that.

The vodka helped.

CHAPTER 7: THE LIES WE TELL OURSELVES.

"Pretending you're okay when you're really not is the hilarious version of normal for the majority of the population."

The next day, broadcast live on primetime news, the interview between CNG war-correspondent Billy Shotcroft and G.O.D. Naval Captain Arthur Brass was conducted in a carefully organized and guarded studio within the CNG tower skyscraper in the heart of London.

The entire event was so perfectly ordered and organized that Arthur couldn't help but feel the individual eyes of everyone positioned outside their carefully orchestrated spotlight. He could barely see the dozens of silhouettes perched all around the set, hidden in the murky black abyss outside the sphere of the stage lighting.

He could feel their presence - judging, waiting, and the Creator knew what else.

His best friend was poised across from Arthur in a pristine white suit, fitted with a black bow tie and kerchief. It screamed "Guardians of Destiny" with all the additional black trim across the rest of the suit, including the cuffs. The finishing touch to his pristine and gently spiked hair was a perfect white lily pinned neatly on his lapel, juxtaposed by his black kerchief in the pocket.

Arthur noted the lily first.

It was clearly another sign or a warning of some sort from Serania, although whether intended for Billy or himself, it was impossible to know.

Arthur Brass was dressed in formal Navy dress attire, clad in the mostly white captain's uniform he wore while on duty. He was sure to wear his *Junktown Blues* cufflinks, and had fastidiously adjusted the new Guardian medal for winning against unfavorable odds he had been awarded for service in battle just before the interview by a random G.O.D. bureaucrat.

Despite the heavy tension lingering in the space, exuded in waves from everyone else, from the moment the camera was rolling, Billy Shotcroft was a man of legend, suave and polite in the extreme. Arthur had missed him so much since he had left, this man of confidence, charm, and passion.

The fierce heat of love and adoration flared in Arthur's chest, and he struggled to keep himself under control in the face of the masses watching from everywhere. The two interacted with such smoothness; it was like they had never been separated as younger men.

Arthur couldn't recall seeing this side of Billy before, so used as he was to the weary war correspondent on the screen. Every time he had talked with him in the past, his face had been sunken, with dark bags under his eyes and dust often coating his sharp cheeklines. He had always looked two steps from death then, and now here he was all prim and proper and dressed to the nines.

He could not imagine a more beautiful man so full of life and charisma.

Billy's introduction was filled with smiles and pride, as he first introduced himself, and then introduced Arthur, poised and plastered as he was in full white dress uniform and adorned with his gleaming new medal. They traded a few gentle comedic quips at first, testing the waters, and Billy served up some softball questions about academy training. But it wasn't long before Billy was forced to touch upon the real reason they were there.

"So, Captain Brass, the real question everybody at home has on the tip of their tongues... How did you first react when you realized your frigate was up against a much larger foe, and that no immediate Guardian Naval help was nearby?"

Billy's first question was one Arthur had been asking himself dozens of times before in the preparation within his head.

He already knew how to reply for the greatest effect.

"You don't have time to think, Billy, you just know that you have the lives of the people under you, both to protect, and to utilize to their full potential as a commander to score a victory for the good guys."

Billy smiled, that same knowing smile that he had perfected whilst signing off in his last several years of work on the front lines.

"Would you say you chose to attack the Black Armada battlecruiser out of duty, Captain? Or perhaps impulse? Or was it something else entirely?"

Arthur thought about it for an agonizing moment - a golden moment, pondering the possible implications of his answer.

Billy had worded the question as if he were truly trying to play the unbiased journalist who could still be asking critical questions.

They both knew the sentiment was false. The only right answer was one that put duty and heroism above all else.

Arthur had been given cue cards and a teleprompter of course, located just out of sight of the camera to answer with if truly needed. He risked a glance over to where they were perched just off camera, held in the arms of a freckled young intern standing on the edge of the spotlight pool between light and dark.

But with that golden moment, he found it was easier to just make it up as he went along. He knew what the G.O.D. leaders wanted him to say, of course.

And besides, the more he got the audience to like him, the more he knew he'd be safer from "disappearing" later on, so he took a risk in appearing casually nonchalant.

There was a certain indignant satisfaction knowing it probably threw Serania for a loop wherever she was watching from.

A small defiance, in that he would refuse to follow her script.

"Well Billy, I did it because I knew that out so far on the edge of Guardian space, by the time reinforcements showed up, the Armada battlecruiser would likely have detected us. And if they did that, well… They'd either hunt us down, or as odd as it might sound considering the size and class disadvantage, they'd flee."

He paused for a second to let it sink in.

"I couldn't risk either of those possibilities… So maybe it was a mixture of both that spurred me to attack. After all, as they used to say a long time ago where I'm from, 'Who dares, wins,' isn't that right Billy?"

Arthur flashed Billy a smile and his friend nodded thoughtfully, giving himself ample time to rearrange the interview for the sudden lack of adequate pre-rehearsed questions to fit the mood.

Arthur was relying on him, of course, but it was a rather safe bet as Billy was a steady old hand within the industry. The reporter had taken note of his use of the century-and-a-half-old military phrase with a polite, knowing smirk.

The glory of a home-field advantage, even if the majority of those that would be watching were from the core world colonies.

"And how did your crew react to your decision?"

Arthur adjusted the cuffs of his white officer uniform while he thought up his answer, hoping to appear suddenly pensive when it came to the lives of others.

"I'd have to say that honestly, some of the crew probably weren't too happy with my choice, Billy, and many of them likely figured that we were committing suicide by trying an ambush instead of retreating and waiting for reinforcements."

Billy grimmaced at that.

"But I'd also like to think that the crew of the *Asalia* are some of the best in the G.O.D. navy, and to their credit they never once questioned my orders. They followed me straight into hell without batting an eyelash."

He smiled, and Billy let out a soft chuckle that was perfect for the moment. He then opened his mouth to speak.

Arthur didn't stop to let him redirect.

"I'd like to personally thank George Durand for taking the first shot that not only crippled the enemy ship, but ultimately won us the battle. I may have chosen the stratagem of attack, but it was his skill with the *Asalia's* weapons systems that really won us the fight."

Billy nodded.

"I'd also like to commend Victor Hammond for his excellent jamming work that let us creep up on the cruiser in the first place. Finally, Jacqueline Harp, Yonathan Halevy, and Hammad Aziz are to be praised for precise following of orders and absolute confidence in my captaincy while under fire. My bridge crew was invaluable, but the rest of the crew really pulled through as well. I hope they'll all be remembered and rewarded some day for their duty out there. I hope I'm not the only one with a medal on my chest when all is said and done."

Arthur had moved the interview in a dangerous direction, pushing the topic away from himself and onto the qualities of others, but it seemed that despite a brief moment of tension in the studio that lingered for but a fraction of a moment, people empathized with his compliments, and even appreciated them to a point.

While his goal was to secure the safety of those under him on the *Asalia,* from being "vanished" or punished, he knew this sort of talk would also endear the audience to him, while alienating his superiors.

Perhaps he had given them the briefest sense of independence and pride, before the guillotine fell on them anyways. They deserved just as much praise as he did, and maybe he'd given them enough celebrity in this interview to promote them out of harm's way.

After a few more easily answerable questions, which he mostly read off the cue cards with as much swagger as he could manage, Billy politely informed him that he had no more questions to ask, and they jokingly ended the interview with a few friendly jabs again both ways.

Their chemistry was incredible, and for the remainder, employees off camera repeatedly gave wildly positive silent gestures to Billy, implying viewership and ratings were through the roof.

The fact that they were such old friends made it easier to keep the act alive without seeming fake. And it had likely paid off.

After the interview had concluded, and the stage-lights had dimmed to a more normal house lighting, Billy flicked off his lapel mike and leaned in close. Did the same to Arthur's. Then whispered in his ear so that the rest of the camera and broadcasting crew couldn't hear.

"Be careful, Arthur… The council, namely Serania, The God of Justice… They have a very close eye on you right now. Can't say much more, but everything you do in the next few weeks will be watched closely to help determine if you're hailed as a hero, or killed quietly for embarrassing Navy Admirals."

He smiled, and pulled Arthur into a hug to disguise the conversation further.

"You're caught in the middle of a power struggle within the council. Not very many people know about the fleet transmission almost screwing up the ambush, and the Navy, and the Bureaucracy want to keep it that way. So, hush hush, got it?"

Arthur patted him on the shoulder to show him he had understood, despite the intense chill settling in all down his spine. He shook Billy's hand, and as much as he didn't want to leave the presence of his friend, decided it was best to disappear as the ripples echoed outwards from this facade.

As much as Arthur tried not to, he thought about the vodka and the lilies on his side table.

Billy got up to leave, shaking hands with various crew members as he went. Arthur didn't speak to him again that day, giving him only one final wave goodbye as he passed through the doorway towards the elevator to his penthouse.

After a few hours, Arthur was re-gifted his freedom, allowed to finally escape from his gilded tower cage and return to a life of relative normalcy. He took his continued "shore leave" at his own meandering pace, staying with Joe Undelwood again in his London West End home for the majority of his free time. Having come to the realization that Undelwood was working for someone on the council who clearly did not wish for Arthur to die, he let himself trust his adoptive caretaker and warmed back up to him again somewhat. He figured that it would do him no good to quietly damn and push away the only man who had originally worked to save his life in that courtroom a lifetime ago.

The Judge made it clear to him that he was working hard on his behalf, and so with Joe's constant coming and going, Arthur spent a night here and there with old pre-navy friends, and even leaned into a couple one-night-stands, although the too-obvious undercover secret police and G.O.D. military tails at bars certainly hurt his overall game.

It also didn't help that he had become something of an overnight sensation to the regular citizens, charmed as they were by his suave interview or their own interpretation of Arthur's heroism or bravery. He was stopped frequently on the street to answer questions or to sign something, which made him question how being a celebrity in the military of the G.O.D. might even work.

It seemed the propaganda and legend-building of the Guardians was just as important as the actual combat itself in regards to winning the eternal war. Both the Guardians and Armada were capitalizing on their devout natures as gods, attempting to win the majority of humanity to their individual causes by playing up a mythos of bravery, heroism, and self-sacrifice.

Undelwood didn't mind his meandering, of course, and was rather open on just about any subject, including openly inviting him to bring ladies back to his home. They had become even closer over the years for sure, and Joe made sure that he constantly reminded Arthur of the fact that he was single.

He also none-too subtly insinuated that in his role as Arthur's adoptive godfather, he would absolutely love some grandchildren to dote on. It was incredibly uncomfortable and awkward every time.

And it occurred much too frequently.

Still, the role Judge Joe Undelwood chose for himself within Arthur's life eliminated any traces of suspicion he had left for the older man, and surer now that Joe wasn't malicious in his aims, he really opened up to this new father figure as a person in ways he hadn't before.

In this new experience of bonding, Arthur learned that Judge Joe Undelwood had lost his marriage earlier in life to a nasty divorce, and never had kids of his own. His work and various connections had kept him quite busy into his old age, and there was simply no time for dating or remarrying.

Walls slowly came down as trust grew like the winding roots of a cedar tree.

There was no threat here.

The old man was lonely.

And it broke Arthur's heart.

CHAPTER 8: FUEL FOR THE FRYING PAN.

"Some people are just unlucky enough to jump from one fire into another for all eternity."

Arthur often felt that Undelwood's poking into his personal life reminded him of an antithesis to his mother's indifference, and left him wondering what kind of relationship his parents had enjoyed.

He tried his best to put Joe's prodding for kids behind him for the most part, and not worry too much about a stable relationship. He certainly wouldn't want to welcome a new girlfriend into his life only for her to witness his sudden execution, or to get caught up in the backroom politics that had enveloped his existence.

However, the fact that Jacqueline Harp constantly sent him messages and e-mails of an increasingly provocative nature definitely didn't help. Their relationship had blossomed during their time together, and she clearly had feelings.

The attachments - mostly pictures, were especially hard to ignore, and he couldn't help but wonder how the G.O.D. and British spies might enjoy viewing them, as closely watched as he might be.

Harp was young and attractive, of that there was no doubt.

Truthfully of course, he had flirted with her indirectly dozens of times during their time together on the *Asalia*. But he had pushed any notion of sex or even a platonic relationship onto the back burner as any smart captain should have with such a subordinate.

There was a gross imbalance of power he refused to abuse.

Fraternization wasn't officially a crime in the G.O.D., probably because the gods themselves often ran around fucking everything under the sun in a grandiose abuse of power.

Consorts were the norm, not the exception on the council.

So yes, he had flirted back, and continued to do so in fun on his leave. But he made sure that he ignored her various prods and suggestions of a more explicit nature, by dancing around the more direct provocations.

While he was increasingly frustrated with his lack of a steady romantic life, which grated on him at times when Undelwood poked at him, he tried his best to focus inwards on his real predicament.

Of course, his biggest problem was the rest of his extended shore leave, and how to avoid getting executed for stepping out of line. It all felt like a slowly darkening shadow as he went week after week without hearing anything at all.

Even his handlers had gone quiet.

He hadn't breathed a word of the transmission that nearly botched their attack, as Billy had cautioned, but he somehow felt that his careful guarding of the secret didn't really matter. Arthur had it set in his mind that he would be killed eventually regardless of what he said, and have it blamed on Armada sponsored terrorists or some such excuse.

As his leave finally dwindled down officially to days from

weeks, he noticed Undelwood absent more and more, as his guardian fought mysterious legal hurdles and stood up for him on his behalf somewhere inside the distant theatre of the Guardian high council.

The bombshell was lurking in the wings, of course.

It was an enormous shock to Arthur when the Judge casually explained to him one day over beers that Serania was actively trying to convict him of false charges.

She was actually trying to kill him off.

Only the intervention of other high council members thus far had stymied her plans, at the specific request of Joe Undelwood.

The day quickly ended itself with an empty bottle of expensive Bourbon, and a deeper sense of existential dread that Arthur hadn't felt since being trapped in prison all those years ago.

CHAPTER 9: DOWN IN FLAMES, UP IN SMOKE.

"When all hope is lost, there is usually enough time for a bit of rabid self-indulgence."

Arthur spent several days in a drunken stupor following the revelation, smoking through Joe's stash of Cuban Cigars on the back deck of the flat and washing them down with half the contents of Undelwood's expensive liquor cabinet. Arthur had always reacted before to these sorts of things with anger, or stubborn defiance, calculating and dreaming up conspiracies he would undo the whole while.

All he felt this time was numb.

There was a notion in his head along the way that he had somehow been fighting for his freedom all these years, when in actuality, it had been the efforts of others to keep him alive this long.

First his mother, struggling to keep him going in a world full of broken people. And when she was gone, it was Judge Joe Undelwood, working on behalf of some higher power to keep him alive and fighting in the most primal senses of the word.

Coming to grips with his helplessness and reliance on others was harder to do than simply getting angry with fate or struggling against the bureaucracy.

He had to try and be okay with not being okay.

And once that was done, he had to let go of the feelings of futility and allow others to support him.

Neither of these things were easy for a young man full of nothing but anger, despair, and self-loathing.

Joe started to be gone longer, often until very late every night, coming home haggard and tired.

Arthur got used to the dull roar of Agatha engines outside upon his return. The Judge didn't drink much anymore, but Joe would often stay up to talk and have a drink with him, making him laugh even through his crushing depression.

It meant a lot that Joe was fighting for him all day, and then staying up with him and his vices even after that.

Arthur was overjoyed to have someone he cared about to actually connect with in person, but…

The act of Undelwood imbibing in something he had mostly quit several years back was simultaneously pacifying and terrifying to him. Did Judge Joe Undelwood know some secret to happiness that Arthur had never discovered? Did he grasp how deeply Arthur felt trapped by all the emotions swirling down inside, that he actively tried to bottle up for so many years?

Joe clearly knew how much Arthur self-medicated with alcohol, didn't he?

Why enable him?

Joe left more and more, and Arthur continued to drink himself stupid to numb the pain and the loneliness.

Eventually his damnation came in the form of a morbid fable.

It came from knowledge that Undelwood had discovered.

Arthur was to be tried and executed by the Admirals of the Naval board on trumped up false charges in a month's time. Part of their accusations involved the nude photos that Harp had recently sent him. The rest was comprised of several fake messages, drafted to imply that he had been quietly and horrifically sexually abusing Harp aboard the *Asalia,* after Arthur had blackmailed and intoxicated her.

She would not be present at the trial to refute the charges, as per the normal G.O.D. method of illegally fixing such things as trials and board hearings, but there would be a written statement she would be blackmailed or bribed into signing.

Arthur felt as badly for Jacqueline as he did for himself. What a shitty situation all around it was.

He couldn't possibly direct his rising anger at Jacqueline Harp, for she was as much a pawn as he was in the gods' games of mortality. She was young, stupid, and naïve, and he had goaded her on like the lonely directionless idiot he had always been.

In a way, he was at fault for her involvement. Yet another person he had failed and let down.

The judge explained it all with a frank and level-headed tone that rendered Arthur incredulous.

Still, Joe demanded he hear him out, without a drink in his hand. Stone-cold sober, he explained the subtle machinations of the charges. It was mostly big words and stipulations that Arthur understood but which he felt mattered little.

However, Judge Joe Undelwood also presented a solution, which ripped the curtain back and revealed to Arthur the object of his salvations so many times previous.

It was a majestic ray of light - one that promised freedom with a new chain, like a true-to-life deal with a devil.

In order to save his life, Joe presented him with an extremely bizarre plan - to marry into the Guardian Council itself.

Not directly, of course.

Arthur would be married as a consort husband to a direct family member of a high council member, and this would prevent the charges from being filed due to an archaic and incredibly old series of protectionist statutes protecting the gods and their families from pretty much any lower level persecutions.

The statutes in question, drafted sometime in the Renaissance, were designed at keeping gods and their loved ones free of almost everything held in the hands of ordinary mortals, which included the courts and bureaucracies of the G.O.D. itself.

Initially, Arthur was disgusted at this clearly broken class system, as much as he was relieved to be informed of at least a single way out. He needed a drink more and more with every new fact Undelwood piled on.

Who did these fucks think they were, making themselves immune from punishment for the disgusting shit they did to mortals?

Joe noted his discomfort, but kept plowing through the details, and it was through this quite-insane plan that he finally discovered his saviour, a far more powerful creature than he ever could have imagined him to be.

The "H" signed on all his documentation all along had been the God of Fire himself, Hewah.

It had been Hewah all along.

Working through Joe, his old friend, as a proxy of course.

Arthur knew him, if only by name and formal title. Hewah sat as a member on the G.O.D. high council, the highest governing body of the Guardians of Destiny - consisting of the most ancient of gods.

The high council directed everything.

The whole of the G.O.D. ran at its whims, with Serania sitting as the figurehead - with the only sole veto power as Prime Triumvirate.

Hewah was also one of the few gods with enough influence and respect to tangle directly with Serania on major issues and disagreements. He was extremely old as well, although Arthur had no clue as to how many millennia specifically.

Arthur stared at Joe for a full minute, agape, when the older man was finished, and then began laughing hysterically.

He just couldn't help but laugh at the ridiculousness of it.

Joe put a hand on his shoulder, deadly serious.

"You must keep all of this to yourself. Don't tell a soul of anything we're talking about here."

Sobered, Arthur nodded, and childishly made a gesture of zipping his lips with his hand.

Hewah hailed originally from the South Pacific, and as Joe explained, was almost two thousand years old, which put him in the middle of the pack in regards to average council age. Joe also explained that this was also the same god who had watched him in the middle of the night in his dark prison cell as a young man, and the same man from his graduation, his "councillor" friend.

A funny joke in hindsight, that.

This was no rookie; this was an old god capable of creating charring heat that could separate flesh from bone and reduce both to ash with a wave of his hands. In addition to his political and diplomatic savvy, there was a clear reason he was informally referred to by some as 'The Volcano God' alongside his more formal title.

It made sense.

Having a member of the high council as your benefactor and friend suddenly explained the weight Judge Joe Undelwood had carried all these years. Hewah was one of the older and more powerful Gods in terms of clout and abilities, but he was also known to be one of Serania's closest allies, which perplexed Arthur to no end.

For the first time in a long while, Arthur Brass' gears began to turn. His brain snapped back to life from the drunken haze previously.

Why the hell would Hewah go against the informal leader of the entire organization to help out guys like Joe or him? Hell, maybe there were gods out there that did give a damn about normal people, unlike Serania and her various puppets.

Arthur felt stupid, and the realizations he was having - that not all gods were completely self-absorbed and indifferent to the common folk, well it had never truly sunk in before, at least not without such clear proof of action.

He was bitter that he hadn't ever been told, as much as he was grateful to suddenly have such a powerful ally in his corner.

But his future was still hazy.

He was still trapped between suicidal thoughts and alcohol-infused nihilism.

Joe Undelwood took on a hell of a time convincing him that the marriage plan was a better alternative than death. Arthur had it stuck in his mind that he'd be a pretty little slave or a glorified escort until he was dumped in an alleyway somewhere, shot dead after his master bored of him.

The marriage, hilariously enough, was specifically to Hewah's only child and daughter, Feria, who was the other dark-skinned beauty of a woman he had met at his graduation.

Attraction was one thing; but being all-in mentally and emotionally for something like a marriage was another completely.

He was aware very suddenly how those trapped in arranged marriages felt...

He tried hard to imagine what his mother would say, and what she might tell him to do. He even tried to ponder what his father might think of it all.

Eventually he drug himself up from the pit of despair just enough to see a point to living, in maybe saving innocent lives with the remaining four or so years of his service. Maybe he could go out like a martyr, in some blaze of glory that helped others far more inclined to live than him? He'd still be in the Navy after all.

Marriage though...

He was uneasy about the whole thing, even though it was the only current option to save his skin.

This plan was actually Joe's brainchild, and the Judge worked hard at getting Arthur to acquiesce to it eventually. Arthur wondered at how Undelwood had sold it to both Hewah and Feria.

It took a lot of clever talent to sell a mortal slab of meat to a god and his daughter.

Despite the idea simmering on the backburner, with Joe leaving Arthur to mull it over further, he was given relatively no information on the marriage or even on his new master herself in the event that he was abducted or interrogated.

If Arthur *was* captured and he talked, he'd screw the whole thing up. The G.O.D. had protocols to follow and procedures to ensure. After all, Arthur Brass was a hero in the eyes of the public.

They needed to discredit him before they did away with him.

From the brief conversations he had with Undelwood, the entirety of the G.O.D. Guardian council was wrapped up in tense and varied negotiations, with members choosing sides and having hushed meetings with one another to decide how Arthur's life would determine future council politics.

A small sliver of amusement came in that Arthur finally felt important for once.

After a few days of warming up to the idea, he could only thank the Creator, non-religious as he was, that Hewah was on his side to give him a choice. Having a choice between life or death was better than not, in the essence of things.

Despite this plan to move him up significantly in the world, there was nothing hidden about the dangers it carried. The higher up one progressed in the organization, the more risk lingered over them in new and subtle avenues. He would be the new plaything of someone who could possibly have lived centuries or more, and his existence would be subject to constant negotiation.

His whole life he had heard rumors that even consorts and spouses of the gods were subject to trade or barter.

But who the hell was he, to question the gods themselves on new-age aristocratic slavery?

CHAPTER 10: PURELY SEMANTIC.

"The Devil you know is better than the Devil you don't, so why not advocate for the former?"

The night that everything started to click in Arthur's head was also the first time he formally met Feria as a real person. That is to say that he began taking the first few steps down the path towards a sort of actual, honest to the gods…

Happiness.

He never expected it until it was already there, pointing an accusatory finger in his face.

The magic moment was at a grand ball style gala hosting a number of significant Central Universe business interests, with most of them seeking impressive military production or research contracts from the Guardian war machine. It would be held in orbit above Earth.

It was a big deal - as there were going to be several celebrities present, Arthur being counted in that number himself.

Even bigger in terms of attendance, the G.O.D. High Council itself and large swaths of the societal upper crust from across Guardian territory and the Earth. The latter being the leeches firmly attached to the former. Several neutral institutions and corporations would also be there - The Junk and Rumblers Guild, The Unitary Mercenary Guild, The Conversion Corporation, the works.

While the gala itself was funded by a selection of those gargantuan businesses in attendance, the funding-slash-donation pool was merely part and parcel of the ongoing bargaining, bribing, or begging for the contracts at hand. The logistics, location, security and everything else would be handled by the G.O.D. for reasons of organizational safety. The donation pool was obviously more for the media than anything else.

All of this Arthur learned from an incessantly chattering Undelwood as they went shopping for attire. His military dress uniform would not do in this case, as according to Joe, he was meant to be seen as an individual of his own celebrity prestige, rather than a mere cog of the Guardian military machine.

Being well-known within the realm of celebrity was a form of protection in and of itself.

Even thinking about attending the event both terrified and thrilled him in different aspects, as he had never met, or even heard of many of these higher ups in the very organization he served in.

Yet...

Most would know who he was quite astutely, from the ever-present media circus.

Arthur was facing the dangerous possibility of meeting the near entirety of the Guardian High Council and a hundred plus others representing some of the most powerful economic interests in all of the Central Universe. These groups were a large reason for the recent timidity of the war, and the existence of the treaty itself was thanks to the influence of some of these powerful individuals and neutral entities that profited eternally off the conflict.

Gaming both sides was clearly expected at this point due to the enormous profits it could generate. And as they were useful, neither the Guardians of Destiny nor the Black Armada wanted to risk pissing any of them off.

Arthur was learning more and more about the delicate nature of power within Central.

Even as a god, one could never be so powerful as to risk angering those with power, influence, and money. And if one did, by accident or not, they were sure to regret it for the rest of their days. As powerful as The Guardians of Destiny and The Black Armada were, it was the corporations and for-hire groups of interest that helped shape the economy at the behest of the gods.

Leeches and mosquitoes mostly, in Arthur's opinion.

For Arthur, his status as a Captain had been stripped, then restored to him as a caveat of council negotiations. That meant he might at least be able to escape quickly after his assumed engagement back out to the frontier, and would be less of a slave out on the edge of space than he would be under the direct thumbs of the gods.

Consort or not, he was starting to feel rather useless with Judge Joe Undelwood doing all the work, and the constant drinking was getting to him health wise, ruining his sleep and appetite.

It was odd to him that such a short time ago he had feared leaving Earth to travel out into the big empty, but now he was scrambling to get back out there.

The older he got, the more the years seemed to blur by at speed, and some memories appeared in his mind to be only months prior to the present. Time was indeed an illusion, more so when one spent much of his free time liquored to hell as a coping strategy.

He was simultaneously ecstatic and disappointed the night before the ball to learn that Undelwood had fought to give him a few more weeks of shore leave, in order to work out the final few kinks of the new "arrangement," and thus this gala would not be the immediate end of his freedom. News of more time to spend liquored up somehow released a load off his back that let him channel the outgoing teenage boy he had once been, which would be a useful trait to have at a party.

The Conversion Corporation was the favorite to win the contracts at the gala of course, being the company with the closest ties historically to the G.O.D., and one of the largest companies with a headquarters still on Earth proper.

They also had more than enough capital squirreled away to put in a low-enough bid to win.
Bidding was funny that way.

It was all about how little you would be willing to charge for the service, not how much time or effort you'd pour into the job itself. It seemed a little backwards if one wanted to achieve quality, and on top of it all, it allowed larger corporations to undercut competitors at a loss to subsidize other endeavours with Guardian money.

While the CC didn't hold an actual monopoly on any one market, Arthur was well aware that judge Undelwood's toaster, window panes, and even his toothbrush were all CC products, if somewhat indirectly through subsidiaries.

The final winners of the bidding processes would be announced at the end of the evening, for a major research contract with a goal of building cheaper plasma shielding for Navy vessels. The G.O.D. would be fundraising and handshaking even as they announced their defacto favorites.

All of this was touted as Arthur's official Naval reason for attending the event, but the event was also supposed to serve as the venue where the G.O.D. would declare the winner of its recent open armaments contract, a weapons manufacturing contract that renewed itself every year.

There were several other smaller contracts that would be announced quietly in comparison, but the buzz was all aimed at who might end up being the big two prize-winners.

This was prime ground for making it a very posh and lavish affair in terms of business presence and an extension of big money. Arthur couldn't help but see the reality behind the *Asalia*'s stupid leather seats displayed in full mockery before him. The eternal stalemate of the war between the Guardians of Destiny and The Black Armada was an excellent war profiteering opportunity, after all.

While Arthur was terrified and excited, a quiet desire not to fuck anything up meant he was planning on migrating to the bar and hibernating there for the entirety of the night, pickling himself in as softly a fashion as he could. Arthur couldn't help but pray he wouldn't spill anything on the nice black-trimmed white suit Joe had paid for.

Undelwood accompanied him of course, dressed in a dark brown suit with a burgundy tie. On the chauffeured Agatha transport into orbit, the Judge chattered as merrily as if he had just won the lottery. Despite being now into his late fifties, with the wrinkles to prove it, Undelwood broke convention and drank quite liberally upon arrival, shaking hands with almost everyone he met.

His cheerful demeanour and posh received pronunciation definitely scored him points with many of the colony-accented English speakers in attendance, many hailing from the G.O.D. core worlds and industrial-minded neutral worlds. Arthur could clearly tell the judge definitely enjoyed faffing about and shaking hands with gods.

He plodded after his protector for a little while, which was at the Judge's orders after he caught Arthur eyeing up the first of several onsite bars. This procession began with Joe lecturing him hastily about not wanting Arthur to soak his nice white suit in bourbon, at least not before he had made a good impression on those he needed to impress. Unfortunately for Arthur, the champagne he was handed on the first floor hardly buzzed him enough to kill his gnawing sense of doom. He was sure the first god he met would explode him into ribbons of tar, or electrocute him to black ash in some obtuse assassination attempt.

The event itself was held on a former cargo freighter, converted into a luxury cruiser at the cost of millions of U.S. dollars, which had been generously donated by the Junk and Rumblers Guild for the event to allow for a neutral meeting ground. The Junk and Rumblers Guild was the face of modern salvage and shipping, and Arthur knew any salvage crew or cargo transporter worth their salt had a guild membership and a neutral passport card.

The J&R Guild was famous for being neutral in the conflict, and were one of the few groups able to move freely in and out of G.O.D. space, the neutral territories, and even into the giant debris field, "The Black," that encircled the known entrances into the mysterious cluster of Armada homeworlds. Not many groups in the central universe could play all sides and win, which in itself impressed him.

It also said a ton about how much both sides of the war valued moving things and how little they cared about recycling their old garbage.

The freighter was set to slowly circle the northern hemisphere in lower orbit, flanked by a trio of G.O.D. battlecruisers and several squadrons of fighters at close following distance. Air-traffic coming and going from Earth would be routed away unless directly connected to the gala.

It was rare that pilots got to meander so casually in orbit around Earth.

Terra, the home world of humanity, spread itself out beautifully below the transparent walls and floors of the central ballroom of the freighter. It hung - a green, blue, and white jewel hiding the entirety of space from sight except for the distantly darkening edges of the horizon.

Arthur wondered if the Navy and Army were still used as glorified bodyguards even when there weren't major arms contracts involved.

Despite the party sprawling through no less than five of the freighter's renovated cargo holds, and trailing up and down across three stepped floors with balconies, he found himself captured by the large observation window on the bottom ballroom floor - stretching three stories up across the grand ballroom wall.

He politely excused himself, finally breaking free of Undelwood's guardianship, and wandered over to it. It was hard not to gawk with his mouth open. All the sights and worlds he had looked out at from the portholes of the *Jalapeño Gold* and the *Asalia* paled in comparison to the fragile homeworld of humanity.

Why had so many abandoned it?

Below, the edge of night was slowly creeping across the planet. On one side of the veil of shadow, hundreds of thousands of lights glimmered into existence against a field of black. On the other, greens, blues, and whitish greys of plains, forests, and oceans. Clouds and seas sparkled like soft cotton and blue sapphire. He knew there were other worlds the immortals had modified over the centuries to look just like it, but something about Earth mesmerized him.

It was home.

It had always been home.

No matter how far away he travelled through the cosmos, he'd always be reminded of the third rock from the sun that humanity had evolved on, whether helped by a Creator or not. There was beauty in that concept, that home was home no matter how you interpreted it.

And there would only ever be this one home, this one place where humanity had a shared history.

Home is a powerful word.

Holy Roman, the G.O.D. core-world and military stronghold he visited for a time on his journey back towards Earth, well it had been nothing more than just a black mass, spotted with a sea of light. He had only ever arrived or departed in orbit with *Holy Roman*'s night side. While impressive, it was still mostly an ecumenopolis, an endless city sprawling across much of the entire sphere.

Somehow Earth was still...

Well, Earth was different.

It was still pristine, at least in Arthur's eyes. And somehow it was largely untouched by factory complexes, too much suburban sprawl or high-rise towers. At first, he figured it was the G.O.D.'s micromanaging that had accomplished that sense of sustainability.

At least they had done some good when it came to protecting it, ensuring Earth was still as much green as it was blue. Maybe sometimes institutions and organizations could still do good.

Sometimes.

Watching the minute details of the gorgeous blue marble

below, his thoughts drifted to and fro, like a lazy river with no determined current.

He had always wondered as a boy why humanity had never encountered aliens or fantastical creatures, aside from the ones they themselves had engineered in labs. He was a little sad that the only creatures they had ever manufactured of note were monstrous bioweapons or new sources of food.

Where was the majesty?

Where was the intrigue of the unknown universe that lay waiting for them?

Were all the dreams of children false from inception? If energy beings could coalesce into existence like the Creator had in Guardian lore, why was humanity the only species plodding across the stars, plunking down terraformers, Earth-seeded ecosystems, and human colonists? After observing so many barren, rocky planetoids or wispy gas giants on his first tour, he felt revived and re-energized somewhat by glancing over at the speck of green that was the U.K. and knowing he still had a place to go back to, even if his mother was no longer waiting there for him.

He was held like that for a time, entranced by every detail he could pick out below. He traced the outline of North America several times with his eyes over the course of a half hour and was just eyeing up the distant edge of Northeast Australia before remembering he was actually at the gala.

He started forcing himself back towards the throngs of people, looking for Joe.

The event had started late in the afternoon to allow additional investors to get nice and drunk enough to mingle "appropriately," and thus he endured several hours of painful meet and greets, interjected every so often with the annoyance of various fans he had accumulated from the media propaganda campaign following his actions aboard the *Asalia*. Some of them were incredibly wealthy businessmen, which left him wondering how much authority they thought he commanded.

He was lucky enough not to run into any gods.

He found, checked in with, and then left Undelwood alone to his schmoozing after only a short reunion, unable to take any more of such endeavours without a sufficiently high blood-alcohol level within his system. Thus, he skulked up to the bar on the tiered ballroom's second floor, trying to drown the seeping feelings of being out of place with a sufficiently high amount of liquid that strongly resembled several gin and tonics.

He hadn't been there fifteen minutes, fending off several more fans, when a strong hand pressed on his shoulder all of a sudden and accidentally zapped him with a slight jolt of static electricity.

Slightly more inebriated as he was, he mildly panicked and then angrily started turning on whoever it was, ready to yell at them to just leave him the fuck alone. All earlier fears of assassination had faded with enough alcohol and more than a few unwanted fans. When he turned and faced a young man with bright sky-blue eyes and dark brown hair, he paled, and his mouth dropped open.

"Hello, Captain Brass, I hope I'm not interrupting."

His voice was silky smooth, and even as he smiled at Arthur, Arthur did his best not to quail at him or either of the companions he had brought with him. He became confident that his brow twitched violently more than once during the conversation as he tried to keep a straight face, or at least a sufficiently sober one.

"No, not at all Sir, what can I do for you?"

Arthur's voice was barely a whisper.

The man was one whom he knew very well from both the media and a wide variety of other stories.

Prometheus.

The blue-eyed god's formal title was 'The God of Electricity', which was most certainly an apt title as his particular talent was channeling and firing electrons, evoking arcs of electricity in lightning bolts against his foes.

The static electricity of his touch suddenly seemed much more intentional...

Not that Arthur needed such a wakeup call when face to face with a member of the high council.

Prometheus seemed so casual standing there, so unlike the videos and broadcasts of him in combat action, with that serious, dangerous look on his face. One he held as he channelled arcs of lightning into Armada ground forces, frying hordes of berserkers into blackened crisps and chaining massive arcs of blue and yellow lightning in the air between several enemy bodies at once.

A god.

It was no small feat of course to turn the word 'god' into a commonplace word, much less begin to call living breathing humans the term, no matter how old or powerful they were. So Arthur remained quiet as Prometheus regarded him for a moment, probably realizing his slightly drunk state. He glanced back at the dark-haired girl with him, expressionlessly, and then turned back to Arthur.

"I've actually come to introduce you to your bride, Feria. Although I secretly only came to keep Hewah from biting your head off for daring to take his little girl from him."

He smiled courteously, and Hewah, suddenly a looming presence of wild black hair behind him, grinned at the joke. The beautiful woman only scoffed loudly and rolled her eyes. Hewah's dark black eyes twinkled and his darkened skin wrinkled along laugh lines with the grin.

This felt like a dream. It had to be a dream. Arthur melted into cohesion, remembering himself and loosening up somehow in spite of the booze.

Then he remembered - these were friends according to Undelwood, despite the vast difference between them in status.

Arthur took them in again, first Prometheus and then over at Hewah. The latter had obviously ascended to godhood at a more middle age, and his Polynesian features had only just started to develop age lines before his ascension. It was perplexing to Arthur how one was simply frozen in time at whatever age they were. Here were two men who Arthur knew had been alive for centuries if not millennia, and they hadn't aged even a day outside of the odd scar. Despite their formal attire, Hewah's jet black hair was still as wild and unkempt as the two times Arthur had seen him previously, and Prometheus sported stubble verging on a short beard. He was racked with the difficulty of connecting the rank of god into a friendly conversation, not sure what to say next.

So he forcefully turned on every ounce of charm he possessed, channeling everything he had learned and experienced from the interview with Billy. Perhaps he'd be overdoing it, but the false bravado gave him a confidence he could never muster on his own.

"I don't think I want to make the God of Fire angry, but I think I'd fear his daughter more in this case."

His joke went over well between them, especially with the accompanying wink at his future bride, and the two gods chuckled at his lighthearted wit. It helped with softening the tension that had accumulated in every inch of Arthur's body without him realizing it. Several tonnes of social pressure slid off his back in the realization that god or not, these were people, the same as anyone else.

He dared a glance over at his future bride to be on Hewah's right, trying to stare at her face and not just the parts of her he desperately wanted to look at in his subtle inebriation. This was a formal occasion, after all. The woman was a definite beauty, the same as before, but at his smile she only bored her eyes back into him with a hollow glance.

His joke suddenly came sullenly true, and he pondered whether she would truly be his salvation or his demise. She perked up, reading his apprehension, and grinned mischievously at him, clearly not intending to alienate him on purpose.

"Considering we're going to get married without even knowing each other, I'll give you at least one proper date before I decide to hate you or not."

Despite her taunting smile, Feria's American accented words were sudden, sharp, and very, very real. Luckily for him, it was her father who stepped in to defend him. He put a large hand on her delicate brown shoulder.

"Listen kiddo, he's not all that bad, you and I both know his track record for only being out of the academy about a year, and from the one time we've met him, he's been a good guy."

She shrugged, feigning a need to be convinced, but made no argument. Prometheus wiggled his eyebrows up and down at Arthur to show his amusement, a small smirk on his face.

"Now, Prom and I need to go off and be nice to all these rich men in order to weasel their money and services away from them, so why don't you two kids get to know each other?"

Hewah's use of the word "kids" was fitting, considering the two gods of fire and electricity were thousands of years their seniors. Arthur nodded and held out his hand, which both Gods took note of and promptly shook before making their way back down to the crowds on the first floor of the grand ballroom.

"Let me buy you a drink."

Arthur offered, knowing full well that she would merely have to ask for one from the bartender and have the wish granted instantly. The entire event was an open bar policy.

"Fine. A long island iced tea."

She was demure, seeming to appreciate his attempt at humor, but her sudden submission threw him off, as he pondered her prior teasing stance.

"Feria, can I ask you a completely honest question? You're free to be offended if you'd like."

The bartender turned away to mix her drink, churning ice into smaller shards. He was clearly paid enough to tune out any conversations he might overhear.

She leaned over the bar, her emotions freezing up again and becoming unreadable. Clearly it was a talent of hers - an excellent poker player, likely.

Arthur stared as if she were the rapture itself.

Her brown skin practically glowed under the shallow potlights above. Unlike her father she was darker in complexion and sharper in her features, and it might just be that he was starting to feel the gin a little more… But she was positively radiant in every aspect he could think of.

He suddenly felt like a boy with a teenage crush.

She gave him a sideways glance and adjusted the shoulder strap of her elegant red dress, taking a sip of the iced tea the bartender handed her all before nodding slightly to him in confirmation of the drink's quality. The bartender took the hint and wandered off to the far end of the bar where a young couple wearing far too much jewellery had sauntered up for service.

Arthur held the silence for a moment, taking another long sip of gin and tonic and contemplating both his recent alcoholism and his question. His eyes were locked firmly on the bar, even as her gaze bored a hole into his skin.

"You're the daughter of a god, so with all due respect; why the fuck would you ever agree to marry me? Surely your dad doesn't have that much control over you?"

She broke out in a loud tinkle of laughter at his uncouth language and brazen forwardness, and just like that, her false icy exterior fell away, to be replaced by warmth and humour again. She pursed her lips at him as she picked her words.

"I think it's because I know you're a good man, at least from everything I've heard about you, and it seems the only way the daughter of a god can really do much with her life to affect this Central Universe of ours is to be married off like a noble in the middle ages, or to follow in their divine footsteps."

She smiled at him.

"I've already finished my master's degree in psychology, and the job prospects are boring and unappealing. Most of the interesting research was done decades ago, and I'm hardly a good fit for a practice. And while yes, I've undergone the ritual, and I have a basic grasp on my powers, I have absolutely no interest in flying all over the galaxy and shooting fire at the Armada from my fingertips, or debating with self-absorbed assholes on council."

She quieted and narrowed her eyes and jutted her mouth to the side. Arthur realized that she was clearly one to think with her face, so to speak.

He could feel it.

His crush was getting worse.

She was direct and honest, and knew where she stood.

"Besides, from everything I've heard, you could really catch a break with everything you've been through in your life. And I reserve the right to divorce you at any time I please, anyways."

Her honesty intrigued him. But led to so many more questions he needed answers to. Why the hell would a god bother to get a master's degree in psychology? Could she really shoot fire from her fingers?

Maybe she lit cigarettes as a party trick?

"So, do you want to settle down via politics? How old are you… 21?"

She laughed at him directly this time, openly and unabashedly. Even her laugh was beautiful. It was then that he understood his folly.

"Wait… How long ago did you complete the ritual, Feria?"

"26 years ago."

"Which makes you… How old?"

She smirked.

"47."

Arthur was awash in a flood of confusing emotions. The fact that she was over 20 years older than him was a shock, despite his prior knowledge that gods who undertook the ritual were essentially immortal. Another inability to clue in, chalked up to and courtesy of, one Arthur Brass.

He took another draw from his tumbler, looking her up and down in a coy manner.

She most definitely took note of it.

He smiled crookedly to himself, closing his eyes in acceptance of how badly he was fucking this up. He made a quick drunken decision and leaned into it, and then prepared to get slapped into putty for what he was about to say.

"So, you're a cougar, I guess?"

He winced.

Instead of the expected slap, at his comment she burst out laughing yet again, and he started to notice the twinkling in her eyes as she gazed back at him.

The funny-guy approach was definitely striking a chord with her.

"Well, to be perfectly honest Captain Brass, knowing that one is immortal definitely gives me a more jaded outlook on life... Because when my husband dies of old age, I can just as easily go find myself someone new."

He bit his lip drunkenly, despite an honest attempt on his part to stay stoic. They both thought with their faces, it seemed.

"So, I'm just your Naval boy-toy until I die? Because I don't know if I can handle that... Maybe I should just go with the execution."

She put her hand on his arm, and her palm was hot to the touch through his sleeve.

"So, you don't want to marry a beautiful woman who will stay this good looking even while you grow old and wither? Who can only die by being physically killed? And who just might... If you dare try taking her home in your inebriated state... Be fun in bed?"

Her forward retort caught him off-guard, as his gaze was definitely tilted from her face when she said the last part. He jerked his eyes up from the folds of her dress to look back into her eyes, and she had a wide childish grin spread across her face.

She had caught him red handed, of course.

From that point of the evening on, she was even more warm, charming, and open, albeit a little cheekier with every drink. They sat at the upstairs bar talking for hours about everything and anything until Judge Undelwood came and interrupted them at around seven o'clock UK time.

Arthur had just found a new fascination with how perfectly white and straight Feria's teeth were in contrast to her brown skin when she smiled, so Joe's interjection was extremely annoying to his younger charge. Joe was also clearly drunk enough himself to do away with cold formality in Feria's presence.

"Come now you two, the main announcement is about to begin."

Arthur sighed and grabbed his glass of gin and tonic, which had sat miraculously untouched for almost the entirety of his time with Feria since she had hit on him. The ice cubes had long since melted, and he carried it with him out of habit more than anything.

There was a flash through his mind at the significance of that.

"Come on, Arthur."

Feria gestured Arthur along with her, exchanging her nearly empty Iced Tea for a glass of champagne lifted from a waiter's unsuspecting tray. Arthur noticed she didn't take a sip from it, realizing the importance of formality in these proceedings.

Feria wasn't just beautiful; she was well-versed in the rules of high-society too.

He was smitten.

The Judge led them back downstairs to where Hewah was patiently watching the centre of the ballroom. He had his eyes fixed firmly on another young couple, a dashing brunette woman wearing thick-rimmed black glasses in an elaborate white dress. Beside her was her equally beautiful companion - a young, long-haired blonde man in a simple black suit with a white tie.

His hair was carefully arranged in a foppish braided contraption as if done by a stylist, and every time he moved, he made sure to avoid displacing it where it lay twixt his shoulder blades. It hung down his back midway in a wave of those yellow braids. The woman sported a severe look on her face, making her prominent cheekbones gaunt and giving her face an even sharper look.

As she looked over the crowd, her consort seemed bored with the whole affair and even openly stifled a yawn in front of guests once or twice.

Arthur recoiled.

This was a fancier, dressed up version of the couple from his court case, and apparently this must be in reality the Prime God and her consort. The photos he had found on the internet paled in comparison to the real person. He made sure to hide himself somewhat behind Hewah, Feria, and Undelwood as best he could.

This entire night was like a fucking reunion of people he had never formally met, but knew all too well. Far too well. His stomach lurched up into his throat and he felt nauseous. Suddenly having sobered up so much was a travesty, and he slugged a hearty mouthful of watery gin and tonic, trying to escape into the blur of inebriation to settle his nerves.

Undelwood leaned in close.

"The Prime God Serania, God of Justice and her consort Julian, The God of Darkness. The former being the unofficial leader of the council with sole individual veto power, and thus the de-facto controller of the entirety of the Guardians of Destiny. Julian runs 'The Eye.' Don't forget, even Hewah has to tread lightly around those two in the council chambers."

Undelwood whispered the explanation in Arthur's ear even with Feria still hanging off his other arm. Arthur hadn't realized that she had taken his arm without him noticing, and he silently panicked, trying to guess or look for reactions in either woman to see whether Feria or Serania had super-hearing or something as part of their powers.

When neither woman made any sign of noticing his quiet panic or Judge Joe Undelwood's whisper, he slowly calmed himself down, comforted somewhat by Feria's hold on his elbow.

But what powers could a god have? He knew that almost every god had radically different specialties in terms of their abilities, but the width and depth of such a talent pool was ambiguous.

It wasn't as if Joe had said anything too inflammatory though...

It was odd to him that he already cared so much about what Feria thought or heard after only having met her earlier that night.

The brunette, Serania, raised her champagne glass and tapped on it loudly with the carefully manicured nail of her right index finger, forcing the room into silence as if carefully orchestrated.

Arthur figured it definitely had been. And it rang clear, as if the sound was softly amplified somehow. It immediately sent a tremble through the entire party - a wave of attention. Serania took a few steps forward, and performed an elegant little spin in a welcoming gesture with her arms extended, without the champagne in her glass so much as rippling.

At least some of these small nuances to the performance had to be influenced by her powers, considering she had something close to a hundred thousand years to perfect them.

Arthur wondered if God-Emperor Xex, Warlord of The Black Armada used these same sorts of party tricks to impress his own minions and allies.

"Thank you all for coming, I appreciate everyone spending their valuable time with all of us, from the heads of the Unitary Mercenary Group, to our friends over at the Junk and Rumblers Guild, who have so graciously offered unto us our venue for tonight. I hope you're all enjoying yourselves, and will continue to do so. But if I may have your attention for this brief moment, we have a wonderful announcement to make this evening, which I do know many of you have been waiting ever so patiently for."

The crowd erupted in whispers, asking questions of their closest neighbour on who might have won, or discussing gossipy rumours that had accumulated throughout the night. Serania had to tap her glass a second time to bring everyone in attendance back into silence.

The sound definitely reverberated even louder the second time around. She didn't have to repeat the action a third time to carefully corral and control the attention of everyone aboard the freighter.

"I'd like to announce formally tonight that the G.O.D. in these trying times of war has finalized the bids for the 'G.O.D. Army Munitions' contract, currently up for tender, and without further ado we would like to formally announce that we are awarding our friends the Conversion Corporation with the contract for this year's sidearms manufacturing. Further contracts are to be determined. Congratulations to this diverse and hardworking company and their fantastic bid."

There was a round of polite applause, during which a balding man in what appeared to be his sixties approached Serania and formally shook her hand for a photo opportunity from a passing CNG camera drone. Arthur could feel the simmering frustration and resentment from many who had gathered in the room, and caught several groups whispering fiercely in the ears of colleagues. No one said anything out loud, of course, especially not with Serania standing right there.

Serania waited for the majority of the discussion to finish, and continued.

"And now to announce the winner of the 'Naval Plasma Shielding Research and Development' contract, put to tender in the hopes of reducing the cost and size of such technologies in order to outfit our smaller G.O.D. ships... We would like to welcome up and congratulate Mr. Hendrickson of Eclipse to accept the contract."

There was a near uproar, which was only kept in check by the formal nature of the event. Arthur's own firsthand issues in the Academy had educated him well to how bizarre this was.

The organization representing a defected G.O.D. scientist was openly bidding on G.O.D. military contracts?

And they had won?

What about the investigation he had been subject to back in school?

No... It was likely more nefarious on Serania's part. He surmised that perhaps it was a sting of sorts to draw whoever this Hendrickson was out of hiding for assassination. Chattering voices filled the room, and Judge Undelwood and Hewah exchanged a single brief glance, tinged with shades of discomfort.

Arthur locked eyes with Prometheus several feet away, and The God of Electricity shrugged at him with an expression that said: "I don't know. Don't ask me."

Once the second round of awkward applause had died down and the photo opportunity with Mr. Hendrickson was finished, Serania went on, somewhat unexpectedly. There was a staggered stop to the conversation that had bubbled up and was rumbling angrily throughout the room.

"And one more announcement, although not at all any less significant, I'd like to extend the G.O.D.'s personal congratulations to the new engagement between our recent war hero Captain Arthur Brass, and the lovely Feria, daughter of their beloved council member and God of Fire, Hewah.

She smiled cordially, shooting Arthur and Feria daggers with her eyes as she did so.

"I wish you all the best, and would like to propose a toast for your new future together."

She raised her champagne glass towards him where he hid, and he could feel every single eye in the ballroom fixate on him in an instant, as if he was merely an obstacle in the way of the gossip continuing. Serania's eyes were particularly unblinking in their stare, and he felt as if he were actually withering away under them.

Only Feria's firm grasp on his bicep prevented him from backing away to hide in the crowd, away from those soul-piercing brown eyes.

He rose his watery glass of gin and tonic in thanks, staring back into her eyes with a frightened but dogged determination.

This was of course the same god who had attempted to have him killed at least once before via the machinations of bureaucracy.

Now she was here toasting him in person, as if amusedly chiding Arthur for escaping her wrath successfully.

For lack of sleeves, what else did Serania have up that dress?

CHAPTER 11: SOMETHING IMPORTANT ABOUT CATS AND BAGS.

"The best laid plans of mice and men mean absolutely nothing when wrenches and works are involved."

After the toast, and the unanimous chorus of demure congratulations that wheezed forth from the throats of everyone in the ballroom, Arthur was allowed to retreat back to the relative safety of Judge Undelwood and Hewah's political shadow.

"I have absolutely no fucking idea how she found out about the marriage itself!"

Undelwood was furious.

The outburst came as soon as they were out of earshot and safely closeted away in a back-parlour room. Joe's voice was cracking and rasping slightly with a double dose of intoxication and frustration, and he would surely lose his voice after tonight with all the vigorous meeting and greeting he had done.

"We were clearly negotiating a little too openly near certain council members. Besides, *Julian is the head of The Eye* - I doubt we could have hidden it from either of them for very long anyways."

It was stated matter-of-factly, while Hewah was clearly musing over something else entirely. He seemed somewhere deep in thought, but was still present, at least in part.

"You're still one of her strongest supporters, dad, in spite of everything she's done. It doesn't seem to matter now that she plotted to have *The Eye* kill Arthur outside of the other bureaucratic proceedings, because her own announcement just now means she's stopped her own public ability to do anything without losing serious face. Seems rather stupid for such a narcissistic bitch, no?"

Feria's sudden revelation that the top dog of the entire G.O.D. had not only wanted him dead formally but had been actively planning to have him assassinated in addition to the bureaucratic approach... Well it was shocking to say the least.

Having multiple irons in the hearth for the same end result seemed to be the new par for the course, at least where Arthur's mortality was concerned.

He threw back the rest of his drink and felt the cold watery liquid burn downwards into his stomach.

The role of Captain Arthur Brass as a piece in a much bigger game of chess between major players had suddenly changed. He was no longer merely a pawn to be lost and forgotten between Navy Admirals, or to be turned into smoke and ash as an annoyance to Serania. He was suddenly the Bishop or Rook in a power play between the members of the council.

The high council *of the fucking Guardians of Destiny.*

This wasn't solely a Naval matter, anymore.

This was a back and forth "check" in a game of chess played between the head honchos of the entire damn organization. Hell, this was the truest of cloak and dagger, spy-game politics.

"Hold on a fucking minute."

He was trying to keep his re-inebriated voice low and failing at it miserably.

"You're telling me that the head of this entire damn bag of shit was not just wanting me dead via a bullshit execution, but was actively planning my death via assassination regardless, and nobody even bothered to tell me about it?"

He could feel his temperature rising alongside his pulse and rate of breathing.

"I thought I was merely a nuisance to some crusty old men in the war room, so she had simply signed off on it all, and now you're telling me the entire damn machine was ready to fall down upon my ass? Sod off!"

Feria gripped his arm even tighter.

She was strong. Scary strong.

He cringed when it became painful..

At least he could write "super strength" up on the mental chalkboard list of Feria's powers. The pain shut him up - as he quickly lost circulation to his forearm. Hewah only stared Arthur down, as if mildly annoyed by an insolent toddler.

He tried to take another nervous sip of the nigh-empty dregs from his flat watery drink, and then wiped his forehead with a sweat-drenched sleeve.

Hewah moved closer, clapping a firm hand on Arthur's shoulder.

He had never been in such close proximity to multiple ascended immortals before.

"Listen kid, I've been playing these games with Ser for a few thousand years before you were ever born. She doesn't give a damn about any of her lackeys down the chain. At least not enough to break a habit of having them wiped off the board at the first inconvenience. It doesn't matter if you're a Super Soldier or an Admiral."

He paused and moved to pour himself a glass of dark red wine from the bottle Joe had liberated from the bar before their retreat.

"You get pretty numb to people dying of old age after a while, kid. Death becomes an inconvenience rather than an inevitability. So..."

He slugged a deep draught, before jabbing the half-empty glass in Arthur's direction.

"If I were in your shoes, I'd just shut up and thank me. If it weren't for Joe being a good friend and ally, I wouldn't have felt the pangs of pity and given Feria your file. I could have just shredded it instead and saved myself the trouble."

There it was.

The full plot, laid bare for him in a matter of simple strokes.

Arthur had somehow pissed off, or annoyed Serania, The God of Justice and sole remaining member of the Prime Triumvirate. That was the long and short of it. His whole life was now simply an annoying sore spot for a woman who wanted him dead - as an afterthought to an inconvenience no less.

His career had been forced from the start, and Judge Joe Undelwood had made a plea to his friends in high places to save Arthur's sorry ass by selling him off as a veritable prostitute to the daughter of a god. To the woman now hanging from his arm, who could likely crush his penis in the palm of her hand as easily as she could choose to fuck it.

He felt overwhelmed, thankful, angry, and desperate all at

once.

"I'm sorry."

Arthur felt himself going red in the face, and his downcast eyes prompted Hewah to clap him on the shoulder again, this time in a display of pitying affection. Arthur kept forgetting and remembering in flashes that Hewah was thousands of years his senior. The millennia must have helped birth this endless fount of patience the god now exuded.

Arthur was no less angry, of course. But he could tell, even while thinking of getting sloshed again, that he would be better off now by keeping quiet.

"Your fire might just prove to be your undoing, kid. With that disposition, my daughter is going to have one hell of a husband on her hands."

A mocking smile.

"In fact, I might even start to like you as a son in law, as you'll do me a favor by keeping her off *my* back."

Hewah's kind, prodding words humbled him, helping reduce the fire of anger in his gut back down to seething frustration. Judge Joe Undelwood clapped him on the back, rather drunkenly. He had been quiet throughout, with a sympathetic look on his face belying his bleeding heart.
"Dammit, go have some fun, Arthur! You should be happy! You're getting married to a beautiful god, and you still have the rest of your life to live while we figure all this out together. Go! Be merry! Kiss her at least once!"

Arthur's future bride winked mischievously at his adoptee godfather, and released her death grip to pull her new fiancé along with only her pinky. She continued in leading him out of the parlour, so the older men could finish talking shop without Arthur Brass getting in their way.

Feria whisked him away for the remainder of the night, before he could tell her he was already worn out. A cup of coffee later, she was feeding him story after story and forcing him into some of the most awkward yet intriguing conversations of his short-lived life. He tried his best to be a grump, half in jest, and half in fatigue, but Feria's wit, humor, and her increasingly volatile beauty prevented it.

"So what are all your powers?"

Arthur finally asked, eased out of his quasi-bad mood by her poise, her grace, and her playful disposition.

She smiled back at him with the cheekiest, biggest grin he'd ever seen anyone produce.

"Well, let's say you don't want to arm wrestle me, for one. And let's also say that I don't exactly need flint and steel to start a campfire. Like father, like daughter, and all that. He showed me some tricks in the first few years after my ascension."

"What else can you do?"

She smirked and put her fingers to her temples, closing her eyes.

"Well, I can read minds, of course."

Arthur freaked out a bit at that one, before realizing the joke.

She peeked out from one eye.

"And I can also kill a man just by looking at him, and fly, and create hurricanes, and make a mean vodka soda."

She was fucking with him. *Of course* she was fucking with him.

"You're heartless, you know that?"

She chuckled at his ignorance and gullibility, clearly doing her best not to guffaw loudly at Arthur's inability to avoid falling for her ruse.

"To be honest? The super strength and the fireballs are about it. As I said - when I first ascended at twenty-two, dad took the time to teach me the basics of his own specialties, like I said before."

She twirled a curl of her hair with an index finger.

"But it takes years and years to actually master and hone your own special abilities, so that you don't blow yourself up or freeze yourself solid or something like that, depending on what you're working on. We're ageless, but not unkillable."

Arthur gawked.

"And with the survival ratios of the ascension ritual and all, we can't afford to lose gods like that. So some of us only ever stick to the basics of the simplest telekinetic powers, because they're fairly easy to get a grip on. I gave up on even trying to train after a few years, and fell into a mix of travel and school instead, because I hated the politics of it all. I kinda regret it now, but I figure I'll always have the time later - when I change my mind."

He was fascinated, like a kid that wanted to collect trading cards. One for every god, power, and ability.

"So really, any god can learn any ability with enough time and training?"

She nodded.

"It's all about patience. But the whole Guardian tradition is that your formal title and any prior family ascension kinda defines the powers you're supposed to use the most, to become a master of. Only the more ambiguous ones - like being a god of emotion or some such shit, then you have much more freedom to explore. It has to do with worship, belief, and public appearance and such. There are a lot of exhausting rules to follow in

The G.O.D. as a god."

He put his hand on her forearm, riveted.

She didn't remove it.

"What do you want to get good at, then? You already have the fire down, what else would you like to explore?"

She grinned again. Leaned in and whispered something naughty in his ear.

The magic "click" from just smitten… Towards being both smitten AND horny?

It happened faster than he could blink, and long before he was really ready for it.

The rest of the night was a happy blur.

Instead of going back to Judge Undelwood's home after the event, via the provided J&R guest shuttles, he was willingly "abducted" via a privately chartered Agatha, and ended up back down on Earth, headed towards a night in the posh part of Chelsea where Feria kept an apartment.

It culminated in the best sex of his life, with a woman who knew exactly the specifics of what she wanted - and who wasn't in the least bit afraid to take it.

He felt more like a schoolboy on a first date than a grown man.

Arthur fell in love with Feria that night, and not just because of her fierce and passionate personality. Her knowledge and her extra few decades of life experience felt enlightening and empowering when gifted freely to someone like him, who had never truly felt in control of his own life.

Later, as they lay awake in her king-sized bed after sex, she promised in a moment of quiet vulnerability to take his name formally, instead of the normally staunch tradition of Gods and their progeny forgoing any legal surnames.

It was a shock.

Yet... He had no idea why he felt so honoured by the offer. He wasn't particularly attached to even his own surname anyway.

"You won't get in trouble?"

She shuffled backwards into him for a cuddle.

"I don't care about getting in trouble."

He made his decision on the marriage that same night.

The next sunny morning after brunch, a rather furious second romp, and some lazy, prolonged goodbyes, he kissed Feria farewell, declined her offer of a taxi or transport, and made the journey via metro to his old home nearby, now left empty since his mother's passing.

Walking in, he was thankful it was kept from dust somewhat by the odd cleaning lady or two that the Judge hired as a small kindness. The furniture was rearranged a bit for ease of vacuuming since his last visit, but otherwise it was left largely the same.

He knew his mother's room hadn't been touched much, hopefully including the primary treasure he was after - her oft-unworn wedding ring.

Hand outstretched, he froze.

Something stopped him from opening her door.

So, he sat on the musty couch in the living room for a while, breathing in the stale air and remembering his childhood, his mother, and his life before the fight that had started it all.

Processing so much all at once was hard, and he actually broke down into tears at several memories.

He was glad that nobody else was there to see him in such a state.

Arthur remained motionless as he reminisced, hands on his face. Trapped, thinking about his family, his mother, and what his life could have been if only fate had chosen another route.

His mother's soft smile in his thoughts haunted him - that same knowing smile that accepted him for who he was, no matter what stupid shit he had done on a given day. The pain of remembering her suicide was far worse than the pain of keeping everything pushed down at the base of his spine. The same pains he had drowned out for so long with alcohol. It was there that he finally let the tears come in a torrent, sobbing heavily all alone in the empty home.

After he had let it all out, tears thoroughly staining last night's jacket - he finally got up the courage to enter his mom's room.

When he opened the lid, it was there - glistening on top of all the other rings, earrings and necklaces she had accumulated over the years. Next to her tiny gold and diamond ring was his father's band, made of plain white gold. It had several nicks and scratches, and he pondered its presence next to hers. His father had shipped it back home one day alongside his cufflinks, in the event he never made it back home.

Home to Earth.

Apparently his parents had gotten matching ring-finger tattoos instead.

Was it some sort of sign from a long dead man, alluding to that man's plain and easygoing nature? And what was the message left from that man, knowing that both rings had remained where they lay for decades?

Arthur took both bands, slipping them with a soft clink into his pocket, and wandered the halls of the apartment for a while, eventually coming back to grab the rest of the box and a few photo-album drives.

The rest, he left behind. A dusty testament to the boy he had once been, and the mother who had raised him all on her own - while her husband sailed the stars fighting the enemies of the gods...

He checked his watch. Realizing he had spent several hours at the house, he finally decided to leave, locking the door again with a resounding click.

He couldn't bring himself to head back to Joe's place just yet, so he wandered his old neighbourhood again, feeling strange and out of place the entire time he was back amidst his old haunts.

Nothing much had changed in his absence.

He had a beer at his old pub, listening to some of the working-class men spatter rhyming slang at each other. Chatting with the barkeep, a fresh face, he learned that the old regular - Mr. Chafer had passed away of cancer. Arthur drank another beer with the barkeep to honor his memory, before finally resigning himself to leave this old life behind him for good.

The metro back to Undelwood's gave him time to reflect some more. He was sure his mother would be proud of him, wherever she was.

Be it heaven or elsewhere.

He thought a bit about his father, too. A man he barely knew.

A marriage in lieu of a funeral?

Well...

Could always be worse.

CHAPTER 12: COME WHATEVER MAY.

"That fateful ouroboros, Jormungandr, will rise up from his home beneath the waves, and release his tail from his jaws at last. In doing so, he will signal the end of the world."

The very next day Arthur's shore leave was rescinded with hardly any notice.

He was suddenly reassigned to a larger ship on the rear lines, which Judge Undelwood threw an absolute fit about - as Joe had fought long and hard for those extra few weeks of leave. However, Arthur was somehow eager to get back to work after sitting idle for so long, and within the span of only half an hour he was packed and ready to go after exchanging a deep, emotional hug with his savior.

He left Undelwood's residence with pangs of longing for Feria, already missing her deeply even as he boarded his military shuttle space-side. She had given him her number, and he texted her a quick explanation and a goodbye, letting her know that they'd hopefully be in touch again soon.

Duty called.

His first order of business was getting in touch with his old Navigator, Hammad Aziz. He waited several minutes en route to the Moon for the operator to finally find and connect him. Aziz had finally earned his promotion to Captain, and being out of the loop whilst on leave, Hammad let him know that change was on the horizon.

According to Aziz, the war had simmered down in terms of active Guardian and Armada warzones, however there were rampant rumours about the sudden loss of a well-populated frontier world - *Seed of The Emperor*, a thriving metropolis planet on the far edge of G.O.D. territory.

The propaganda machine, with a tone of spiteful hope, was saying that the Black Armada had decimated large swaths of the Navy and Army and taken the world, but rumours abounded amongst several prominent captains that there was talk of traitors, and even of mass defection.

The Eye was working hard to squash any contradictions to the official story of course, as any proper spy agency might, but the implications of something that big...

Arthur thought back to Eclipse winning the plasma-shielding contract out of the blue, and couldn't help but feel the two were somehow connected. Perhaps Eclipse had been bribed with the contract to get back on the side of the G.O.D. due to wartime losses?

He thanked Aziz for what he could share, and let him get back to his duties.

Arthur spent the next few hours contacting other old Academy and ship-colleagues, seeking any information he could on the warfront before an official briefing might take place. Something made him doubt that he could trust the honesty and effectiveness of the Navy, now knowing Serania and her spymaster consort Julian, God of Darkness had it out for him via more nefarious methods.

He tried not to gossip with other Naval officers too much, and only shot for facts, especially since his return to duty had come with a sudden and strange bumping up in rank. Upon his arrival at the Naval base on Luna he was assigned as an

OF-4 Commodore to a battlecruiser; *Princely Disposition Under Duress*.

While he was mainly part of the defence fleet stationed in and around the Guardian core worlds, he was moved to the front on a few occasions. Mostly these missions were as a subordinate captain participating in small fleet-based hit and run attacks under the direct command of Vice-Admiral Delki.

First, there was the destruction of a small Black Armada scouting frigate - an easy battle for a plasma-shielded full-size battlecruiser against an unshielded smaller vessel.

The opposite scenario to his own victory aboard the *Asalia*.

A grim reminder.

The costs of such protections as plasma shielding was high, and he was grateful for the added layer of protection in the short skirmish.

His next combat experience would be surviving another brief offensive, a forward fleet skirmish with a well-organized fleet of pirates inside the neutral territories, followed shortly after by even more daring harassments of Armada frontier colonies closer to their end of the neutral zone.

Princely Disposition Under Duress was almost never working alone like the *Asalia*, and never once did they find themselves in any real trouble. To Arthur's mystery, the next year would pass by dreadfully slow. No assassination attempts ever came, and aside from his infrequent fleet actions, his new battlecruiser and crew hardly ever faced a real risk or challenge.

Of course, Feria and Arthur soon craved every second of contact they could get, be it via video calls or in-person. The pent-up frustration of his absences was worked out in full during every single shore leave he got.

Regardless of physical contact, he could feel himself growing closer and closer to her, and while he never told her out loud, he knew he was falling in love with her. He wasn't sure if he had ever known what it felt like to actually love someone before, outside of his casual dalliances born of lust.

He didn't know how or when he might appropriately drop a bombshell like: "I love you" on her...

Engagement or not!

In between the sexual encounters, they spent almost every waking hour possible together, and she facilitated his transitions back to a more normal life when on shore leave. She introduced him to her friends, many surprisingly mortal like him, and regaled him of the tales of her inner colony explorations and other crazy adventures.

Hell, she even battled the bureaucracy of the G.O.D. by taking on the brunt of planning their wedding, which was hell regardless of whose daughter she might be.

Their relationship was interesting in terms of celebrity, too, as he was oddly the more famous of the two. Whereas he had been the hotshot young captain plastered across propaganda only a year ago, she had somehow evaded most fame for the entirety of her life outside of the Guardian Council itself.

The magic moment came exactly as he planned it.

He gave her his mother's ring at twilight, as they wandered the Royal Botanical Gardens. This was after telling her that he loved her for the first time. It was highly unorthodox, considering the nature of their arrangement, but it was the first time he ever saw a god cry.

In return - tears still slipping down her face, with his mother's ring on her finger, she pulled out a box carved in yellow cedar, lightly stained.

They stared at it for nearly a minute before she began grinning at him like a child, and fell to one knee.

Arthur cackled and covered his face in embarrassment with a palm to the forehead, feeling the pricking of tears in his eyes.

"I never did formally ask you to marry me Arthur Brass, and somehow you beat me to it."

She opened the box with a gaudy flourish.

"Will you marry me, Arthur?"

He grinned ear to ear like an idiot.

"Of course."

Her flowery summer dress billowed out around her in the breeze, as she took the gleaming ring from the box and put it on his finger.

He fingered his father's ring in his pocket, helping her to her feet. Took a minute to look over the ring. It was almost black, a solid band seemingly composed of two parts.

"Titanium on one half, and Tungsten on the other, with something special binding them in the middle. My father forged it himself. He wouldn't tell me what the middle segment was made of."

He smiled and rubbed it softly. He was wearing a ring crafted by The God of Fire himself.

They continued their walk, wearing the two rings hand in hand.

He never thought that they would work out, but somehow, they did. She had chosen him knowing his faults, his strengths, and his nuances. What he had feared would be a one-sided relationship of subservience was blooming into truest romance.

She wore his mother's ring from the day he gave it to her.

Arthur Brass was smitten like a schoolboy, hopelessly lost in love.

He had his father's ring split in two and converted into two matching necklaces, one of which he gave to Feria on her birthday. She cried then, too. It was another sign that this wasn't just some comatose fantasy, but that it was real, it was tangible, and it was hopeful.

He hadn't felt hope in a long time.

Life was solidifying, and he had Billy, Joe, Hewah, and now Feria to thank for that.

He was finally finding a sort of peace.

CHAPTER 13: RAGNAROK.

"Any one of the larger factions in Central has the technological and financial capability to crack apart a planet, effectively converting an individual apocalypse into a tradable commodity. It's lucky that colony worlds capable of being more easily terraformed and colonized are still in such high demand."

On his twenty-eighth birthday, a year and a half after the gala, he was given yet another extended leave of absence, which Hewah played a large part in getting.

The war front was still relatively stable, and despite his rather significant gains in combat experience from just a few years of captaincy, at least in comparison to others his age, he had become regarded as something of a phenom, much to his guilty pleasure.

He was hardly the stuff of legends, but regardless of however many compliments and kudos he dismissed in humble sheepishness, he was filled with a growing sense of confidence.

He was *good* at this whole "captaining" thing.

On top of a sense of accomplishment and pride in his work as captain of *Princely Disposition Under Duress*, he found himself constantly eager for his time with Feria, and even more eager to be able to call her his wife.

Some of his friends such as Billy found it odd that he had so quickly fallen for a woman who had basically forced him into a shotgun marriage in order to save his life, but he was happy, in all honesty, and it was easy to sway their opinion after meeting her only once or twice.

It meant everything to him to build a family of his own now that he had no blood relatives to connect with.

Feria was a woman he could have long philosophical debates with, although she was always quick to lay on the psychoanalysis and make him look more the fool. Yet something about that fired him up about her, so they'd be able to kiss and make up fairly quickly most of the time.

Disagreements were never permanent.

Feria had her weaknesses, of course. But a lack of courage was never one of them. She never backed down, and never gave even an inch if she felt strongly enough about something.

They had a particularly fierce debate on the ethics of public versus private education once. It had the unintended side effect of prompting him again to think about children. He had been so worried for so long about his job, or his survival, or about Feria.

It was something he had put on the backburner.

He finally gathered the courage and asked Feria about it.

"Arthur, I'm almost forty-nine, you don't think I might have thought already about having kids by now?"

Even now, he was forgetting about the enormous age gap of two decades between himself and his fiancé. Her body was eternally frozen-in-time at twenty-two, after all. It would stay like that forever, insofar as she continued living.

"But… Would you ever consider having them with me?"

She tormented him, reaching over and pinching his cheeks,

lifting up tufts of his hair, and spreading his eyes open with her fingers. She continued this fake inspection for almost a minute.

"Yes, I might consider you to be suitable breeding stock."

He was exasperated already.

"Feria."

She smiled and quietly kissed him on the lips.

"Yes Mr. Brass. I would."

A pause.

"When... I can be certain that you're around to stay, and can actually play father."

It was good enough for him.

Plus, this final extended shore leave had become the windup to their wedding.

Hewah told Arthur personally that he'd largely be in the clear politically once the marriage was settled. Yet despite the sense of relief it brought, Arthur still shied away from calling Hewah his father in law unless he absolutely had to.

Being called up to drink with Hewah, Prometheus, and other minor gods had become something of a commonality in recent months when coming and going, and Arthur's social status crept slowly upwards as a result, no matter how much he avoided the spotlight to keep a sense of normality.

More awkwardly, while Feria hardly ever used her powers, Hewah, Prometheus, and others were fond of using their powers for party tricks when amongst the company of gods.

Oftentimes it became a competition of sorts, an awkward wagging of ego.

Exactly what percentage of their skills from the repertoire of powers had been perfected by such flights of fancy, anyways?

Feria herself was swamped, and even though she had personal assistants, couriers and other lackeys - all on loan courtesy of the G.O.D. to do most of the legwork and errands, she was constantly left to stew in her own rising panic. Every time he tried to inject himself into the Arthur-Feria wedding equation to help, he was ejected out of the situation forcefully by an irate wife-to-be. He was asked questions on his own preferences, of course, but not once was he ever given much of a choice in the actual logistics of it all.

Their plan was to have a relatively small wedding inside an old church in the Scottish countryside. It was idyllic and pastoral, standing all alone in the middle of an open and beautiful grassy field full of wildflowers.

Hewah had pulled all the strings necessary to allow them to prepare back in London and then board on-loan Guardian military transports to arrive at the church in time for the ceremony. The reception after the ceremony would take place beneath a series of large popup tents set up in the field outside the church specifically for that purpose. Since it was so small, with only Joe, Billy, and Rebecca on his side and Feria's closest family and friends on the other, they hardly expected any trouble.

Arthur was most excited to meet Feria's older half-brother Amar and his family, through her deceased mother's side. Amar worked for a large law firm in New York. Ever since hearing about him, he wondered how Amar's life had progressed, being related so closely through his mother's second marriage to the leaders at the top of the Universe.

Amar had refused an attempted ascension like his sister when given the opportunity, clearly not wanting to take on the high risk of death. In Arthur's eyes, it must have been nice to be given a chance at immortality and immense power just by being nebulously related to a god. Still, Arthur sure as hell would never want to risk his own neck for immortality, with the chances of survival being so low.

Besides, unless you died via combat or assassination, it meant a literal eternity of serving the G.O.D...

Arthur knew the nature of the gods - to come and go as they pleased. It was likely hard on a family at the best of times. Thus, questions abounded.

How many other children had Hewah sired over the millennia? What percentage of the human population was the unascended offspring of gods? What was it like to watch your children die of old age?

Feria had never told him of any other ascended siblings, so he was under the assumption that aside from being taken care of financially, none of her family had chosen the risky path of immortality. Thus, they were likely living the lives of wealthy heirs, unremarkable otherwise. Feria, while mostly free of direct Guardian trappings, could still find herself beholden to them in times of strife.

A life of obligation.

Feria confided in him eventually, when he asked about her mother – confessing that she had passed away undergoing the ascension ritual, and Feria's choice to follow in those footsteps was partly to honor the immortal life her mother was never allowed to live.

Arthur was undoubtedly curious, but he was smart enough to keep those curiosities to himself around such a sensitive matter. Discussing the particulars of the ascension ritual with mortals was strictly forbidden as heretical.

Everybody knew - the bodies of those candidates who failed were cremated almost immediately after death. Their existence was unofficially blacklisted. Aside from official records, no evidence existed of such candidates after failure.

Her mother's name was Farah. A secret Feria shared in confidence.

The day of their wedding arrived at last, and Arthur and Feria discovered via Joe and Hewah that the ceremony and reception had been forcefully escalated from the quiet ceremony they had planned into quite the grand affair, in that almost the entire G.O.D. high council and upper echelons of the Navy were to be in attendance.

While he was hardly surprised at such a last-minute imposition, he was frustrated at such a snub and belated rebuttal to their wishes. After all, he could hardly protest the bastards - they could freeze him solid or cut him in half with air pressure as they so wanted.

Refusing a god directly without being a god yourself was the riskiest proposition around, short of flying a G.O.D. branded ship directly into Black Armada turf. There was always an unspoken taboo in polite society around mortals contradicting, disrespecting, or going over the heads of immortals. When Serania herself pulled the strings to inject the entirety of the council, well…

Even with Hewah and Feria's involvement, Arthur's status meant the couple lacked the social standing to refuse, as he was a mere mortal.

With so little time before he was in the clear marriage-wise, he found himself filled with the blind self-confidence to stand up for himself and his new wife in a more subtle way. Arthur may not have been immortal, but an immortal had chosen him as a partner or consort, and that meant more than anyone gave it credit.

He was going to get as cheeky as he could away with.

Thus, as he stood at the altar waiting for Feria to begin being walked down the aisle by her father, he made sure to nod directly at Serania in the front row on his side of the church, noting her presence in his court and grinning at her in stupid, happy, insolent defiance.

She had clearly not expected such an open display of swagger.

He raised his eyebrows in expectation, but she just stared Arthur down with so many others watching, not once removing her eyes from his, even as Julian whispered something in her ear to elicit a soft smile.

Billy and Rebecca, Billy's wife, sat to Serania's left, and Julian sat on her immediate right.

Arthur thanked the stars that Billy had become famous enough in his line of work to ensure his protection already. He had become the biggest, most major CNG Anchor for their primetime news slot, and his face was known across Earth and the colonies.

Not everything was triumphant bragging and joy, of course, but it made Arthur happy to defy Serania in such a small way, as stupid as it was to do so. The God of Justice had already chosen to sit on Arthur's side, as some threat or coded message.

And then it began.

Hewah walked his daughter down the aisle, and handed off Feria at the altar. Then took a seat next to Julian in the front row, seeming to forget he was on the wrong side of the aisle.

Maybe he did it to protect Arthur's friends against Julian and Serania, or to send a message.

Who knows.

From there, the wedding proceeded normally, or as normally as a high-profile wedding can go.

Arthur stumbled over his lines here and there, but he didn't care. He was happy to be alive, happy to have lucked out with such a beautiful, intelligent, powerful woman, and happy to be standing there in that exact moment to revel at it all.

Serania's angry hate-on for love and awesome relationships couldn't stop those feelings in that moment no matter how hard she projected it.

Of course, what happened next had nothing to do with Serania.

This was because everything came crashing to a halt as Feria and Arthur were in the middle of exchanging vows. There was an enormous bang, and the back of the wedding hall exploded.

Despite what one would expect when there is a bombing at a wedding, there were relatively few screams. It seems the bomb had been relatively low yield - a charge designed to blast open the doors leading inside. In the first few seconds after the first bang, Arthur instinctively threw himself over Feria, as the stained-glass panels cracked in the center window above them from the force and started to break apart, spraying both the bridal party and the two front rows with coloured shards of glass. As Feria was the one with super strength, she quickly swapped spots with Arthur and he realized his initial instinct had failed to meet with reason.

Billy also covered Rebecca the minute glass started falling, obviously still carrying his own lived history of front-line experience, but Serania and Julian had already projected strange, vibrating, semi-transparent shields out of buzzing air to cover the majority of the guests from harm. It was a simple task afterward of collecting the shards into a ball and dropping them harmlessly in the corner.

What followed after the initial blast was chaos, and while most of the gods in attendance had been quick enough to throw up some defence or another, a few minor gods and some Navy officers near the back doors of the chapel had been killed instantly, unable to conjure whatever telekinetic shields or protections they could in time to stop blast shrapnel from piercing their well-dressed, albeit unarmoured bodies.

Gods had accelerated healing to a degree, Arthur was later to find out, but the sudden shock and trauma was just too much for some injuries if inflicted on them unprepared. And of course, gunshots and puncture wounds could kill them just as easily as any normal person if they hit the right spots.

Just because you could heal flesh wounds in a few days instead of a few weeks, well that didn't exactly mean nicking a crucial artery wouldn't cause one to quickly bleed out.

Even as those in the chapel were all reacting to the initial attack, the secondary assault began.

The rest of the guests began panicking as the sound of gunfire erupted from outside, and suddenly Captain Brass clued in to what was happening. In the first few seconds, Arthur had interpreted the bomb to be another elaborately disguised G.O.D. attempt on his life. But with the council and high-value military targets in attendance, he quickly quashed that train of thought.

Instead, somehow, someone had likely found out about the last-minute attendance of the council.

This was a planned attack on the core of the G.O.D. high council, hoping to sweep the leadership away in one fell swoop while they were gathered together in a less defended location.

The chapel descended further into disarray as others came to the same realization. Those without powers who foolishly panicked and bolted to escape through the now open main entrance were gunned down, as several Black Ops teams converged on the damaged church from somewhere outside.

A glance through a now paneless window by Arthur belied a lack of any specific Black Armada ostentation. Regardless of who might be behind the attack, attendees of the wedding quickly took the hint that exiting the building equated to death, and hid behind whatever they could find.

Rounds were raining in through the fragmented stained-glass windows at anything and everything that moved within.

Despite a lack of armour or weapons, the gods had their powers, and the first few assailants to burst through the door guns blazing were brought down by stunning volleys of fire bursts, ice spears, and everything else imaginable that could be conjured.

"Barricade the exits. Cassius, block the windows. Somebody, get the backup security detail here *now!*"

There had been guards outside, but calling for such backup without an immediate answer implied they were already dead. More orders were given by Serania even as Feria helped Arthur to his feet. A shard of stained glass had grazed his forehead in the initial blast and he was now bleeding fairly heavily. His bride's white dress was stained dark crimson with Arthur's blood, smeared all across the front. He held her close for a second, thankful that she was safe, and then rushed a few steps down the aisle, scanning frantically for Undelwood.

Arthur ducked down low as a smattering of white-hot plasma bolts arced dangerously close to his head, fizzling into the wall behind him. He dropped and crawled the rest of the way, finally spotting Joe lying face-down beneath an overturned pew in the second row, lying in a pool of blood.

Arthur nearly lost it then and there in his anger.

He struggled to lift the damn thing off his foster parent with no success, covering both of them uselessly in forehead blood. Luckily for the two mortals, a nearby god, who looked to be a young teenage girl, spotted his effort and hefted the pew off the unconscious judge with her telekinesis.

She left him alone to tend to his fallen friend and moved her floating cargo towards the barricade several gods and military personnel were attempting to build at the damaged church entrance at the end of the aisle.

Arthur knelt at Joe Undelwood's side, as gunfire and plasma bolts continued flying through the windows and into the churches' engraved steel doors from outside. One of the heavy doors was now stuck half-ajar in a splintered mess, with a man's fallen body and a twisted steel chair both preventing it from closing properly. None of the gods seemed to want to touch either obstacle for fear of disturbing the door even more and reducing the available amount of cover, as even now the doorway was being speckled with even more bullet and plasma holes. A few of the plasma bolts had started a fire on the outside of the door where they had recently punched through, and the barricade was soon aflame - helping obscure those inside, but simultaneously filling the church with thick black smoke.

"Joe, please be okay, come on."

Arthur lifted the older man by his armpit, tenderly, looking for where the blood was coming from. With both of them coated in fresh blood as they were, he couldn't tell much of anything, and as Joe was unconscious, it took rolling him over to find out where he was bleeding.

To his horror, there was a large fragment of wood embedded in the center of Undelwood's back, and Arthur dared not move it, so instead he dragged him towards the front of the church on his stomach, hiding his unconscious body with Feria behind the front-most row of pews.

He knew it wasn't smart to move someone with a back injury, but if the choice was death or paralysis, he knew he'd take the chance. The officiant of their wedding had taken cover behind the altar itself, and was too busy having a nervous breakdown to help in any way whatsoever.

The strike team tried several times to force its way inside, to kill or capture the gods hiding within before any help arrived. However, despite their best efforts, every offensive quickly stalled, and a few black-clad bodies soon lay around the entrance and some windows as a result - repelled or felled by the angry powers of the gods within.

The valiant defense of the main entrance now being fought by some feisty lesser gods deterred the enemy, and the assault concentrated on the windows instead, with several weapons being appropriated by military officers or gods from the fallen enemies who had attempted to clamber over the glass-strewn windowsills.

The open space where the stained glass had been was now an open corridor for gunfire and projectiles being sent back and forth, with most grenades redirected by telekinesis before they detonated.

At least the height from the ground on the other side prevented clambering invasions.

"I'll take care of Joe, see how you can help my father!"

Arthur got to his feet and scanned the entry points in an attempt to scavenge for some sort of weapon. His lack of experience on the ground outside of basic academy training left him next to useless outside of some simple weapons knowledge and emergency boarding training.

Regardless, he scrambled to the barricade where Hewah was directing the efforts of other gods and Navy staff.

There were only so many gods in attendance, and they flung bolts of fire, arcs of electricity, and bursts of highly pressurized air out the windows around him, with some even hurling objects with telekinesis at random out whatever entryway they could fit them through. Apparently, nobody had thought to bring a gun to the wedding, save the few fallen security guards killed outside the main doors. The ammo in the few captured weapons was also quickly running out.

"Somebody shit the bed here."

A grotesquely obese God in a white suit wheezed the complaint, even as he grunted to telekinetically hurl pew fragments out the window closest to him with far more force than his compatriots.

"Shut up Bub."

Julian commanded, and the rotund man fell sullenly to his task of defence, his body continuing at sweating profusely through his white suit. He continued murmuring unhappily to himself as he fought.

That's when Arthur noticed one of the two dead security guard's submachine guns lying just outside the chapel doors, easily a quick sprint and a jump over the flaming barricade. The strike team was pressing, and a middle-aged looking asian god shrieked as a bolt of plasma caught her in the side of the ribs. She went down gasping for air as her pale blue dress instantly burned through and her skin bubbled and blistered open. The bolt crackled out of existence, and blood poured from the puncture and over the burned edges of the gaping wound. Arthur didn't look to see if she was healing or not.

"THOR, get Ares into cover."

An older, greying man dragged her back, attempting to staunch the blood and pus flowing from the freshly burned hole. Despite the well-coordinated defence, the enemy was getting more and more aggressive as it too dwindled in number. Outside, attackers threw grenade after grenade at the barricades in an effort to blast them apart, and the enemy even had some brave melee-quarters in packs to rush the windows and door, likely in an attempt to break the stalemate.

Several of those without powers were quickly killed by grenade shrapnel or stray bullets from what the gods missed, with the survivors beginning to fall back and seek shelter at the back of the church.

The gods dragged the remaining pews around the altar for a second line of ramshackle defence as they went.

Arthur looked from face to face.

He had to do something.

Anything.

He waited for a brief lull in the firing, and then sprinted towards the propped door, leaping the barricade and reaching his arm out through the flames to snatch up the SMG from the dead security guard outside, their nearby body riddled with shrapnel and bullet wounds. He pulled back and stalled once he had it, blinded by the sudden light outside and pondering the propped open door he had emerged through.

Bullets and plasma rounds peppered the space around him.

He considered falling back to the altar, but ended up leaping backwards in a mad scramble as two men in black combat armor rounded the corner of the nearby hedges just past the flames and started shooting. There was a muffled thud from further inside the church, and he fled from them backwards, through the gap and further into the church, spraying the SMG in short bursts through the barricade behind him.

Everything had changed in the few seconds he had been gone, with several people bleeding out on the floor, including several lower gods. The attacking soldiers had moved just outside the windows on the sides of the church, actively ducking out from the edges and firing into the room. Arthur could see the muzzles of their guns flashing in the light just beyond the windowsills.

"ARTHUR."

Feria's shriek caused him to look back at her, right as a plasma bolt breezed past his head. His cheek instantly flushed bright red from the super-hot blue-white energy and blistered slightly in small bubbles. He instinctively turned on his heel and squeezed off a short burst into the black armored man now standing and firing through the gap in the door, who had begun following him inside.

The first few slugs hammered into his padded combat vest, knocking him back, but the last few pierced through the goggles of his visor, spattering blood and brain matter backwards across on the brick steps.

It was not the most intentional of volleys, but it had worked regardless.

He started firing at the second man he saw, but his shots were irrelevant, as an enormous fireball thrown from Hewah to his left soared past and caught the second attacker in the chest. The man made an effort to duck uselessly to save himself, but he was much too late as the ball erupted on contact, blowing apart the majority of his torso. His corpse fell uselessly over the corpse of the comrade as his remains continued to smoulder with a wet crackling sound.

Arthur continued his retreat to Feria backwards, swinging the barrel of his SMG wildly from window to window, waiting for any sort of shot. The blood on her wedding dress had dried slightly in the last minute or so, fading to a rusty brown, and he damned everything he could damn, remembering that this should be his wedding day.

Of course there had to be an attack on his fucking *wedding day*.

No time for thinking.

Arthur spun and hit another soldier with a quick-trigger burst as he clumsily attempted to scramble over the nearest windowsill, pouring at least four bullets into his shoulder and neck. As he redirected to a clatter at a window to his right, however, his gun clicked harmlessly with the next pull of the trigger.

"I'm out!"

He shouted to the gods nearby, and scrambled backwards, deeper into cover next to Feria as the gods continued their defense without him. There was no way he could grab another weapon without taking a bullet himself.

The enemy was getting desperate, and pushing their advantage.

Undelwood was still bleeding, and Arthur placed a bloody finger on Joe's neck for a brief heartbeat check. The pulse was sluggish and weak at best. The younger man started compressions as best he could from Joe's side, cursing brutally with every chest thrust to stay alive. It was all more difficult to do while actively trying to avoid thrusting the shard of wood deeper into his back.

The sickening thing about proper compressions, Arthur learned at the academy, is that it often required one to break several ribs to be effective. But it was the only way.

Feria continued defending them with streamers of fire, even as Arthur frantically pumped Undelwood's chest, but the Judge made no immediate signs of reviving.

The god in the blue dress had stabilized herself, getting Hewah to cauterize her injury somewhat via flame with a pained scream. She was now staggering over to them, even as she was still clutching her side and weeping pus.

Her makeup had caked across her cheeks with a mixture of sweat and blood. She took one look at Undelwood, and gently pushed Arthur aside.

"What are you…?"

She simply shushed him and put her hands on Undelwood's chest. Her hands began to glow a soft yellow and Undelwood's skin tightened as whatever powers she utilized began to work on him. Arthur pressed his head against Joe's collar and tried to listen for a heartbeat. With the touch of his head, Joe jolted, and started breathing faster, making quick sputtering sounds and coughing up sputum.

The shard of wood remained, but the blood stopped seeping as heavily.

The woman leaned back and clutched her side, emitting the same yellow glow to her own injury now that she was in cover.

"He's stable now, but he's got a puncture wound to the spinal column. My powers are no good for serious spinal injuries, only flesh wounds and organ failure."

Arthur made a pained face, wanting to protest her angrily in the heat of the moment, but she shook her head dejectedly and that shut him right up.

"There's only so much my powers can do. I've stopped the bleeding, and settled his heart-rate, but I can't just heal damage wherever I want, it's too risky. The stress might kill him when he's like this. Guardian medicine is better for mortals."

Arthur rubbed his temples, a roaring pain searing with every one of his own heartbeats. The goddess noticed the fresh blood on his forehead, and the burn blisters on his cheek, and moved his hands away to complete the same healing on Arthur's forehead gash and blisters. The blisters faded down to the white of dead skin, and the gash shrunk smaller and stopped bleeding as heavily. The thumping in his head faded away somewhat.

"Arthur, are you okay?"

Feria asked the question, and he had to shake his head to clear the buzz of sound in his ears to hear her. The gunfire had only intensified, but the attackers, despite their apparent urgency, were hesitant to venture into the chapel head-on, en masse. Serania was still shouting orders, snapping at those without weapons to help build the defences, but only a few scattered non-god survivors were actually following her commands. Many were frozen in fear or huddling into cover, content to let the immortals do the fighting for them.

"I think so."

Feria gripped his arm tightly, before slapping him lightly in the face.

"You're a fucking idiot for being so risky. Not to mention that burn would have scarred the hell out of your face if it weren't for Aeres."

He smiled slack-jawed back at her and she forced his mouth to hers for a sloppy kiss that tasted of blood and sweat. Dizzy, he hesitatingly got to his feet. The ringing hadn't stopped, so he must have been deafened somewhat by the explosions, because a slight buzz, albeit faint, was ongoing. Aeres, surprisingly, had passed out again next to the judge. Arthur huddled down and ducked over to the God of Justice. She barely seemed to notice him as he approached.

"Serania, m'am, how can I help?"

She looked back and stared down the rims of her black-rimmed glasses at him.

"You've already scored at least two kills, so you've done far more than the snivelling cowards hiding in the back, Captain Brass. Go sit down and tend to the wounded. There's a force en route to deal with the Executioners, so all we have to do now is survive until they get here."

His mouth dropped open slightly.

Serania had been busy.

However, she seemed to take his pause as ignorance.

"Black Armada's assassin unit, Brass. It's why we haven't finished them off already. They're trained as God-killers."

He nodded. The plain black armor without the famous black "X" of the Armada finally made sense – if they were indeed Black Armada, this could be a treaty breaking situation, and things would get far worse.

She smiled at him, which was unexpected for how brutal she had always been wherever the topic of Arthur Brass was concerned.

"I'm sorry this had to happen during your wedding, Captain. Julian will be chastised for his failure here."

Her apology was completely unexpected, delivered in a somber tone, as if it were merely a flower mix-up or somebody hacking too loudly during the vows.

"It's *all right* m'am. I apologize for the grin earlier."

She waved him absentmindedly back toward the altar with the others.

Maybe... Maybe they'd be able to see eye to eye after all?

Undelwood was regaining consciousness, and was now frantically looking around for Arthur, very obviously concussed.

"Arthur. Arthur. Thank the gods you're safe."

He knelt down beside Joe, just as a rocket propelled grenade exploded against the barricade, sending shrapnel in every direction. Most of the gods were ready enough to put up shields or hit the floor, but one poor god was too slow, and Arthur watched as several pieces of shrapnel entered her and then exited the opposite side of her body in a spray of bloody fragments.

She arched backwards as if it were all happening in slow motion.

"ATHENA."

Screamed the grey-haired older god, Thor, and he rushed to where she lay, pooling blood on the floor in excess.

A younger man in his thirties also sprinted to her, but even as the two knelt by her side, attempting to take her pulse, everyone in the church could see that she was already dead.

Aeres hadn't regained consciousness, and was the only healer from what Arthur had seen.

"Barriers on those windows, NOW."

Shouted Hewah, and the gods began a ploy to simply cover the windows against any other explosives. They switched tactics, blocking the enormous windows with telekinetically held barriers and objects, rather than actively attacking anymore. In reply, rockets and explosives began slamming into the heavy stone sides of the church itself even more ferociously, and concrete, stone, and plaster sprinkled and fell from the arched ceiling like fresh snow.

Part of the roof near the door collapsed, but the heavy timbers bracing it failed to budge and bring the rest down. Arthur watched as one unlucky man was killed outright from a large piece of stone debris hitting his head with a gruesome crunch.

He wasn't even able to shout out a warning in time.

This final stalemate continued for several more tense minutes, before help arrived at last, a mixture of jet engines roaring and rotors chopping the air outside in a frenzy as the sound of high velocity anti-infantry rounds cracked in staccato.

A matter of minutes later, G.O.D. Seraphs and Shocktroopers in white armour stormed the church, forcing the partially blocked door open with a hydraulic battering ram and scattering the flames to either side to make an escape route.

None of the attackers remained alive, with most of them spread in pieces across the wildflower fields of grass outside from the firing of the anti-infantry guns.

Things slowed down from there, once the building was secured and a perimeter was established, and field medics followed the troopers in to tend to the wounded. The first priority was evacuation, and civilian survivors were quickly escorted outside to waiting transports which arrived and departed like swarming bees.

People in white combat armor were everywhere, most of them G.O.D. soldiers tasked with escorting the higher-profile guests to immediate safety, or who held the defensive perimeter around the badly damaged church.

The idyllic church in the middle of the field had been reduced to a smoking husk, with gaping holes where the various stained glass windows had been, and black soot caking the majority of the walls.

Gunfire and explosions had been replaced with a mess of barking orders and the roar and thumping of transports. The ceremony and reception grounds had become a warzone.

What should have been the happiest day in Arthur's life had been completely and utterly ruined.

CHAPTER 14: HAIR OF THE DOG

"Honeymoon is a funny word. The moon isn't made of cheese, so why the hell is there honey involved?"

The gods moved to circle their fallen comrades.

After Arthur made certain that Undelwood had been placed on a stretcher and evacuated, he too wandered tentatively over to the group of immortals, waiting quietly behind his wife in somber silence.

None of them seemed to notice his presence, or even care that he was still alive.

"Athena was our historian, so we'll have to announce her research projects to be on hold."

Serania was nonchalant in musing over the options. Her voice lacked empathy of any kind for her fallen comrade, even as she lay there circled by peers. Only the older man, Thor, was welling up. The rest seemed more frustrated and annoyed, than actually trapped in the early stages of grief.

This was a normal that Arthur was struggling to process. Perhaps when one lived thousands of years, even the lives of immortal colleagues were easy to disregard as irrelevant in the grand scheme of things.

"Well, I'm not sure Odin is ready to take her council seat yet. He's barely into his apprenticeship, and has several years of training to complete, first."

Hewah murmured his reply as half-answer, half protest.

"We should use her body for propaganda. Embalm it perhaps? Maybe use it as some sort of paraphernalia for possible investment? We can say she died in battle; that much is true. And it looks to be a thinly veiled Armada attack. They were Executioners, I'm sure of it."

The obese god speaking waved the end of his ivory walking cane at the corpse as might a butcher regard a cut of meat, and the reaction was mixed. Odin, the 30 something looking God, glared at him with pure unadulterated hatred in his eyes.

The rage at such indecency was clear.

"I'll permit propaganda if it aids the war effort, but I will NOT shame her memory by slapping her face on T-Shirts or by putting her corpse on display. We must uphold our status as hallowed immortals in the eyes of the public. So show some respect, Beelzebub. She served with us for over seventeen-hundred years, and I doubt she'd appreciate your ideas, were you lying on the ground and not her."

Serania was curt and cold, so Beelzebub huffed loudly without responding and waddled away from the circle, obviously annoyed with her. His white suit was stained terribly with more sweat than blood.

"Well, I think Odin would be fine for the job."

Explored Ares, now awake but clutching her side through the hole in her burned blue dress. Her breathing still came raggedly. She had woken up after help had arrived, yet was struggling even now. Clearly her powers couldn't completely heal the damage, merely make it tolerable as her ascended form stitched up the damage.

"We could say that with her last breaths, she asked that Odin take her place."

The probe came from the fop, Julian, and there was a chorus of murmured agreement.

"Brass."

His name snapped him back to reality, and Arthur suddenly came to the conclusion that he probably shouldn't have been listening in on this private gathering of ascended souls, even with the shields of his wife and father in law.

Serania was staring at him with that blank gaze she seemed to do so well. The one that burned holes in his body.

"I want to thank you again Brass, were it not for your help, Ra would be dead along with Athena."

A dark-skinned Arabic man wearing a dark grey suit with gold trim, adorned with various necklaces and bracelets stepped forward and took Arthur's hand to shake with both of his own.

"Yes, Captain. I indeed thank you. You killed the man who had me in his sights as he came through the window. There was no time for me to turn and defend myself, according to Kellen, and I would have joined our comrade Athena, had you not killed him."

Arthur continued to shake his hand noiselessly, equal parts humbled and terrified by the acknowledgement. His hand kept shaking on autopilot long after it would be polite to cease.

"No problem, sir."

Serania was still gazing at him wordlessly and he continued to wither under her sight. No matter what, he was still unable to read her expressions, and after gloating so openly before everything went to shit, he was sure there would be hell to pay somehow.

"How long have you served in the Navy again, Brass?"

Serania asked the question rather carefully, already knowing the answer and only asking for the sake of formality.

"About three and a half years, m'am. Give or take, since I left the Academy."

Arthur looked to Hewah and then Feria for reassurance. Feria's eyes narrowed in suspicion, fearing for how her partner might be manipulated next, but in the end, said nothing.

"Well, Brass, it seems you're more capable than you look. Perhaps a seat on the admiralty board might be a suitable reward for your efforts over the last three years, as we seem to be missing some of our admirals after today… Especially a key admiral responsible for sending a certain transmission that almost lost us the *Asalia,* once upon a time."

She smiled at him, breaking the somber tone. Her smile terrified him more than the stern librarian expression she usually wore on her face.

"Your actions on that frigate proved you to be more than capable at the helm of a ship, and your experience on the *Princely Disposition Under Duress* gives you fleet action experience… So perhaps you might have the same touch with a fleet of several ships under your own command."

The smile turned upwards, into a sort of morbid amusement.

"We need skilled leaders in difficult times, especially after we lost *Seed of the Emperor.*"

She turned to the rest of the gods.

"Would the council support my decision?"

The majority of the inner circle nodded their heads, with the lesser gods still in attendance standing idle. Arthur noticed that Hewah failed to nod, and The God of Fire's irises now dug into him as Serania's had previously. Arthur was left trying desperately to ascertain what he might be thinking.

Feria gave him a worried look.

"My son in law still needs to be married properly before we send him out into space to die with a fleet, councillors."

The injured god Ares, wincing as she moved to him, leaned on Arthur's shoulder with her free arm for support.

"We'll have to reschedule your wedding, no doubt, as I hardly think you'll want this fiasco to mark what was supposed to be your happy day. I second Hewah's modification."

Arthur broke into a small smile at her comment, because Hewah was right. He had no intention of being shipped out to the frontier again the very next day before he was properly married to the love of his life.

The gods nodded assent, and began to file out, with the exception of Serania, Hewah, and a bald god who had stayed silent for the entire duration. He was a serious and dangerous looking man, but spoke with wisdom and discipline.

"I see potential in him. It's a pity that the public can't know what happened here today."

The bald god spoke the latter part of the sentence aloud to nobody in particular, and Hewah smirked. Serania became suddenly pensive at his involvement, with her face going solemn and still.

It was a subtle change, but it was there.

It seemed like this bald, dark-skinned god might have a considerable amount of sway within the high council.

Arthur bowed his head with fatigue, and after a brief moment, took Feria by the arm, intending to lead her away. However, trying as he might to stay upright and support her, he leaned on her heavily instead, suddenly overwhelmed. She made no signs of discomfort or effort, strong as she was.

The benefits of her ascension were coming into play yet again to flip the script on Arthur's expectations. It was a pleasant surprise with how fatigued he felt. It was nice to be supported once in a while.

The black god turned to him before he could retreat, and offered his hand.

"You can call me Cassius, The God of Earth."

Arthur shook it.

"Come see me on The Hub sometime. I'd love to speak with you more in-depth. And I do sincerely apologize on behalf of my colleagues and I for what happened here today. If we hadn't been in attendance, this wouldn't have happened."

Arthur shook his head to dismiss the apology. The man seemed soft spoken and sincere. Arthur couldn't help but feel humbled at his earnest nature despite the mixture of fatigue and a pounding head. It wasn't often an immortal god put themselves on the same level as a mortal.

Cassius turned and strode from the church, and the gods slowly trickled out behind him.

Arthur and Feria were some of the last to leave, and it was then that his vision began to blur.

Feria caught his arm as he slumped, half-conscious against her side.

"I think you lost a lot of blood."

Feria murmured in his ear even as she helped him hobble past the coroners coming to remove Athena's body. The couple limped over to a waiting transport, one of several more Aggies and Betties that had landed in a defensive position around the church.

There were now Seraphs, Shocktroopers, Medical Corps, and a new addition – bureaucrats, everywhere. The latter were doing everything that one would expect after a major skirmish. Personnel in white darted to and fro, tagging enemy bodies and weapons, loading corpses into body bags, tending to the wounded, and helping the last few guests previously trapped inside the church into transports after initial screening and interrogation.

"All this reminds me of my earlier days traveling the frontier. You'd constantly see scenes like this in the middle of the street. Always for something different. Terrorist bombs, drug deals gone badly, hits, the works. This one time on Greasy Knuckle I watched a purple haired woman with a cleaver take out over 10 gang members in a drug-fuelled rage while I watched from a second story window."

Arthur's head tilted almost 90 degrees. He felt delirious.

Was all of this real?

"Really?"

"Oh yeah, every neutral territory planet has its share of raiders, revolutionaries, pirates, and the like. People die all the time out there. Had to kill a few bad men and women myself."

It was hilarious how Feria could so calmly discuss murder after such an event.

An event on their *wedding day.*

He staggered again, starting to collapse completely this time. He kept trying his best to hold onto his vision as it went dark and blurry, shrinking to a pinpoint with orange and black skirting in around the edges.

Feria caught him under a single arm and hefted him up through the side sliding door of an Agatha with a gentle push.

Arthur vaguely recalled her talking to the pilot, and then she got in beside him.

Arthur felt frantic all of a sudden.

"Joe. I need to know if Joe is going to be okay..."

He remembered speaking the words, before immediately afterwards slumping into her blood-stained bosom.

He blacked out completely then, with the sudden lifting of the Agatha and the forces of gravity pushing his body to its limit.

What the hell had happened?

CHAPTER 15: A LOVE OF MASKS.

"It's often easier for the unscrupulous to tell a smaller truth and keep the bigger ones hidden away for later. Technically... You aren't telling a lie that way. You're merely lying by omission."

Arthur would go on to drift in and out of consciousness for the rest of the week, waking up several times in an unknown hospital only to pass out again. He received several blood transfusions over the course of his stay, but his D-level celebrity status and apparent value to the G.O.D. kept him stuck in bed until he was deemed one hundred percent fit for duty.

The next couple weeks after the hospital were somehow even more hectic, as the bureaucracy stormed his world in force for a second time now that he was able to move and talk. There were legal documents, non-disclosure agreements, medical waivers, marriage re-arrangements to work out, and numerous legal hurdles to jump in order to get himself more time off duty.

Funny how the gods often said one thing, but the bureaucracy then did the exact opposite.

On top of it all, there was the effort of trying to find time to fulfil the mysterious summons he received repeatedly every few days from the office of one "Cassius, God of Earth."

One would think that an attempted serial killing at a wedding should be devoid of any paperwork afterwards for the victims, but there it all was.

Arthur was getting very good at paperwork, much to his disappointment.

As Joe was bedridden, Feria stayed with Arthur at Undelwood's home. But she was often off doing her own thing on the few days when she wasn't running around the house playing nursemaid and treating him like a helpless infant.

He could tell she enjoyed babying him, as much as he despised it.

Despite the "big bad immortal" she was in reality, Feria loved throwing on the disguise of a concerned partner in micromanaging his recovery.

Of course, the various media agencies threw him and Feria into the spotlight again after his
"injury in the field." It started with running biographies, old newscasts, and interviews of his past Naval actions, including the now famous post-*Asalia* meetup with Billy. The propaganda machine plastered his face across the galaxy *again* for his "heroic actions while being boarded by pirates," sold part and parcel in the mainstream media thanks to the scab now healing across his forehead.

The media circus didn't let up as easily this time, either. Doctored biographies, inquiries into Feria's life, and conspiracy theories or rumor mills popped up on every channel and internet blog. Even worse, the public lapped up the controversial fact that Feria was not only an ascendant but also two decades his senior, spreading some awkward bad press due to her status as an adored celebrity and sex icon in the media.

For most gods, this would hardly be a problem, as the G.O.D. could just lean heavily on the media. But Arthur's inclusion seemed to change the narrative of the story, and allow for an ascendant god like Feria to really be scrutinized for the first time in post-veil history. What were the power imbalances and dynamics of gods dating or marrying mortals, let alone the highly controversial norms around taking mortal consorts?

It was amusing and frustrating that he wasn't even allowed to do another interview to clear anything up, despite the news being leaked by someone within The G.O.D. that an Armada assassination attempt on the gods had been foiled at his wedding.

The propaganda machine had to work overtime to quash the rumors, and when the rumors proved impossible to quash, it worked double-overtime to pretend that the fabricated "pirate boarding" and the wedding attack were separate events.

It continued to get messier and messier, angering the general population at such double standards, and even led to a push by the high council to reinforce cultural norms for immortals.

Almost always, gods preferred to take consorts rather than marry, or at the most, they only intermarried to other gods of various ranks - knowing it would eventually end in divorce however many decades or centuries later.

But this time, possibly for the first time since the factions and immortals had become public in the 2040s, the propaganda machine had failed, and it opened up the love-lives of the gods to the public for consumption.

There was open public outcry at both Arthur and Feria of course, with many young men who pined after her as a celebrity demanding the marriage be cancelled or disallowed. G.O.D. channels pushed the consort angle, which didn't help their case.

It made Arthur want to marry Feria all the more, if only to be defiant.

And now, Feria herself, who before had merely been a footnote to the Guardians of Destiny, was now forced to fight for the right to make her own decisions and break with tradition. She was absolutely outraged at mortals wanting to dictate her love life, but was forced to keep quiet, hidden outside the public eye as much as possible at the request of her father.

Hewah himself was used to the fame, which was much easier to ignore when he was often far away from everyone else in the depths of space. But this was an entirely different sort of fame - one that he was completely unprepared for. Worse, getting involved in his daughter's affairs would only make the situation far worse and open up the high council to more scrutiny.

Something the Guardians couldn't tolerate.

Perhaps it was better that the public simultaneously loved and hated Arthur and Feria as a couple, as an alternative over the whole of the populace panicking, knowing the truth.

The location of their wedding on Earth itself was still secret.

The public couldn't know.

Knowing Earth was a battleground again, and that the core worlds were unsafe would surely incite mass hysteria. The Guardians preferred to keep the treaty, at least for the time being, so the Armada's brazen breaking of The Sol Treaty in an attempt to wipe the Guardian leadership off the board was a quiet debt to be called in later.

It was stressful, to say the least. Arthur's clique suspected Serania's subtle legal involvement against them almost the entire time as each small new development surfaced. Her false praise of him after the attack was revealed through Hewah to be an attempt to endear him to her and thus more easily dispatch him as a tool of the opposition block.

Cassius was now involved, a "neutral party" on council, but Hewah declined to state how The God of Earth factored in exactly, aside from letting him know that the two were "friends."

What it boiled down to was that Cassius would play the cards Cassius wanted, regardless of what Serania or Hewah desired.

The G.O.D. hierarchs could certainly be of many minds all at once.

Through the chaos, he felt terrible for Joe Undelwood, his guardian and pseudo-godfather, as the judge underwent procedure after procedure to try and fix his damaged spinal cord from the injury that had mostly rendered him a parapalegic.

Despite highly advanced medicine, Joe was only able to regain partial use of his legs, and swapped often between crutches and a wheelchair just to get around. He had made a point of declining the prosthetic replacement limbs and exoskeleton offered to him, not taking well to the idea of 'noisy machinery' that required recharging, or the notion of having himself, a "strong man approaching sixty" relying on cybernetic augmentation. He even declined the proposition of experimental nanobot injections that would work from inside his natural body to let him walk again, citing fear of "creepy crawlies."

Arthur never would understand the machinations in the minds of some.

Arthur spent much of his free time at Undelwood's bedside. Between the surgeries and Arthur's legal meetings, the young charge did his best, choosing to keep Joe company by chatting over games of chess and cards. Arthur lost almost every game of chess he ever played against Joe; a skill he swore he would improve insofar as he saw it related indirectly to his skills as a naval commander.

Upon Undelwood's release from intensive care, he was gifted an early retirement from the British and G.O.D. joint legal systems for a vague sentiment of "services rendered." In addition, there was a sizable fund granted to him through a British Government and G.O.D. joint disability pension that would allow him to live fairly lavishly despite his situation. His inability to work within the G.O.D. any longer bothered him to no end, but no amount of preaching to Hewah would change things, as Hewah was forced to keep out of the affairs of Arthur and anyone close to him for as long as the media circus was playing itself out.

Arthur saw the forced early retirement as Hewah protecting Joe, even against the man's own wishes. It led to some deeper thoughts. What might he himself do were he to somehow survive his five-year tenure with the G.O.D. and be similarly dismissed into retirement? Would a position as an admiral mean he was beholden beyond his five years of service?

The great thing about a military career, he realized, was that while one was on duty, there was no way to easily spend your money, and you were completely taken care of in regards to room and board.

So of course, your wages just kept piling up back home in your accounts.

He had never been great with money, so this suited him just fine. He swapped between staying with Joe and Feria during his leaves, and continued the habit of hardly touching his rapidly accumulating wealth, which spiked upwards sharply with the change over to an Admiral's rate of pay.

He begrudgingly accepted that his life was not entirely his to control anymore, so money was the very last thing on his mind. Even more hilariously, the G.O.D. hired ghost writers to begin selling a heavily doctored version of his life story, and he'd stand to receive a tiny portion of the profits, not that he wanted or needed *that money.*

He was reminded of the excessively fat Beelzebub, God of Pestilence, wheezing about income for the Guardians of Destiny coffers in a similar fashion as to how he had sought to sell the corpse of a god back to the public at profit.

All this talk of finance annoyed him, and he began to think about the near-possibility of his leave ending and rejoining the Guardian Navy as an Admiral proper, something he could hardly be mentally prepared for in any honest method.

A month after his botched wedding, after finally being cleared for travel by a doctor, and sorting out the numerous book deals, interviews, propaganda pieces, and other media issues, he was cleared medically to travel via space-flight.

The doctor who assessed him for duty was nice enough, telling him in a worrying voice that she hoped he would reconsider space travel so soon after the injury, as she couldn't accurately predict how it would affect his blood pressure or his equilibrium.

He smiled at her politely and agreed, but went to book the flight to The Hub through his Naval channels shortly thereafter anyways. He left for the space station the following morning on a Sophie transport, outbound with supplies for the station.

Feria made an enormous fuss about the visit when he told her of his plans for the short trip, yelling at him for almost an hour.

"We aren't even married yet, and you're already zooming off to space again?!"

"Feria, he-"

"No Arthur Brass, I'm pissed that you'd even consider trying to head up there while you're still healing from an *assassination attempt*."

He let her keep going for a long while, only saying key points in-between segments of her extended lecture. Eventually, she noticed his polite silences, and knowing they were equally stubborn, she gave in and let him go.

She did give an ultimatum that he check in with her via text message the minute he left the station for the return trip home.

The Hub was a large orbital installation hidden in high orbit above the Earth near a Lagrange Point, permanently cloaked via an array of light diffuser relays spread out in a grid around the station proper. It was the former centre of the G.O.D. leadership and military, since long before the organization went public. Despite being the site of such great battles as *Lamentation Day*, it was now largely defunct as a result of the Sol Treaty.

However, it was still no joke as one of the most protected installations in all of G.O.D. Space, with damn good reason.

The Hub was almost holy ground to the Guardians of Destiny. It had been their headquarters for centuries - the earliest permanent space station in the Solar System, and the home base of the Guardians long before they ever revealed themselves to the general population below amidst the dropping of the veil.

After Lamentation Day, the Armada had tried to attack the station at least once more in the station's recorded history, at least as far as Arthur knew.

Officially, the second battle for The Hub had led to the Sol Treaty being signed, and the G.O.D. had very rapidly decided to withdraw from the station as a central seat of power, deeming such a vulnerable position to be too hazardous in the event that the Armada attacked a third time.

Arthur knew from his studies at the academy that after the treaty, the Guardians of Destiny chose to move the bulk of their military to *Dhekar-Qiraj*, a previously seeded and excellently terraformed tropical world that hosted the largest Guardian military-industrial complex in Central Universe.

Dhekar-Qiraj was even more defended and jealously guarded than even the mighty G.O.D. inner core world colonies of *Holy Roman, Gift of the Ancients*, and *Peace Cross*. He himself had only ever been to *Holy Roman*, but every military man knew of *Dhekar-Qiraj*.

It was possibly the safest planet in the G.O.D. territories.

Perhaps when he started work as an admiral he'd be relocated there. Sitting back at HQ, which also doubled as a tropical paradise? Well, that sounded far better than floating out in the black, patrolling forgotten backwater worlds and rocky asteroid belts.

The initial move from years back, and the logistics of *Dhekar-Qiraj* were a fiercely guarded secret to all but the captains and crews of the relocation fleets assigned to the task. One more reason to keep his head down on the trip to The Hub. Julian and The Eye had numerous strings woven throughout the transition and relocation, so it was pretty clear even to the lowest of grunts that anyone who blurted something out too loudly was quickly vanished.

He found it odd that even though The Hub was the ancient technological centrepiece and marvel of the G.O.D. - work was still going so damn slow in relocating it as a seat of power.

He could grasp the other nuances, or at least the religious ones - like the station being extremely holy ground. Hallowed, with the ripping up of the original Nepalese Guardian Temple from antiquity to build parts of the station with.

But why not just abandon it outright if the Black Armada could hang out on your doorstep?

Religion or not, it seemed like an enormous liability. Earth was so divided faction-wise that it seemed far too risky to hang onto the station at all, especially with the duty of having to defend a piece of religious history that didn't give you much of anything strategically.

Arthur would take the thick armor plating of a starship over a cobbled together mix of stone and steel precariously orbiting Earth any day of the week.

Or maybe it was all really just another propaganda psych-out for the people down below? Some misdirection for the public?

He knew that The Hub would be dangerous to visit from the start. Wandering around an active military base in transition was risky already without all the gods meandering to and fro in the middle of the process. If he ran into the wrong one, he could end up as a splatter on the wall with a quickly fabricated story to cover the tracks.

Serania would likely be properly pleased at that, no matter what she had said to him in person.

As he walked down the enormous bay door of the Sophie and into The Hub's central hangar for arrivals, he made note of the mixture of old and new. The entire place was built from a weird patchwork of the ancient, modern, and every era in between. He was getting chills down his spine already, and he had barely even left the arrivals hangar yet.

He was fascinated to say the least.

All of his previous Navy dispatches had been to and from crisp, clean Naval stations or refuelling and resupply depots. *Holy Roman* had been the newest of the new, and every installation there was close to spotless and well-lit. The walls were usually coated with a blinding shade of white or cream, painted or lacquered on top of the metal. Yet here on the station, most surfaces were scrawled with different languages, symbols, and iconographies. Mostly they were all relating to Guardian history and beliefs.

Despite being mostly metal and plastic, there were stone relief carvings and even wood mouldings along many of the walls and roofing panels, and fake fluorescent torches lit the corridors rather than traditional projection lights. It gave a spooky, archaic sort of feel, which he assumed was the ultimate goal for a cloaked space station that had been hanging around in orbit since mankind warred with flintlocks.

Superstitions and things only the ramblings of a madman could produce.

Each piece of artwork looked to be hand carved, representing some archaic ritual or hidden spell incantation. Scenes from Guardian history were splayed out in the varying artistic interpretations of zealots and artists.

The deeper one went into the station, the dimmer the lighting got and the more the eerie wooden and stone panelling showed up in excess.

Doing his best to shake off the unease, Arthur followed the signs leading him from arrivals to the crew quarters and bureaucratic offices, which ended up leading him on a wild goose chase. Before long, he was zig-zagging past doorways guarded by ceremonial soldiers in fancy white cloth regalia, who double and triple checked his identity card. Backtracking through the maze of art-panelled hallways, he wandered the endless ocean of corridors, completely at a loss, until a helpful engineer asked him where he was headed and pointed him in the right direction.

The Hub was maddening. Every so often, he could swear he heard chanting, as if he was being stalked by a distant mass of ghostly Gregorian monks. Coupled with the increasingly mystical décor, it simultaneously freaked him out even while it awed him.

Even though he was on the right track, he was constantly

checking over his shoulder as if a shadowy creature might materialize and drag him back into a secret passageway behind some mysterious bookcase. Nobody else he passed - bureaucrats, soldiers, or other personnel seemed to hear the chanting, as it began fading in and out of earshot intermittently. It was always just a twist and turn out of reach, and he couldn't help but paint it as a figment of his imagination.

Maybe he was going crazy after all?

He became lost a second time, as he found himself chasing the haunting sound, ignoring the engineer's instructions.

By the time he abandoned his hunt for the chanting, he had reached a uniquely god-oriented section of The Hub, based on the shifting in reliefs. This section transitioned again, with corridors and doors even more elaborately carved and decorated than what he had seen before. He was already dog-tired, having been lost for at least an hour now in the winding labyrinth.

His forehead was now pounding with every footstep he took, but he soldiered on. It took him another several minutes of wandering back and forth through this new section, staring at the titles and names on the doors and plaques in rows before he found the right one, labelled in sharp black text on a reflective gold background.

Cassius, God of Earth.

He knocked politely and entered the office with a puzzled expression on his face, wondering why such a powerful god would keep such a tiny office. It lacked any extra room or elaborate luxuries when compared to the other offices he had seen, mostly filled with white-collar workers.

Arthur was also certain he had been travelling deeper into The Hub, moving towards the center of the station... And yet there was somehow a viewport stretched out across the entire back wall behind the desk, with Luna hanging there in the distance.

The office was a soft difference from what he expected.

Plain. Orderly.

He crossed the threshold, and the mysterious chanting flared up once more behind him, scaring him half to death. When he turned to look for the source - it faded a final time, and then was gone for good. The god failed to notice it whatsoever, so Arthur shook his head and tried his best to put it out of sight, out of mind.

He saluted, remembering protocols in a formal environment, and the man finally looked up from his writing.

"Sir, I came as you requested?"

Cassius' dark brown eyes locked onto Arthur's for a moment, taking him in.

There must be something going on with these gods and their tendency to stare people down. Arthur was growing tired of the immortals' inquiring looks and these severe staring contests. The whole thing had gotten bloody annoying, and he regretted coming.

Why had he even come? Hewah's help had been enough thus far in his life, hadn't it?

"How can I help you sir?"

Arthur was hoping to break the stare, and Cassius gestured to a seat across the desk before looking down once more and continuing with his writing. Arthur tried not to smile at his use of a quill and inkpot.

Such old-school tools baffled him almost as much as Cassius' tiny office.

"Sit down Admiral. I called you here for two things, and your delay in visiting has unfortunately made one of them worse."

Cassius began his initial speech before Arthur could interrupt him with other formalities, still writing away busily even as he spoke. Arthur did as he was told, sitting in the plush, worn velvet chair across from The God of Earth.

Arthur clasped his hands together, as if that would stop his nerves from firing at lightspeed as they were now.

"The first issue is fairly simple, so let's get it out of the way first. I'm going to throw some of my weight behind your marriage fiasco, and make sure everything else goes ahead without any interjections or interference from Serania. I will make sure you are married to Feria quickly and quietly, exactly how it should have been in the first place."

Cassius' unexpected kindness broke Arthur somewhere inside, and he couldn't stop the tears from rolling down his cheeks. How could he have expected generosity from a god he barely knew?

Arthur wiped his eyes, and thanked Cassius profusely for the next minute, blubbering like a moron until the god broke his stoic silence by raising a hand to shut Arthur up.

"I have no idea why Feria is such a firecracker, but I've always liked her, much like I liked her mother. From what I've seen of your service... I find that I like you too, Arthur Brass."

Cassius smiled.

"Still, I'm not one for the politics of court and council, and so usually I prefer to remain neutral through all this council *bullshit*. I frequently have to remind my immortal colleagues that our job is *protecting humanity and their future*, not squabbling with each other over their favourite little mortal toys and playthings... Uh... No offense. Consider this as completely out of the ordinary for me, and not something to be invoked or requested again. This is a 'one and done' as far as I'm concerned."

Arthur nodded respectfully, not wanting to piss Cassius off by ranting and raving again out of turn. He quickly wiped his face clean and did his best to collect himself.

"However, the second thing we need to discuss here today is both dangerous, and risky. It's the real reason why I called you up here to meet with me."

With a wave of Cassius' hand, the door behind Arthur slid closed and a locking mechanism clicked firmly somewhere inside the wall, as the god continued.

"This will likely be new information to you. However, your new position as an admiral permits access to one of the most carefully guarded secrets within the Guardians of Destiny. So… Let me make myself clear…"

Cassius glared with the force of a thousand daggers.

"What you learn here today will not leave this room or escape your lips in public unless you are in the strictest confidence of other admirals, generals, or those on the high council. If you leak this, even by accident, I'll kill you myself, for our entire organization could be put into jeopardy."

Arthur tried not to squirm in his seat as he nodded back in the affirmative.

"Well… You are likely not aware of them, since they've been so careful to censor and obfuscate their movements and territories, but there's a third faction mucking about out there in Central."

Arthur figured he meant the various pirate alliances and smuggler enclaves he had battled before, but then he remembered what Hammad had told him before about Seeds of the Emperor falling to the Armada under suspicious circumstances.

A lot of things suddenly clicked into place.

He had to ask.

"Who, sir?"

Cassius smiled with a wistful longing.

"The Resistance, Admiral."

Arthur scratched his head thoughtfully, trying to remember his high school history days, or any other Academy tidbits he could scrounge from his brain. There had been an insurrection on Mars several decades back, even before even his father's time in the navy… But it had all transpired long before he was born, and had been quelled by the Guardians, with the hero of the day being… Some obscure soldier? Frederick Fontaine?

Who… Subsequently vanished by dying on the front lines as quickly as he had emerged.

To be honest - his upper level history classes had mostly breezed over the 2040s and 2050s sections of the course. Modern-ish history was hardly as important as the older stuff in the eyes of all his teachers. The Alexander the Greats and Napoleons of the ages. The World Wars. Age of Turmoil. Small insurrections didn't often make the cut, especially when they failed.

"I don't understand sir, it's been something akin to 40 years, hasn't it been crushed yet? Wasn't all that just before the G.O.D. went public?"

Cassius sighed and shook his head.

"I said the Resistance Brass, not the Insurrection. They're two different groups, although your timeline is mostly correct."

Cassius suddenly grew grave, and flicked the feather of the quill absentmindedly. He spun in his chair to look out at the moon, not saying anything for several minutes.

He now had Arthur's full attention.

"Your father, Captain Bradley Brass? He died in one of the first Naval actions ordered by Serania against the Guardian Resistance Army, Admiral. The Black Armada was not involved in the slightest. He specifically died in an offensive push against the defector world of Petronova, formerly a G.O.D. colony world."

Arthur was struggling to process it all.

"It was one of the first colonies to turn against us, and it was entirely unexpected that a G.O.D. fleet might not succeed at defeating the rebels. Serania and her supporters, well... They fed your father and thousands of others to the wolves, along with billions of dollars in equipment and ships. All because the council, foolishly, failed to expect any real challenge in re-acquiring the planet."

Arthur felt... Betrayed somehow.

"It wasn't an accident, and it wasn't a casualty in an offensive against the Black Armada, as we pass off most Resistance deaths to be. Apparently Serania, in her wisdom, would rather our organization be thought of as incompetent, throwing lives and resources away blindly rather than expose the real truth. The Guardian Resistance Army is a threat, so long as neither us, nor Xex can effectively pivot to deal with them out in the neutral territories."

It was several bombshells to process all at once, and Arthur tried his best to keep up. So many years of conspiracy theories, struggles, death. How many more secrets was the G.O.D. keeping?

What else was happening out there beyond the edges of their control?

"How long, sir? How long have they been out there? How have

they survived for so long? Have they allied with the Black Armada?"

He had to ask the questions. There were so many more he had to ask.

Even if he had never been close to his father, even despite the fact that the man had died when Arthur was still so young, he could hardly leave the issue untouched. He felt a wave of guilt and resentment for the G.O.D., knowing that his mother had suffered so long without knowing the truth. Arthur needed to know everything, if just to make sure his father hadn't died for nothing.

"The infamous Xex Project..."

Cassius broke Arthur out of his tornado of thought.

"You see, Brass, your father died in 2058, some years after the Resistance was formed. You mentioned the Insurrection. Ever hear in school about our trump card in putting it down?"

"Frederick Fontaine, sir?"

"Ah yes... One Frederick Fontaine, the one man who led the charge, who almost single handedly took down the entire insurrection on Mars. You ever find it odd how he just disappeared one day?"

History had lied.

"This all happened before we were forced into the public eye by Xex, so we were able to write our own history of how things transpired before anyone knew the nature of The Insurrection, none the wiser that we even existed. So how could Fontaine be a hero one second, but then get himself killed on the front lines when you yourself know that the G.O.D. loves using war heroes for our propaganda?"

Arthur already had his answer ready.

"Well, sir, the propaganda was likely changed in all that time between then and now, or made up after the fact. Frederick Fontaine probably never existed at all. He was created to save morale, as that would be the smartest idea, wouldn't it?"

Cassius nodded, solemnly.

"Gods are immortal, Brass. We remember these things. Despite the niche research arguing it, we don't forget, or go mad with time. We remember, and everyone *else* who could know the truth as well, we make sure they repeat the same history, or we silence them. That's how it's worked for centuries."

Arthur recoiled at how candid Cassius could be about it. That notion that had kept flickering to life at the back of his head for the entirety of his life, that mortals were just meat for the grinder.

It was all true, and it horrified him, even if he somehow knew the truth the whole time.

"See, these sorts of people that are the unfortunate victims of 'incorrect' history... I prefer to pay them off and settle them somewhere they can't be found - out on the frontier. When they die of old age, they take the truth with them to the grave and history is protected. But failing that, we have no choice but to dispose of them."

Cassius was speaking at the moon now, barely acknowledging Arthur's presence in the room.

"There's no statue for Xex Project One, Admiral Brass. There's no damn statue because he never died and he's still out there. Defeating the insurrection on Mars was merely his trial run."

Cassius shook his head, recalling a loss of some sort.

Arthur had no clue what the hell he was talking about.

Xex Project?

Who never died, exactly?

"X-1 defected when it came to understand the brutal necessity of our organization and what we need to do to keep order in the Central Universe. I was against the project from the start, of course. After those initial few failures, the council decided to keep the rest of the Xex Project iterations under wraps from then on. We changed that little section of history when we went public, as it was well enough after X-1 had vanished from the recent collective memory within the ranks of our organization. So, the council came to consensus. We made up Frederick Fontaine and gave him all the credit. A fake soldier taking credits for the exploits of a laboratory experiment."

Arthur had hundreds, if not thousands more questions. These were the types of secrets that kept many of the governments of the galaxy carefully eating out of the G.O.D.'s hands. And here the God of Earth was just laying it down before him as if Arthur had asked him out for a beer and they were shooting the shit.

"You keep referring to the Xex Project sir, and you keep talking about it as if it's still active. What is it? Why is it named after the head of the Black Armada?"

Cassius spun in his chair and looked pensively at Arthur again, carefully placing his fingers together in a steeple upon his desk.

Considering.

Deciding on how much he would reveal.

He eventually shrugged after a few tense seconds.

"The Xex Project was a top-secret attempt to develop a technologically advanced bioweapon. A thinking bioweapon designed to assassinate Xex in a one-on-one combat scenario. A way of ending the war, ideally. It was an unprecedented success on the battlefield, but after a while it and the little A.I. inside it figured they didn't like how we operated, in how we do our job of keeping humanity safe by imposing on it a little and keeping some secrets here and there."

Cassius grimaced.

"And at the time, some of our ranks were thinking similar thoughts. Therefore, it was easy enough for that half-metal thing and everyone else in the G.O.D. it could convince to turn traitor."

Arthur gaped.

"It was the story of Xex' defection from our ranks all over again, only with stupid ideas about 'true democracy for the masses' in lieu of Xex' obsession with authoritarian dictatorship."

Cassius sighed heavily.

"Despite it all though, at least that *thing* didn't defect to the Armada, thank the Creator."

He burst into laughter for a moment as if this top-secret universal security issue was merely a nuisance or a joke, an insect to be swatted with a bug zapper.

"We built it in a lab, with Shifter at the helm. Easy enough, right? Grow a fetus in a tank, mess with the genes a bit, and when we had grown it big enough and perfected the organic parts for a few decades, we hacked it apart and implanted it with cybernetics and weapons systems. Integrate an A.I. to share a mind and handle all the back-end systems management, and there you go."

Cassius guffawed, as if toying with life itself to create Frankenstein-style monsters was a simple joke. Arthur wasn't sure now if he liked Cassius or despised him. The God of Earth was losing more and more of his composure, chuckling and increasing in mania as he went.

He was now far from the stoic soul he had been when Arthur first entered.

Arthur was afraid. Extremely afraid.

Cassius was almost spitting the words out now with the force of his projection, and his desk was trembling without either of them touching it.

"That *thing* and his *resistance army* have been gallivanting out there in neutral space around the frontier and border colonies for *decades*. Not only did they all turn traitors, but they've been building fleets and armies to fight *both sides,* as if they *could win.*"

The increasing mania of the god was starting to make Arthur feel oddly better about his father's death, if only slightly. It was an old wound, but at least his father's enemy hadn't been a pirate or a mercenary.

If only the death of Bradley Brass hadn't been just some suicidal rush at the enemy lines.

"When that *cybernetic piece of shit* went, he even managed to convince half the damn research division, several prominent gods, and a chunk of the army and navy *to go with him.* Obviously even the rotting carcass of the Insurrection went and joined the cause too. Shifter stayed with us for one more iteration of The Xex Project, before he turned traitor too and absconded to form The Eclipse."

Cassius was starting to calm down. It was as if he was realizing what was done, was done. The desk stopped shaking, and Arthur felt his nerves settle as the tension subsided in the tiny space.

Cassius couldn't change the actual past, despite the G.O.D.'s power to rewrite history or manipulate humanity.

"While I absolutely hate the fact that we now have to bring the fight to several people I used to call my friends, Serania is forcing the rest of us to do something about it, in the name of solidarity. I'm completely fine with crushing a tin can, no matter how sharp the edges on it might be. But having to eliminate ex-colleagues is always difficult for me."

He flicked the feather of his quill again.

"And you know what, Brass? Serania is right about that. Solidarity is important to the Guardians of Destiny after two major defections in a mere five centuries."

Cassius finally started looking at Arthur again, taking in his presence and role in the room.

"Still, her wasting of resources is something I can't condone. Both The G.O.D. and the Black Armada have been putting pressure on the G.R.A. since Petronova, but the war between us and Xex stops us from wiping them out, and as a result they've grown unchecked, getting more sympathy and support in the neutral territories with every passing year."

Arthur finally understood.

All the rumors he had collected were piecing themselves together. Why the war had been stalemated for the last long while. Why neither the G.O.D. or the Black Armada had really expanded into the neutral territories much. Why *Seed of the Emperor* had been so rapidly taken off the map. Why his patrol as captain of the *Asalia* had passed by such a remote section of space near the neutral territories. Why a Armada Battlecruiser was scouting in the same region.

Arthur was now fighting against people who were fighting for what they believed in. Rebels fighting against the clandestine nature of the G.O.D. He couldn't help but feel the irony seeping into his bones, and he remembered sitting in prison for very similar reasons of defiance all those years ago.

Could he hate them enough to kill them?

All they wanted was to live independently of the immortals who had controlled every aspect of humanity for millennia, was that so wrong? These immortals like Serania who saw themselves as superior to the rest of mortal humanity because they could live forever.

Well, at the end of the day, gods were human, just like the rest. Stuck in the same cycles and psychologies. No matter how badly Serania and the council wanted to keep themselves on some magical pedestal above everyone else.

Cassius picked up on Arthur's hesitation immediately. The blood vessels were bulging in his forehead as he clenched his jaw repeatedly again and again.

Arthur wasn't sure if he was outraged at him, or at the scenario itself for a moment.

"I'm not going to tell you that we're the good guys and they're the bad guys, Admiral Brass. Good and evil *do not exist.* They are *concepts* and *nothing more.* If you looked at the whole thing philosophically, yes, all the GRA wants is democracy; some actual political representation for mortals. But look at Britain or Blend. The citizens there still vote for representatives, they still go through the process, and they *believe* they have a choice, even if we're really keeping an eye on things to keep them safe. No matter how much power we give them, we will always be the big bad authoritarian bastards in their eyes. And we're not even half as bad as Xex. He actually *mind controls his populace.* That's why I'd rather the GRA just surrender, and fight the Black Armada with everything we have."

He sighed.

"Still, if we let them get too cozy, they could cause us serious problems."

He leaned forward, and Arthur had to try his best not to instinctually recoil.

"At our core, that's what makes us different. The Guardians of Destiny are the *only* group that has Humanity's best interests *as a whole* close to our heart. Xex and his Black Armada? They want him to rule humanity as a Creator-level dictator. The Rebels? They want a shiny new form of democracy and the freedom to live however *they* want. But *we* are the ones who want everyone to flourish and thrive *together* as only humans can."

Arthur swallowed, trying to ignore the spittle that flecked his face.

"I understand, sir."

An eyebrow raised in response, and Cassius slumped back into his chair, deflated.

"*Do you?* If we're not around to stop the Black Armada, what prevents Xex and his fanatics from rolling through the core worlds, raping, brainwashing, burning, looting, and pillaging as they go? Because you should already know that is *exactly what they do when they take worlds*. You haven't seen true depravity until you see an Armada occupation. Watch the horde of mindless berserkers swarm through the streets, stabbing innocents with the *bones of their loved ones.*"

Arthur had to admit, he could see what Cassius was getting at, but even Cassius seemed to have visible doubts. The God of Earth looked distraught at the chaos of all of it, and Arthur could see the trauma that lingered there. Cassius was reliving painful memories even now.

It made sense in a sick sort of way.

"Arthur – I will repeat to you. What I'm about to say will not leave this room. Are we clear?"

Cassius waited for the nod.

"Myself and a number of the elder Gods serving in this organization lost faith in Serania a long time ago. She has too much baggage she is unwilling to let go of. The betrayal of a lover, the defection of traitors, all are commonplace in this fucked up world we live in. And she can't see the forest for the trees anymore."

He snorted with indignant frustration.

"Myself, Hewah, and others know for a fact that even if we don't agree with Serania most of the time, the G.O.D. is the only way to stop Xex and his Black Armada. We fight for the innocent just as much as we fight for the faithful. And, as I said, I dislike fighting old friends. But we don't have a choice. If we want true peace, we'll *kill them all* if we have to."

This was a fanaticism of its own, really. Gods like Cassius were far more dangerous than a mindless berserker murdering women and children in the street in the name of their god-emperor.

And that was because in their minds they were justified no matter what actions they undertook. Arthur couldn't help but wonder how close Hewah was to Cassius when it came to wartime philosophy and the nature of both the Black Armada and the GRA.

"Hewah's loyalty is worth more than mine to Serania, as she knows how dedicated I am to the cause. I won't *ever* do anything that jeopardizes the big picture. But that neutrality in being committed to a cause rather than being committed to people is worth more than anybody knows, because at the end of the day I know where I stand, and I can tip any decision the direction it needs to go once I get involved. I don't give a fuck about their petty arguments. That's because *I have a goddamn war to win.*"

Arthur's anger emerged from the hole where it had been hiding, and the emotions at his spine uncurled like a cobra ready to strike.

"No offence Sir, but you called me up into space, broke the illusion of my father's death after I had buried it, and then told me all about a conspiracy I probably shouldn't know anything about. Didn't you think that I might need some time to fucking collect myself after I was almost killed *on my wedding day*, while the entire world is debating about my status as some boy-toy prick? *What is the point?*"

Cassius stood up abruptly and slammed a fist into the table with such force that white spiderweb cracks began spreading out from his fist across the smooth granite top. Arthur could tell by the veins bulging bigger than ever before in his bald forehead that he had worked hard to control himself and not cause any further damage than just that.

"Don't you get it Brass? Can't you look at the bigger picture? *I'm doing you a favor*. I'm not telling you any of this because I give a shit who you are or what you believe in. I'm telling you this because Serania is going to issue you an official order *the minute you've been publicly promoted*. She's going to send you marching right into Resistance territory at the head of a half-assed fleet, and I'm going to be forced to watch as you get your ass blown out of the sky."

He thumbed the cracks in his desk, clearly annoyed with himself.

"And just guess who will then have to pick up the pieces, and figure out why we wasted time, money, resources, and *solid officers like you* on suicide missions against the G.R.A. when we should be fighting the fucking Armada. When the dust settles, you'll end up with the exact same obituary as your father in our record books. I don't want that, do you?"

So. There it was.

Again.

Serania.

AGAIN.

"Why? Why the fuck does she want me dead so fucking badly? Hewah is on her fucking team. It's not like he works for Xex or the Resistance or fucking *anybody*."

Cassius sat back down and rubbed the cracks in his desk a second time, annoyed that he had lost control and damaged it in the heat of the moment. The fire was gone in him, replaced by an exasperation.

The weight of centuries that Cassius had been carrying all this time.

"Brass, you remind her of the exact same people who have fucked her over in the past. You stick to your moral code regardless of what others think, you refuse to bend the knee, and as a result of both that and your stubborn anger, you refuse to keep your mouth shut when it matters most. In combat, being clever and decisive like that makes you a good leader. In this shitty political game that we gods have to play with each other, it makes you a liability, despite what you have to offer us. It's easier for Serania to direct your talent at brick walls to rid herself of people like you, the people that remind her of her weaknesses. And she will do so every single time, with complete and utter disregard for *my* war machine."

Arthur crossed his arms and tried to think of some way he could save himself with words.

"So how can I ever hope to get out of this?"

"I'm trying to give you a chance to do that."

Cassius sat up straight and leaned across the desk towards Arthur again, this time with determination rather than fatigue, anger, or frustration.

"I called you up here into space because I'm trying to rebalance the power between Serania's ass-kissers and the rest of the council. Serania's biggest issue right now is that she's flirting with emulating her old squeeze Xex, and that *fucks up my war effort.* Gods like Hewah who have the balls to disagree with her while still being allies are locked in a power play every second of every day, trying to save her from becoming what she detests most. And we all have a role in it, by doing what we can to prevent her from becoming a female copy of the one god she hates more than anything else in this god damn central universe."

Cassius fell silent, and so did Arthur.

The god turned back towards the window behind him and they sat there in silence for a while, both staring out into space in discomfort.

All the jitters Arthur had upon entering were gone. He had long since stopped caring that Cassius was a god.

Every god had been a normal human at one point.

But it definitely felt to him like some of them had forgotten it.

CHAPTER 16: BETTER THAN A POKE IN THE EYE

"What is better? To guess a hundred times and only get one right answer? Or to never guess even once but never answer wrong?"

"I'm going to provoke the Armada to give you a chance."

The God of Earth finally admitted.

"If we can press the need for an offensive, or even a false defensive against the Armada, the councillors with any sense can argue for an alternative to Serania's current Resistance proposal. We could send not just you; but entire battle-groups against our *real* enemy, rather than allowing you to be sent out completely unprepared against the Resistance to die without any real value. The Resistance is entrenched, focused on defense. You're a smart man, Arthur, and we need you in charge of fleets, not on some fucking *kamikaze run* headlong into the G.R.A. defenses, just to meet a yearly quota for attacks against the fucking rebels."

Cassius got up and moved to the whiteboard on the left wall of his tiny office where various dates and ideas were scrawled in a mixture of Latin, English, Arabic, and Spanish. Arthur was perplexed by his sudden gumption. The god grabbed a whiteboard marker and began drawing a crude map of the Milky Way, using differently colored markers for military checkpoints or bases, and marking down with red where the Armada territories and general traffic routes were. After that, he marked in black where the G.O.D.'s own borders, traffic routes, and defences were mostly positioned as countermeasures. Arthur was surprised he knew even half of what the god was drawing. Apparently, he had learned more in all his schooling and few years of experience than he had thought.

Arthur stood up and joined him.

"What are you doing, Brass?"

Cassius paused to look at his sketching.

"Planning a military offensive, Sir."

Cassius observed to the side as Arthur squiggled on the crude map, paying special attention to the direct route between Earth and *The Black*. While also an informal piece of slang for the farther reaches of space, *The Black* was the primary name for the large swaths of shipwreck graveyards, asteroid belts, and other randomly circulating debris The Black Armada used to limit access in and out of its territories.

No smart navigator, captain, or pilot would open a rift anywhere but the main Armada shipping and entry routes, as a single piece of debris or an uncharted asteroid could scuttle an unprepared ship, and that was *if* the Armada defenses didn't notice your rift and blow you apart first.

"See, we're going to have to stage the fleet buildup somewhere clearly in the Armada's sightlines. While we've traditionally wanted to keep our attacks a secret, it'd be far faster and more noticeable to the Armada to start building up a fleet right here in the Solar System, around one of the outer planets. That way we wouldn't be directly breaking the trade treaty by having too many ships in Earth's orbit, but we'd still allow the Armada to see that we're planning an attack. They might see it as revenge for the attack on my wedding that broke the treaty."

Arthur could see that Cassius had started to grasp the plan.

"I see. The Black Armada, being what it is, doesn't like to sit still and wait to get hit. Xex almost always counterattacks to force our hand early. And he'll especially want to hit first this time when he hears this specific fleet is to be headed by our most recent and most capable war-hero, one of the fastest to ever move up through the ranks."

"Exactly. So while he's bulking up defenses for his two major traffic routes leading in and out of the Armada core worlds via *The Black*, and looking for a place where he can strike at us to force our hand, we're actually gathering our strength as a *defensive fleet* from the outset, and establishing rapid response routes for wherever the attack might be. Which, honestly, is probably going to be one of a handful of frontier colonies, as they've hit *Holy Roman* and our other core worlds a dozen times at least over the years and know that they're only going to inflict minimal damage. He won't know we're baiting him, so we can hope for a sweep and then organize a real offensive afterward when the Armada plays its hand too early."

Cassius began circling possible worlds that could be hit in green.

"We're not going to draw any defensive ships or resources from anywhere serious - we'll merely syphon a few ships each from the patrol lines and major worlds, likely the ones facing Resistance turf. The Resistance might think that we're going to attack them though... The treaty is public knowledge."

Arthur frowned at the last sentence, and Cassius explained.

"Well... I normally wouldn't be able to tell you what regions the resistance holds, but, since you're the admiral in charge of this operation now..."

The god took a blue marker and drew a large circle around a

good portion of the whiteboard which was labelled as neutral space, some of which Arthur was surprised to see intersecting with their own official borders.

"So when they defected..."

Cassius nodded.

"They managed to get a few big worlds to support them almost immediately. *Petronova, Boldinstad, Gibraltar's Might...* We had to take a step back and reassess, especially after the first couple pushes to stamp them out got obliterated. We horribly underestimated them and got our asses handed to us as a result, largely due to planetside weapons batteries that make it incredibly difficult to land an invasion force. Right now, they're entrenched, especially because they have such solid production planets right in the well-protected centre of their territory."

Cassius continued drawing.

"Of course, for propaganda purposes, the G.O.D. never redrew the galaxy maps when it happened; we simply kept it a secret to everybody except a small minority at the top. We boxed them in on our side of the neutral territories instead, using Xex as the other front, and occasionally our ships out in those territories risk brief trips close to their outer lines, just to check in on and harass them. Every so often we try and invade one of their outer resource colonies to clip their wings a little, but we haven't had much success outside of keeping them contained."

Arthur dotted the line, making a mental note to draw in a few reminders.

"We *do* have a few active war-zones with them, but The Eye is careful to monitor any soldiers who fight Resistance forces, and eliminate any who risk exposing their existence. Julian is good at spreading tales about the extremely well-equipped and well-organized bandit and pirate clans in that area, so most of the time our Guardian troops see their forces as such. We funnel support to some of the larger mafias and political parties on key neutral worlds like *Greasy Knuckle* to help that process out."

Arthur began circling secondary rally points for the attack, trying to cut down their response times. Cassius threw in changes of course, pointing out where the Resistance and Black Armada were deadlocked against each other, or where Resistance shipping lanes might be located based on recent intel.

He even explained to Arthur the unique nature of the neutral, unaligned groups such as the Unitary Mercenary Guild or the Junk & Rumblers Guild and how they worked for the Resistance and Armada just as equally as The Guardians, making profits in the billions.

The general guidelines for neutral groups was that as long as they kept their mouths shut in public about their clients and contracts, the G.O.D. mostly left them alone.

They were too useful to risk alienating.

Arthur was also astonished to learn that the G.O.D. even traded with the Armada through neutral proxies in the unclaimed neutral territories at times. Which... Seemed hypocritical to an extreme.

Arthur kept working with Cassius for hours, building onto his whiteboard plan every possibility and fallback he could think of. When they were finally done, Cassius was visibly pleased, and had his assistant A.I. Terminado make a copy and forward it to Hewah, Prometheus, and a few other names in the council bloc that actively resisted Serania's dictatorial efforts. Then, he carefully erased the files and washed the entire whiteboard until it was a pristine white once more.

"I won't be able to guarantee your safety in this, Brass."

Arthur nodded in solemn acknowledgement.

"And don't forget, this might only buy you time as I bring it up to the council at the next meeting. Baiting the Armada has worked before to suck up their time and resources, but Serania will know the true ploy of it, and she's going to stick you in command of that response fleet without a doubt, which nobody will be able to stop. You have time for a wedding and not much else. And it'll be on you in the heat of battle to ensure everything goes according to plan, and that you don't die, of course."

They clasped forearms in a farewell handshake, and an odd feeling of solidarity welled up inside Arthur.

Cassius broke a smile and patted him on the shoulder. For all their differences in philosophy, they did share an affinity in some indirect way.

Arthur could feel the immortal opening up a little.

"I grew up on the Iberian peninsula, you know. Back in the Roman days before the Christians moved in. I watched my people later as they were torn apart by the fighting. Hell, watched entire family trees and portions of my own bloodline get wiped out by those Christians. So believe it when I say I don't want to see the same happen to yours."

Arthur thanked him and left with a sense of fierce resistance.

This was a way he could fight the system from within it, and not have to defect or die to get out of the council's warpath. Maybe he could even save the lives of innocents along the way that would otherwise fall victim to the Black Armada's cruelty.

He saluted Cassius appropriately as he went to leave, and started working his way back through the hallways, with the chanting picking up at the edges of his hearing again.

Even the eerie sing-song illusion couldn't defeat his sense of optimism.

At least until he ran into the last person he expected to see.

The smile on his face vanished entirely when he ran directly into Julian, the God of Darkness striding down the narrow corridor towards him.

Why were there still so many gods hanging around this abandoned space station?

"Afternoon, Admiral Brass, what brings you up into this neck of space?"

Arthur's heart was wrenched into a knot, but he tried his best to be polite.

"Just visiting The God of Earth, like he told me to do on my wedding day, sir."

Julian sighed.

"Yes, quite a pity, seems the Armada couldn't get its act together and cull the weak amongst us quickly and efficiently."

His voice was smug in that archaic, high regal, received pronunciation that Arthur hated.

His arrogance…? Well, immortality had obviously changed him for the worse.

"What do you mean, sir?"

Arthur grit his back molars and did his best to be cordial.

"Well, if The Executioners had been any bit as efficient as they were touted to be by our military advisors, perhaps I wouldn't have to watch you slink away from the station today like a snake. And perhaps that thorn in the side that you were going to marry could have been dealt with in the same stroke."

It didn't matter how stupid it was. Arthur lost it.

His fist was flying at Julian before he even realized how pathetic and futile of an action it was.

How dare this pompous piece of shit insult Feria in any way whatsoever?

Julian raised his arm, but not to deflect or stop the punch. Instead, when he closed his fist, the corridor snapped to black, long before Arthur's raised fist was even close to connecting.

His entire body constricted, as if the darkness itself was crushing every bit of his being like a boa constrictor.

Invisible hands wrapped like a vice around his throat, and he stopped dead in its tracks.

"Well aren't you slow?"

Julian's voice hissed from everywhere all at once, and the sheer stupidity of his action hit him like a brick to the face. Julian could easily kill him, crushing the life from his bones. Then he could blame it on Arthur attacking first, which the various security A.I.s and camera records on the station would somehow prove true.

Everything would end because he got mad at an immortal for talking shit about the love of his life.

The chanting grew louder and frenzied, scaring Arthur even more, trapped as he was in this pitch-black hell.

"I'm the God of Darkness, Brass. You're just a mere mortal. Just a helpful reminder. I *could* kill you, but... I'm not sure I'd get as much satisfaction from it as watching you be tossed around as a plaything by the rest of the high council."

Arthur gasped for breath as the physicality of the darkness found his mouth and began coldly coiling its way down his throat in order to begin squeezing the air out of his lungs from the inside.

It felt like ice water was being poured down his esophagus.

He sputtered helplessly.

"But, perhaps…"

The darkness withdrew in an instant, and light returned to the corridor, leaving him gasping for air on the floor.

"So, I guess it's a matter of waiting then."

Julian murmured to himself, standing where he had been previously, as if he had never moved a muscle at all.

"But aren't you Serania's boy-toy?"

Arthur wheezed, quietly, but defiantly.

"I am exactly what I wish to be, and while yes, I do enjoy the benefits of being the bedfellow of the prime god, I find it more prudent to stay aloof as well. I get to put her face to the pillow and keep my independence at the same time. *You?* Well Arthur Brass, *you* get to die out in the cold inky void of space."

That smirk of his never left Julian's face as he tossed his long blonde hair back across one shoulder and straightened the dark purple vest over his upper-class attire.

"I think I'll leave you alive for now. Serania gets annoying when she's angry, and who knows what she still wants from you before you die, *little puppet.*"

And with that, he walked right past him, stepping over Arthur's tangled legs as if he were merely the upturned corner of a rug he wished to avoid tripping on.

Arthur remembered cursing him with every expletive he could remember after he had gone, and then staggered to his feet afterward with every effort he could muster.

His head was pounding again worse than before, and he started to clue in as to the differing power of gods. His fiancée might have super strength and the ability to shoot off streams of fire, but she had nowhere NEAR the power and skill some of the council-members had.

The darkness had been horrifying, and *very, very real.*

It was a brutal reminder of his place in the hierarchy.

CHAPTER 17: A HARSH REALITY.

"Taking a long hard look at yourself can be more damaging than anything else in existence."

When he arrived home, Feria was frantic.

Even before he called ahead to let her know he was on his way back, she had somehow heard about his meeting with Cassius through her own methods, likely via her father.

She forced him to sit down and immediately threw cup after cup of hot tea his way upon arrival.

He only managed to finish the first half cup, and a few soon sat scattered across the coffee table haphazardly. She hardly seemed to notice, eventually realizing, taking, and replacing each one as soon as it was stagnant for more than a minute.

She was clearly busying herself to calm down, which was surprising considering how rarely she was ever fazed. Here was his soon to be wife, the powerful goddess without a title, waiting upon a mere mortal.

Were his chest not so damn cold, he would have laughed.

"This is getting dangerous, Arthur. You can say whatever you want, but I don't want you to die."

She had that look in her eyes he knew now by heart, where they would sparkle ever so slightly when she really wanted something badly enough. He was never sure when she did it if it was an optical illusion of his brain or not, because she usually asked him for something important after he noticed it.

Could be powers for all he knew.

"Arthur, you need to tell Serania to her face that you're willing to retire, or that you're ready to just lay down and give in to her. It's the only thing she'll understand. She sees you as a wayward toy, a man being used as a tool against her in the sandbox. If you were subservient, if you just became *her* tool, you might survive all this. My father is still known as one of her staunchest supporters publically."

Her words went right through him.

He stared first at her soft face, her dark black eyes, and the light tanned brown of her skin.

Perfect.

Immortal.

He, on the other hand, was already developing laugh lines and crow's feet from all the stress.

And yet she was the same eternal twenty-year-old who could spit in the face of mortality. No matter how much he loved her, he knew she was immortal by choice. She was given the privilege and the power to choose, and he didn't have that same privilege.

He felt guilty at his sudden jealousy.

And maybe that was quite possibly the true point in her suggestion. Did he want to grow old with her at the sacrifice of his own independence?

He couldn't think. His head was foggy. He felt trapped, like there was some obligation to the dead hanging over his head. What would his mother think? What would the man who was his father think? He needed to stand up for himself, didn't he?

"I can't do it."

She stared at him for a long time, and as if she knew what his argument would be before he had uttered a word. She stormed off into the kitchen, and started delving into the mundane act of starting some dinner as a means of cooling herself off.

Arthur was supposed to cook that night, of course.

There was an uncomfortable silence, and he came back from the washroom slowly. Caught her eye from the couch. Perceived the pure venom in it, before deciding he should leave for a little while.

They had fought before, but never over something so serious as his very life.

It was sobering, that.

He knew that somehow, he was the source of this strange weakness, and she needed space and something simple to do as a form of therapy.

It always seemed to Arthur that when someone loves someone else, they open up gaps in their soul that allow the self to bow in areas it wouldn't before. In a way, he knew he was a weakness that Feria was experiencing, and not the other way around. Feria was giving up a small piece of her immortality to a person who might just be her downfall.

A weakness for the first time in a long time.

But… He had only ever known weakness from the very beginning.

"I'm going to the pub."

He muttered it loud enough for her to hear him over the banging of pots, pans, and other kitchenware, and then winced as several pieces were audibly dented and broken in her cold fury.

He grabbed his jacket and threw on some boots without another word between them.

She made no reply to him, but as he opened the door, they locked eyes through the gap between the entryway and the kitchen.

There was a moment of crystal clarity, where they realized that they understood the point of the argument the other was trying to make. He knew he loved her. He really loved her, and he loved her especially in that moment because he felt in a roundabout way that she was promising him her immortality for as long as he'd stay with her. Regardless of whether he died tomorrow or eighty years from that very moment.

It was a monumental promise to make to a lowly mortal like Arthur Brass.

He felt selfish, and he knew she took his answer to be a rejection of her own self in some fundamental sense. Would their marriage fail as a result of her being unwilling to let him go, or would it be due to him being unwilling to let go of what he saw as his strange destiny?

Arthur left quietly, and wandered the streets around his house for a while, trying to figure himself out before going towards the nearby commercial area. When he had moved in with Feria, he had quickly scoped out the local public houses, so he knew by rote where he was headed.

He passed the giant billboards and holographic propaganda of both the "official" British government and of the G.O.D. Proper, and yet even on the civilian streets, he was haunted by the faces of generals, admirals, and other men he had known, especially the few of those who had died on his wedding day.

To make his sense of guilt all the worse, there was always that same face of the God of Justice, Serania. Her black rimmed glasses didn't help to hide that stern glare, the one that even the media couldn't help but capture as if it were right there in front of you boring holes into your flesh. The media hardly captured the beauty, either, to be honest.

It was frustrating to be murdered by such a beautiful woman.

So, would he drag as many men down with him as possible before he died? What kind of person did that make him? How many other men had died in the line of duty in the time since he was freed from prison so long ago?

Eventually he couldn't take the gnawing questions and self-doubt and moved on his parting words to Feria; hiding himself away in a pub filled with as much working-class chatter as he could find. He blended in well with his casual wear, despite lacking the grease stains and rusty coughs of most of the middle-aged men who filled the bar.

"What's with the glum face, friend?"

A particularly worn looking older man, with a large orange beard flecked with patches of grey and white. Clearly pretty liquored.

Arthur smiled, and being several beers in himself by this point, bought him a round for his bother. He did his best at answering the questions that came vaguely, but honestly.

Sure never to touch too closely on his problem, for both security and also for sheer shame.

If the man recognized him... He didn't show it, which Arthur was thankful for.

"Well son, the way things are looking right now, the working-class folk like us only have our personal lives to worry about these days. You might be lookin' kindly on your lady troubles later down the road when the gods have won the war and you and I are slaving away in some iron mine in the boonies."

"What do you mean?"

Arthur enquired, too drunk to realize what he was getting at.

"Well, the higher ups don't give two shits about the working man, and they don't even give a shit about the middle-class folk that DO make ends meet. Once the big blonde bastard Xex gets jogged, we're proper fucked, just a different way than if he wins instead. We're nuttin' short of bodies to them anyways. They crushed the Insurrection 'cause they don't got no mind for democracy. Proper democracy mind you, not the fucked sense of pollies they have now - rigging 'lections and licking the boots of the G.O.D."

Arthur gaped at his forwardness.

"Aren't you scared you might be sniffed by the quiet cops?"

Arthur asked, making sure to use the old 2060s slang and keep his voice low.

"Nope, cause even if they do sniff me out, rotting in jail sure beats welding gun parts together ten hours a day. At least this way I got a voice, even if me and the 'missus eat cabbage and piss soup for the rest of our days. They can take everything away, even kill me, but I know that there's more to life than what they got to offer us. Fuckers killed the Neanderthals, I read online!"

He roared with mirth, and Arthur thought back to what Cassius had told him, about how a large block of the council really didn't believe in how things worked, and how they only did it out of necessity to avoid anarchy, or worse - the fascism that loomed if Xex came out on top.

The drunk old man's words hit somewhere close to home, and knowing there were others out there who thought so openly, it cheered him up. They swapped buying rounds as the night wore on for three more hours. Near the end, he was rather drunk, and he shook the man's dusty, grease smeared hand before they finally parted ways, humming old drinking songs on the way out. Most were from his younger years, that he had learned working the agencies and shops of an old, forgotten life.

"The Frosty Bitch Up Yonder!"
Arthur finally staggered home, quietly tiptoeing into the dark house at a far later hour than intended. He must have sounded like an elephant despite having sobered up some on the walk.

The first thing he noticed was the stale smell of garlic and red wine in the air. The hair on the back of his neck tingled as he finally noticed the silent presence sitting alone in the dark living room.

"Arthur."

His wife spoke his name with resolution, scaring the shit out of him even after he suspected her to be there. He must have jumped half a foot and had to grab the wall to avoid falling in a stupor.

She tried to suppress a laugh.

"Feria."

He replied, doing his best not to slur and to stand up straight.

"Sit down."

A demand.

He obeyed, after fumbling a bit for the arm of the couch in the darkness.

"Arthur. I love you."

He blushed at her quick change of tone. A warmth filled his chest, and he felt suddenly happy in his drunken state.

"I love you too."

Her presence didn't soften.

He could tell she had been crying by the way she sat. He moved to sit beside her, tenderly putting his arm around her and trying to pull her close. She offered slight resistance and she reeked of red wine, and he realized she had followed exactly in his footsteps as far as intoxication was concerned.

Usually she was the smart one.

It was his first indication that ascendants could even really get proper drunk, but then he noticed the four empty bottles on the coffee table, outlined in the darkness.

It definitely took a lot to get there.

"I don't want you to die, Arthur."

She murmured.

"I won't let her kill me, Fer. I won't."

It seemed odd for the first time in a long while, that an immortal goddess capable of so much was so deeply rooted in him: a stupid, stubborn, ignorant, arrogant, selfish, and completely ordinary mortal man.

He tried to figure out what he gave her back, and what the cost of emotional support was to a woman like Feria.

Even the strongest needed a pillar now and then, he guessed.

"Listen, I've got this plan. I don't know what your dad told you, but the plan… Well… It's dangerous, but it's the only thing I've got going for me to get out of this alive."

He offered it up as gently as he could, but she only stiffened and started sobbing loudly, doing her best at the same time to choke back and wipe away any evidence of her tears.

She was a mess.

"The bitch won't have me that easily."

He cooed like a moron, to the tune of "The Frosty Bitch Up Yonder", and coaxed a drunken laugh out of his wife-to-be. There was a flash of comprehension, and in his own drunken state, he came up with the simultaneously most brilliant and ridiculous thing he could think of.

"Why don't we have a shotgun wedding tomorrow evening?"

He asked, and she giggled as might a schoolgirl, not the ascendant twenty years his senior that she actually was.

"I'm not pregnant, you dope."

She batted his arm softly, and it felt like she had slugged him in the shoulder. He was willing to bet it was largely due to the wine. He didn't know many normal humans that could tuck away four bottles of wine and only be moderately drunk.

He was willing to bet it was true after the pain flared in his bone. Gods were terrible judges of strength whilst intoxicated. In his inebriated swaying, he was actually a little afraid she might splatter him by accident one day.

He sucked in breath through his teeth and rubbed his tricep. Feria leaned over to kiss it better in jest.

"I mean, we'll have a fast one. We'll invite your dad, and Prom, and Joe, and your best friend Carrie if she's healed up enough, and Billy and Rebecca, and not tell anybody. No pre-planning, no worrying about a bombing, no nothing. It'll be great. We could have a single Seraph or Chayot with us if they demand protection."

He slurred the last part, but found he was sobering up just thinking about it. She snuggled her nose into his pectoral, and he squirmed at the sudden discomfort.

"I'm drunk."

She slurred, suddenly happy, as if she had noticed her state of inebriation for the first time.

"I know. You reek like red wine, and there are four empty bottles of it on the table."

She sat up straight, and smeared the long-dried remnants of tears away from her eyes in the darkness, mockingly offended.

"Yeah well you reek like cheap shitty beer."

He kissed her in the darkness.

She pulled away again.

"And I have to drink two whole bottles before I even feel a buzz."

He kissed her a second time, and she didn't pull away.

It progressed, until they were both quite naked on the living room couch in the darkness, and then it progressed some more beyond that.

He remembered it being very akin to the night he had first met her.

In her drunken state she was a tyrant the entire time, but... He did everything she asked regardless.

He woke up the next morning with several dark bruises that he couldn't recall getting. Feria was still asleep and he rolled over in bed to cuddle her.

Somehow, he always felt he owed her more.

CHAPTER 18: EVERY DOG, EVERY DAY

"You can't help but smile seeing young folks having a good time together, even when they're blitzed."

The next day was a whirlwind of hung-over calls and hasty preparations with a conveniently unscheduled British government marriage counsel. He was a stuffy old man, but he got the job done. As the G.O.D. held its own citizenship status, they opted for a dual union. Arthur would pick up the additional citizenship of his employer and Feria would be henceforth partially British, bringing her down to Earth in a very literal sense.

The wedding ceremony took place in a tiny U.K. courtroom, with Hewah, a recovering and wheelchair-bound, but largely stable judge Undelwood, Prometheus, Feria's old friend from university Cassie, now in her mid-thirties, Billy and his wife Rebecca, and as a last minute addition; Billy's mother, recovering from her alcoholism with the professional help her son could now afford for her.

It served as a sort of wakeup call for him, seeing Billy's mom looking happy.

He vowed to get his own coping mechanisms under control, for Feria's sake. Perhaps the biggest secret commitment of the day.

Feria finally tied the knot with him that day, amid much applause from the small courtroom audience.

Arthur bent her over almost to the ground when he kissed his new wife, and even the stuffy old British marriage counsel broke into a foolish grin at the sight when she did the same to him even more effortlessly in return. The power balance of their relationship was undoubtedly amusing to everyone else, but Arthur wouldn't have it any other way.

Their "honeymoon" as they joked - was a gathering with their guests sans Billy's mother, who went home to rest, at a local Chinese restaurant Arthur had frequented in his teenage years. It was a rather small group, with the newlyweds, the gods in attendance, and Billy all belligerently wearing caps, sunglasses, and other wacky disguises to avoid being pointed out.

Not that the awkward Seraph on guard duty outside in full power armor tipped anyone off with that plasma lance of his.

The restaurant throughout the entire night was almost always empty save for their party, and they ate, laughed, teased, and told stories for hours. After nearly three dozen bottles of beer even Hewah was drunkenly kidding around with them as if they were old friends, and not hundreds, if not thousands of years his junior. Arthur made the active choice to drink hot green tea instead, and somehow found himself none the worse for wear. Billy got along quite well with Prometheus, babbling on about some of the more dangerous experiences he had found himself in, slightly altered and censored to avoid attracting any serious attention from either the old woman serving them or the ancient looking cook who they presumed to be her husband.

At the end of the night, Arthur called the attention of the table by tapping a wooden chopstick against his teacup in a comedic display of solidarity. The motion was repeated by everybody at the table to much sloppy applause, with the exception of Joe, who had a piece of sweet and sour pork halfway to his mouth and who adamantly refused to drop it.

He wasn't very good with chopsticks and was deathly fearful he wouldn't be able to lift it again were he to give it up in the moment.

"I wish to propose a toast."

Arthur began.

"To everyone here, and to my beautiful new wife. It may have taken years and a special *arrangement* for me to settle down properly, which some have made a point of noticing quite loudly..."

Joe Undelwood cackled with nearly senile laughter at the statement, knowing full well he was the target of such a jab. He dropped his pork in doing so and swore loudly, eliciting even more laughter.

He finally gave up on it and raised his own glass of whiskey to join in.

"We're finally here. I just want you all to know, you're very dear to me, as friends..."

Arthur caught himself, because that wasn't how he really felt.

Everyone waited in silence, looking at him. Tears were starting in his eyes. Feria put a hand on his back.

He took a deep breath.

"No, I love you as family. You're all well aware that I don't have anyone else in the world except for you, and if anything happens to me... You all need to do something important for me."

He paused for effect, the crowd expecting some big epitaph.

"Make *damn sure* my wife never ever *ever* remarries. For like a hundred years at least."

He was blubbering even as he got the joke out, and the table burst out into a mix of tears, wheezes and cackles, not expecting something so crass.

Feria raised an eyebrow and gave him an amused glance, but he moved in and kissed her before she could say anything to retort.

After another few hours, near midnight, they finally decided they had lingered long enough, and got up to leave. Arthur remembered seeing the look on the old woman's face when she read the tip. He started panicking at first and thought they had given her a heart attack when they confirmed the number was not a mistake.

It was known at the table that between the combined wealth of the two gods in attendance, judge Undelwood's joint G.O.D./U.K. Government pension, and his generous new admirals' salary, her and her husband who ran the place were now hundreds of thousands of dollars richer. It was a small method of giving away what he could before he ran the risk of dying, and the others were glad to oblige him in granting an old neighbourhood couple an early retirement.

They bickered jauntily over whether to take a cab or limo, and Billy offered his nearby apartment and couch to the two gods in attendance as well as to Undelwood, forgetting their stature in society. The two Gods politely declined, and after a fairly fierce and intoxicated debate, it was arranged that Prometheus, the less drunk of the two council members, would volunteer his civilian model Agatha he affectionately nicknamed: "Deborah" to transport everyone safely to their own homes.

The perks for them of being in such company was that it was equipped with a Pilot A.I.

As only Arthur was sober enough to fly, it was a very welcome development in terms of transportation.

He and his new wife were the first to be dropped off, which was entirely intentional, but by the time Feria and he were halfway through the complexes' front door his arms were around her back and her legs were wrapped around his waist, accompanied by the cheers of everybody still watching from Deborah's open side doors. Her creamy brown skin positively radiated under the dim lights, and he couldn't imagine himself wanting to be anywhere else than right there with her.

As the transport lifted off with a muffled hum of thrusters to deliver its other passengers, he and Feria retired to yet another passionate night, both quietly and wordlessly scared of Arthur's departure in a few days' time. It was a departure to what they feared could be a final deployment in his short few years of service.

If things went poorly, it might leave Feria a widow just days after her wedding.

They passed the remaining time with sex, stupid hobbies, and various newlywed activities in an attempt at both ignoring the danger and trying to create a sense of normalcy.

In another universe, she might be just another captain's wife married to just another grunt.

It was a fantastic few days of playing house.

It was almost like he could just tell by her touch, her voice, and even her actions, that she had clearly reneged on her words and motives the very first night they met. She didn't view him as her boy-toy anymore, which was a bizarre comfort to a frightened mortal man.

She cherished who he was as a person, and gave him a sense of worth that he had never realized for himself.

If only his eighteen-year-old self could see him now.

For her to break down sobbing as he left... It was probably harder for him to watch than for her to do. Feria was a goddess; powerful and immortal, and this was clearly torture for her.

Alone, she was in control of only herself. With him in the picture, she could be hurt in ways that neither her super strength, nor her fire throwing, nor immortality could ever prevent.

And he knew that's what bothered her so much, being completely helpless against her emotions despite having so much power everywhere else.

He boarded the Navy shuttle that would take him unto his fate, and stared out through the window to where Undelwood in his wheelchair sat consoling his distraught wife.

Seeing this weakness in plain sight brought forth his own uncertainties and doubts.

The shuttle engines flared, and then two of the most solid rocks in his life were gone, shrinking down quickly into tiny dots on the tarmac far below.

They couldn't help him now.

He could only help himself.

CHAPTER 19: OUT TO THE BLACK.

"There is no lonelier realm than the one out in the empty space between stars. No sound, no life, and only the twinkle of distant galaxies to keep you company."

Arthur felt empty, in a sort of transition state between being "off" and being "on".

On a ship, he could feel in control, because he knew what had to be done. At home, even though there were no set schedules or strict rules, he was at peace emotionally thanks to Feria. On the shuttle, the "off" and "on" persisted.

He felt uneasy, as if he was in a purgatory of sorts.

Yet his unease slowly faded as the shuttle approached the forming fleet - a handful of ships hanging in the grey skies high above. He gaped at how big some of the ships were. If not for their anti-gravity engines, the sheer mass of some of them would have an effect on the planet itself most likely.

It was truly a miracle of science, technology, and engineering that such enormous pieces of metal could hang in the atmosphere like leaves on the wind.

Even with these few battlecruisers and frigates, the sheer size of what would ultimately be a fleet under his command still staggered him.

The *Asalia* wasn't even a fifth of the size of the largest ship in the fleet, and it had been a kilometer long. *Princely Disposition Under Duress* had been at least twice her size, and even it was a dwarf of a ship while looking up now at what would be his headquarters on duty.

His flagship was one of the largest in the entirety of the G.O.D. fleets, a heavy assault carrier named *The Chrysalis*. Despite his absence from duty, everything came back to him the minute he set foot on the bridge in uniform, even though he had never served on a ship of such a size.

The uniformity of The Guardian Navy made the transitions easy.

As he stood surveying his new ship and trying to get a handle on yet another gigantic leap upwards in terms of responsibility, he had a pensive moment.

Free of emotion or doubt, fueled entirely by logic.

Observing this "First Expeditionary Fleet" that suddenly answered to him and him alone, he was aware of all the small things that annoyed him. The starched white Admiral's uniform chafed his skin after weeks of wearing casual civilian clothes, and his hat was slightly too small for his head, thus it left a furrowed red line in his brow after only a few minutes of wearing it. If he wore it long enough, he got headaches.

He developed the bad habit of leaving it sitting in the captain's chair.

Another small frustration was the mandatory requirement for all high-ranking Captains and Admirals to be implanted with tracking and navigation chips as a safeguard in the event of capture. He was implanted upon coming aboard, and his skin still itched where the menacing needle had entered his arm and placed the trio of small microscopic chips. Arthur kept running his fingers over the small mosquito sized bumps on the skin of his forearm without meaning to.

The first expeditionary fleet, despite an impressive first glance, was actually a hastily manufactured conglomerate of three unique patrol or rapid response battle-groups. The vast majority were battlecruisers and assault cruisers, dotted with all manner of support ships and smaller frigates in between. *The Chrysalis* was undoubtedly the largest of them all, and served as the central command center of the small fleet.

Arthur's first task was dividing the fleet up into more manageable divisions, as he had been subject to himself under Vice-Admiral Delki on his last tour.

Cassius had expertly arranged for some of the best and brightest young captains to be transferred to this unique battle-group, and as such he was able to rely on several hungry youngbloods as well as a few war-hardened veterans who quickly helped him acclimatize to the situation.

He placed two of the longest serving men, Captain Anderson and Vice-Admiral Long in command of divisions two and three respectively, keeping command of division one for himself.

While the fleet already looked somewhat impressive when he first took command as leader, its ranks were only just beginning to swell; as Cassius and Hewah won council battle after council battle and fought hard politically to keep building up his forces for him.

The treaty stipulations, despite the Armada breach, forced the First Expeditionary Fleet first into orbit around the moon, and then farther out into the outer rim of the system.

Arthur soon came to expect a new ship to rift into orbit around Pluto and join the fleet every few days. With every ship reassigned to his new fleet, or ordered fresh from the various dock-worlds and stations, he felt more confident in the stratagem of baiting The Black Armada into an attack.

Despite the boost in confidence, he had never captained a Carrier before, and the first thing he familiarized himself with were the plasma shields and lack of multiple heavier offensive armaments in favor of extra defensive batteries and equipment plus troop carrying capacity.

Carriers were designed to fulfil a specific role - to hang back, command fleets, launch support fighters and boarding craft, and soak up damage far better than they dealt damage. *The Chrysalis* could fight, outsizing most other ships as it did, but he wouldn't be doing his job if he charged headlong into the fight with the carrier when push came to shove.

His fleet experience with Delki had been invaluable.

After a few weeks of gathering forces, Arthur declared the fleet to be of a large enough size to move from the first rally point around Pluto, shifting into a quick patrol location above Mars.

And soon after that, they moved again to criss-crossing orbits around Saturn's rings, which definitely got the Armada's ears burning. The media made sure to slather the Guardians of Destiny with praise and amazement for building up one of the largest fleets in the recent history of the G.O.D.

After over three and a half months of waiting, in which time Arthur had moved the fleet again as planned into a defense position in high orbit around *Holy Roman* - Xex finally took the bait and moved first.

Clearly the emperor and his Navy wouldn't dare let Arthur build up his forces any further.

He cursed how fast they had moved, but was forced to act with what he had, with additional reinforcements on standby to act as a pincer after first contact.

Arthur had added several more ships to the fleet since moving to *Holy Roman*, and hoped he would have the numbers his fleet needed to fight the Black Armada off. There were other defensive fleets active, of course, but he needed to save the First Expeditionary Fleet for wherever the main force materialized.

The Armada started an offensive first, by staging lightning fast raids on *Bukaviev, Heartland*, and a few other core planets, bombing them from orbit without much actual effect. It was strange that they also did so without committing any single heavy force. The Armada actually lost more than it gained due to the G.O.D. 's planetary batteries, orbital defense stations, and naval ships already nearby to both worlds.

Arthur refused to take the bait, watching as there were some hard fought skirmishes and even a few initial ground invasions of some outer rim resource colonies. However, the major attack they expected was withheld, and he surmised that the Armada was likely hoping to prod them into a wrong move or a misplay.

Serania and her supporters used this waiting to their advantage, trying to argue for the redirection of the First Expeditionary Fleet toward the original targets of Resistance holdouts near the taken worlds, or at the very least towards a direct attack on lightly defended Armada worlds on the edges of the neutral territories.

Despite the reports and casualty lists Arthur was forced to review with each new engagement, he knew the small excursions and raids on some of the outer worlds wasn't the major attack Xex was sure to launch. While there were voiced concerns from some other fleet commanders - forced to pick up the slack of the missing ships that instead swelled Arthur's ranks, he refused to risk springing the trap too early.

Arthur wasn't exactly making friends in the Navy by bleeding the G.O.D. slowly and promising a mysteriously big payoff later.

Tension mounted as another week passed. When Arthur baited the Black Armada even further by ordering the now battle-ready defence fleet to rift into orbit around the recently bombed *Heartland*, Xex finally started to make his move.

Arthur was forced to hop around the Heartland system, watching and waiting as false positives and reports from all directions came in fast and frequent. The Armada's white rifts, signalling feints and wild goose chases added more polka dots to the dark of space and the twinkling of distant stars, and for another day they drifted, expecting at any moment to have the Armada drop down on them.

The holographic projection screens were slathered with false positives and FoF registrations.

The attack came furiously, unexpectedly, in the void between the *Heartland* system's furthest gas giants. Despite his work with The Eye to try and catch it early, the Armada somehow moved faster than the G.O.D. could communicate.

Or was it that Julian had messed with the reports on purpose?

The Armada began by sending heavier assault ships to crush any remaining weakened defences on the patrol routes to and from *Heartland*, succeeding with only a few ships.

The fleet received the distress calls far too late.

There was nothing they could do but sit and wait to avoid stretching the fleet too thin, whilst listening to the comms - G.O.D. people on the other end, dying in droves.

When the attack came for the larger of *Heartland*'s moons, it was time. Arthur moved the fleet as fast as he could upon hearing the emergency beacons activate.

Having experienced the failures of communication and proper backup on his tour with the *Asalia*, rifting into a sea of debris and broken ship skeletons near *Heartland*'s moon was somewhat sobering.

The risky gamble to save a single man's life, his own, had lost them no less than four ships with all hands here, and the lunar base on the larger moon itself was all but destroyed. It was bizarre... The Armada attackers were nowhere to be found, leaving only carcasses in their wake.

It could only mean the worst.

Even this rout had been a ruse.

Arthur ordered the First Expeditionary Fleet towards a deployment of ground forces and the securing of a defensive orbit around *Heartland* itself, knowing that crippling Guardian patrols and the lunar base was only the first foray. Other G.O.D. fleets in the core systems were scrambling to adjust their strategies to the evolving situation around *Heartland*, so his backup would definitely be delayed. After all, rift generators could only bridge space so far apart without an overload, and multiple jumps and cool downs were a tad too precarious for rapid relief.

When early warnings came in of rift activity just outside *Heartland*'s gravity well, he felt a twinge of contentment knowing that his plan had worked, even as he prepared himself for the worst.

Arthur ordered the fleet into the assigned divisions and formations.

It was the moment of truth.

Even as he gave the general order for all ships to arm weapons and to prepare for a direct assault upon the incoming invasion fleet, he was made aware from their now miraculously bountiful comms reports that it was almost double their size.

For all their preparation they were still marching in under-gunned, pretty much headfirst into a possibly suicidal fleet engagement. How could the Armada have assembled a larger fleet than this one in so little time?

Had they been preparing for an attack already?

Arthur had to stall for a few tense minutes while waiting for the smaller ships to get their rift generators spinning up to speed, but they finally moved forward as a unit, careful to do so all at the same time. He hated the wait, but it was a countermeasure to avoid crashing into one another when exiting the blinding white rifts.

The second they slipped through their exit portals on a far-side of *Heartland*, they were attacked.

The Armada had split itself up, with one half waiting for them to emerge from their rifts, guessing almost exactly what vector they'd attack from through some trick or clever planning.

It was not a good start to the battle.

The other half of the remaining Armada ships not directly engaging Arthur and his fleet were working away busily in low orbit and down in-atmosphere to cripple planetside defense batteries and land as many ground troops down onto the surface as it could. He was thankful that G.O.D. ground forces were already dug in, but if they failed to protect the batteries on the ground, it meant more losses for them up above.

Their only advantage against superior numbers could be lost.

The Armada ships on blockade duty against his fleet didn't even wait for them to finish emerging from their glowing white rifts before firing; and he watched a smaller frigate take a rail-gun round to the bow and then slowly shear itself into two pieces by lurching off course, connecting with the edge of the jagged white circle it was attempting to exit from.

The Armada didn't seem to care that they were taking heavy

fire from the planet below, focused as they were on scuttling Arthur's fleet.

It was a quick and dirty attack, because every Naval commander knew about disrupting rift travel. If their ships touched the edges of the rift, there would be no recovery. They were birds made of clay, flying through hoops ringed with razor wire.

A single failure meant you'd simply be sliced into neat pieces.

He made a mental note of the frigate's name as he watched the bow split apart from the rest of the ship.

Churchill's Liquor. Somewhat ironic for Arthur.

"Sir, we've lost three ships in the 2nd division already, one from a rift collision, and two from rift generator failures from direct hits."

Rift generator failures were terrible things, as rifts were dangerous at the best of times. When the portals collapsed or closed for whatever reason, it had a guillotine effect. Arthur watched at least one of those poor ships have that happen before his eyes.

The back half of the battlecruiser was nowhere to be found after a flash of brilliant white light, and without the engines, gravity generators, rift generators, and power systems in the stern, the bow was without power, life support, lights, or elevators.

It would be a deathtrap to escape as it vented.

Whenever he thought about it, the mental image popped into his head of a razor swiping down through an apple in midair. The two pieces were then stranded hundreds of light-years apart, drifting helplessly.

It was his first time seeing it happen for himself.

"*Tympanic Roar* and *Constellation* are down in the 3rd division from Armada fire, Admiral, and division one captains are requesting orders."

Arthur had hesitated too long already, in taking stock of his fleet's first losses. Hundreds of lives lost for mere moments of hesitation.

"All ships, break rift formation, assemble battle-group divisions. All division one ships may fire at will. Let Long and Anderson know they have command."

The Armada was in no noticeably tactical formation, and the battle thereafter devolved into a hodgepodge of broken ship frames and fierce small craft battles. Their first few salvos crippled or destroyed several enemy battlecruisers, but the size of both fleets soon made proper strategy useless aside from the odd attempt to flank the edges of the battleground. Arthur made sure his division quickly closed the gap between their two opposing fleets, and precision shooting devolved into a complete melee, his vain attempt at evening the odds and forcing the Armada to inflict friendly fire by accident.

Hopefully the planetside batteries checked their aim.

The Armada clearly outnumbered them in terms of smaller frigates and attack craft, he noticed, despite his own slight advantage in having more large cruisers and ships. It made such a close-range battle extremely dangerous.

"*Edge of Abyss* is crippled, bombers hit her engines, sir."

"*Devotion* is gone, clean hit through the bridge."

Every ship they scuttled or lost was a pyrrhic victory or a horrific loss. The space all around the two fleets got smaller and smaller, and was soon filled with a sea of husks, debris, and destroyed attack craft filling the length and width of the battleground.

Some damaged ships were also in danger of being pulled down into Heartland's gravity well.

Arthur continued to weave his fleet in and out of formation as they closed distances to mere hundreds of metres at times, and they lost a few more small ships simply to collisions with various pieces of wreckage. *The Chrysalis* was holding up well, with mostly superficial scarring to her armor-plated hull and no direct damage yet. The plasma shielding had only failed twice, and recharged relatively quickly by diverting power from the rift generators.

A blessing for his own safety, but not many of the Guardian ships possessed such defensive boons.

Arthur started to get the upper hand, by using his fleet's own crippled or destroyed ships as cover. It wasn't long though before the alarms started going off on consoles all across the bridge.

He sat down in the captain's chair, for the first time since the battle had begun, expecting the worst.

"New fleet rifting in near low orbit sir."

"They're Armada sir, a relief fleet, mostly frigates."

"A third fleet, sir. Rifting in near the first."

He calculated the numbers and knew it was over. Their fleet had slightly outmatched the first enemy battle group despite its superior size, due to his risky close combat strategy and the use of debris. But even if they managed to quickly defeat the remnants of the first wave and move on to engage the relief fleet, there was little to no hope of defeating a third.

"Sir, the last fleet to rift in is engaging the Armada. They're sending us a friendly call-sign. Unknown FoF tags."

What?

He was flabbergasted, and he stalled for a few seconds, valuable time lost while they were still in the middle of a firefight. He stuttered a few times, before finally getting out what he wanted to ask.

"W-Who is it.? Is it the core defense fleet?"

The rhythmic thumping of their weapons firing and chattering somewhere below was the only answer for a tense moment.

"The FoF tag isn't working sir. Friendly call-sign is all we have. The God of Death. Question Marks otherwise for unknown."

Arthur had no idea what it meant or whose call sign it indicated, as there was no such thing as a God of Death in the G.O.D. The core fleet's call-sign was "Relentless", and they hadn't shown up to reinforce *Heartland* as of yet.

Still, he made sure to remember the new call sign in case he ever got the chance to thank the commander personally.

"Send them a friendly G.O.D. call-sign from *The Chrysalis*, and keep an eye on them for me Davis."

The young woman went back to her duties at communications and he continued barking out orders, reinvigorated with the new prospect of possible survival.

"Move us into firing range of the second fleet, and unload on that central Armada carrier."

He had no sooner finished barking the order when *The Chrysalis* lurched forward, and a deep groan emanated from somewhere below and behind them. The entire bridge shook, and before he knew it, Arthur had flown up out of his chair, his entire body weightless. His abandoned hat floated off to the side. He could feel his form tremble and his abs clench as gravity flickered in and out in rapid succession, falling down a few inches each time.

"We're hit, admiral. Clipped on the stern. Artificial gravity is down, engine three is sputtering."

Arthur cursed, even as he flipped himself around to plant his boots on the ceiling and gently push himself back towards where the floor had been. A tinny voice began to play through the bridge loudspeakers, that of assistant-engineer Greene.

"Bridge, we've been holed through all decks on the starboard side down here, and the gravity generator is completely gone. We've also lost both atmospheric anti-grav and on-board grav generation. I have crews putting out plasma fires, sealing breaches, and hauling out who they can from the holed areas, but engine three was grazed. Don't push the engines too hard or they'll blow and risk a fuel cell rupture."

He clenched his fists.

While most of the bridge crew remained strapped in and working, he and a few others were drifting around, having no set station to be at other than relaying orders and giving miscellaneous tasks. One crewman had accidentally puked from the sudden gravity spasms, and was now trying to gather the globules up with an emergency spill kit.

He was only partially successful.

"Where's head engineer Morton, Greene?"

Arthur enquired, as one of the two on-board Class 6 Artificial Intelligences spattered more detailed damage reports at him in his other earpiece. Dominic, maybe?

"He's dead, admiral, he took some shrapnel to the head and got spaced shortly before we could re-pressurize the observation area. The plasma shielding breached outside, but soaked up most of the hit, and we've got it back up and running."

Arthur let him get back to work and reassessed.

"Start moving us at half throttle towards the edge of the debris field; we need to get the hell out of the middle of this firefight or we're an easy target with only three engines and directional thrusters. Switch to emergency power for lighting and life support and cut whatever power was coming and going to the Grav-Gen. It's wasted fuel now. How is the situation planet side?"

The Chrysalis started moving again, although the engine vibrations had dimmed down to a bare whisper.

The second communications officer whipped around.

"Admiral. Ground forces have already been pushed back to the capital and industrial cores on the main continent, sir. Field commanders are requesting air support as they retreat. We've already lost most of the orbital batteries on this side of the planet. Reinforcements are moving around the planet, but with only small aircraft to shore up the ground, it'll take a while to retake their positions again."

Arthur winced.

"Deny their air support requests, let them know our hands are full up here. But try and get anything VTOL off the ground to help them."

There was an alarm and a series of muffled explosions.

"Strafing fighters! Boarding craft are moving to our hangars on the port side."

There was a second tremble, and a few screams.

Then the faint hum of the three remaining engines cut out completely. An eerie silence settled over the bridge.

"Greene, what's going on down there?"

He could barely hear Greene's voice over the roaring of something in the background.

"One of the other two engines took a hit sir, all main engines are down aside from directional thrusters. We're fighting to cool her down and keep the fuel cells from going."

The Chrysalis, the largest ship in the First Expeditionary Fleet.

Dead in the water.

"Fuck."

CHAPTER 20: THE WORST POSSIBLE OUTCOME

"When the going gets tough, there isn't always an option for the tough to get going. Often the tough are the first to die instead, and the weak must continue fighting alone."

Arthur stalled for a moment, trying to figure out what he could possibly do to fix the shit-show that the battle was quickly becoming. He still wasn't sure who The God of Death was, so he didn't want to risk pulling the battle between them and the Armada relief fleet any closer.

He had no one else to ask for help. And besides, he was starting to have an inkling as to who this Death Fleet might be.

"Give the order for any available ships to cover us, and start deploying explosive decoys, missile flares, and anything else we've got left. I want every single defensive battery manned somehow, by an A.I., or a damn crewman if it has to be. Have fireteams move to the portside hangar bays and prepare to repel boarders."

The immediate situation remedied, the outside of *The Chrysalis* lit up with reinvigorated streams of battery fire, and Arthur felt himself fall into anxiety.

Images of his loved ones kept flashing through his head.

Feria, Joe, Billy. His mother.

The meaning of life seemed very much a pointless endeavour to try and figure out when you were staring death in the face.

The ship was rumbling more frequently now, and he could see flashes on all the video screens from where their plasma shielding was struggling to hold under sustained fire. The pilot was doing an excellent job of keeping *The Chrysalis* continuing along its previous path due to inertia, and the ship navigated the debris as best it could with what few directional thrusters it had left.

A.I. and manned gun batteries joined in by the dozens, attempting to fend off the swarming attackers, but were clearly fighting a losing battle. The Black Armada smelled blood, and fighters and bombers swarmed Arthur's ship, trying to bring down its' shields for the boarding craft to begin capturing the ship.

The Armada had obviously keyed into the fact that *The Chrysalis* was the command carrier simply by how large it was, and how fiercely the rest of the fleet was fighting to guard its escape.

The Armada's insistence on boarding did help them avoid being fired upon directly via rail gun rounds or plasma and missile barrages, but essentially the entire Armada invasion fleet had deployed whatever it could muster to capture the high-ranking personnel who might be on board.

It dawned on Arthur that he was now one of those high-ranking personnel, which added to the bathtub full of anxiety he was trying to force into the recesses of his gut.

"Sir, the plasma shields have overheated."

That report signified their approaching doom. Their munitions-deflecting plasma shielding had gone down from absorbing too many hits and overloading the shield generator, and assistant-engineer Greene was far from being able to start a shield cool down with the engines at risk of exploding at any given moment. The majority of the nearby escort cruisers and frigates had been crippled or scuttled, and almost every one of their defensive batteries was quickly damaged or destroyed, an easy task when the target was moving as slowly and predictably as they were.

"Deploy any of the Skyjacks we have left. Have our A.I.s focus on downing any boarding craft moving for hangar access points and airlocks, and then seal the blast shields across the entire ship. If we have any mech pilots left, have them rally inside the hangars with whatever troops we have left backing them up."

He had saved one last reserve flight of Skyjacks, the small A.I. controlled fighters with lower-class A.I. Only installations, capital ships, and carriers were usually equipped with them due to manufacturing costs. He had saved this last flight until his ship was on her last legs, as she was now. They were solely defensive, and would not stray far from the ship.

"The reserve Skyjacks are deploying now sir."

"Hangars 8 and 9 have been boarded sir, before they could be fortified."

Well, with boarders now on his ship, the anxiety was mutating and migrating from a pit in his gut to a martyr-like bravado and a rage in his head. Nothing stoked fire in a person more than the knowledge that they are now a cornered rat.

He was damn sure that the Black Armada wouldn't board his ship and take him prisoner without *The Chrysalis* putting up one hell of a fight first.

Arthur gave the order for response parties to push back, forming defensive lines along all the access points to the bridge.

The Chrysalis wasn't left with much in the way of defenders, as they had sent most of their ground forces to the surface, but there were still two companies of Shocktroopers aboard, and more than a dozen power-armoured Seraphs on board to repel the Armada's boarding parties.

He crossed his fingers that Tyrone Wells wasn't one of them.

He cursed his lack of any combat ready gods on board, of course. Who wouldn't want someone capable of decimating thousands? A superhuman fighter to hold back a tide of invaders? Feria's fire streamers would work wonders in the corridor fighting that was to come. She would obviously…

He pushed the thought of her out of his head.

"Have Greene pull his men back to the observation area and seal off engineering completely. It's too late to try and effect repairs with Armada crawling all over the carrier. Tell him to use A.I. robots and drones for the engine upkeep. Have the crew evacuate all nonessential other areas. Get escape pods down towards *Heartland* as soon as we can."

A crewwoman spoke up.

"Sir, callsign God of Death has eliminated the Armada relief fleet with partial losses, and is asking permission to assist."

Even as his ship crawled with Armada soldiers, he considered who could possibly have drummed up another fleet. Hewah? Cassius? No… He was always daydreaming, and when faced with certain death at the hands of an overwhelming Armada force, and not seeing Feria again…

This wasn't the time to daydream.

He watched another one of his own ships erupt in flames and plasma as it tried desperately to help them, and he knew he couldn't refuse the help if he wanted to make all of this worth it. No point in assembling this fleet in the first place if he was going to be carted back to Xex for brainwashing and lose a core world in the process.

"Give them permission to engage any and all Armada hostiles."

"Sir, they're failing to broadcast any proper G.O.D. call-sign?"

"Blimey girl, *just do it*."

Another rumble from belowdecks shook the bridge, and he tried to guess how long *The Chrysalis* had left.

"They're Resistance."

A shrill voiced crewmember protested, and he whirled around to face the man, doing his best to channel an inner Serania and death glare him into the ground.

"Fuck it, who cares at this point?!"

The outraged young officer unstrapped himself from his station at weapons and pushed off towards Arthur, drawing his sidearm. Arthur could see a fury in his eyes, and he was suddenly reminded how fanatical parts of the G.O.D. were. Gunshots rang out without him saying a word, as another member of the crew drew his own weapon and sent the enraged officer spiralling off towards the back of the bridge, trailing droplets of blood behind him in the zero gravity.

"Stand down!"

Arthur waved an arm and broke the momentary silence that had descended over the bridge with the young man's death.

He was filled with pity and remorse.

The crewman who had defended him holstered his sidearm and moved to strap himself back in as if nothing had happened, as two other crew members grabbed the corpse of the offender and gently pushed it towards the cargo elevator to be hauled off somewhere below decks.

Minutes passed, and there was almost nothing left for them to do on the bridge. Their Skyjacks had fought valiantly, but were quickly all but decimated, and their forces onboard *The Chrysalis* were being forced back towards the bow of the ship and up towards the bridge. Arthur couldn't even imagine what the corridor fighting below was like, especially sans gravity like the ship was now.

Minutes passed in a fervor as battle reports from the soldiers dying below them were recanted in his headset.

"Armada forces are pressing the main elevator shaft sir."

The Black Armada had broken past a section of their defensive line on the carrier, and the lack of gravity meant that the invaders only had to torch their way through a few blast doors into the useless cargo elevator in order to get up the shaft to the bridge. Shutting down the elevators would do absolutely nothing without the help of gravity. It also meant they couldn't drop the damn things on the enemy either due to failsafe mechanisms designed to avoid injury.

It wasn't often that a carrier was boarded by hostiles in zero gravity.

Arthur flicked the loudspeaker button on his collar mic, and his voice reverberated across the ship, echoed through the speakers on the bridge around him.

"Any G.O.D. Army units left aboard, fall back to bridge defense positions. Transport pilots, you have *five minutes* to board survivors and wounded. All non-essential crew, abandon ship. I repeat, *abandon ship*. Forward bow escape pods are being unlocked."

The words trickled out of his mouth and amplified themselves, coming to a stop at the same time as his own voice stopped over the loudspeakers. Hearing them echo back sickened him.

He felt grim when he gave the order for the escape pods to unlock. It was an anti-desertion scheme, to give him and him alone the master keys to escape, but it still felt wrong somehow. He knew the Armada onboard would have heard the announcement, but at that point it didn't matter. They wanted him and his bridge crew, and would gun down anyone else that got in their way.

Better to save lives at this point.

"Sir, this is Engineer Greene, the Armada have cut off access to the escape routes. We're trapped in the observation area."

Arthur shook his head, and began calling out names. The bridge crew reacted quickly, as he went down a list of names and let them know who was to flee, and who he would need to stay behind.

The young woman feeding him comms alerts stayed where she sat, as did the primary pilot.

Since the majority of their weapons systems were down and they had already lost one of their operators to insubordination, he had the rest of the weapons crew flee as well, leaving the few remaining guns to the A.I.s.

He tapped furiously on the touch screen on his arm, and rerouted weapons control to comms. She was hardly trained, but it was better than nothing, and she could let the two Class 6 A.I.s man the handful of guns they still had operational.

If the two bodies left behind with Arthur on the bridge felt any fear, they did well to hide it.

"Greene, hole up in the observation area and repel any boarders that come your way. Do you have vacuum gear?"

The reply failed to come back instantaneously. When it did, he could hear muffled gunfire in the background.

"Yes sir, we have some vacuum gear but not enough for everyone here. The Armada are pushing back the fireteams in the maintenance hallways. There's only a handful of troopers left."

Arthur knew what he had to do, but felt sick to his stomach in doing it. He'd be boxing them in, in hopes of a miracle.

"Greene, you have two minutes to choose who puts those suits on, and everybody else needs to arm themselves and go aid the fireteams. Seal the blast doors to the observation area afterward."

Greene offered no protest, and had likely come to the same conclusion as Arthur. Saving the lives of some at the cost of others.

Minutes passed.

The solidarity in the decision made him feel no better in performing the action. He released himself from his hold on the rail nearby and pushed his way over to the ship's access controls. Maneuvering through a seemingly endless series of menu options, he was finally presented with a large red confirmation button.

"Greene, I'm opening the airlocks in engineering in thirty seconds. Is everybody suited up, and are the blast doors sealed?"

"Yes sir."

Arthur waited fifteen more seconds and then hit the red confirmation button with a bated breath.

"Greene, still with me?"

"Yes sir."

Greene's voice was somber, and Arthur could hear the whistling in the background as the atmosphere was sucked from the observation section. He could only hope the soldiers defending Greene in the maintenance hallways had sealed their gear or died before they suffocated or were spaced. It meant that Greene and whoever he had suited up were now trapped with a finite air supply, with only one way to go – out into the void of space.

Arthur knew venting the atmosphere from the rest of the ship would be largely futile after that, as by now the Armada goons belowdecks would be tapping into *The Chrysalis'* subsystems to prevent it. So instead, he sealed every blast door he could access from the bridge and sailed back to his captain's chair to plan his final few minutes.

"Any pilots still near *The Chrysalis*, there are evacuees at stern, near engineering, do your best to reach them before you get yourselves planetside."

Arthur hoped someone was still out there to hear him. He didn't relish the thought of saving Greene and a handful of others from being gunned down in engineering only to have them suffocate out in space, or worse - drift towards *Heartland*, sucked down into the gravity well to burn up in the atmosphere.

It wasn't long after Greene's exodus that a half-squad of Shocktroopers and a single Seraph joined the survivors on the bridge, emerging from the emergency elevator behind him much the worse for wear. Several had seen some brutal fighting, and many were already wounded, with some of the more fit soldiers pulling or pushing the wounded along. Arthur took note of what should have been pristine white combat armour and looked down the line at the plethora of gas masks, visors, and helmets. Almost every set of armor in the group was dented, blackened, or bloodied in some way from defensive action across the carrier.

How did they feel knowing the blood of their fallen comrades coated their armor? Arthur rubbed his own hands, feeling imaginary liquid between them as if Joe Undelwood's blood was still sticky and fresh on his palms from the day of his wedding.

The Seraph's lanky power armor clambered in through the elevator last, and it and the shocktroopers took up defensive positions, with the most wounded of them all activating the deployable cover installed all over the bridge and crouching or propping themselves up behind the bulletproofed steel panels for the coming last stand.

"Where are the other fireteams?"

Arthur asked, as the Seraph engaged the magnetic floor locks in his spurs and clacked down onto the bridge floor beside him.

"We're all that's left of Echo and Charlie, Admiral. I think we're all that's left on the whole ship."

The Seraph's tinny reply was surprisingly calm, even as it paused for a moment to examine the blackened burn patch on its breastplate from a plasma bolt.

"You're the senior officer?"

The Seraph's armored head bobbed in a slight nod, the servos in his armor's neck whining quietly.

"Lieutenant Douglas, sir."

Arthur shook his hand, and took a moment he didn't have to wonder how the powered mechanical fingers of Douglas' suit differentiated between a handshake and a lethal chokehold.

"You're more experienced than me on the ground, Lieutenant, so you're in charge of bridge defense as of right now. I'm going to try and get us out of the debris field and make sure we put up a fight outside."

Douglas bobbed his head again and began barking out orders.

"Alright people, I want to cross-cover in case they get smart.

Adams, Duncan, you're far left. Vigneault, Juarez, Kosta, you're far right. The rest of you, fill-in the middle. They have three entry points - maintenance access, and the two elevators, main and emergency. Open fire the minute you see their beady eyes pop up the main elevator shaft. They're likely to hit there first, and we need to keep them bottlenecked."

The Seraph clonked over and took a kinetic needle rifle from one of the wounded Shocktroopers, a simple looking metal gun with a long barrel that fired long, thin, steel composite needles in a semi-automatic fashion. He handed it to Arthur, ignoring the fact that Arthur had a holstered plasma handgun.

Arthur had trained with one a few times before in the academy years ago, and knew how deadly it could be against infantry, especially the unarmored Berserkers that made up the majority of Armada ground forces. He had thought them to be banned from Naval use in favour of plasma weaponry for how gruesome and inhumane they could be.

War was like that sometimes.

Killing a soldier took them off the battlefield, no extra effort required. Wounding a soldier in a grotesque and horrific fashion required an entire medical team, and someone to try and extract the wounded.

It was the brutal calculus of war.

Too bad The Black Armada treated their soldiers like fresh meat.

Arthur shook his head free of the mental image of the needle rifle in action, and tried to get Greene back on comms for a check-in. There was no response, so he turned his attention to the two crew still under his command, trying to have some oversight in some attempt to push the coming siege from his mind.

Distraction was a hell of a drug.

Two troopers sealed the doors to the main elevator shaft with an override code as he gave the order to the pilot to keep *The Chrysalis* on a course out of the primary debris field. Moving with only directional thrusters and previous momentum was a painfully slow process for such an enormous carrier. Every piece of material they impacted slowed their already agonizing pace even further.

They were trying to traverse thousands of kilometres, and it felt like shoving a few firecrackers out the back end of a minivan, trying to get it rolling uphill.

More boarding craft soon caught up with them rather effortlessly, and began the process of unloading wave after wave of Armada forces somewhere into the bowels of Arthur's ship. By this point, every weapon *The Chrysalis* had was offline, so Arthur tried and failed again to get Greene back on comms. It was all he could do while he waited for the enemy to come.

"They're breaching the bottom of the shaft now, sir."

Reported Douglas, crouched half behind a console in the move to take up firing positions. His Seraph armor was too big and gangly to properly hide itself very well, and he stuck out at odd angles like a terrible game of hide and seek. As Douglas was unwounded and heavily armored, he had chosen to perch his lanky white form behind the closest piece of cover to the doors.

Arthur tried not to laugh, picturing him as a monstrous white rabbit, the kind pulled out of a magician's hat. He only lacked the tall floppy ears.

It was uplifting for his final moments, knowing his dark sense of humor hadn't completely failed him.

The bridge dropped down a few steps from the elevator access point, so the enemy had the advantage of height.

He cursed whoever designed these ships.

They had thought of deployable cover on the bridge, but had not thought of basic firing lines in the event of boarding. If he were to somehow magically survive this, he swore on his status as a puppet of the gods that he'd rectify that error with whichever engineer would listen.

He huddled down behind a console and switched his collar mic and earpiece to local comms now, tapping into the same frequency as the soldiers. This would avoid having the Armada boarders overhear their conversations via tapping the ship's comms.

The lack of gravity made it hard to stay behind his chosen piece of cover, and he knew the minute he began firing his needle rifle he'd have to hang on for all he was worth to avoid drifting backwards from the force. Lack of gravity certainly was a bitch, as was the lack of recoil dampeners in such a cruel weapon.

He couldn't help but cringe at the notion of ricochets and broken fragments of needle coming back at him.

Each of the surviving crew had a trooper apiece nearby to cover them, as they were trapped helplessly out in the open at consoles with minimal deployable cover protecting them. Arthur wasn't sure how much it would even help. The debris had lessened somewhat outside the bridge, with only a few larger husks left in their path as the carrier trundled along back towards open space. Once they were in the open, it could be that the Armada would abandon the boarding maneuver and hole their ship regardless of who was left alive. It would be easy enough to do without their plasma shielding crackling in a protective sphere around them.

"Hold us steady Hartnell."

His order was simple, but his voice was partially drowned out by a series of clangs and metallic banging from the Armada beginning their ascent up the quarter-kilometer long cargo elevator shaft. They would start by torching their way through the bottom of the elevator car hanging on the floor just below the bridge. It was a useful stopgap, hanging stalled and unmoving outside the blast doors.

"Anybody with a plasma weapon could open fire the minute they start torching, maybe they'd blind them with plasma spray."

A trooper mused, and despite the severity of the situation, the bridge chortled with laughter at the futility of it. When the Black Armada did break through both the elevator floor and then the roof with the scrape of moving metal plating, there was a pause. A minute or two later, they finally started to cut through the door to the bridge, with several troopers acting on the earlier suggestion and opening fire at the peeping white torch. It was useful in buying them what seemed to be fairly useless extra time and a few fatalist laughs as the enemy started and stopped the task amidst loud curses and screeches from the other side of the blast doors.

Arthur readied his needle rifle and took aim.

They didn't sound like the mindless axe wielding berserkers he had been taught about in the academy, who ran around half naked in a bloodthirsty rage. These Armada soldiers sounded like average infantry.

"Ready yourselves."

Douglas ordered sternly, as the Armada finally finished the torching. A second or two of tense panic passed through the room as the boarders beyond clanged and prepped themselves, but eventually the elevator door groaned and a large plate was forced inwards, drifting weightlessly into the bridge.

The whole bridge was spontaneously deafened with weapons fire the millisecond the piece of blast door was clear.

"WATCH THE GRAVITY!"

The shout came from somewhere in the enemy camp down the shaft, as bullets and other projectiles whizzed randomly by Arthur's unarmoured head. He started firing at the gap with squeeze after squeeze of the trigger, aiming into the jagged circular hole, hoping that ricocheting needles might score kills further down the shaft.

"Hartnell, close the blast shields."

The view screen behind them, facing the bow of the ship in front of them, was reinforced with a heavy blast shield that could be closed in case of major battle damage from enemy ships, and Arthur preferred not to take any chances with the viewport buckling and sucking them all out into space.

There were screams as bullets, slugs, plasma bolts, and needles ricocheted around in the space beyond the doors, and slowed the Armada even further. Arthur was forced to duck several times as the odd projectile bounced back his way and continued to bounce around the room, losing a piece of momentum on each surface it contacted. Arthur figured out damn quick why there was a push in the G.O.D. to convert entirely to plasma weaponry for small arms on ships. The ricochet was just as likely to kill you yourself as your enemy if you were a poor shot or failed to grasp the rudimentary concept of angles and physics in zero gravity.

Each squeeze of the trigger rocked him back, and his left shoulder was close to pulling out of the socket after so many jolts backwards. He readjusted himself on his piece of cover just in time to watch something small and round arc through the air from the abyss of the elevator. He failed to notice the soldiers around him averting their eyes and hunkering down. The blinding flash of light that followed both stunned and blinded him, and he lost his needle rifle in a flailing sprawl backwards through the air, connected to the gun only by the strap he had wrapped around his shoulder.

Someone grabbed his arm and yanked him to the side as he flailed around visionless, and the rifle swung back into his head, butting him on the jaw painfully.

He was blind for a good half minute, unable to figure out what was going on over the sounds of gunfire.

When his vision finally cleared, red emergency alerts were flashing across almost all the bridge consoles in front of him. A trooper had tucked Arthur in behind him and was strapped to the railing nearby via a clip-harness. He continued to fire with his one free hand and hold Arthur with his other until Arthur patted his arm to let him know he was fine.

"Sir. Call sign God of Death is sending several dropships straight for us."

That explained which possible scenario the alarms and flashing red lights were warning the bridge crew of.

Did the Resistance want to help…?

Or did they want to make sure the commander of the G.O.D. fleet was truly down for the count…?

Did the Resistance have the manpower to take and keep Heartland for themselves?

"We can't do anything about it now. Better they hole us and take these Armada bastards with us out into the black."

There was movement at the elevator, and Arthur spun around just in time to witness an enormous figure move up into view and grab the edges of the torched hole. It was shirking off the needles, plasma bolts, and bullets the G.O.D. soldiers launched at it as if it were a soft spring rain bouncing off an umbrella. Death had arrived, with a matte black finish.

CHAPTER 21: THE GOD OF DEATH.

"Bury dem bones, dem bones, dem bones. Bury dem bones down deep, down deep."

"DREAD KNIGHT!"

Someone screamed, as an enormous shoulder plate was thrust in through the torched gap. It was followed by the biggest and bulkiest suit of power armor Arthur had ever seen in his life.

The heavily armoured figure scanned the room, taking their time despite being pelted with gunfire. It wasn't really doing any lingering damage anyways. Arthur had never seen a Dread Knight in person before, so couldn't help but gawk at it stupidly from his hiding place, looking for weaknesses.

Easily at least seven feet tall, the battered matte black armor was graffitied with Armada iconography and skull motifs.

When the gaze of the Knight's helmet settled on him, the enormous figure changed tactics from scanning, to attacking. Whoever was inside this black-metal giant proceeded to unholster a brutal looking hand cannon with a hammer the size of Arthur's thumb and open fire, spattering with only two shots the shocktrooper to his left who had helped pull him into cover.

The shocktrooper died agonizingly as he choked on his own blood – the two gigantic slugs had implanted through his armor and into his torso, spraying blood up into drifting globules around his corpse and onto his face.

Arthur ducked down for fear of being next, trying not to look the dying trooper in the eye.

The sound of the hand cannon was deafening.

There was a lull in the shooting, and then a second bright flash he was smart enough to shield his eyes from. One of the troopers on the far side screamed and went limp in a ragdoll of flailing limbs. Arthur had been smart enough to cover his eyes for the second flash bang grenade, but his ears and skull still echoed, as if his head were stuck in the middle of a church bell being rung.

The pounding of the hand cannon continued.

The bridge was still awash with noise and light, as the Dread Knight killed a third defender while still only seeming to take glancing damage. Each shot they threw at the Knight impacted and deflected off his chest and shoulder armor, many leaving scorch marks or dents but not seeming to be able to punch through properly.

The Knight stood there in the open middle of the firefight, blocking the elevator. Its' boots were magnetically clamped to the floor like the Seraph's.

Douglas was facing it, unloading his plasma rifle into the behemoth's joints and face while trying to stay behind his own tiny excuse for cover. Other Armada soldiers were taking the opportunity to move up and use the colossus' powered suit of armor for cover.

Arthur tried to remember his Academy training while frantically searching for a bigger weapon.

The needle rifle had worked its way free from his shoulder and was floating near the bow, gently bouncing off the closed blast shield.

The dread knight kept firing, and shock troopers kept dying everywhere around him with each few thunderous pulls of the hand cannon's trigger. Not a single round came his way and Arthur realized it was saving him for last. For capture.

He dared to unholster his sidearm and duck out to send a few small bolts of plasma at it, only to have the shots sizzle and melt superficially, twisting and melting the outer layers of plating. The giant black suit of armor turned to face him, casually slipping new slugs into the open cylinder of the hand cannon from a pocket at the waist. He could feel it taking stock, measuring him for his worth as it reloaded.

Being regarded as nothing more than meat to be collected sent waves of terror through his whole body.

Dread Knights were twisted genetic, surgical, and pharmaceutical nightmares of the Black Armada, the most fanatic of the Armada's soldiers. They were chosen after numerous close calls or victories in battle as Berserkers, Soldiers, or Harlequin Knights. After they had survived hell several times over, they were ramped up on drugs, stimulants, and enhanced with gene splicing, risky surgery, and other implanted technology akin to Harlequin Knights - those horrific experiments in cyborg soldiers.

If it all wasn't horrific enough, they finished off the process by encasing the person in an enormous powered combat suit for the rest of their war-mongering existence. A Seraph could remove the suit, but a Dread Knight lived for all eternity in theirs, serving their god-emperor until they breathed their last gasps.

He glanced over to the Lieutenant, who was still taking potshots at the gargantuan slab of black armour plating to minimal effect. Douglas had several deep dents and breaches in his armor from the hand cannon.

Arthur had read somewhere that Dread Knights were originally based on Chayot armor.

Normally, only G.O.D. specialist units with similar powered armour like Seraphs and Chayots could go toe to toe with them and win. And even then, a Dread Knight's sheer size, determination and fanaticism often forced even the best G.O.D. soldiers to early, brutal deaths.

"Follow the Lieutenant's lead. Aim for the head."

Shouted one of the senior troopers over the gunfire, and suddenly every weapon was trained on the Knight's helmet. The Dread Knight barked an order in response, muffled by his helmet, and other Armada berserkers and infantrymen poured in behind it. It was odd to see the Dread Knight itself being used for cover, but it was crushingly effective.

The last few Guardian troopers were suddenly dying left and right, as more corpses filled the weightless bridge even further, along with floating spheres of blood and shrapnel.

Arthur realized the uselessness of his handgun, and snatched up a rifle floating by.

The Admiral aimed it at the Dread Knight's head and pulled the trigger again and again as fast as he could.

It took all he was worth with his one hand to hold onto the railing and keep himself from flying off into the bridge-wide view port behind him, where he would likely become an easy target for the Armada. While the low caliber rounds alone didn't accomplish much, the mixture of various weaponry smashing and sparking against the helm eventually did, collapsing the bullet-proof glass and metal of the faceplate inwards upon itself with the help of Douglas' superheated plasma bolts.

There was no scream, and via some sort of witchcraft, the Knight kept fighting and shooting even as it died, fanning the trigger of its enormous hand cannon like a cowboy at a shooting gallery.

Eventually it slumped in place, with the magnetic boot locks stuck where they were.

"It's down!"

The Seraph was still pumping plasma bolts into the corpse to make sure.

The Dread Knight's body shifted, and then the helmet fully gave way, ensuring whatever horror inside was reduced to plasma charred ash and a disgusting mixture of brain matter, circuitry, and bone. The armor's magnetic boot clamps released with the death of its occupant, and it drifted backwards towards the entrance hole, pinning an unlucky Armada soldier against the still glowing torched corner of the door.

The ranks of the enemy were being replaced with Berserkers.

These were men and women clad in nothing but rags, bones, and the most rudimentary gear imaginable, brainwashed to serve Xex and the Black Armada to death and beyond. It became more and more of a shooting gallery than a real battle thanks to the narrow corridors and the single bottlenecked access point, although now and then a Berserker would be fast enough to pop off a shot their way before they were gunned down.

"Callsign God of Death has launched some small attack craft. The boarding vessels are almost here."
Arthur was surprised to see the woman on comms still strapped into her seat despite the dozens of floating stray rounds and corpses.

The Berserkers cluttered the entryway, and their fallen comrades were unceremoniously tugged back down the shaft so that more could enter in a never-ending stream of bodies.

He suspected they had broken into one of the floors below the bridge and established it as a mustering point.

"Whatever!"

He shouted back, but his words were already falling on deaf ears.

"Nonononono."

Her call had attracted the attention of the enemy, and she was already slumped over in her chair from several rounds that had pierced through her back. The offending Berserker guilty of the deed, a man wearing a human skull as a faceplate, had already been killed in retort, but she was still limp.

Arthur swore, and slapped on the safety of his rifle, flipping the strap over his shoulder and pushing over to her.

It was tough attempting to unstrap her from her seat in a zero-gravity environment, and he had to duck several shots that came his way as he did it.

"Hold on."

She couldn't if she tried.

There was a wet hack, and she sputtered up blood and air.

Then she stopped breathing altogether.

Arthur pushed off from her console, pulling her along by her collar and sailing to a safer place behind one of the deployable cover segments. It was a struggle to keep her from drifting away again, as her blood had quickly stained his white admiral's coat and made his hands slippery.

Two growing globs of sticky red liquid were accumulating on her uniform all around the wounds.

He realized the futility of his actions as he watched her die.

He continued to keep pressure even after he knew she was gone.

"Admiral, we need an extra gun. Jacobs and Yeltsin are dead."

He left her floating in a constellation of her own blood - eyes open, and moved hand over hand up a safety rail back towards the firefight, doing his best not to retch. His hands slipped, incessantly coated as they were in sticky drying blood that clung to his hands in huge drops.

Most of his upper torso was also covered in the girl's blood, a simple force of cohesion sticking the liquid to his body and the fabric of his uniform. He discarded his hat and started stripping his torso down to the black undershirt. The blood soaked into his jacket was making it impossible to move around.

In a small act of defiance, Arthur threw his heavy soaked jacket at the elevator in some feeble attempt at screening. The soldier at the railing nodded as he grabbed the kinetic rifle from Yeltsin's corpse and continued shooting.

The Armada had wizened up by now, and was breaking through other entrances. A simplistic ploy that Arthur was surprised had taken them this long to figure out. They were seeking to divert gunfire from their initial breakthrough and break the bottleneck for their unarmoured forces who were dying in droves.

The emergency elevator shaft was rapidly torched open, as was the maintenance access leading back into the bowels of the ship.

The ship was eerily silent as they did so, save the casual click or pop of a brief weapon exchange, the flaring noise of the plasma torch, or the shuffling of their careful movements. The Armada had sustained heavy losses, with bodies, blood, and fallen weapons from both sides still drifting haphazardly around the bridge and obscuring vision to a frustrating degree.

It was a massacre.

"Sir, we have incoming. Two new contacts are closing."

The pilot had taken on the fallen ensign's duties at his own side console, and was trying to handle manoeuvring the crippled carrier and also tracking hundreds of different conversations at once with the help of the ship's dual A.I.s Dominic and Kyros. The two A.I. constructs were largely responsible for keeping them in the fight outside and delaying the enemy onboard, having taken over many of the ship's systems at great strain to processing and memory. An A.I. running the basic maintenance and subsystems of a ship was one thing, but trying to operate a badly damaged carrier needing thousands of individual fixes without any crew?

It was straining them to an error point.

"Keep it moving. Dom, Kyros, vent anywhere you still can at this point to kill as many of the Armada as possible."

Arthur hoped Greene and his engineers had been picked up by someone.

"Two battlecruiser contacts, no callsigns, moving to intercept, the rest of the God of Death fleet is engaging the Armada in pursuit."

The ship rocked, and the air trembled and started to pull towards the elevator shaft. Somewhere in the rear of the ship there had been an explosion. Arthur didn't bother to ask where they had been hit. There was a second rumble and then a sudden rush of air.

His ears popped as he was nearly ripped from cover.

"Kyros, seal whatever blast doors you can for that breach."

The air pulsed on the bridge, and then stopped moving. Arthur breathed a sigh of relief that they wouldn't suffocate in a vacuum for at least a little while longer. The rifle he had recovered had quickly run dry, and the replacement plasma rifle he had snagged from an Armada infantryman's body was running close to an empty magazine as well.

It had become a battle of attrition.

The entire bridge was filled with floating projectiles spinning and bouncing in the zero-g. The air pressure change had scattered everything around yet again.

Bullets and casings, needles and blood droplets, all of it mixed in with bodies and debris from plasma charring.

There were only a handful of G.O.D. soldiers left fighting out of the two dozen soldiers. Even in a space as large as a carrier's bridge, Arthur and his survivors had lost the option to move around with ease… At least not without causing themselves harm.

"Admiral Brass, callsign God of Death. It's a pre-recorded message."

Kyros' synthetic voice was calm and polite as it informed him of the development over his earpiece. Arthur ducked down as a stray round whizzed past his head and sunk into the back of the pilot's shoulder. He screamed in pain as his entire arm went dead and slapped the controls.

The Chrysalis lurched, beginning to ever-so-slowly twist around them.

"*Fuck.* Play it!"

A weathered older voice began playing into his ear, crackling heavily due to all the jamming and intense plasma interference from the battle outside. Arthur remembered that they were isolated from it all in their current firefight. Sound didn't travel in space, and the naval battle hadn't stopped just because their ship had been incapacitated.

Maybe it meant that somewhere out there, Captain Anderson and Vice-Admiral Long were still commanding the tattered remains of the First Expeditionary Fleet, taking as many Black Armada ships down to hell with them as possible.

"Admiral Arthur Brass, I'm aware of your predicament. Please be advised, I am plotting your extraction even as you receive this message. While some of the soldiers with you are likely equipped for zero pressure, I assume yourself and any surviving bridge crew are not, so I highly suggest you make yourselves ready for such an event in a timely fashion."

He wondered what it could mean, but then it hit him like a freight train.

"Double check the blast shields, prepare for breach."

It was crazy and dangerous – pretty close to insane.

One of the A.I.s confirmed that more transports and fighters had been launched from one of the two intercept cruisers. Shortly after, he heard several resounding thumps on the thick armor plating of the blast shields.

He frantically looked around for a helmet, a suit, *anything.*

"Douglas, we're about to lose pressure, is everyone strapped in?"

Douglas couldn't answer, as another batch of soldiers mixed with Berserkers charged the entryways to break the brief silence that had been.

Gunfire chattered into the breach once more.

Arthur pushed over to Hartnell, the pilot.

It was bad, and the man's arm hung limply from the socket, the bullet embedded into the shoulder blade. Looking over the injury and realizing there wasn't much he could do – Arthur paused. That was when he noticed the series of quiet clicks on the blast shields behind them.

Arthur hadn't moved his hands so fast in his whole life as he helped unstrap Hartnell in a hurry and seek shelter with him by the railing.

"Sir, according to Dominic there is a small team on the outside hull setting breaching charges around the external blast shields."

"*I know.* Fuck."

Arthur felt helpless, effectively out of any logical decisions to make. Should he charge the Armada and maybe save the fireteam and his one remaining crewman onboard? Or should he let the Resistance space him, for gods knew what ends?

Well…

Suicide was always an option.

"Kyros, do we have any means of getting them off? This 'rescue attempt' sounds like liquidation."

"Negative."

Replied the A.I., this time over the loudspeakers.

Arthur thought hard about what to do next. It was unlikely they were to be killed intentionally if the bridge was vented, as this God of Death fellow had suggested they suit up before his teams breached the shields. But suiting up was impossible under the current circumstances.

He had already relayed the coming danger to the soldiers around him, several of whom lacked sealing headgear or whose armour had already been holed or damaged. There was a rising sense of panic within everyone on the bridge. Arthur could feel it.

Well, except for the Seraph, Lieutenant Douglas. If he was worried, any expression or fear was encased firmly inside his Seraph armor where nobody else could see it.

"Dom, Kyros, set us on the best trajectory you can to get us out of the debris, then start a wireless data transfer to the closest command ship still fighting. Split yourselves up to different ships if you can. Can't risk your capture."

"Yes sir."

Arthur hoped that whatever was coming was fast, or they'd all be sucking nothing but vacuum in a matter of seconds. Or the vacuum of space would be sucking them.

Not much of a difference, really.

Arthur struggled to make any sense of his life, and could feel every single regret in his life pouring into his head from somewhere warm inside his chest. What was the point of life, when it was going to be snatched away from you right when you started to realize what it's truly worth?

He had been fighting stubbornly against fate for so long, that perhaps now was finally his time to go. He would join his family and find some sort of peace from this chaotic existence. He would miss Feria, Joe, and everyone else.

At least Joe might join him someday.

And at least Serania and Julian would get their long-awaited wish?

He didn't know how he had time to think about it, but he thought about God, and then about the Creator.

Were they the same thing? Were they watching?

The ultimate question, then, for a stubborn soul - in a universe where gods walked around with the rest of them, who should he beg supernaturally for help in his dying moments?

"Ashes to ashes."

The Seraph called.

"Dust to dust."

His few trooper comrades finished the phrase in recital, and Arthur realized that unlike himself, they had clearly adapted to this lifestyle of death. Hell, they had probably seen dozens of their friends and teammates die already.

In that moment he felt shamed in front of these hardened men and women who felt no fear, and for whom death was merely a side note to a career choice.

Despite his years of Naval experience, he was afraid. He could feel tears drifting off his face, and rushed to wipe them away before it could demoralize Hartnell. Almost in defiance, Hartnell drew his kinetic sidearm with his remaining arm and blind-fired the entire clip at the nearest torched entry, in a dogged display of determination.

Arthur had to admire his gusto, at the least.

"Alright, on the count of three, they're goi-"

Before he could finish the sentence there were a series of nearly simultaneous dull thuds at his back, and an enormous roar of sound. The shaped charges had detonated on the blast shields behind them, cutting away the entirety of the material separating them from the void outside. The steel blast shields and fused silica viewport sheared away from the ship, and everything pulled out into the abyss.

Bodies, shells, blood, all.

Arthur gripped the railing with both elbows as hard as he could, to avoid the sudden pull of force - locking his legs around Hartnell's stomach.

One of the troopers attempted to yell over the roaring din of air escaping the ship, but he was far too late. The kilometres of air still encompassed within the ship prevented an explosive decompression, but the situation rapidly grew much worse as air was ripped from within out into the hungry maw of void.

One of the troopers' grip slipped, and he was drawn backwards as he screamed for help over the screaming wind. The lack of gravity made even the moderate pull of the vacuum outside impossible to fight against, and Arthur watched him flail uselessly, spinning in all directions.

Arthur watched his fall. The man slammed brutally into a control console somewhere halfway to the viewport with a sickening crunch and a breaking of glass, before being drawn out of the ship into the darkness beyond as if sucked up by a straw.

Arthur could see shadowy figures waiting for him at the edge of the light outside, latched onto the edges of the gaping maw into space. He closed his eyes and held on as tightly as he could against the rushing air as the lights flickered on and off across the entire bridge. Bodies, shrapnel, and stray weapons from the breaches all zoomed out into the inky black space above *Heartland*, pulled out with the escaping atmosphere.

The second trooper to go was a victim of the debris being pulled through the wind tunnel effect, as a stray needle struck his shoulder sideways and dislodged him. He, too, was shunted out into space and rapidly vanished from Arthur's sight.

Arthur's legs were tiring and next to go was Hartnell, yanked out of his grip without a word between them.

Arthur was going red in the face, trying his best to remember his training and breathe properly in the rapidly vanishing air. Being right next to the breach, those on the bridge faced the worst of the vacuum's pull, as air was siphoned out from the kilometres of corridors or breached blast doors the Armada had torched open on their way up.

That was a stroke of luck, in that they were clearly being affected too.

Arthur watched as several soldiers and berserkers were ripped from the elevator shaft and shunted beyond the chasm of dark.

The skin of his face felt like it was being ripped right off with the force of the wind. Almost everything aboard the bridge was already gone to this gaping maw of black space and flickering stars that beckoned him.

Bodies of both living and dead were drawn past him into the starry abyss.

The Armada obviously hadn't prepared for this sudden turn of events, and the holes they had cut now became their doom, as soldiers from each breached opening into the bridge quickly found they were being shot out past their foe into space. Many of the Berserkers scrabbled to grab anything and everything.

Few of them would survive long without helmets, armour, or space-sealed gear.

There were flashes outside on occasion, as the suited-up Armada and the mysterious breaching force engaged each other in a vacuum. It was more of a shooting gallery, as the shadowy figures magnetically locked to the hull took pot-shots at helplessly drifting Black Armada soldiers spinning out of control.

It was the most morbid skeet shooting Arthur had ever witnessed.

Arthur could only imagine what would happen to his body without space gear as he simultaneously asphyxiated, boiled in his skin, and then froze to death in a matter of minutes...

He knew full well about ebullism from the naval academy, and it didn't sound like a great way to die. He hoped he fell unconscious first, as boiling to death was surely one of the more terrible ways to go.

The lack of pressure in a vacuum like space ensured that any liquid could boil out from within his body in a matter of seconds.

The trooper to the far right of Douglas lost his grip, and vanished next through the hole.

Douglas didn't even make a move to grab him.

The Seraph's magnetic clamps were securely locked to the floor, and he was standing up straight at the full height extension of the suit, swiping at each Armada soldier that flew past with a brutal jagged kukri the length of Arthur's arm.

A gruesome stream of red accompanied every slash.

Arthur could see more bright flashes outside the broken viewport, and wondered if the flashes were the ongoing battle, or the Black Ops team ensuring there would be no survivors. As time passed more slowly, more of the troopers were pulled towards the makeshift exit, failing in their grips due to the blackouts and hypoxia setting in. His own arms, locked around the railing by the elbows, were screaming at him in protest, the ligaments and tendons searing with pain.

He refused to let go, but his vision was rapidly blurring and he could feel his heartbeat pounding in his head.

There were only two troopers left. These were the troopers who remained vacuum sealed, and of course there was Lieutenant Douglas, fully suited for almost any environment in his cybernetic Seraph power armor suit.

Arthur's vision flickered again, and he began pressure breathing as the air current slowed. The Seraph's clamps detached. It turned out the Lieutenant was waiting for the air to vent so he could leave the ship without being slammed into anything. A smart move really, to avoid the risk of compromising his armour's seals. The Seraph pulled a looped cord from his waist and drifted it over to the two troopers as his soft blue thrusters across the armor flared to life.

Arthur felt his vision going just before the air was completely gone and let out every iota of air in his lungs in one big breath, a tactic to avoid rupturing his lungs that he had been taught in the academy.

He was seconds from blacking out, and Douglas knew it.

The Seraph moved first.

It was lucky the remaining bridge heating still worked, but it was barely fending off the angry cold that now seethed in through the open hole where the view ports and blast shields had recently been.

The Chrysalis struggled valiantly, pouring heat out into cold space in a futile battle against the endless starry backdrop. It was a final defiance of the ship against the cold hateful fury of space. How long would the carrier's husk draw power from the subsystems and the damaged engine's fuel cells before they failed?

Weeks, months?

It could go nuclear any moment, really.

Arthur's vision was going, and consciousness was slipping away. He felt his body churning, as the lack of pressure allowed his body to start boiling at room temperature. He struggled to move his hands up to his face, and in his sudden blindness he could feel his body going numb from the exertion and waste of resources.

It was like swimming through sticky black tar.

He became vaguely aware of something moving him off to the left with a gentle tug, but he knew he was helpless to save. Douglas or whoever it was would watch him boil and suffocate to death.

In the blackness beyond consciousness, something grabbed at his legs behind him, and the sudden shock on his tortured, dying body made everything go white.

The last thing Arthur Brass remembered seeing were the four glowing red eyes, two on each side of the Seraph's helmet as it moved him towards the pulling hands on his ankles.

Those four red lights haunted his last waking breath, red slits against the cold and the dark.

He saw the four horsemen signalling his own personal apocalypse in each one.

Death had come at last.

CHAPTER 22: THE LONG SLOW GOODBYE

"You fade into darkness only to be presented with a bright white light? I don't buy it. I'd expect death to be more like an endless dream instead, one you can never hope to wake up from."

Arthur Brass figured death would be far bleaker than a simple dream after that, but he did dream, which was somewhat comforting to a dead man who feared the worst.

He failed to arrive in a stereotypical place like Heaven or Hell, and so he dreamt mostly of his mother, long passed on, and of Feria. He missed them both so much that his heart wouldn't stop aching. Sometimes his father would be there, a shadowy figure with an arm around his mother's waist.

But his memories as a young boy failed him and he never appeared as solid.

His father was forever a hazy shadow, some metaphor of the subconscious for his real-life lack of person in Arthur's own existence. Arthur was envious of his parents in those dreams, that they should get to spend eternity together and he was damned to only see his wife Feria in passing swirls when his subconscious allowed it.

Feria would never die. And as such, they would never be reunited.

After a time, he assumed this place of never-ending dreams was purgatory itself. His vision was foggy and the edges of his sight were shadowed ever so slightly as to always remind him that nothing was real.

He dreamt of how Feria would take the news of his death, and of places they'd never get to go; to the ancient Guardian temples of Nepal, old when the first civilizations were young. Or perhaps to *Love*, with glowing pink skies and orange-lit seas. Or maybe even to the gaseous shaded Nebulas amongst the furthest stars of the Milky Way. He dreamt of everything they could have had, but were now denied, even as worried pitifully about what it meant to be dead.

Serania had gotten what she wanted, finally. And maybe she'd leave his loved ones alone at last - taking his sacrifice as penance enough for the defiance she felt exuded from his very existence. And maybe Feria would finally be rid of the one weakness she was forced to protect, free to return to a life of individuality and freedom.

As much as he pined for her, he thought it best.

Perhaps that's why he struggled to find her in his death dreams? Her continuing life was free of his longing for her in death.

He wondered if his soul core would be pulled out of his corpse, some strange husk of his very essence. He wondered if it would please the researchers who pricked him with needles and ran him on treadmills at the academy so long ago. Many of his death dreams were familiar moments of reliving, like those lab tests.

He doubted they'd even find his corpse, let alone manage to harvest it before it had boiled away and frozen beyond the point of autopsy.

A morbid amusement in that.

He felt an enormous sense of loss throughout those death dreams that he could never identify, but which never went away throughout. Arthur assumed it was the part of him that acknowledged his death and was trying to come to peace with it.

Would he go to Heaven, or Hell, or Valhalla, or Shangri-La after he came to terms with being dead?

And what of fate?

He kept looking for where he had gone wrong in his life to cause him so much trouble. Did that Creator bastard, somewhere out in the stars, damn him for some predestined crime? The absence of such a true god amused him, but perhaps going to church would have given him a different experience in the great beyond than the one he faced now.

There were large black patches where he could feel what he thought was his body moving around. He assumed they were merely phantom images, just as an amputee might feel a phantom limb. Maybe the mind still had some biological connection to the corpse, and could feel it breaking down as the brain itself eroded.

It was in one particularly long dream, where he was standing in a happy fleeting moment with his wife, overlooking an enormous peach orchard that the most extraordinary thing happened.

He woke up.

His vision was locked on a single nearby tree at that moment, its fuzzy ripe orange-red fruit looking decadent and delicious.

He loved peaches.

The image of them on the tree burned into his brain, and even as he was gently sucked back into a brutally bright light, it remained.

It only slowly began fading out once the new image had taken its place.

"Can you hear me, Admiral?"

The voice was familiar, edged with some far-off accent he could hardly understand; but that was also strangely similar in a reassuring way. He had known false awakenings many times before in his death dreams, but this was a new scene, and not one of the places he had reawakened to previously.

Arthur huffed and stared at the ceiling, praying for the peach orchard and for his wife to come back into his vision. He had been deprived of so many of his dreams with her halfway through, and he was always angry to be torn from Feria's side.

His thoughts were mashed together, disjointed for a long while with anger and confusion. The ceiling wasn't fading.

Usually he could focus hard and change the dreamscape.

There was a realization that sent an involuntary jolt through his body, as he started recognizing the familiar feeling of a body again, clearer than in some of the more lucid dreams. As he rediscovered his fingers and toes, it suddenly hit him that this was a particularly clear dream, lacking the strange milky fog and dark edges that obscured others.

"The God of Death."

He spoke it aloud, just to see what would happen.

It hurt.

His throat tightened, making him cringe in pain. He was confused when his sentence rang back into his ears, hoarse, rather than fuzzily echoing into nothing as it always did in dreams.

"*Former* God of Death, actually. The callsign is for the sake of ease."

The voice was soothing, scratchy and old. It had that faintest trace of an accent of someone who had learned a language second but been forced to speak it their whole life.

It became more and more apparent that this was someone he had never met face to face in his former life, but who was standing at his bedside now in death - a kindly old balding man in a three-piece suit. He found it hilarious that this was the image his death-brain had conjured up to match the voice, and guffawed at the sight.

Damn did it hurt.

A bowler hat was perched in the man's left hand near his lap, and he held a dress cane in his right hand, although he was leaning on the guardrail of Arthur's bed with his elbow instead.

"Who are you really though?"

Arthur asked, making sure to gather enough saliva to help ease the pain of speaking.

He wondered if this was just death playing a morbid sort of subconsciousness game on him.

Still, it was a new experience, so he explored it for what it was.

"Tarnos."

The vision of death replied, failing to elaborate further, and Arthur slowly wandered off into another sleepy daydream, remembering the happy peach orchard. The visage of the old man faded, and the peaches transformed into blurred shapes with tails made of soft white light.

Peaches made of shooting stars. Next, he drifted into a dream about an ocean full of coral and brightly coloured fish, like one of the holograms from back at the Academy in Maxwell Mons.

The name rang in his head though. And several dreams later, he took heavy breaths and tried to get a sense of where he was, as his vision suddenly started blurring back and forth between the brightly colored coral and the strange old man again. Thinking and observing at the same time, he forced himself to sit up, aware of the pounding headache and severe discomfort in his lungs that jarred his dreamy head with fatigue.

He coughed and brought up phlegm, which helped him feel better somewhat, although it hurt like hell to do so.

"You were in a vacuum environment for over two minutes. Usually mortals die from less."

The man explained.

Arthur was annoyed, because he had been well aware of how he died. He didn't need some figure from his subconscious explaining it again and bringing up the fact when Arthur was trying to remember the peaches.

A sweet taste filled his mouth and he wiped saliva from his cheek. The taste helped the pain in his throat.

Delicious ripe peach flesh filled his mouth and he licked his dry lips, half-trapped in fantasy.

"Our medical experts were quite baffled at how you were quick and intelligent enough under that much situational pressure to gauge your breathing and lung pressure appropriately with the last major drop of pressure. Luckily you remained inside the bridge or you may have freeze-dried completely before my men reached you."

What...?

Arthur panicked, and jolted his head around, making his

now horrendous headache worse by trying to determine the difference between dream and reality. The peaches faded completely, and the old man and room came into focus again. He had put the black bowler hat on his head now, covering his bald head.

The room was basic, with what he assumed to be state of the art medical equipment and a very simple medical bunk. He wasn't strapped in, so he chalked that up to still dreaming, as if he refused to acknowledge he might still be alive.

"Am I alive or am I still dead?"

His voice rasped, with a bone-dry throat, his hands moving to rub his face with a forearm and straining at the effort it took to do so.

His skin was mottled pink and white, and felt raw.

He stopped to examine the flesh of his palms, wrinkled and mildly disfigured as if he had been in a bath for too long. Everywhere he examined, his skin was red and irritated, although it was the worst on his face, neck, and hands.

The world came into focus again suddenly, baffling him as to his real identity and place for a second time. The deep comforting voice with a soft foreign accent still belonged to that same old man in a bowler hat and his three-piece suit, leaning forward now onto his cane as if his legs were about to give out.

His face was fixed on Arthur's and his lips were softly pursed.

"You are quite alive Admiral Brass, although if I recall correctly, you suffered from onset ebullism, asphyxia, and hypothermia, all of which could have killed you individually had you remained in the vacuum much longer. As I mentioned previously, you are very lucky to have exhaled, or one or both of your lungs might well have ruptured. The medical team was still forced to use an experimental nanobot medical treatment to repair much of the tissue damage caused by the liquid in your body beginning to boil. You almost lost your fingers to it, actually, not to mention the doctor's fears of brain damage."

Everything was fuzzy and he struggled to comprehend that some of the dreams he had may have been real, and not what he had perceived as actual death. His fingers did hurt, and he examined the backs of them slowly, noting the fresh pink skin and lack of some previous scars and wrinkles.

"Had you suffered the same fate and been in the G.O.D.'s hands for your recovery, I can say with some confidence you would have surely lost your hands and digits at best, and been forced to use the dreadful excuses for prosthetic limbs the Guardians are still peddling these days."

"Where am I?"

Arthur asked, and the man called Tarnos smiled politely, seeming to realize Arthur was still filled with all manner of questions.

"You're on the G.R.A. Command Carrier *Killing Kingship*, or as some of the boys like to call it informally: *The Double K*. As I said before, my name is Tarnos, former God of Death, and also former member of the G.O.D. High Council, or at least I was long before you ever came into the picture."

"The Resistance has carriers?"

He asked without thinking, and Tarnos patted his leg, smiling bemusedly.

"So you know who we are. And you're already trying to interpret our combat strength while you're recovering from a near death experience, bedridden on one of our flagships? You're more capable than you look, Admiral, although you might want to keep the plotting quiet. At least around the enemy leadership."

His voice was almost too cheerful for such an old man.

"Arthur."

He was annoyed at the formal pretext. He felt a slip of consciousness come back as he said his name.

"Okay. Arthur it is."

Arthur rubbed at his eyes and tried to swing his legs over the edge of the bed to stand up. It was difficult. There was no telling however long he had been bedridden and motionless. This god seemed to hardly care about his own safety in the event Arthur were to attack, as he saw no security stationed anywhere in the room. Arthur could hardly guess what powers such an elderly god could muster. Remembered Julian's crushing darkness and made a note to remain civil.

He must have ascended at a very old age, which was astounding.

How had he survived the process at such an old age?

"I know you are still recovering, but we have some important things to discuss, Arthur."

Tarnos pointed it out as a matter of fact, and Arthur was suddenly aware of the conundrum this would undoubtedly result in. He just wanted to go home and see his family and friends, and to get rid of the headache that was developing. He had *absolutely no desire* at that point to play politician or diplomat.

His body was coming into focus more clearly, and it ached and burned as if it was being dunked in ice water and lit on fire simultaneously.

He longed for the numbness of his dreams.

"How much do you already know about me, Tarnos?"

He slowly eased himself onto his feet, making his best effort at ignoring the raging pain. He was happy that he was able to stand, albeit tenderly and with agony, but was worried at the lack of feeling in his toes. He pulled at the simple grey shirt and sweatpants he was wearing and got embarrassed, bristling at the thought that they had undressed him and possibly examined him, even if they had saved his life as a result of it.

"Well, we know that your fleet was originally intended to attack us, and for some reason, it was drawn into a conflict with the Black Armada over *Heartland*, a conflict which you initially lost, although not without inflicting great damage to the Black Armada."

Arthur swore, loudly. And Tarnos wasted no time in whacking him across the backs of his knees with his cane when he did so. If standing was agony, falling to the floor was a searing, white-hot crucifixion. He remained there, crumpled to the floor, and took an extremely long while to get back up.

"You're a diplomat for the Guardians now, Arthur, so watch your mouth."

Tarnos' demand for manners was aggravating, especially as he had slipped back into some sort of accent in his warning. It brought up memories of Judge Joe Undelwood.

"Fuck off."

Arthur spat back, and Tarnos narrowed his eyes, far more severely than the judge ever could.

"Do you think I risked and lost the lives of my people to save you merely because I wanted to revive you and then have a chat over tea, Arthur? Do you think I lost the lives of those under my command, and several Resistance ships above a G.O.D. core world for nothing? I advise you not to waste my time, or I'll certainly waste yours in a less than amicable fashion."

His sudden fury broke the illusion of manners and brought

Arthur to his senses. He remembered the other name this old man had gone by.

"You're a god."

He pointed out, and Tarnos sighed, exasperated at Arthur's sudden manifestation of pointing out the obvious.

"Of course I am, and I used my old title as a call-sign in the hope that one of my old colleagues somewhere on your fleet would recognize me and accept my help in denying Xex a major victory and a pressing advantage in the ongoing war. Unfortunately for me, there were no gods anywhere on your fleet to talk to, and instead I got stuck with you as the highest-ranking surviving officer. Although it was lucky in that you are, or I should say *were* also apparently the commander of the entire First Expeditionary Fleet."

Tarnos fell silent after that, allowing the words to sink in and hammer home the point he was trying to make. He wanted to talk shop, not dabble in niceties.

"So, what happened?"

Tarnos motioned for Arthur to follow him, turning towards the double doors which hissed open at his proximity. Arthur followed him in a hobble out of the room, legs searing with pain. He felt like a lost puppy as they navigated the corridors and past various Resistance crew members.

Outside the door were two Black-Clad Shocktroopers, similar to Guardian ones in armor and weaponry. His feet were tender, but even without shoes the floor was clean and smooth enough, and he was careful to avoid getting in the way of the heavy boots and dress shoes of those they passed. He did *not* want to find out how much having his feet stepped on would hurt right now.

"Well, upon rifting in, we noticed the Armada relief fleet right next door and engaged them before they could identify us and engage our fleet effectively, as I'm sure you're aware - you being in the middle of the fighting and all when we arrived. The Armada was unprepared for such a sudden attack so close to their formation, and we blew them out of the sky without much issue."

"And then all hell broke loose."

"Yes, Mr. Brass, all hell certainly did break loose. We rushed to your fleet's aid, doing our best to navigate the debris field, but at that point most of your fleet had been outgunned and beaten back, in the middle of a retreat to regroup on the opposite side of *Heartland*. The few ships remaining in the melee were hard pressed to fight off the swarms of fixed wing fighters and the various mechanized forces, all of whom descended down upon them in the chaos. From our intelligence, the First and Third Divisions were largely destroyed and the Second was retreating from the wreckage. Anderson took command of the surviving forces after Vice-Admiral Long was killed."

Tarnos coughed and hacked for a minute, but continued.

"By the time we ascertained which ship of the G.O.D. fleet was the command and HQ vessel, which was your ship *The Chrysalis*, you were in the process of being boarded and overwhelmed. With that being the case, I had two cruisers and two Blue Flame teams deploy into the heart of the conflict and blow a hole in your bridge with charges to rescue you. For some reason you were able to hang on until the atmosphere had vented, which my teams hadn't expected. They had assumed you'd pop out into space nice and quick so they could grab all remaining survivors and go. They were also largely unprepared for the Black Armada that came pouring out of the hole alongside you, requiring elimination."

Arthur smirked at his last comment.

"The Armada was spreading across the interior of the ship, or at least across the sections that hadn't been vented, so my teams had to hurry to you, albeit stopping briefly to rescue a batch of survivors near an airlock by the engines. With such overwhelming forces, my people could hardly engage and fight through the entirety of the Armada onboard, so breaching the bridge was the only option. After they hauled you onboard a transport with a little help from one Lieutenant Douglas, we provided the remnants of second division with enough covering fire to regroup around Heartland, and then together our Navies eliminated the Armada fleet in a cross-fire situation."

"Wait, so we won then? What about the others?"

"We're not monsters who leave people to suffocate out in space... My team grabbed the Troopers and your pilot and made sure they were oxygenated and pressurized aboard the transport. Unfortunately, we lost many of them due to exposure or prior wounds. The problem came when the second Armada relief fleet rifted in."

"The fleet that rifted in just before you WASN'T the only relief fleet?"

Had the gamble for his own life lost *Heartland* completely?

If he ever saw home again, he'd likely be court martialed, put on trial, and executed faster than Serania could snap her fingers.

"The fleet was lightly equipped - it was merely another deployment of ground forces for an invasion. In addition, the section of the Armada fleet that we noticed dropping a ground force onto the surface quickly wrapped that little job up and made a beeline into orbit towards our two joint fleets when it noticed we were winning."

The Guardians, and Arthur, had been duped.

All those months of planning and struggling to divert attention away, to actually try and make the threats on his life useful, an attempt to actually put a dent in the Armada... It had all been useless, as Xex had been biding his time waiting for an opportunity in the first place...

"And then?"

Arthur was trying his best not to dwell on the consequences that losing *Heartland* and having his fleet ravaged would undoubtedly bring. The loss of thousands if not tens of thousands of lives was hanging heavily over this enemy debriefing, not to mention the millions of civilians living down on the planet proper. Tarnos shifted uncomfortably as he walked, and he started using his cane heavily almost out of habit rather than any perceived need.

"Well, that's when things went wrong. We gave them a full salvo on our side, working with whatever was left of your G.O.D. fleet, under Anderson. Together we managed to eliminate about a quarter of the Armada's strength, but after the Armada lost those ships they actually began to evacuate, leaving their ground forces behind."

He smiled, sadly.

"With Captain Anderson ceasing all communications with us shortly thereafter and a G.O.D. relief fleet pending, I called for the retreat myself. The seventeen-odd G.O.D. ships remaining, mostly smaller frigates, were turning to face us, so I opted to retreat to Resistance space, back to *King Albert*."

"There were only seventeen ships left out of so many?"

Arthur gaped, struggling to see where he had failed so badly as a commander.

"Your fleet had some difficulty after your carrier was disabled. Captain Anderson took charge of the First Division remnants once you were under siege aboard *The Chrysalis*, and once Vice-Admiral Long had his battlecruiser destroyed with all hands lost, Anderson absorbed Third Division command as well."

"Do you have a casualty list? Do you even know who might still be alive and who might be scuttled?"

"No, the G.O.D. fleet only barely tolerated our presence. There was never an open dialogue between us, outside of that which was absolutely necessary. We were allies of convenience for just a brief moment in Anderson's eyes I presume. It's just as well, I suppose. I doubt that the G.O.D. would allow the Armada to take such an important core world without sending reinforcements for your fleet once they heard things had turned. And I'm almost sure that this attack has reignited the larger war somewhat from its previous stalemate, something Serania is likely pleased with."

Tarnos' roundabout method of reassuring him was futile.

"So then where are my men?"

Arthur's blood was boiling. Knowing the loss of so many men under his command was partially his fault for engaging in a melee both hurt and enraged him. He wanted to pick up a blunt object and beat the shit out of this asshole, just to have someone to act against in his anger. For the first time in a long while, he needed a stiff drink.

"Those recovered from the bridge are safe, Arthur. Those who survived the vacuum, at least. Right now, we're in talks with the G.O.D. upper echelon, trying to secure a round of peaceful negotiations for a possible prisoner exchange. Technically you and your men are now prisoners of war, after the G.O.D. initially refused to barter for your return peacefully. The Guardians seem to want to keep us as an enemy, rather than solve their differences politically through negotiation and diplomacy."

Arthur stared him down, and it came to mind at last that he lacked restraints. It crossed his mind that perhaps if he moved fast enough, he could incapacitate the immortal before he could muster his ascendant powers against him. Maybe it wouldn't be a second Julian incident...

Arthur decided on attacking him just as Tarnos was turning to face him.

Tarnos' mind moved faster.

Just as when he tried to attack Julian, his entire body was locked up, only this time it was pressed up against the side of the corridor by an invisible wall of force.

He screamed in pain.

Arthur's arms pushed up behind his back painfully. And he had also bit his lip in the process of slammed up against the wall. Blood was dribbling awkwardly down his chin and into his scruffy stubble that he had sprouted while bedridden.

Tarnos hadn't even moved his body, and still wasn't even fully facing Arthur's direction. Arthur had never seen a god muster up such fine control without any body movement to accompany it, even at the wedding attack.

He figured Tarnos must be ridiculously old or ridiculously skilled to not even have to use his arms or hands to properly direct his powers.

"Arthur, you have to understand. It's not I who needs to play this negotiation out like my life depended on it. It's your life and the lives of your subordinates on the line, and I'm honestly surprised that not both of us seem to know it. If I were merely to hand you back to Serania unopposed, she'd merely have you executed for failing to fire on us as an enemy of the state, officially or not. I am informed enough to know your personal history with her, despite Julian's best attempts to shut down our spies and agents."

Tarnos sighed, and grasped his brow in a sigh of exasperation. The tension holding Arthur failed to lapse in the slightest.

"You have no argument for your survival as a free man at the moment. If I declare you a prisoner of war, and then trade you for men and women who I *know* are Resistance, and I *know* are rotting away in Guardian prisons... Well, you might just survive long enough to tell Hewah and Cassius what really happened, and barter with the council for your life while I free good mortal folk who are worth the weight of any council member twice over."

Arthur stalled. This god's logic was both brilliant and oddly fair. Why the hell would he care if Arthur lived? Why would he care if Arthur's subordinates lived?

This was framed carefully. It wasn't a stroke of goodwill.

Tarnos' aim all along had been to kill two birds with one stone - to stop Xex from taking *Heartland* and shifting the stalemate, but also to try and gain an advantage for The Resistance.

"I have an interest in keeping the two sides equal for now, while we build our strength and support in the neutral territories. If any one side gains too much of an upper hand, they will split their forces to harass us. This was a calculated loss."

"Why would you give a shit about what happens to me personally?"

Arthur was struggling to speak while pressed up against the wall, and a decreased pain tolerance was outstripping his hostility.

He needed to fish for information.

But god damn was he sick of being disabled and imprisoned by ascendants.

Tarnos turned to face him, and released his grasp on Arthur's body slowly, letting him slide to the floor. Arthur hauled himself up by a handrail on the wall and wiped the blood from his chin.

His legs were visibly shaking. The pain in his body was terrible, but it was easy to ignore within the greater gravity of the situation.

"Because I also owe Hewah an old favour. And I always try to repay my debts when the opportunity presents itself. Now I am free of one more string tying me to the Guardians of Destiny."

Arthur was quiet, because if Tarnos knew Hewah, well… It had some serious implications. Which was the priority? Was he really trying to kill two birds with one stone?

Or did he actually save him primarily as a favour to his father in law?

What favour could be worth dozens of ships and so many lost lives?

CHAPTER 23: ALL THAT REMAINS.

"Ashes to Ashes, Dust to Dust."

At that point Arthur made the choice to offer little in the way of a struggle.

Tarnos continued down the hallway, Arthur plodding along behind him like a dog on a leash.

They eventually reached a series of holding cells in an area that resembled a brig. Despite Arthur's lingering mistrust of Tarnos, the hope of seeing his wife and adopted family again and his curiosity at Hewah's involvement drove him to comply. He was examined by one last medical staffer, and deemed fit and recovered enough.

He was designated to rejoin the other prisoners.

All of the cells were empty save one isolated at the very end of the brig. Within that single large cell were his subordinates who had been "captured" with him at the same time; the surviving Shocktroopers, the Seraph Douglas who had stayed with him on the bridge, and the pilot Hartnell that Arthur had surely taken for dead. He was relieved to find Engineer Greene and a single junior engineering crewman as well.

He didn't recognize any of the troopers or Douglas without their power armour or combat suits, but also wasn't surprised to see them stripped of it and wearing the same plain clothing he was. He wondered if Douglas had gone down fighting, and what it took to subdue a Seraph in full power armor.

"Good to see you're alive, Admiral."

The pilot greeted him with a wave, and Arthur shook his good hand. Hartnell sported a number of scars and disfigurements from the battle, primarily due to encounters with shrapnel that had followed him out of the bridge. His arm was hanging in a sling and gauze padded out his shoulder.

Obviously the G.R.A. hadn't expended as much effort to fix Hartnell as they had Arthur, which was yet another source of guilt.

With Hartnell's help, he quickly built up a rapport with the other surviving troopers, especially Lieutenant Norrin Douglas, the Seraph who had stayed behind to see if he could save him somehow. Most of the troopers had perished when the blast shields were blown out; but the one with the wounded eye was alive.

Greg Strept, his eye carefully bandaged.

He'd likely have either an eyepatch or a cybernetic replacement when all was said and done.

Which one?

Well, it likely depended on how much the G.O.D. liked him.

They had mourned the loss of their comrades while he was still unconscious. Arthur had apparently been laid out for almost three weeks as the nanobots fixed his various bits and bobs and slowly replaced much of the flesh in his hands in order to have him keep his digits.

"So, we're officially prisoners of the Resistance, sir? These folks clearly aren't Black Armada or we'd be drugged up and brainwashed by now. Or we'd have holes in the back of our heads.

Are the rumors true?"

A young private by the name of Ferio Jaures was the one who asked it, and Arthur nodded respectfully, rubbing his chin and sitting down on one of the boxlike bunks provided to them.

Those in the cell likely figured Arthur's split lip was from interrogation, so it was easy to garner an extra level of respect in addition to that afforded to him by his rank. He didn't feel it would change anything to bother correcting them, but he felt guilty about leading them on.

"Looks like it, private. At this point I've been informed by the oh-so-generous God of Death that if it's possible, we're to be part of a prisoner exchange with the G.O.D. - despite the strangely friendly nature of our encounter at *Heartland*. However, with how Serania operates, I'm not willing to put any of my eggs in that basket. I know her personally, and she's not quite the generous type."

There were a number of muffled whispers at his statement, and finally someone spoke up, one Sergeant Vela Thatch.

"Sir, I would appreciate it if you didn't blaspheme the gods."

Her sudden request took him aback, as he had thought everyone to be of the same mind as himself, an unwilling pawn. He regarded her closely, but her face was set and she was dead serious.

He was reminded of the man who had tried to kill him in mutiny over his choice to let the Resistance help.

"I can respect that."

Arthur conceded, and the cell moved into quiet conversation, trying to get to know each other.

All told there were ten of them, including himself in the rather large double cell.

Douglas, Hartnell, Greene, Jaures, Thomas, French, Strept, Cherque, and Thatch.

Most of them were Earthborn, with the exception of Thatch, who was from Blend, and Strept, who was from the neutral stretch of colonies along the Junk & Rumbler Guild trade routes.

They all had various reasons for joining the G.O.D.

Some had joined for debt problems, Greene for adventure, and others for a sense of duty or religiosity. The younger engineering crewman Markus French was from the moon's main city - Luna, and unfortunately for him he had only been enlisted a few months prior.

He had only gone through basic training. *Heartland* had been his first actual battle.

Arthur felt sorry for the kid, trapped as a prisoner due to the connivings of himself and parts of the High Council. He was seeing the ripple effect of his actions in real-time, but didn't want his fellow prisoners to know he was largely responsible for their current predicament.

He did struggle with the idea of telling them the truth, but chose to stay silent for sake of morale.

It was important that the battle for a planet like *Heartland* had meant something.

They had been defending home turf from the enemy.

Sergeant Thatch, who had called him out on his anti-Serania statement was certainly an interesting case, and he had to toe the line to avoid offending her and losing any respect his position afforded him. She had never met the council like he had, so everything surrounding them was tinged with a hallowed aura of reverence and hallowed divinity.

It seemed Sergeant Vela Thatch was the single soldier who had joined out of sheer religiosity, which explained her devotion to Serania and the gods. The way she talked, Arthur figured she was probably prime Chayot material if she kept on her current path, where she would join the corps of walking artillery suits and risk burning to death on some dust-ball somewhere. After all, you only needed three things to be a Chayot as far as Arthur knew: A healthy dose of fanaticism, a willingness to be in slow, bulky power armour, and just a smidgen of pyrotechnics or explosives training, which was mostly optional.

He was thankful Tyrone likely ended up a Seraph and not a walking bomb like the Chayots.

They spent the days getting closer to each other, playing twenty questions and other games, and they even devolved to charades at one-point, in-between routines of sleeping and eating. It was just like being back on the *Asalia* those short years ago on their boring patrol route, except this time they were confined to a cell.

He found being a prisoner was boring more than anything, as there wasn't much to do. His short prison life as a younger man awaiting trial at least had a mystery he could try to decipher, as where aboard the *Killing Kingship* he was waiting on those in power to figure everything out.

He had begun in a jail cell, and maybe he would end in a jail cell.

There was simply nothing for him to do.

The rations and conditions weren't terrible, and thus he didn't complain out loud. Besides, he couldn't help but wonder how the Guardians of Destiny might treat its own prisoners back home.

One of the hardest things to adapt to was the open bathroom, as there was absolutely no privacy whilst using it. Greene,

French, and Arthur were somewhat privileged and restricted in their mannerisms coming from the Navy, used as they were to the formality and relative cleanliness of ship-life. Rules were strict and distance between crew was mandatory to avoid contagion spreading like wildfire.

Arthur himself was especially mortified, having exited the academy as a ship's captain and being privy to private quarters for his entire career.

Resistance soldiers would come by every so often and take one or two of them away for "interrogation", but Arthur doubted they ever learned much, as none of them had ever really taken part in any action against the G.R.A. proper, and only the army folk had heard any of the rumours of their actual existence.

They didn't torture them, thankfully, which made the stay more tolerable mentally. It actually seemed bizarre that they were willing to be so cordial and easygoing on enemy prisoners.

Perhaps it was why defections were likely so common to the Resistance cause once army grunts got out to the neutral territories?

Would any of those in the cell seek to join their captors if they were unable to be freed?

They tried to learn about the Resistance as best they could in the event that they ever made it back home, but there was a clear lack of opportunity with how carefully they were interacted with. Cherque, the oldest of them all, had fought remnants of the Insurrection a few times back in the day - twenty years ago. But that was old news by now with its apparent integration into the G.R.A.

It seemed only Arthur was ignorant to the truth.

Only a specific group out of the Insurrection command structure had even independently survived the move, common knowledge amongst the army folks already. It didn't really matter too much about the enemy leadership's makeup, because they knew so little about their worlds and forces to begin with as grunts. They just knew the Resistance was another enemy to fight, like the Black Armada, Mercenaries, or pirates.

After a few weeks, Tarnos took Arthur back to the interrogation room, and bade him sit, offering him a hot cup of black tea. It was a welcome comfort after the long period of relative boredom and stagnation, and he quickly warmed up to the immortal.

It was a stark contrast to the relationship after the uncouth violence of their last encounter.

The God of Death beat around the bush a bit - allowing Arthur to enjoy his tea.

He was careful in doing so to avoid revealing much.

It was only when the tea was half gone that he got to the heart of the matter. Tarnos let him know that the defense fleets had indeed shown up after the retreat and smashed what was left of the Black Armada invasion, an easy task after their combined efforts at softening them up in orbit and enabling a one-sided game for air support.

Captain Anderson had been promoted to a Vice-Admiral for his efforts, likely taking Long's position. It was widely known within the G.O.D. that Arthur had been captured by the enemy, but apparently the Guardians were still trying to spin the story so that the Resistance would remain invisible in the grand scheme of things. Arthur would be a Black Armada captive by most accounts when the propaganda roared into action.

"So, there's to be a prisoner exchange, Arthur, which we have achieved after bartering back and forth with the G.O.D. through their secret channels for the last while. Four of your people alongside yourself will be traded in exchange for three of our highly valued Resistance thinkers and scientists."

Arthur stopped with the cup of tea halfway to his mouth.

"Only four?"

Arthur knew full well that all told; there were nine others. He made ten. Five of the total would have to remain in G.R.A. custody.

"I handled the negotiations personally, along with the rest of the G.R.A. Leadership. We tried to get more out of the council, but they refused to budge, thanks in a large part to Serania's stubborn attitude. The God of Earth was far more vocal than I remember him being in his efforts to secure your release though."

Arthur set the cup of tea down and scowled, thinking hard about what to do. The hot beverage completely disinterested him all of a sudden, and he wanted nothing more to do with any creature comforts while his fellow G.O.D. members sat in a cell, some for a now indefinite period of time.

"If we gave all of you up freely, the Guardian Council would have known you were not worth as much to us as their own detainees are. And thus, they would have declined to deal, regardless of Cassius' or Hewah's voice in the matter. I did the best I could for both the Resistance and for your group simultaneously, insofar as my debt is concerned."

It seemed unfair, but Tarnos clearly had a grasp on the situation. After a brief mental calculation, Arthur figured he would have likely come to the same conclusion were the roles reversed. He was an Admiral, after all - valuable through rank alone. And he was also a minor celebrity of the G.O.D. war effort against The Black Armada. Declaring him KIA would be a massive blow to morale. "Liberating" him from the Black Armada would be much more beneficial as propaganda. The rest were hardly valuable in the greater scheme of things to the G.O.D.

Engineers and soldiers were a dime a dozen in the Central Universe. Even a bare bones trade in terms of securing their release was more than the G.O.D. would ever agree to.

"So, I have to go back and tell my people that I'm going to leave half of them behind? To rot in your prison cells?"

Tarnos sighed, seeming almost apologetic about it.

"There is no other alternative without diplomatic repercussions on both sides, I'm afraid."

Arthur was discontent. Even though he could parse the logic in these actions for himself, and while he certainly craved a reunion with his wife more than anything else in the central universe, he could hardly get angry with anyone but himself at yet another failure. He had slowly heaped guilt upon his own person for the entire fiasco, and this was just another addition to the list that he felt was somehow his fault. Arthur knew that he shouldn't be in the position of having to face other human beings and tell some of them that they might never see their loved ones or homes again.

"Fine."

It was so quiet that Tarnos barely heard him, and he threw back the entire half cup of hot tea, scalding his throat and mouth. He felt it was a stupid sort of small penance for what he was still unprepared to do, and the coming conversation filled him with dread.

Tarnos took him back to his cell in silence and locked it behind him as Arthur entered with a resounding clang.

Arthur appraised the group of soldiers who were all looking to him for any scrap of good news he could give them. His reign as a golden child of the gods had finally come back to haunt him by having him address his favored status personally.

"I have some good news, and some bad news, so what do you want to hear first?"

Classic, but clean. He could think of no better way to put it.

He sat down on the nearest bunk, scratching his head while trying to choose his next words based on either possible answer. They all immediately focused on him, curiosity filling the cell more than dread. He could tell by her posture and dark look that Thatch was preparing for some sort of religious martyrdom in the event that he was to announce their execution.

They looked at each other and after a brief and honest discussion, with him remaining silent throughout, they decided to hear the good news first, probably hoping to get whatever morbid joke he had prepared out of the way.

They had picked up on that much of his personality over the time spent together in confinement.

"Four of you and myself are to be given back to the G.O.D. in a prisoner exchange."

The room fell into an awkward silence, instead of the angry outburst he had expected. It made him feel even more depressed and guilty - having admitted that he was somehow special enough to be freed based on rank.

"I can already see what the bad news is."

Murmured Jaures, and fell forward onto his hands, rubbing his face thoroughly as if to stir himself out of stupor.

"So, who's it going to be, Admiral?"

Thatch asked, prodding Arthur indirectly to try and assume some responsibility.

"You want me to pick and choose who gets to come back with

me? You're really just going to fall back onto the chain of command?"

They exchanged a few glances, and then all shrugged or nodded, as if they could hardly care what happened to them. Even knowing their backstories, their apathy pained him.

"You've got to be kidding me…"

He shook his head slowly, burying his head in his hands. It wasn't the greatest show a leader could put on in the face of a huge decision, that was for sure.

"Sir, the Guardians of Destiny haven't survived this long by drawing straws. The organization has survived by making the tough choices, and doing the right thing for the majority. We protect Humanity. We protect the future."

Douglas' words were sincere, and Arthur had half a mind to listen to him. After all, the Seraph had been in the military a lot longer than him in terms of years served, second only to Cherque.

It made him think.

Was there even a "greater good?"

Could there ever be, with people like Serania at the top who had long since grown disinterested in the value of mortal lives? Or was there more emotional vehemence behind her ideas, decisions, and plots? Even Arthur was guilty of the same thing, weighing his own life and value against the numbers that had died on the surface of, and in orbit around *Heartland*.

He mulled it over.

"Douglas, Hartnell. You two are the highest ranking Naval and Army officers here, and the G.O.D. needs your expertise for the future. Good Seraph and ship pilots are hard to find."

He paused after stating his first two choices, looking over the remaining Troopers and crew.

"Are there any volunteers to stay, before I make my next choice?"

Arthur was hoping to avoid delegating any more names.

Only silence answered him.

After a few brief moments of this silence, Cherque spoke up.

"I will stay, sir. I have been in jail before. I joined the army to get out, and now I am back. I have been fighting a very long time, and somehow, I have always survived. I am tired. This being back in jail, it is a sign. That's life, no?"

Arthur got up and shook his hand in thanks. Similar stories seemed to latch onto each other.

So...

He had to choose between Greene, Jaures, Thomas, French, Strept, and Thatch. He wanted to use the same logic to take Thatch, but somewhere in the back of his mind he knew that was somehow a mistake. He knew she'd somehow react poorly to it unless he justified his decision.

"Thatch, why did you join the G.O.D.?"

She didn't even blink at his question, nor did she hesitate.

"The rest of my family were murdered by Insurrectionists as a child. A car bomb, sir."

"Why are you still here in this cell, living and breathing, now that the Insurrection is part of the Resistance?"

She glared at him, as if he had slapped her across the face.

"Because when you commit to something, you never back out, sir. Xex has done worse than car bombs."

A wicked grin spread across her face.

"He's worth killing, and I want to kill him."

She was deadly serious, and he couldn't help but smile at the severity of such a woman. Strept was smiling too, and he could tell that Strept admired her fire, even if he shared Arthur's lack of zealotry for the G.O.D itself.

"Ashes to Ashes."

Strept spoke the words with reverence, as if in support of Vera's motives.

"Dust to Dust."

Came the instant reply from every other Army soldier in the cell, and Arthur was given a feeling of family in the space. It wasn't so much as they were all equally committed to the G.O.D. as an organization, but that they all had their own reasons for being there. They were definitely committed to each other through some military bond, which forced him to think about it in terms of their bonds to each other.

Strept was the only shock trooper proper who wasn't a part of this particular squad.

"I've built my own family."

Arthur mumbled to himself, and then made his decision.

"Greene, French, you're coming too."

There was a nodding of heads from everyone in the cell, and he could tell that he had made the right decision. He guessed that Jaures was the youngest and newest member of this particular squad, judging by how the rest of the team looked at him and by how he acted.

As for Strept, well, even though the Resistance had fixed him up, there was a good chance the nerve damage to his eye was permanent, as far as the medics had told him. He wasn't part of this particular squad, either, but he would be forced to keep fighting with one eye or retire back home in the G.O.D. core worlds with pay. Here, he could rest.

"You're learning how us army dogs work, Admiral."

Strept beamed, patting Arthur on the shoulder with his good arm.

Arthur still felt sick at his judgement.

"Us grunts are different on the ground, Admiral Brass. We live together, we fight together, and we die together, because we don't have anybody else to worry about us except for each other."

Arthur couldn't help but smile sadly at the sentiment, but said nothing. He missed Joe, Billy, and more than anyone his wife, at that moment. He thought back on the mental image of her crying on the tarmac as he left.

Arthur Brass was her one weakness.

The backbone of the army, the Shocktroopers, would stay strong together in Resistance prison.

The rest of them would return to the Guardians.

It was decided.

After a few more days of waiting, the five of them committed towards the exchange were transported off the *Killing Kingship*, and onto *The Sun*. Apparently it was the first capital ship of the G.R.A., and one of the first defecting vessels those decades ago, by what Tarnos told him.

There was a proud significance at that, at the resistance needing to keep a forty-year-old carrier in service.

Arthur could only chuckle at their foolish pride.

After they were transferred on-board, they rifted directly into space near a neutral Junk and Rumbler space station. It was a location specially picked as it was just inside the neutral zone, closer to resistance territory. The J&R guild was as always one of the few truly neutral organizations in the central universe, a position he envied.

You could hardly expect truckers or salvage crews to care who they were being paid by, insofar as they still got paid. And of course, J&R would likely be paid by both sides for the use of their station as a trade-off location.

A small standoff between the G.R.A. And G.O.D. fleets was occurring as they both waited for *The Sun* to arrive. However, the Junk and Rumblers guild had been paid handsomely, and thus neither faction wanted to risk either the cash held as deposit or any needless losses due to itchy trigger fingers.

A risk to any beneficial relationship with the J&R was bad for business.

"Homeward bound."

Greene spoke the magical words upon seeing G.O.D. branded ships through the window, bringing an ease to the tension that had built up in waiting. As they passed the other shuttle crossing no man's land, he locked eyes with a young, curly haired blonde woman with glasses through the opposing viewport. Feeling some sudden solidarity between prisoners, he waved at her tentatively. She waved back with a smile, likely surprised to see comradeship from one of her many enemies.

They passed the security screening on the primary hangar of a battlecruiser, *Machiavellian*, similar to his check-in above Venus prior to the academy.

From there the bureaucracy descended as always like a rabid demon hungry for blood.

The prisoners were carted off to be cross-examined and debriefed separately, and Arthur was cut off from the others, subjected to hours-long interrogations, lack of food and sleep, and psychological warfare that was a far worse form of torture than he had ever suffered from the Resistance.

Likely it was all sponsored or encouraged by Serania herself.

He never saw the other prisoners again during the bureaucratic process, but he did what he could to protect them within his examinations and interrogations, as he had learned to do after the *Asalia* incident.

He hoped they were as honorable to him as he was trying to be for them.

A final hiccup came when Guardian tests discovered that the Resistance nanobots were still active and replicating inside his body somehow. While they found there were no spy capabilities or other nefarious goals hidden within the microscopic robots aside from basic body maintenance, he was surprised that the G.R.A. had so carelessly left them inside to mindlessly putter around his body.

When he asked if they were going to harm him, the scientists laughed.

It was exactly the opposite.

He was told they'd likely keep him alive longer, and help heal any wounds quicker.

Was this an extension of the favor Tarnos was repaying, by giving him several extra years with Feria thanks to a gift of Resistance science?

It was an unexpected boon for the G.O.D. as well, as the Guardians had been unable to refine their own nanotechnology much whatsoever. A small bonus to his return.

After a little over a month of due process and tacked on fluff, he was finally cleared for a high-level meeting, and was able to meet with Hewah for the first time since the initial mustering of the fleet about five months prior.

The God of Fire had come for him at last.

CHAPTER 24: BLACK HUMOUR.

"Oil and Vinegar taste great together, but they never mix properly."

"I'm glad you're alive, kid."

They were seated at a steel table in the interrogation room. One Arthur had become very familiar with throughout the bureaucratic process, following his return to Guardian hands.

Without skipping a beat, Hewah noticed the sleep deprivation in Arthur's eyes and movements, gesturing at him vaguely. Arthur was sure that the dark circles under his eyes were enough of a clear indication of the abuse he had suffered.

"I can see that Serania wasn't very kind in her attempts to get some scrap of evidence out of you for treason..."

Arthur smiled despite his fatigue.

He was never so happy to see an immortal in his entire life.

Hell, he might have just started praying to Hewah right there and then he was so desperate for sleep.

"I gave her everything I could possibly give her in terms of what she might want, from the Resistance ship's layout as best my memory could describe, to how they handled their prisoners. I never got a glimpse of military activities nor their true intentions for getting back those Resistance people."

Arthur leaned in close towards his father in law.

"And I only withheld one single thing the entire time."

Hewah looked startled, obviously thinking hard about what might be so important that Arthur would soldier on through a month of old soviet style interrogation to hide it.

The god glanced up at a corner of the room where a pinhole camera lurked. Arthur had noticed it sometime during one of his interrogations and nodded back.

A snap of Hewah's fingers was all it took to light it ablaze.

The small fireball's combustion sent plastic and glass everywhere, destroying the ability to record what was said next.

When it had ceased to smolder, and nobody burst into the room afterwards with a gun pointed at him, Arthur spoke as quietly as he could.

"Tarnos said that allowing me to come back was his way of paying back a personal favour to you."

Hewah gaped at him wordlessly, and then roared with laughter, slapping the table again and again with such force that sparks and flames flew from where he connected with it. His powers never usually flared unless he wanted them to, so the action startled Arthur into quiet submission.

He needed to sleep so badly.

"That wily old bastard."

Hewah roared, and continued laughing for a solid minute or two before finally composing himself.

"You know what that favour was, Arthur?"

His father in law asked the question with tears of mirth starting in his eyes, after he had finally finished his fit of laughter.

Arthur tried his best not to be offended at his humour, as the favour had granted him his freedom, but he was a little bitter after keeping the secret for the past month of torture and interrogation at the hands of his own faction.

"I let one of his apprentices win a sparring match against me when it was first created, and I let him know afterwards that he owed me a favour, as it influenced Serania's decision regarding the kid. It was a project they had been working on for a very long while, and Tarnos really wanted it to pay off."

He sat back in his chair, smiling.

"Funny how shit comes back to bite you in the ass. What a stickler. I can't believe he held onto that bullshit for so long."

Arthur didn't really understand, but smiled and nodded in his fatigue, leaning forward heavily and starting to nod off even as Hewah began chattering at him about the logistics of the past month. The final burden free from his shoulders, Arthur wanted nothing more than to crash.

He had another vision of peaches and his mouth tasted sweet.

"I'm going to take you home, Arthur."

Hewah interrupted his visions of peaches with a soft pitying smile, and hauled Arthur Brass bodily to his feet with one hand, his wild jet-black hair dancing out at all angles as he did so.

"Your wife misses you terribly, and I'll make it my personal mission to take care of all the other paperwork and red tape, damned be whatever Serania wants."

Arthur realized what that sentence meant even through his exhaustion, and due to the mixture of sleep deprivation and the joy it brought, he began sobbing uncontrollably. Hewah hefted the grown man's arm heavily over his shoulder as if he were a mere feather, half dragging and half carrying him along.

"You're the best father-in-law a Navy man could ever have, Hewah."

He remembered telling him, before passing out and drooling into the harness of the Aggie that was going to take him home. He didn't even remember arriving fully, but he did remember waking up the next morning with Feria draped over him like a rug, her brown legs tangled around his as if she was never willing to let him go again.

He was happier than he ever remembered being in his whole life. When he woke her up with a soft kiss, she almost crushed him to death, hugging him wordlessly for a long time.

Tears poured from both sets of eyes.

The next couple months were a mess of more hearings and more bureaucracy, but Hewah used his council clout and fought off the lawyers, justice ministers, bureaucrats, and other military tribunals with a greater ferocity than Arthur had ever been witness to.

It was a clash of the titans, the God of Fire versus the mighty bureaucracy of the G.O.D.

At the end of the long series of battles, he was granted an honourable discharge from the Navy after Serania and Julian's cronies had finally given up on trying to pin him with something. If there was an assassination attempt, he wasn't privy to it, and he guess they had finally grown tired of even dealing with him.

He was the thorn in their side that hadn't gone away, and it must have been easier just to let him go than to try to snuff him out any longer at great pains and cost.

In the eyes of the media, Arthur was a war hero, one who had won every battle up until the battle of *Heartland*, and then who had suffered cruelly in Black Armada prison. They fabricated a beautiful story about how he was captured and tortured mercilessly, until a daring rescue attempt by Guardian Special Forces saved him from certain doom.

The core world of *Heartland* had been defended by the combination of the First Expeditionary Fleet and the core world defense fleets, rushing to help finish the battle he had begun - outmanned and outgunned. According to the "official" story, the Black Armada Navy now lay in tatters, suffering losses so catastrophic that the overstretching of resources for an attack became a colloquialism – "Shooting for *Heartland*."

The officially quoted reason for his discharge was Shell Shock and Post Traumatic Stress Disorder related to his enemy imprisonment, the circumstances of which were a closely guarded secret he was forbidden from discussing.

It hilariously wasn't far from the actual truth.

According to the news stories that emerged, it was one of the shortest and most successful careers of any G.O.D. Naval Officer in history.

Serania and her army of bureaucrats and propagandists wouldn't dare throw him under the bus.

He was too valuable after surviving the fires he had faced.

Along with his discharge, he was bestowed with a new prisoner of war acknowledgement medal that the G.O.D. Naval Branch was coerced into presenting him with.

"The Scarlet Flame of Freedom."

The media lapped it up.

Billy definitely helped with his new media clout inside CNG, of course, for he had worked his way up to a senior network manager position after a previous promotion. He too had disengaged himself from the spotlight at last.

For a while; the glowing propaganda prompted Arthur and

Hewah to ponder if Julian had abused his power as head of "The Eye" purely to amuse himself and get back at Serania for some slight. His public exoneration and the shit-storm that ensued between warring media agencies of different ideals, all combined with Serania's reported fury? It gave him a smug satisfaction.

Arthur enjoyed his ridiculously early retirement by utilizing his sizable coffers to move into the countryside with Feria. The size of their funding allowed him to start construction on a beautiful new estate home.

It came complete with a cultivated peach tree orchard, the same one he had obsessed over in his dreams.

He was finally able to make the oft-remembered taste in his mouth finally go away, by devouring juicy ripe peaches whilst in season at a near-unhealthy rate, either fresh from the orchard or imported from somewhere else in the off-season.

The climate of the UK made it rather expensive, of course, but it made him happy.

In a strange and unnecessary act of generosity, Hewah forcefully chipped in money for both the estate and the peach orchard, despite his and Feria's more than ample funds. No amount of arguing on Arthur's part would force him to take it back, even with his daughter screaming at him at the top of her lungs and threatening to break his legs - her body wreathed in angry orange flames.

In order to placate them, or rather calm Feria and eliminate her leg breaking threats, Hewah suggested that they donate whatever portion the couple would have spent on the estate towards charity-work, helping young children get into higher education. Arthur named the various grants, awards, and bursaries after his parents, with the most prestigious low-income recipient receiving "The Junktown Blues Memorial Award."

Judge Joe Undelwood by that point was growing older, and due to his disability was becoming more and more dependent on hired help. Arthur talked it over with Feria, and they formally invited Joe to come live on the estate, an offer which he accepted with much hesitation and loud protest.

He maintained a private disability aid worker; but after several months of their prodding, eventually gave in to the idea of prosthetic legs, and was soon able to walk and jog again. He kept his old aide Gloria on staff at the estate out of kindness, and she grew accustomed to playing tennis and squash with him every morning.

In his free time, the honorable Judge Joe Undelwood opened a private school in London to help troubled youth find their true calling, with the help of the Brasses' charities. It was an attempt at trying to help people like Arthur avoid the path he had been forced down - as a pawn of the council and a victim of fate. With all the side projects in education, Arthur quit drinking completely, with his one replacement vice being fresh peaches of course.

Time passed, and Arthur Brass finally found a semblance of lasting peace.

At times, however, he found himself asking questions in quiet moments. Questions with no answers, of course. Not that many of them needed answers... Outside of cordial visits, he had escaped the yoke of the Guardians of Destiny, at least publically.

Some of these questions pertained to technology, and Arthur couldn't help but wonder what the G.R.A. alternative was to Joe's prosthetic legs, with the sorts of scientific advancements that Tarnos had implied. Was the resistance so technologically advanced, at least over the strained and overstretched G.O.D. - that their quality of life was tenfold the Guardian territories?

Arthur was quietly forbidden from giving blood transfusions, of course, but if he matched Joe's blood type, and if he could give him some of the nanobots, would he have been able to walk without his exoskeletal legs?

By the sounds of it, Tarnos had described the God Resistance Army as some sort of newfound utopia, struggling for a place in Central.

Had his father really given his life to fight against something so noble as what Tarnos hinted towards, all those years ago?

Regardless of his own personal musings on ascendant biology or technological advances, Feria and Arthur decided to start a family sooner rather than later, and at her insistence she became pregnant a year and a half after Joe moved in with them.

They began the task of preparing for a baby, although with her ascended status there was yet another media fiasco as few other ascendants had ever become publicly pregnant, often hiding for nine months instead.

It was a normal enough pregnancy, as there were very few complications. After all - Feria was a young woman frozen in the prime of her life. She could shoot flames and was blessed with miraculous healing and rejuvenation powers.

What had the couple to fear?

It was decided that they would choose not to know the child's sex, and Feria and Arthur battled over names constantly.

Somehow, even the fights were full of passion and vigor.

He couldn't have imagined he would ever be so happy, at least not after being a puppet of the gods for so long. And this happiness came from an arranged marriage designed to save his life, of all things!

That said, for the next many months, he was still subject to late night craving runs, with Feria refusing out of pride to hire any house help other than Gloria.

His life had finally settled into a state of bliss.

He had family. He had friends. He had security emotionally, financially, and physically.

Life was perfect.

Perfect.

CHAPTER 25: THE MARIONETTE MAN

"Who says that a good joke needs a punchline?"

To expect that such a state of happiness might continue forever was naïve and simple-minded, as Arthur had already learned so many years prior on his journey. Somewhere deep in his heart he knew that happiness was always meant to be a temporary reprieve for someone like him, subject to the whims of those who saw themselves as his ascended betters.

When things are too easy, things go wrong.

On his thirtieth birthday, a month and a half before the baby was due, Arthur received a letter from the G.O.D. bureaucracy, telling him that while his exemplary military service ensured his honorable discharge, he had been selected, assessed, and pre-assigned to fill one of the most prestigious new roles in the organization's entire history.

He would be the first of firsts.

Both a result of his valiant wartime efforts, and as a personal thank you from the council gods for his service.

It stank of Serania before he had even finished reading it.

According to a listed yet obscure legality in Guardian service laws, he was unable to decline or postpone such a prestigious and generous offer.

This precedent went back thousands of years of course.

According to the letter, he was to be ascended post haste and awarded a post as a non-combat consultant in an on-Earth diplomacy role.

It was the very first statement that scared him shitless. Hidden in the phrasing was a death sentence. It dropped a bombshell on their relationship that would yet again reverberate through their lives.

Arthur floundered, as he struggled to contact Hewah, Cassius, and anyone else he could possibly ask for help.

All were powerless to help him, try as they might. The law was clear, and it was a very old law, dredged up from the earliest days of recordkeeping.

On the surface, it sounded like any normal person's dream, the very thing most other mortal humans prayed to be selected for.

And it served as one final, spiteful attempt at something Serania had been hunting without pause for over a decade.

One last "fuck you" from a seventy-five-thousand-year-old bitch.

He would be "ascended posthaste."

The ascension ritual.

He already knew the success rates.

He would become an immortal. A god. A living deity.

Or?

Well…

He would die.

Manufactured by Amazon.ca
Bolton, ON

28809077R00224